**"I'm not going to decide one day that you are more trouble than you're worth. I'm not going to walk away."**

She wished she could believe him, but she knew so much that he didn't. She knew the truth about the kids, this house, and, worst of all, about herself.

He removed one glove and touched her face. His fingers were warm against her skin, and they made her tremble. She should stop him, should run from him as far and as fast as she could, because whatever there was between them—and he was right; there *was* something—couldn't last. Once he knew what a fraud she was, he would never forgive her. He could never love her.

But when she raised her hand to his, she didn't push him away. When he tilted her head back, she let him, and when he kissed her, she let him . . .

*more . . .*

"This one will make you sit up and take notice quickly and then you're hooked for the duration. Ms. Pappano's superb handling of the complexities of the plot and characterizations makes this story a compelling one. A mix of mainstream, murder, and romance, PASSION is a winner in any genre."

—*Rendezvous*

❄

## *IN SINFUL HARMONY*

"A wonderfully wicked web of intrigues and passions as hot as a Louisiana summer."

—Tami Hoag

"[A] well-plotted tale of twisted passions and murder . . . a dark and intriguing mainstream romance that is as sultry as its setting."

—*Library Journal*

"A stunning and potent debut in women's mainstream fiction."

—*Affaire de Coeur*

❄ ❄ ❄

Also by Marilyn Pappano

*Suspicion*

*Passion*

*In Sinful Harmony*

Published by
WARNER BOOKS

# MARILYN PAPPANO

## Season for Miracles

**WARNER BOOKS**

A Time Warner Company

WARNER BOOKS EDITION

Copyright © 1997 by Marilyn Pappano
All rights reserved.

Cover design by Diane Luger
Cover illustration by Ben Perini
Hand lettering by David Gatti

Warner Books, Inc.
1271 Avenue of the Americas
New York, NY 10020

Visit our Web site at
http://warnerbooks.com

W A Time Warner Company

Printed in the United States of America

First Printing: December, 1997

10 9 8 7 6 5 4 3 2 1

# Chapter One

*Bethlehem, 5 miles.*

If she hadn't been so close to crying, the legend on the highway sign would have made Emilie Dalton laugh. She'd known she had made a mistake when she exited the interstate a couple hours back for gas and there wasn't an access ramp back onto the freeway. She'd known she was taking a chance on getting lost when she'd decided to forge ahead on unfamiliar state routes until one of them eventually led back to I-90. She had known that with the snow falling the way it was and the kids tired the way they were, it would be best if they stopped right where they were, checked into the motel near the turnoff, and waited for morning.

But where they were had been too close to where they were fleeing. The snow, which had been falling sporadically throughout the day, hadn't looked as if it had any intention of stopping, and, according to the map, she'd needed to go only about fifteen miles on the twisting highways to reach the interstate again, and so she had pushed on. Her second mistake.

*Bethlehem, 5 miles.*

She'd never heard of Bethlehem, New York, but she wasn't familiar with this part of the country, except for Boston, where she'd lived the past twelve months. She was a Southerner, Atlanta-born and -bred, who, until last year, had never traveled farther north than North Carolina. And now here she was with three exhausted, hungry, frightened kids, lost in western New York, driving through a snowstorm toward a little town called Bethlehem.

A strangled sound, part hysterical laugh, part despairing cry, escaped before she clamped her mouth shut, but it was enough to rouse nine-year-old Alanna in the seat beside her. The girl straightened and looked around. "Where are we, Aunt Emilie?"

"A couple of miles from Bethlehem."

"Bethlehem . . . Pennsylvania?"

"No, honey, New York." At least she hoped so. As far as she could recall from last year's drive up from Atlanta, Bethlehem, Pennsylvania, was in the eastern part of the state and a long, long way from where she needed to be. She prayed she hadn't gotten so turned around that she'd messed up that badly.

Not that it would be the first time she'd done something incredibly stupid. Moving to Boston hadn't been her brightest decision. Helping Berry hadn't been too brilliant. Running away from Boston was pretty darn stupid—to say nothing of criminal. Oh, yeah, she was great at making messes.

Emilie looked around, searching for something that indicated a town nearby, but the only things around them were forest and hills. There was no other traffic, no houses, no turns leading off the highway. Just wilderness, loneliness, snow. And them.

"Are we lost, Aunt Emilie?"

She opened her mouth to deny it, then sighed heavily. "Yes. But only for tonight. We're going to rent a room in Bethlehem and get some dinner. Tomorrow morning, I'll get directions to the interstate, and we'll be on our way home. We'll be fine. I promise."

"Home," Alanna echoed in a whisper, as if she were testing the word. Nine years old, and she'd never had a real home. From the time she was a baby, Berry had dragged her—and later Josie and Brendan—from city to city, state to state, house to apartment to shelter. There had always been a man involved, of course. Berry needed a man in her life the way most people needed food, and she always picked the wrong men, the ones who cultivated her own weaknesses for the easy fix, the easy oblivion, until she was no longer capable of caring for herself, much less her kids.

Emilie understood, forgave, and forgot a lot about her sister, but that was one thing she would never understand: how Berry could care more about the men who were temporary parts of her life than she did about the three innocent children she'd brought into the world. It was the one thing Emilie couldn't forgive, especially now that her sister was locked up in a court-ordered substance-abuse program and Emilie's own life was on hold while she took responsibility for those kids.

A year had passed since her sister's frantic call for help. Emilie had tried to talk her into moving back to Atlanta, where she could better help them, where she had a home and a job with a good salary. With the great lack of wisdom that colored most of her decisions, Berry had refused. The love of her life was in Boston—the man who had been preceded by two dozen other great loves, the man who had just thrown her and the kids out on the street—and she had been convinced that, with just a little help, she could get straightened out and win him back. She'd had no place to live, no money for food, and a job that paid minimum wage—on the days she was able to work—but all she needed to make things right was Emilie, just for a while.

In her heart, Emilie had known Berry wasn't going to change. She could devote herself twenty-four hours a day to the task and even achieve some degree of success, but it wouldn't last. It never did. Before long, there would be another man, another bottle of booze, another dealer of drugs, and another frantic phone call.

But she had heeded Berry's call anyway. After all, if

she hadn't, what would have happened to the kids? She had quit her job with no more than a day's notice, had sold her furniture, closed out her bank accounts, and gone to Boston. She'd done it for the children. They were the only family she had, and she would do anything for them—give up her job, leave her home, move across country.

Defy a court order.

Gripping the steering wheel tighter, she turned away from that line of thought. She hoped Bethlehem was around the next curve, hoped it was big enough to have a motel and a restaurant that would be open tonight. She hoped the motel was clean and cheap—really cheap, since she had only $132 to get them back to Georgia. She hoped the people in town weren't nosy about strangers and that whatever law enforcement they had was home for the night, where all people of good sense should be on a snowy Thanksgiving evening—

As they rounded the next curve, she stared in amazement at the sight ahead. One second there was no hint that they were within a hundred miles of civilization, and the next an entire town was spread out in the valley below. It looked like a scene from a glass paperweight, bright, welcoming, and oh, so charming. But that was from a distance. When the road descended into the valley and they saw the town close up, it would be exactly like every other small town they'd passed through today—shabby, worn, showing the effects of tough times.

Like her.

"Pretty. It looks like Bedford Falls in that movie you like so much—the one with the angel named Clarence."

Emilie's smile was thin. Alanna was right. With the lights and the snow, Bethlehem did remind her of the town in *It's a Wonderful Life*. But Bedford Falls existed only on the screen, and she had learned all too well in the last six months that angels didn't exist at all. Neither did miracles, not even in the holiday season. In the last few months, she'd even begun to doubt the power of prayer.

The road snaked down at such a gentle descent that by the time they reached the valley floor, they had circled halfway around it. From a distance, Bethlehem appeared a place of fantasy. Close up, it was even better—a Norman Rockwell painting come to life. It was decorated for Christmas with wreaths and big bows on every streetlamp. Holly with bright red berries hung in shop windows, and clusters of mistletoe were suspended over the doors. Six-foot-tall nutcracker soldiers painted in bright blues, reds, and greens and wearing black-plumed caps stood guard over each block, and evergreens up and down the street were decked out with velvet bows, silver bells, and glittery gold ribbons.

It *was* a fantasy, Emilie thought as she drove slowly along the wide thoroughfare appropriately named Main

Street. A lovely, charming fantasy. Tomorrow morning, though, when the sun shone and the snow melted, all the shabbiness would be revealed. The decorations would have been defaced and vandalized by the young punks who roamed the streets at night, and the quaint little storefronts would show signs of peeling paint, dirty windows, and economic depression.

But tonight, in the glow of soft lights, it was lovely.

The businesses they passed were closed for the holiday, and there was no sign of a restaurant that might be open, no sign of a motel, cheap or otherwise, where they might find a place to sleep. Emilie was about to give up hope and accept that she would be driving miles more in the snow when suddenly Alanna spoke. "Look, Aunt Emilie, that place is open."

Sure enough, lights were on in the diner in the middle of the block, and a half dozen customers were visible through the plate-glass windows. She parked in front and immediately felt a little stress drain away. She'd been driving for hours in weather that was best enjoyed from a snugly warm house, and she felt it in every muscle.

But they didn't have a house. They'd spent the last seven nights in a shelter. Only a year ago she had berated Berry for allowing things to degenerate to the point that she'd been forced to take her children to a shelter for the homeless, and yet with her own expert management, that was exactly where *she* had landed them, right back in the same shelter.

In her entire adult life, she had never needed help from anyone. She had worked since she was eighteen, paid her bills and her taxes, built up a tidy sum in savings, and still had money left over to give to those less fortunate. She had been a responsible member of society. How in the world had she gone from that to standing in the cold asking a stranger to please give the kids a place to sleep and something to eat?

It had been humiliating.

And it wouldn't happen again. She would get them safely home to Georgia, find a new job and a new place to live. They would have to be satisfied with cramped quarters and lots of spaghetti and other cheap foods, at least until she got back on her feet, but it wouldn't take long. Atlanta was her hometown. There was nothing she couldn't accomplish there with hard work and determination. Unlike Boston, where hard work and determination had gotten her nothing but trouble.

And that was very definitely spelled with a capital T, she thought as a police car pulled into the space beside her.

Sitting very still, she watched as the officer got out. For a moment, he simply stood beside the black-and-white Blazer, fat snowflakes shading his brown hair white. How long would it take the authorities in Boston to discover that she and the kids were missing? When the social worker had arranged for her to retain custody over the Thanksgiving holiday, she had counted on four days of freedom, to get home, get settled, and get started on keeping the promises she'd made.

But what if Social Services had decided that putting the kids into foster homes was better than leaving them in a women's shelter with her? What if they'd gone to the shelter to pick them up, only to find that they'd disappeared before the turkey dinner? What if they'd turned over her name, description, and the license number of her car to the police? What if the police officer standing only a few feet away and looking in her direction had seen such a bulletin?

After a moment, he shook off the snow, clamped his hat on his head, and went inside the diner. She watched him slide onto a stool and pick up the coffee cup the waitress had waiting before she blew out her breath in relief.

"Josie, Brendan, wake up." She leaned over the seat to shake first one child, then the other. "Come on, guys, it's time to eat."

Six-year-old Josie sat up from the pillow she'd been sharing with her brother, yawned, and asked, "Are we there yet?"

"No, sweetie, but hopefully this is as far as we'll have to go tonight. Brendan, are you awake, baby?"

The three-year-old sat up, yawned, then took a look around. Emilie wondered what he thought of all the lights and decorations. She wondered if he was still tired, if he was hungry or needed to go to the bathroom. She wondered if he missed his mother or if he understood that for now Emilie would be doing all the motherly things for him. She wondered, but didn't ask. It wasn't that he couldn't talk. He could, and on the occasions that he did, he did it quite well. He just seemed to have a preference for nonverbal communication.

It was one of the many consequences of his mother's lifestyle. Emilie had no doubt that Berry loved her little boy. From the moment she'd discovered she was pregnant, she had remained scrupulously clean, just as she had with Alanna and Josie. Unfortunately, after Brendan was born, she went right back to her old ways. Cuddling, loving, and teaching were tough to do when you were drunk or stoned as often as she had been during his short life. It was just one more thing for Emilie to deal with once they got home.

"Listen, guys, we're going to go into the restaurant and have dinner, and we're going to be on our best behavior. No fussing, no fighting, no crying. And no talking to strangers—*any* strangers." Especially cops.

"But the waitress is a stranger. How can I tell her I want a hot dog and a sundae if I can't talk to her?"

That was from Josie. Like Alanna, she'd been forced to grow up far too soon. Unlike her sister, she could still be perfectly childlike at times. Emilie hoped that was a quality Alanna would regain once they got settled in a stable environment.

"Don't be difficult, Josie." Alanna sounded a hundred and nine instead of just nine and so much like her mother. Don't be difficult, Berry had pleaded when she'd called to ask her sister to move to Boston. Don't be difficult, she'd told the kids whenever they had behaved like kids as well as whenever they hadn't. Don't be difficult, she had begged of Emilie before telling her that she'd been arrested yet again on drug charges.

*Don't be difficult.* Berry was always making the request—or demand or plea—of someone, when, in reality, *she* was the one who was difficult. *She* was the one who made everyone else's life hard.

"Josie's not being difficult, Alanna," Emilie said gently. "It's a very good question." From the sheltering hood of a coat that was much too big for her, Josie stuck her tongue out at her sister. With a faint smile, Emilie opened the door to a blast of icy air. "Let's get inside, kids, before we freeze."

Nathan Bishop was starting his second cup of coffee when the restaurant door opened, lowering the temperature a few degrees before it swung shut again. He knew without looking that the new arrivals were the woman in the wagon and her kids. He wondered what was so important that they would travel in weather like this. It was bound to get worse before it got better, and that car of hers didn't look particularly reliable.

But as long as they weren't doing anything wrong, they weren't his responsibility. If they did do something wrong, he could probably muster the energy to call Sadie Simpson, who was dispatching for both the town and the county tonight, but that was about the extent of his willingness to act. He'd put in a full fourteen hours today, and he was tired. He was the only one in the department without family in the area, and so he had volunteered to work what had come close to a double shift. He worked long hours through all the family holidays—Thanksgiving and Christmas, Easter and Father's Day and the Fourth of July.

Still, he didn't mind the job. Law enforcement in Bethlehem was a snooze in a hammock compared to big-city police work. Today his first call hadn't come in until after dinner, and it had been no big deal—a minor fender-bender in front of the nursing home. After that, he'd made a routine patrol, taken a report about a nuisance dog, and chased a few kids from the roof of the carousel house.

A typical day in Bethlehem, which was exactly what he'd moved here for.

Shrugging out of his jacket, he draped it over the stool beside him, then gazed around the dining room. With the exception of the woman and kids, he knew everyone. There was Harry Winslow, owner of the restaurant, who opened the place every day whether he was likely to have customers or not. He said he did it because any town that was fit to call itself a town had to have a place to eat every day. Nathan thought it was because, with Harry's wife dead and his kids moved to bigger and more distant places, home was too lonely a place to stay.

Nathan knew loneliness. He recognized it when he saw it, and he saw it on just about every face in the place.

Dean Elliott sat at Harry's table. He was one of the few people in town who had come to Bethlehem from someplace else. He was an artist whose sculptures had bought him fifty acres halfway up the mountain and a home too elegant for the description suggested by its log-cabin construction. But his art and the comfortable living it afforded hadn't brought him happiness. He worked alone, lived alone, and acted as if he expected to die alone.

Over by the door was Sebastian Knight. He lived outside town, too, just down the road from Elliott, on the farm his family had settled over a hundred years ago. Although he hadn't carried on the tradition of farming, Sebastian still worked with his hands. He was a carpenter, and a damned fine one. He'd been married, but one day his wife had packed up her clothes and walked away, leaving him and their little girl to fend for themselves. Chrissy must be at his parent's place, where the rest of the family had gathered. Why wasn't Sebastian with them, instead of over here looking morose and ignoring everyone around him?

Nathan gave the rest of the diners—Holly McBride, old Jeremiah Dent, and Colleen Watson—a brief glance before his gaze settled on the strangers in a distant booth. They looked even more tired than he felt, especially the littlest one. He leaned against the middle kid—a boy or girl, Nathan couldn't tell. The face was perfectly average, too young and unformed to lean toward masculinity or femininity, and the blond hair, cut in a careless, shaggy unisex style, offered no clue.

The older child was definitely a girl, about ten, pretty, delicate, and solemn. Their mother was also pretty, delicate, and solemn. Other than the color of her hair, she bore little resemblance to any of the kids. As far as that went, beyond the hair, the kids didn't look much like each other, except in that unfinished way that all kids looked alike.

Wherever they were headed, the woman should have planned better. This wasn't a good night for driving, and, except for Holly's inn, there wasn't a motel for miles. Judging from their clothing and the condition of the car outside, they probably couldn't afford Holly's place, not with rooms starting at ninety bucks a night.

"Are you sure I can't get you anything?"

He looked from the strangers to the waitress in front of him. Maeve was old enough to be his mother, widowed, and more than a little sweet on Harry. She thought she hid it pretty well, but Nathan was used to watching people, learning what he could from the way they looked, moved, and acted. For example, the mother in the corner was weary—not just tired from hours of travel, but weary from the inside out. Soul weary.

"Some turkey and dressing?" Maeve coaxed. "A sandwich? A piece of pie?"

"No, thanks. I'm heading home to bed."

"Not after drinking two cups of Harry's coffee, you're not. It's got a kick, it's so strong."

"Yeah, but I've been working since six this morning. I don't think I'll have any trouble sleeping." Sliding from the stool, he pulled his jacket on.

"You have tomorrow off, Nathan?"

"I've got the whole weekend off. Want to run away with me?"

She laughed. "If I thought you meant it, I'd take you up on it."

"If I thought you'd take me up on it, I would mean it." He started toward the door. "See you next time, Maeve."

"Have a good weekend."

Nathan returned Harry's and Elliott's farewells as he passed their table, acknowledged Holly's wave with a nod, then stepped outside. The temperature felt as if it had dropped another ten degrees while he'd lingered over the coffee, and the wind had kicked in, too. The valley would be snowed in before morning. Until the state got the highway cleared—or until the sun did the job for them—no one would be coming to or leaving Bethlehem for a while, which suited him fine. With three days off and no way into or out of town, he could hibernate. By Monday morning, when he had to return to work, the holiday would be completely past, and he wouldn't have to face another one—the worst one—until Christmas rolled around.

His boots crunched on the snow as he ducked his head against the wind and started toward the four-wheel-drive Blazer. Back in the city, he'd hated nights like this. People didn't have enough sense to stay home, traffic was god-awful, and the simple act of getting to a call was nearly impossible. Nothing ever went right on nights like this in the city. But he was in Bethlehem now, where nothing ever went wrong.

After starting the engine and turning the heater to high, for a moment he simply sat there, shivering inside his jacket. Directly in front of him inside the diner, the mother and her kids were talking to the waitress. How had he failed to notice that Harry had hired a new waitress? This woman, like her customers, was a stranger. Young, slender, with pale brown hair that had a silvery tinge under the fluorescent lights, she looked too fragile to hold on to such a job for long. Harry's was a busy place, and waiting tables was tough work.

Not that she was working hard tonight. She had served the family their drinks and was now chatting. Something she said made the older kids laugh and coaxed a smile from their mother that, somehow, made her look sad. After patting her arm, the waitress left the table, and the mother turned to stare out the window. Her gaze met Nathan's for only an instant, then she immediately returned her attention to the kids. Immediately. Almost guiltily.

Pushing the clutch in, he shifted into reverse. When he began second-guessing the behavior of tired mothers traveling with three kids on a nasty wintry evening, he'd been working too long. He needed to go home, get out of his uniform and into bed. He *needed* this three-day weekend.

Home was on Fourth Street, on the east side of town. The neighborhood was one of Bethlehem's best—although, in all fairness, the town had no bad neighborhoods. People in Bethlehem took pride in their town and in their homes. The properties were well maintained, clean, and in good repair. Even the shabbiest house in town was one he wouldn't mind calling home.

He lived where he did only because the two elderly sisters who owned the house had taken him in. Miss Agatha and Miss Corinna lived across the street and over one house in the Winchester family home, a rambling Victorian, and rented its toy-sized duplicate to him for a fraction of its value. It was big enough for a family, but he lived there alone.

Alone and lonely.

He let himself in the back door, flipping light

switches until the darkness was banished from the first floor. The light showed the way upstairs, where he traded his uniform for sweatpants and a T-shirt and put his gun belt on the top shelf in the closet. Back downstairs, he stopped for a moment in the front entry. Such quiet. At one time Miss Corinna and her husband had raised four kids here. They had raced down the halls, slid down the banister, and swung on the front-porch swing. They'd had camp-outs out back, sleepovers upstairs, and first kisses on the porch. They'd left echoes of themselves in the very structure of the house. Echoes of laughter, of arguments, of life.

Nathan had lived too many years with echoes of another kind.

When he had first moved in, the stillness had taken some getting used to. He'd passed many midnight hours on the porch, seeking distraction, but his neighbors were quiet people. In six years he hadn't heard one shouting match, hadn't seen one neighbor come home drunk, hadn't had even one mildly irritating experience with any of them. They were home early and in bed early. Their dogs didn't bark, their cats didn't stray, and their children were unfailingly polite.

On the street where he'd lived in the city, something had always been going on. It'd been as busy at three in the morning as it was at three in the afternoon. Loud music, blaring TVs, domestic disturbances, squealing tires, sirens—those had been his music to sleep by. He had been comfortable with his environment . . . at least, until the last year he was there. Sleep had been a problem then. Misery had been a problem. The noise, the crowds, and the hustle of the city had begun to grate. He had been unable to deal with it any longer, unable to become a part of it.

And so he had come to Bethlehem looking for quiet, which he'd found, and peace, which he hadn't. He had accepted that life was never going to be good again, but at least here, it was better. It was livable. It was bearable.

Most of the time.

And the rest of the time? He survived. It wasn't easy, but he did it. He'd been doing it for seven years.

He would be doing it for a long time to come.

A table full of dirty dishes in front of her, Emilie stared out the window at the snow that had turned the car into a long, featureless lump and felt its chill all the way through. When they'd arrived forty-five minutes ago, she had been able to see clearly all the way to the far side of the square. Now, if she squinted, she could just barely make out the tall, round gazebo in the middle of the block. They needed to find a place to spend the night, before conditions got any worse.

"Can I get you anything else?"

She glanced up at the waitress and tried to smile. "Just the bill."

Noelle, as she had introduced herself with a million-watt smile, pulled a pad from her apron pocket, tore off the top page, and did some quick figuring before laying it on the table. "I'll take that for you when you're ready. Just let me clear these dishes first."

Emilie checked the total. Eleven dollars and forty-seven cents. The amount made her wince and wonder where they could have saved a little. Maybe by ordering water or skipping dessert. But the kids needed milk, and their child-sized sundaes had cost so little. Besides, they had missed Thanksgiving dinner. They'd deserved a little splurge. Tomorrow was soon enough to start scrimping.

She counted out the money, then added a small tip for the waitress. When the woman returned, Emilie asked, "Can you direct me to the nearest motel?"

Noelle paused, balancing a coffee cup atop three sundae glasses. "That would be in Howland."

"Where is that?"

"About forty-five miles west of here. There's an inn here in town—Holly McBride's place—but it's usually booked over the holidays. She may have something available if you want to go by, but I doubt she has any vacancies and . . ." She tried not to be obvious in her appraisal of their worn and ill-fitting clothes, but Emilie felt the assessment all the way down to her toes. "The inn is awfully expensive. It'll run you over a hundred dollars a night. It's a beautiful farmhouse that's just

meant for lots of guests. When it's all decorated for
Christmas, it's absolutely breathtaking. Next to the
Pierce house, it's the most beautiful house in town."

Emilie felt numb. Forty-five miles to the nearest
motel. Under good conditions it would take her nearly
an hour to get there, and conditions tonight were about
as far from good as they could get. She had to find another way—*had* to find a place to stay. But where?

The inn was out of the question. Her cash had to be
saved for gas and meals, and her only credit card had
been canceled after she'd missed the last three pay-
ments. The only place likely to be open all night in a
town like this was the police station—certainly the last
place *she* wanted to be when the state of Massachusetts
might have issued a warrant for her arrest. But where
*could* she go?

Through her despair, she realized that the waitress
was still talking. To keep the panic at bay, she forced
herself, just for a moment, to listen.

"It's a wonderful old Victorian," Noelle was saying.
"It's stood empty for about seven years. Mrs. Pierce left
it to her niece, but the woman has never come to even
see it. She lives somewhere in Massachusetts, but no
one in town has met her. A trust pays the taxes and pro-
vides for routine maintenance, but the house needs a
family, someone to take care of it and give it life." She
paused, then her eyes brightened. "You know, you really
should see it before you leave. It's at 311 Fourth Street.

You go straight down Main, then left on Fourth. It's only a block or two over. Even though it's nighttime, it really is worth seeing."

Emilie returned to the original subject. "I don't think we could make it to Howland in this weather. Are you sure there's no place here in town, besides the inn, where we could get a room for the night?"

The light in the waitress's expression dimmed. "I'm sorry."

"Maybe . . . maybe we could stay with you?" Emilie's voice quavered with pleading and barely disguised desperation. "I would pay. I don't have a lot, but I could give you something. . . ." Her voice trailed away as Noelle shook her head. There was genuine distress in the woman's eyes, but she was still turning them down.

"I'm sorry." Noelle scooped the money from the table, counted it, and returned the dollar tip. After sliding the rest into her apron pocket, she laid her hand on Emilie's arm, her fingers curving in a tight squeeze. "Go see the Pierce house. Please. You won't be sorry."

The insistence in her voice lingered after she walked away. Why should she care if Emilie took the time to see someone else's house when she desperately needed a place of their own for tonight? Unless . . . Could she possibly have been hinting that the Pierce house might be that place? Was she suggesting that they stay in a place that didn't belong to them, that the house's emptiness and their need made it all right?

More likely, Emilie thought, her own desperation was reading something into the words and gestures not intended by Noelle. Besides, borrowing someone else's house, even just for one night, wasn't all right. It was breaking and entering, and the last thing she needed now was more trouble with the law. She had enough already.

"Aunt Emilie, what are we going to do?" Alanna's voice was pitched low to avoid frightening her brother and sister, but the softness didn't disguise her own fear.

"I'll think of something. Don't worry. We'll be okay." She took a look around the room and saw no sign of Noelle. The other customers were getting ready to leave, and the older waitress and a gray-haired man were turning chairs upside down on the empty tables in preparation for closing.

"Put on your coats, kids." She gave Josie and Brendan her best smile. "It's time to head back out. Enjoy the snow while you can. Once we get back to Georgia, you'll see it only once in a blue moon."

"What's a blue moon?" Josie asked as she struggled into Alanna's hand-me-down.

"It's just a saying." Emilie went to the opposite side of the booth to help Brendan with his coat. Chocolate was smeared around his mouth, and his blue eyes were glazed over. The poor kid was asleep on his feet. She didn't ask him to walk, but lifted him into her arms. He immediately snuggled close, turned his face into her neck, and went limp.

They were almost at the door when the gray-haired man spoke. "You folks have far to go?"

She looked at Josie and Alanna, felt Brendan's weight in her arms, and knew what she had to do. No matter that she didn't want to, no matter that it was going to break her heart. The kids were her first priority.

"No," she replied quietly, the word very small. "Not far at all."

She hustled the kids to the car, settling them in the backseat so they could snuggle. After starting the engine so the heater could warm, she began clearing snow from the windows. The storm was bad and getting worse. There was no way she could go on.

By the time she joined the kids in the car, she was shivering, and her ungloved hands were numb. She backed out of the parking space, the tires bumping over the hard-packed ruts, and headed at a crawl down Main Street. To go to Howland, they had to drive east, until the road slowly curled its way back up and around the mountain.

But they weren't going to Howland. They weren't leaving Bethlehem.

She should have asked for directions to the police station, but it couldn't be too hard to find. Still, when she left the business district and headed into a neighborhood of neatly kept houses, she didn't turn around. She was delaying, looking for the courage to turn herself in and the kids over to total strangers who could provide for them better than their own family could.

What failures she and Berry were.

Realizing that she'd reached the edge of town, she turned, drove a few blocks, then turned again. Her intent was only to delay the inevitable, but she succeeded in getting herself lost. Three times she thought she made the proper turns to take her back to Main Street, and three times she was wrong. Street signs were of no help. The snow had turned them into white-frosted ornaments atop tall poles. Tears of frustration choking her throat, at last she pulled to the side of the street, bent over the steering wheel, and fought the sobs. Only when she was sure they were under control did she look around.

They were parked in front of a house, with brick columns supporting a wrought-iron fence. Recessed into one column was a plaque painted with birds and an address: 314 Fourth Street. According to Noelle's directions, they were only a block or two from Main, and the wonderful Pierce house must be . . .

Without seeing the numbers on the fence, she easily picked it out—across the street and one house down, the only house on the block that didn't have welcoming lights in the windows. It *was* a beautiful place—three stories with towers and turrets, fish-scale shingles, rambling verandas, and yards of ornate gingerbread—but it looked abandoned. Forlorn. Definitely empty.

For a moment Emilie envied the woman who owned it so deeply that it hurt. How full this stranger's life must be that she could own a house such as this and not even want to see it . . . and how empty her own life felt in comparison. Right now she had nothing, *nothing* but this beat-up old car, $121 dollars and change, and three frightened kids.

She glanced over her shoulder at them. They were all asleep, an old quilt tucked around them. The car was warm. Spending the night in it would surely kill them—there was no way they could keep warm with the few clothes they had, and in this old rattletrap, running the heater through the night would put them at risk for carbon monoxide poisoning—but for only five minutes, they would be fine. They probably wouldn't even awaken, and she could delay losing them by that much.

With the driveway blocked by drifts, she pulled to the curb in front, shut off the engine, and quickly, quietly, closed the door behind her. Forging through mid-calf-deep snow, she followed the driveway to its end. The snow in the backyard was undisturbed except for a three-foot-tall hump that snaked along the back fence. It was a woodpile, an immense supply of firewood that could heat even this big old house through multiple hard winters. If it had been there since the old lady's death, it was undoubtedly as dry as paper and would need no more than a match to set it ablaze.

Now all she needed was a fireplace, a match, and four

walls to contain the heat. Then she wouldn't have to worry about the kids freezing to death. Then she wouldn't have to turn them over to the police. Then she wouldn't have to break the promises she'd made them.

*Go see the Pierce house. Please. You won't be sorry.*

Noelle's insistent voice echoed in Emilie's mind and brought her slowly around to face the house once more. Would it be so wrong if, just for one night, it was used for the purpose for which it had been built, if it provided shelter to a family who desperately needed it? If she paid for its use, if she tossed in a few bucks extra for the wood they burned?

Yes, it was *wrong*, she insisted as she made her way across the yard to the side steps and over increasingly higher mounds of snow collected there to the partially protected veranda. Even if everyone would understand how desperate she was to take care of the kids. Even if she apologized, made restitution, and asked God to forgive her.

Even if it just might be her last chance to keep her family together. If she lost the kids now, she would never get them back. The state would put them in separate homes, always promising them that when their mother was better, they could be together again. But *she* knew a few things the state didn't. She knew how it felt to be forcibly separated from the only family you have. She knew how it felt to live with strangers, always to be apart, never to belong, no matter how many weeks or months you lived with them. She knew how it felt always to come last, always to be the outsider.

And she knew that Berry might never get better. Her sister had spent most of her life desperately seeking some bond, some tie that would stop people from always leaving her. It had been with her since she was seven years old. It had made her neglect her children and waste her life, and it had landed her in a psychiatric hospital at the age of thirty-one.

It could have been worse, Emilie knew. The judge would have been justified in sending Berry to prison after this last conviction on drug charges. In fact, he'd given her a five-year term, along with five years' probation, but he'd chosen to defer the sentence and send her for treatment instead. Treatment was no costlier—and hopefully much more effective—than imprisonment.

Dual-diagnosis inpatient treatment—that was what they called it. The hospital's first priority was getting her off the drugs and the booze, but at the same time, their psychiatrists were treating the emotional problems—the low self-esteem, the sense of abandonment, the depression, the feelings of worthlessness and hopelessness—that underlay her addictions. The length of her stay at the hospital was open-ended—the terms of her sentence required a *successful* completion of the program—but her doctors anticipated that her treatment would last about six months. They were hopeful.

Emilie wasn't. Too many times she'd seen Berry

clean up, dry out, and make a fresh start, only to be right back where she'd started within a few weeks. Maybe this time would be different—the treatment was certainly different—or maybe it wouldn't. Either way, Emilie had a responsibility to the kids. This house might be her last chance to fulfill it.

She came to a stop at the front door. Staying here, even for one night, *would* be terribly wrong, but she was desperate. And once she made it safely to Georgia, she would make it right. The owner would forgive her. The children would forgive her. And because she truly was sorry, God would forgive her, too.

Reaching out, she wrapped her fingers around the doorknob. If only it would swing right open, she could take it as a sign from above that what she was considering was excusable. But the icy metal didn't turn. It simply froze her fingers.

She was turning away, her heart even heavier, her spirits lower, when a breeze blew across the veranda. It wasn't a hard wind, not even enough to make her shiver. It came with a sprinkle of snow and a whoosh of sound, passing from one end of the long porch to the other before disappearing.

Emilie stopped where she was. Her breath grew slow, shallow, and for one moment she forgot the cold and the hopelessness. For one moment she believed that the kids would be all right, after all. *She* would be all right. Heavens, maybe even Berry would be all right.

If the door were unlocked, she had thought only seconds earlier, she could accept it as a sign from God that it was all right for her to claim shelter in this house for the night. The door hadn't been unlocked. The sign hadn't appeared.

Or maybe it had. Because that slight little breeze that had blown along the veranda had left a gift for her. With no more strength than a child's puff—than an angel's puff—it had uncovered a key on the windowsill buried in snow, and *that,* she wanted to believe, did believe, was a sign.

She wrapped her fingers around the old-fashioned brass key, then inserted it into the lock. It turned easily, the door swung inward, and her heart grew about a million pounds lighter. She stood motionless a moment, her eyes squeezed shut, then started away with an energy she hadn't felt in weeks. At the top of the steps, though, she paused to direct her gaze to the snow-obscured heavens and whisper a heartfelt prayer.

"Thank you."

# Chapter Two

In the middle of her favorite dream, the one about home, Alanna jerked awake to find herself shivering in the backseat. Josie was snoring, and Brendan was asleep, too. The kid could sleep through anything, even Josie's racket. Apparently, so could *she*. Where were they? Had they already driven all the way to the next town, or had they never left Bethlehem? And where was Emilie?

Straightening in the seat, she used her sleeve to wipe the window enough to peer out. The snow was still coming down hard, and they'd been sitting there long enough for the car to get cold. There was a house at the end of the drive, a big one, like rich people lived in. Maybe Emilie had found someone to take them in for the night. Surely whoever lived in a house that big could spare a room for them. They didn't need much—just some floor space and some heat. Pillows would be nice, and a blanket for each of them. They only had two blankets, and Josie hogged the one Alanna shared with her.

Then she noticed the one thing that set this house apart from its neighbors: no lights. No one was home.

So why were they there? And where was Emilie?

A shiver swept through Alanna that had nothing to do with the cold. It made her fumble with the door handle and sent her scrambling out into the deep snow. "Aunt Emilie!"

Footsteps dotted the snow from the car to the backyard. She followed them, reminding herself that Emilie wasn't her mother. Being sisters didn't mean they acted alike. It didn't mean Emilie would ever leave them the way their mother had. She wasn't like that, Alanna told herself, and she believed it. Still, she felt a dizzying relief when her aunt appeared around the corner of the house, her arms cradling something heavy and dark.

"What are you doing out here?" Emilie asked without stopping.

"I wanted to know where you were. What are you doing? What is this place?"

"A house."

"Who lives here?" She followed her aunt onto the porch, stomping her feet to remove the snow before it soaked her only pair of shoes.

At the front door, open wide and leading into a dark,

smelly hallway, Emilie looked back at her. "For tonight, we do."

When Alanna finally managed to speak, it was in a whisper. "Aunt Emilie, we can't break into someone's house just because it's empty and we need a place to stay! That's stealing . . . isn't it?"

Emilie tightened her hold on the logs she was carrying. "Listen to me, darlin'. We've got only two choices tonight: either we stay here in this house, or we go to the police."

The color drained from Alanna's face. If they went to the police, she and the kids would be sent to stay with strangers—a different home for each of them, the social worker had said—and Emilie . . . They would take Emilie away. She would have to stay in jail because she didn't have the money to get out, and sooner or later they would send her to prison.

Josie might not mind staying with strangers so much. She liked everybody and thought everyone liked her, too. Brendan didn't like *anybody*, except their mom, Emilie, Alanna, and especially Josie. She was the one he talked to the most, the one he wanted when he woke up in the middle of the night. What would happen if Josie wasn't around any longer? Who would he talk to? Who would cuddle him when he cried?

*She* would hate it. As the oldest, she had responsibilities. She had to look out for the others, but she couldn't do that if Child Welfare gave them to different families.

And Emilie . . . She hadn't done anything wrong. Mama's drugs, losing her job, getting evicted, running out of money, this snow—none of that was her fault. Why should she go to jail for being a good aunt?

"What about the owners?" Alanna asked in a small voice as she reached out and took the top three logs to lighten her aunt's load. "What if they catch us?"

"According to the waitress, the owner lives in Massachusetts. She's never been here before, so it's not likely she'll show up tonight." Emilie started to turn away, then looked back. "For the record, I didn't break in. The key was lying on the windowsill. And as soon as we get settled at home, I'm going to send the owner money to cover our use of her home, because you're right, darlin'. What I'm doing here is wrong. It's stealing, and Daltons don't steal. We'll make it right, I promise."

Alanna gazed at her in the thin light from the streetlamp, then nodded. Emilie never broke her promises. She shifted the logs so the bark didn't bite into her hands. "We'd better hurry and get more wood so we can get the kids inside. It's getting cold in the car."

As she passed through the door, her aunt bent and kissed the top of her head. "I appreciate your help," she said in the quavery sort of voice that meant she was awfully close to crying. In the last three weeks, Alanna had heard that voice a lot.

The hallway was dark, with a flicker of light about halfway down. Her eyes adjusting to the night, she found the door that led into the living room. The light came from the fireplace, where a couple of logs were burning. More logs were stacked on the big white cloth spread nearby. Emilie had been busy, she thought as she added her few logs to the pile, then paused for a moment in front of the fire and gazed about.

The room was big, the windows rising to the lofty ceiling. There were curtains—thin lacy ones peeking from behind the thick, heavy ones—and furniture, big and lumpy underneath white dust covers. It all smelled old and musty, but she'd lived with worse smells—sour food and moldy dishes, backed-up toilets and mildewed carpets. In one building there had been a really bad smell, and when the police had come, they'd found a neighbor who'd been dead for days. There hadn't been anyone to miss the guy—no family, no friends. He must have been a sad man, she'd thought, but that would never happen to her. She had her family. They had to stay together no matter what, no matter how many laws they had to break.

"Why don't you stay here and get warm?" Emilie straightened after neatly stacking her latest load. Looking at her, Alanna saw that her aunt's eyes were heavy, and there were lines around them. When she had first come to Boston a year ago, she had looked so good, like someone who didn't drink or use drugs, who didn't party and stay out late and have some guy knocking her around. When Alanna had realized that Emilie was only two years younger than her mother, she had been shocked. Her mother looked almost old enough to be Emilie's mother, too. She looked worn-out.

Lately, Emilie had been looking a little worn-out, too. Mothering three kids who weren't her own couldn't be easy. Or losing her job. And her apartment. And facing jail.

"I'll help you, Aunt Emilie. Then we can both get warm and get some sleep."

They made four more trips to the woodpile before Emilie estimated they had enough for the night. Leaving Alanna to make their bed, she went to get the kids.

After adding another log to the fire, Alanna closed the heavy drapes more tightly, then made a pallet from the canvas dust covers. Four pillows from the sofa and chairs completed the bed. By the time Emilie returned, carrying Brendan and leading Josie by the hand, Alanna had already removed her coat and shoes and staked out a place on the side nearest the windows.

Without speaking, they settled the kids, Josie next to her, then Brendan, with Emilie on the opposite side. The door was closed, the fire was crackling, the room was getting warm, and Alanna was almost asleep when she roused herself to speak. "Aunt Emilie?"

"Yeah, honey?"

"Everything's going to be all right."

"I know, honey."

"Aunt Emilie? I love you." She turned onto her side,

tucked her hands beneath her head, and closed her eyes. She didn't wait for an answer—didn't need it to know— but it came anyway, as she knew it would, a soft whisper in a quiet room.

"I love you, too, Alanna."

Morning came too soon for Emilie. She had slept fitfully, awakening to add more wood to the fire every time the room started to cool. She was as weary this morning as she'd been last night and not at all sure she could force herself up from the floor and into the car. She needed long, uninterrupted hours of sleep, but she couldn't have them now.

Ignoring the stiffness in her body, she slid out from under the blanket she'd shared with Brendan and went in search of a bathroom. She found a small one back by the kitchen, home to dust and spiderwebs, with a pedestal sink and a toilet empty of water. A twist of the cold-water handle confirmed that there was no water service to the house.

No problem, she thought, returning to the parlor for her coat. She would melt snow over the fire until she had enough water to fill the toilet tank and the bowl.

It was a miserable task—traipsing outside to freeze, warming by the fire while the snow melted, carrying the pots of resulting water into the frigid bathroom, then starting the process over again. Still, the end result was

worth it. She came out of the bathroom for the last time
feeling a hundred percent better able to face the day.

Back in the parlor, she nudged aside one velvet drape
at the window. The view outside was breathtaking in its
beauty and, at the same time, the most depressing sight
she'd ever seen. Piles of snow obscured the front steps,
blotted out the path she'd worn across the yard, and covered the car. The wrought-iron fence across the lawn had
turned white, and the street beyond it was also unbroken
white. Not a single car had passed during the night—
maybe because none had been able to get through.
Maybe they were snowed in. Maybe they were stuck in
this house they had stolen with no food, no way to escape, and neighbors sure to get curious about their in-
trusion. Maybe—

A knock at the front door made her jerk back. The
curtain fell into place, sending a cloud of dust into the
air, making her sneeze. She clamped her hand over her
nose and mouth.

"Aunt Emilie, who's at the door?" Though Alanna's
voice was sleepy, her eyes were wide and alert. She
knew too well what unexpected guests could mean. A
knock at the door had preceded Berry's lawyer when
he'd told them she was going away for an indefinite
time for rehabilitation. There'd been a knock from the
landlord notifying them that he had started eviction proceedings, another knock when the social worker had

come to report that Emilie's custody of the kids had been revoked.

"I don't know, darlin'." And she had no intention of finding out. If they stayed quiet and didn't answer the door, their unwanted guests would go away.

Another knock sounded. Maybe they wouldn't go away. After all, they had surely seen the car parked out front and probably noticed the smoke from the chimney. What if they had a key—neighbors gave other neighbors keys, didn't they?—and they let themselves in to make sure everything was all right? Worse, what if they called the police to report a suspicious situation next door?

Reluctantly she started toward the door. "If the kids wake up, keep them in here and quiet, all right?"

A third knock came as she hurried down the hall to the front door. She twisted the lock and swung the door open, half-expecting to see the policeman from last night with a warrant for her arrest or the house's angry owner standing there. Instead, there were only two elderly women, so bundled that little more than their eyes showed.

"Good morning, dear. I hope we didn't wake you—"

"Of course we woke her, Agatha. The poor girl didn't even have a chance to comb her hair."

Emilie raised one hand to her hair. She must look a sight—her face without makeup, her hair standing on end, her clothes wrinkled from a night's restless sleep.

"I'm Agatha Winchester, from next door, and this is my sister—"

"Corinna Humphries. And you must be Miriam's niece. How nice it is to finally meet you." The woman extended her hand, realized it was full, and laughed. "We brought you a little something for breakfast. We thought you might not be prepared—"

"Having just moved in and the snow and all." Agatha offered a foil-covered plate that was still warm, Corinna a tall thermos. "Hot cocoa and cinnamon rolls. We baked them ourselves."

"We won't keep you, dear. You go and eat while it's warm. By the way, what did you say your name was?"

"She didn't say, Corinna. We didn't give her a chance." In spite of the knitted scarf that covered the lower half of her face, Agatha's smile was apparent. Emilie found herself wanting to smile right back. "We're just so happy to have a neighbor again. Dear Miriam had always hoped that you might come for a visit, and we could have met you then, but you didn't, and, of course, we understand that you were out of the country when she passed on and that's why you didn't come to the funeral. It was a lovely service, dear—What *is* your name?"

"Emilie Dalton," she said, not thinking to lie until it was too late. But apparently neither sister remembered dear Miriam's niece's name. Their only reaction to her own name was a big smile from each.

"Welcome to Bethlehem, Emilie. The whole town's going to be excited to hear that you've come."

"Yes, you've been such a mystery and all. Why, I don't think anyone in town has ever met you, not even Miriam's attorney."

Corinna gave her sister a chiding look. "She knows that, Agatha."

"Of course she knows it, Corinna. I was simply making a comment." To Emilie she made a shooing gesture with both hands. "Go on now, dear. Enjoy your breakfast. We'll have plenty of time to talk later."

Emilie watched until they were out of sight, then closed the door. She felt a twinge of guilt for accepting the sisters' hospitality while deceiving them, but the cinnamon rolls smelled wonderful. The kids were sure to be hungry when they woke, and this would save her the cost of a breakfast she could ill afford.

When she returned to the parlor, Josie was sitting on the hearth while Brendan remained silent and drowsy on the bed. Alanna was at the window, trying to peek out the tiny crack she'd made. The moment the door closed behind Emilie, she whirled around. "Who was it?"

"The neighbors from next door. They brought breakfast." She laid their offering on the hearth, then picked up Brendan's jacket. "Alanna, the bathroom's down the hall by the kitchen. Get your coat on—you, too, Josie—and take Brendan. There's just enough water for one flush, so be careful, okay?"

"What are you going to do?"

"I'll get the snow cleaned off the car so we can get out of here." Provided the roads were passable. If they weren't . . . No use borrowing trouble. She had enough already.

She stuffed Brendan's arms into the sleeves of his coat, zipped it up, and pulled the hood over his head. Once everyone was dressed, she led the way into the hall. "As soon as you're done, get them back in the parlor and feed them. Let Josie and Brendan share the cup on the Thermos, and you can drink from the bottle. I'll be back as soon as possible."

It seemed even colder outside then before, though the sun was shining brightly, reflecting blindingly off all the white. Wishing for sunglasses—and gloves, rubber boots, a warmer coat, and a heat wave—Emilie made her way through knee-deep snow to the end of the driveway. There she stopped to study the street. The snow was smooth, marred only by footprints. It wasn't nearly as deep as in the yard behind her, but she had no idea if that meant it was passable. She'd never seen so much snow in her life except on TV, and all she knew about driving in it was what she'd learned yesterday.

Movement down the street caught her attention—a pickup backing out of a drive and heading away, its rate of travel slow but steady. She could handle that. Besides, this was a residential street. Main Street and the highway would surely be in better shape. After all, everyone up here had snowplows, didn't they?

Turning to the car, she began sweeping snow from the driver's door. Opening it required effort, but when she managed, she climbed inside and stamped her feet to remove the snow. Her breath forming clouds in front of her, she fumbled the key with frozen fingers into the ignition and turned. The engine sputtered, coughed, then died. When she tried again, she got the same response.

Emilie sank back, her chest tight, her eyes burning. She knew even less about cars than she did about snow. Gas, oil, and insurance—that was the extent of her automotive knowledge. Oh, and one more thing. She knew repairs cost money. Lots and lots of money.

Her hand trembling, she gave it another twist. It sputtered, clicked a few times, then went silent. Damn it, she *needed* this car! How in the world could she possibly get the kids home without it? How could she do *anything* without it besides go to jail?

Tears filled her eyes, and a sob escaped before she could stop it. All she'd wanted to do when she'd left Atlanta was take care of the kids. She was twenty-nine years old, a mature, capable adult, old enough to be a mother herself. Instead, everything had gone wrong. The salary at the best job she'd been able to find had been half what she was accustomed to. For a time, Berry had straightened up, but then she'd started drinking and using drugs again. She'd stolen money from Emilie, had drunk or snorted away the rent money and the grocery money.

They'd already been in serious trouble by the time Berry had been sent to rehab—more than a month behind on rent, nearly two months' past due on utilities. Then had come the kicker. Emilie had gone to work one rainy Friday payday to find her coworkers milling around and new locks on the doors. Without even a hint that there was trouble, the owners had packed up and left town, leaving her and everyone else with nothing to show for their last month's work.

Then the landlord had evicted them. Social Services had reclaimed the kids. She had kidnapped them, gotten lost, and now was stuck in a place she had no business being. How much worse could things get?

A rap at the window answered the question for her. Through the ice that coated the glass, she could make out a distorted view of one of the sisters—Agatha, she thought. Since the electric windows wouldn't work without power from the battery, she opened the door, climbed out, and shoved her hands into her pockets. "Ms. Winchester."

"Oh, call me Miss Agatha."

That was a custom alive and well in the South. Emilie had grown up with a host of Misses—Rosalie, Ginny, Mary Pat, and Annabelle, among others. Some had been kind, good-hearted women doing their best. Some had been more interested in the money paid by the state for each foster child and the free help Emilie had represented. At best she'd been an interloper in a home where she could never belong. At worst she'd been unpaid labor. Always she had been an outsider.

"It's not a good morning to be out and about. Of course, you'll need some of these drifts shoveled before you can get out, anyway. I imagine Nathan would be happy to clear them for you when he's finished with our driveway." Agatha raised her voice to carry past the hedge that separated the two yards. "Wouldn't you, Nathan dear?"

Emilie became aware of the distant scraping of metal against stone a moment before it stopped. "I appreciate the offer, but I'm sure I can handle it myself. Do you know if M—" She stopped herself before *Mrs. Pierce* got out and substituted her benefactor's first name. "—if Miriam had a snow shovel?"

"Oh, I'm sure she did, but it's such difficult work, and you're such a slender thing, and Nathan doesn't mind at all, do you dear?"

"Nathan doesn't mind what?" The question came in a deep voice from somewhere behind Emilie, who automatically turned, then froze inside. He was dressed differently—heavy boots, jeans, and a parka—and she'd paid him little enough attention last night, but she would have recognized him anywhere. How much worse could things get? she had asked. How about stealing a house that had a cop for a neighbor?

"Nathan, this is Emilie Dalton, Miriam Pierce's niece. We need the snow cleared around her car. She intended to do it herself, but there's no need for that when you're already here." Patting his arm, Agatha said confidingly to Emilie, "Nathan came to Bethlehem not long after dear Miriam died. He helps us with heavy chores and keeps an eye on everything. He's a policeman, you know. He lives right across the street, so if you ever need anything . . ."

Last night, in finding the key to the house, she'd thought she had everything she needed. Now she needed the snow to disappear. She needed the car to start, and she needed to get out of Bethlehem without rousing anyone's suspicion. Failing that, she needed the courage to make the best of the situation, to take this unexpected gift of mistaken identity and use it to protect the children and herself. As the first step in that direction, she smiled the best smile she could manage. "I'll keep that in mind."

Beside her, Agatha shivered. "My, it's a bit chilly out here. I believe I'll go inside. You should, too, dear. Stop by when you're finished, Nathan, and pick up the cake we baked for you. It's your favorite."

Once she was gone, Emilie looked at the cop. He had dark brown hair, mostly covered with a knitted cap, and darker eyes. His cheeks were red from the chill, his jaw strong, his expression neither overly wary nor overly friendly. He looked like any other person would look, meeting a neighbor for the first time. Just a little hand-somer.

The thought made her go still. How long had it been since she'd noticed a handsome man? *Months.*

Switching the shovel he carried to his other hand, he offered his right hand. "I'm Nathan Bishop."

"Emilie." She took his hand, strong inside the thickly padded glove, then quickly slid her own back into the slight warmth of her pocket.

"Everyone's wondered about our absentee neighbor. You spend last night here?"

She nodded, hoping her expression gave no sign of the uneasiness she felt. If she was going to stay here, whether for a few hours or, heaven help her, a few days, she couldn't flinch every time she was asked a question. She couldn't give anyone a reason to believe that she was anyone other than Miriam Pierce's niece.

"Kind of cold, wasn't it?"

"There's plenty of firewood. Seven years old and so dry that it flashes, then it's out. But it puts out a lot of heat with that flash. We were fine."

*We.* Nathan remembered the kids who'd been with her last night—the little boy who'd looked tired enough to cry, the pretty older girl, the in-between child. "Fine" was probably an exaggeration. It must have been an un-comfortable night, but at least they'd been out of the snow and cold. "Where are your kids?"

"Inside eating breakfast. Miss Agatha and Miss Corinna made cinnamon rolls and cocoa."

He'd had two rolls and a mug of cocoa himself before starting work this morning on the sisters' driveway. Being well fed was one of the benefits of doing heavy chores and keeping an eye on everything. Having his services offered to a new neighbor—a pretty, blond-haired, blue-eyed, delicate-looking neighbor—might be another. With one gloved hand, he gestured toward her car. "Where do you need to go?"

"Home."

"I thought this was home."

Her cheeks, already pink from the cold, darkened. "This is Aunt Miriam's house. I'd heard so much about it that I wanted to see it, but we're not here to stay. We're not moving in."

"Miss Agatha seems to think you are."

"Miss Agatha never gave me a chance to say otherwise." The dry comment was offered with a smile that took the sting out of it. It eased the weariness in her face and lightened her eyes a shade or two, but it couldn't hide the fact that she was freezing while they chatted. Her face was a stark contrast of unnatural paleness and cold-induced ruddiness, her Cupid's-bow mouth a faint shade of blue. Her teeth were chattering, and she was trying hard to contain the shivers that made her tremble. She should be inside with the kids, wrapped in a blanket in front of the fire, instead of out in the snow in clothes that were never intended for weather like this.

Still, he didn't send her there, not yet. "Where is home?"

"Massachusetts."

"And you think you're going back there today?" He shook his head. "Sorry. The highway's closed."

Worry crept into her gaze. "What do you mean, closed?"

"As in not open. Impassable. Snowed in. With luck you might make it to the turnoff for Dean Elliott's place, but that's as far as anyone's going for a few days."

"But I can't stay here a few days! I've got to get home! We can't—" Abruptly she turned away, raising one ungloved hand to sweep snow off the car. "Damn it," she whispered so low that he barely heard it.

He looked at her clothes, faded and worn, then her car, so old and beat-up that it hadn't been worth more than a few hundred dollars for more than a few years. He'd rarely given much thought to the Pierce house and its owner. He'd known what everyone else had known and assumed that she was one of the privileged few for whom money was never a problem. He had never imagined her as someone so far down on her luck as Emilie Dalton appeared to be.

"Will the car even start?" He'd heard her trying while he'd been shoveling the sisters' sidewalk. The coughs and sputters had sounded like the motor's last dying breaths.

In reply, she slid behind the wheel and turned the key. More coughing and sputtering.

"Pop the hood." Letting the shovel fall, he cleared the top layers of snow from the hood, then released the latch and lifted it. The rod was missing, so he braced it with one hand while he poked around. He knew just enough about cars to keep from getting ripped off too badly by unscrupulous mechanics, which wasn't a problem in Bethlehem.

He also knew enough to recognize that maintenance had never been a top priority with Emilie or anyone else who'd ever owned the car. Dirt and grease coated every surface. The air filter was black. The belts were cracked, held together by sheer luck. More than likely, the tires were bald, the brake pads worn through, the oil dirty and a perpetual quart low.

Stepping back, he let the hood drop as she climbed out again. "I can recommend a mechanic. He's good and reasonable. I'll give him a call Monday morning, and he'll send the tow truck over."

"*Monday?* I can't wait—" Her words trailed off as she stopped herself and her face closed in.

"You don't have a choice. This is a holiday weekend, remember? There's not a garage in town open until Monday. And it doesn't matter anyway, because there's no way anyone's getting out of the valley before then."

For a long time she stood motionless, then her shoulders sagged. She closed the door quietly, went to the back, and lifted out two suitcases and a smaller bag. When he silently offered to take them, she tightened her grip and nodded toward the open rear window. "Could you close that for me when you go?"

He watched her climb the steps, then disappear inside before he picked up the shovel and moved to the back of the car. With a cop's curiosity, though, he couldn't just push the window down. He had to look inside.

In the cargo area were three open boxes holding pots, pans, and dishes; two laundry baskets filled with odds and ends; and a lumpy pillowcase shoved full of towels. It looked like everything a down-on-their-luck family might own.

Surely not. Surely they'd just gone to spend Thanksgiving with family and were on their way home again. But who took their own dishes and towels along when they visited family? Who packed laundry baskets with silverware, an iron, a couple of tattered books, a stack of framed photographs, and an envelope marked Personal Records for a short holiday trip?

Maybe someone who didn't have a home to return to.

But if that was the case, why didn't she plan to stay here? The house was hers. Except for utilities, she could live there free. If that option was unacceptable, then she could put the place up for sale. It might take time to find a buyer, but she would end up with a nice chunk of change.

When she suddenly appeared at his side, he was startled. He hadn't heard the front door open and close, and the snow had muffled her footsteps. Although he hadn't touched a thing, he felt guilty for snooping.

She didn't say a word, but reached past him, pulled a scruffy teddy bear from one basket, closed the window, and returned to the house again. That grungy little bear had been the only plaything he'd seen. She had three little kids in the house and apparently everything they owned in the car, and only the one toy.

Something was definitely wrong. Of course, as long as it wasn't illegal, it was none of his concern. Just to be on the safe side, though, when he went to work Monday, he was going to stop by the county tax assessor's office. He was going to check the records on this house and make sure that the rightful owner was, in fact, Emilie Dalton.

He chided himself with the fact that she probably was. People just didn't break into other people's houses and take up residence, not even people with no place else to go. He was being overly suspicious, but life— and his ex-wife—had taught him that things often weren't what they appeared. He would check the property records, just for his own satisfaction, and when he found out that she had a right to be here, end of story.

She wouldn't be his business, and she certainly wouldn't be his problem.

Aware of her stomach's hungry rumbling, Emilie went into the parlor, where once again she found Alanna peeking out the window. Josie and Brendan were playing on the floor, and the plate with one last cinnamon roll sat on the hearth. She dropped Ernest the bear between the kids, then went to the food, breaking the roll in half and washing it down with a gulp of lukewarm cocoa. She took the other half with her as she joined her niece at the window. "You don't have to hide. The neighbors know we're here."

"Who is that man?"

Emilie looked out above Alanna's head at Nathan Bishop, shoveling snow from the Winchesters' driveway. He didn't seem to mind the cold at all, while her feet were numb and her fingers were tingling. "His name is Nathan. He lives across the street."

"I saw him in the restaurant last night." Alanna glanced at the little ones, then lowered her voice to a cautious whisper. "He's a cop, Aunt Emilie."

"I know."

"Is he going to arrest you? Is he going to take us away?"

"No." She swallowed the last bite of the roll, then wrapped her arms around her niece. "The woman who owned this house died a long time ago and left it to her niece in Massachusetts. She's never visited Bethlehem, so no one here knows her. They don't even know her name, except, I guess, the lawyer. The ladies next door assumed that I was her, and they told him."

Alanna turned to hug her tightly. "Let's get out of here, Aunt Emilie. Let's go someplace where no one will find us, please! I don't want you to go to jail, and I don't want to be split up from Josie and Brendan. They need me, and we all need you. Let's go now before he finds out that we don't belong here. You finish eating, and I'll get the kids ready. We'll put the suitcases back in the car and the key back where you found it and go."

Emilie brushed the girl's hair back from her face. "I wish we could, but the road out of here is closed because of the snow, and the car won't start. It'll be towed to a garage Monday morning. We're stuck, sweetheart."

"Can we afford a garage?"

"No, but we have to have the car."

"So what are we going to do?"

"We'll manage."

"How?"

"Don't worry about it, honey. I'll take care of it."

"But *how*?"

"I'll take care of it," she repeated. The car was her first priority. She would find out Monday how much the repairs would cost and how long they would take. If her luck held, it would be something simple and inexpensive, and they would be back on their way by Tuesday.

And if it was neither simple nor inexpensive? She would get a job. It would mean staying in town longer—pretending longer, lying longer, and running the risk of exposure—but so far everyone she'd met believed she belonged here. She would just keep them believing it.

Actually, she thought with a shiver, her *first* priority was keeping warm, and that meant braving the backyard snowdrifts for more firewood. There was just one other important first to take care of.

Where are your kids? Nathan Bishop had asked, making a mistake that many others had made. People took one look at her and the children, all blond-haired and blue-eyed, and automatically assumed they were hers. Sometimes she corrected them, and sometimes she didn't. Back in Boston, it hadn't mattered. Here in Bethlehem, in their stolen house, with a cop who could ruin all her plans, it mattered.

She drew Alanna to the hearth, scooped Brendan into her lap, and pulled Josie close. "Listen, kids, we're going to have to stay here a few days, until some of the snow is gone. While we're here, we're going to play a game of let's pretend. We're going to make everyone in town believe that I'm your mother."

"But you're not," Josie said flatly. "You're our aunt."

"I know that, honey, and so do you, but we want to fool everyone else."

"Why?"

"It's just a game, Josie, but it's a very important game. Do you think you can do it?"

"Yup." Her head bobbed up and down, making her hair swing.

Emilie knew better than to leave it at that. "*Will* you do it?"

"Nope. Don't want to."

Brendan wriggled free to stand beside his sister and echoed her rebellious response in baby-soft tones. "Doan want to."

It was Alanna who replied. "All right, then you guys can't play. You're too little anyway. You'd forget to call her Mom 'cause you're just babies."

Josie gave her sister a shove that tumbled her back against the marble surround. "I am not a baby! I'm six years old! I want to play, Aunt—" Catching herself, she gave Alanna a flinty look. "Mama, tell Lannie to let me play her stupid old game."

"If you promise to always remember to call me Mom, you can," Emilie said, and the younger girl stuck her tongue out at her sister. So did Brendan. "Okay, now you guys stay here with Alanna. I'm going to get some more firewood."

"Okay, Mama." Josie's words were repeated with a giggle by her brother as they returned to their play.

Emilie steeled herself for the cold. The hallway could have sprouted icicles if there was a drop of water in the house, and her first step out the back door was even worse. Resisting the urge to flee back inside, she ducked her head and made a path through the snow to the near end of the woodpile. She moved three logs at a time, laying them haphazardly on the kitchen floor. It was a tedious and miserable job, but she was grateful for the drudge work. She didn't have to think about what she was doing. She could simply shut her mind off and do it.

She needed desperately to shut off her mind for a while.

Time and again, she trudged back and forth, packing down the snow. She had gathered yet another armload and was turning toward the house when her temporary neighbor came around the corner. The mere sight of him was enough to make her nerves jump.

He stepped onto the path in front of her, blocking her way, and took the logs from her. She didn't have the strength to stop him. "Where do you want it?"

"In the kitchen." She watched him for a moment, then returned to the woodpile. Once again he met her halfway, but this time he didn't offer to take the logs.

"Go inside and get warm. I'll do this."

The part of her that had learned when she was only five that the only person she could count on was herself wanted to refuse. But the part that was neck-deep in misery, that could no longer feel her fingers or toes, was perfectly willing to let the job fall on his more-than-capable shoulders. While she debated the two choices, he went inside with an armload of logs, came back, and picked up another. Finally, knowing she'd reached the limits of her endurance, she followed him into the kitchen.

He was stacking the wood neatly against one wall. As he added her logs to the pile, she summoned the energy to ask, "Why are you doing this?"

His gaze skimmed over her. "Don't people in Massachusetts offer help when their neighbors need it?"

"Sure. The boys next door helped us move once. They moved our belongings into their possession." It had happened on the last move, when their grace period before eviction expired. The boys hadn't gotten anything of value—the kids' toys, some books, a few pieces of worn clothing. None of it had been worth more than a few dollars, and the punks, discovering that, had probably thrown it in the trash. The incident had shown her how little anyone cared about anyone else. It had convinced her that she never should have left Atlanta. It had been the final blow to her naive, everything-will-be-all-right faith in others.

Nathan looked at her again, his gaze steady, dark, sympathetic. His voice, when he spoke, was quiet. "People aren't like that in Bethlehem. Believe me, I know. I'm a cop." He smiled faintly, then gestured toward the hallway. "Go on and warm up before you get a bad case of frostbite."

With a weary nod, she went to the door, then looked back. He was still standing there watching her. "Thank you." After his nod of acceptance, she walked, zombielike, through the house and to the parlor, where Alanna had opened the drapes and folded last night's bed neatly away. Their blankets were tucked over the sofa, the pillows had been put back in place, and everything breakable had been moved out of the kids' reach. Josie and Brendan were playing in front of the windows, and Alanna sat on the hearth, lost in the worried thoughts that occupied too much of her life.

If only Alanna didn't look so distressed, it would be a homey scene. The scent of woodsmoke had finally overcome the musty odor. The room was cozy, warm, and bright, and Josie and Brendan were being as well behaved as they ever were.

Alanna jumped to her feet, adding two logs to the fire for a sudden flare of heat. It was as painful to Emilie as it was welcome as she began the slow task of unbuttoning her coat. Her hands were purplish white, her fingers stiff and icy hot, her toes beyond feeling.

Alanna hung her coat on a coat tree she'd dragged in from somewhere, helped Emilie remove her shoes, socks, and jeans, then wrapped a blanket around her. "Go sit by the fire. I'll get you some dry clothes."

"Just socks, honey." Her feet stinging with returning sensation, Emilie sat down in front of the fire, then slid bonelessly to the floor. The last thing she remembered was a pillow placed underneath her head, then gratefully she slept.

# Chapter Three

Nathan added his last load of firewood to the stack on the kitchen floor, then closed the door. The house seemed as empty and still as always, but it was only an illusion. Emilie Dalton and her kids had taken up residence somewhere in this frigid, uninhabitable place. There was no electricity—a flip of the wall switch confirmed that. The lack of gas service made the furnace useless, and there couldn't be water without heat to keep the pipes from freezing. What a way to live.

Down the hall, the bathroom door was open. The lid to the empty toilet tank leaned against one wall, but the bowl held a few inches of water, probably melted from snow, with a thin skin of ice across the top. On the opposite side of the hall, another door opened into the formal dining room. The next door was warm when he touched it. With a rap on the solid wood, he swung it open.

There was a difference in temperature of a good sixty degrees between the parlor and the rest of the house. He quickly closed the door behind him, giving the room a quick sweep. The younger kids were playing and ignored him. The older one was between him and them, eyes wide and as blue as her mother's. She looked frightened but determined to stand her ground.

"Hi. Where's your mom—" Just then he saw the blanket-covered figure in front of the fireplace. Emilie lay on her side, covered with a blanket from her nose to below her knees. Her legs were bare, slender, pale, and splotchy red from the cold, and her feet looked small inside two pairs of thick socks. She was motionless, in the sort of deep sleep brought on by exhaustion.

He stepped forward and offered his hand. The kid didn't accept it. "I'm Nathan. I live in the blue house across the street."

"I'm Alanna."

"I was going to ask your mother if she wants the firewood in here, but I won't bother her now." He turned back toward the door, then stopped. "When she wakes up, tell her to let me know if she needs to go anywhere."

"Where would she go?"

There was fear underlying what should have been an innocent question. It made him wonder just how tough life in Massachusetts had been for them. "I don't know. Maybe to the grocery store for food? You guys do eat, don't you?"

She looked as if she didn't quite know how to answer. Finally she blurted out, "I'm not supposed to talk to strangers."

Would it make any difference if he told her he was a cop? Maybe. Or it might make her even more nervous. Who knew what this family had been through?

"Okay, I'm going. If you need more wood, it's in the kitchen. Don't forget to tell your mother about the store. If she sleeps a long time and you guys get hungry, let me know. The two ladies next door would get a kick out of cooking for you. Okay?"

She nodded, but he suspected it was a meaningless gesture. Like her mother, Alanna was wary of people offering help. If Emilie slept all day, Alanna would let her. If the kids got hungry, they would stay hungry until Emilie was awake to feed them.

He left the parlor door open a crack. At the broad kitchen door, he turned and saw that she was watching to make sure he left. A cautious kid. He supposed it was necessary in this day and age, but it was a shame. Kids that young shouldn't have to worry about being safe. They deserved some measure of security. Adulthood was soon enough to deal with the uncertainties of life.

After too many years of uncertainty, his own life had gotten pretty secure in the last few years, though it wasn't the life he'd expected. Fourteen years ago he'd had his future planned: a job with the New York City Police Department, working with his best friend, marriage to the girl he'd loved since they were kids, promotions, babies, and more promotions until, finally, retirement. It was all he'd wanted. Diana had claimed that he and the babies were all she'd ever wanted.

He had never asked when she'd stopped loving him. He hadn't wanted to know if it'd been a year, two, or, hell, maybe even all the way back to the beginning of their marriage. Maybe she had never loved him. Maybe she had only used him until something better had come along.

Something better *had* come, and it had ended in tragedy. Nathan had lost everything—his home, his best friend, his job, and his family. Diana, who had promised to stay with him forever, and sweet baby Elisabeth, who'd never been his to lose. He had come to Bethlehem to deal with the bitterness, the anger, and the sorrow. He'd wanted a place where he could work and live alone, and he'd found it. He was lonely, sure, but that was something he had to learn to live with. Without trust, there wasn't much chance of anything else, and after Diana, he didn't have much trust. He didn't have much of anything.

He went next door, ringing the old-fashioned bell, and waited for Corinna, dressed in green as always, to answer. In spring and summer the shades were paler, growing darker through the fall. By Christmas she would be wearing deep, dark greens that, paired with Agatha's cherry reds, were appropriate to the season.

"We thought you had forgotten your cake." Corinna ushered him in, helping him remove his coat, brushing a few drops of melted snow from his hair.

The only grandmother he'd known had died when he was just a kid, but he remembered her as being like the sisters—kind, generous, loving—though maybe he was kidding himself. Kindness and generosity didn't run in his family, and, while they'd all been fond of each other, there'd been no deep emotional attachments. His parents hadn't been the least bit sad at seeing Nathan and his brothers move away from Pennsylvania. It didn't bother them that years passed without seeing the sons they knew no better than the grandchildren they'd never met. They didn't even seem overly attached to each other. He'd always thought that one could simply disappear, and the other would miss him for a while, but not for long. Life would go on.

No doubt about that. Your life could get shot to hell, but at least it went on. He was proof.

"I was next door," he said, following Corinna to the sweet smells of the kitchen.

"Getting acquainted with the new neighbor?"

He knew that tone in her voice. In addition to housing and feeding him, she and Agatha felt it was their duty to find a wife for him. They had presented every single young woman in the county for his approval. He'd dated some and gone to bed with a few, but he'd never met one who'd tempted him with more. Emilie Dalton, pretty as she was—wary as she was, mother of three as she was—wasn't likely to be an exception. "Don't get your hopes up. She was inside. I just carried some firewood in for her and the kids."

Both women turned to him, disappointment in every line of their faces. "Kids? She's married?"

"Now, Agatha, you know one has nothing to do with the other, not these days," Corinna chided as she set a cup of coffee in front of him. "A lot of modern women choose to have children outside the sanctity of marriage."

"She didn't strike me as a very modern woman."

"You saw her for—what? Three minutes? Hardly long enough to tell."

She didn't strike Nathan as very modern, either. She did have an independent streak a mile wide, but so did the sisters. Mostly Emilie Dalton struck him as needy. Disillusioned. Down, but not defeated.

"How many children does she have?"

"Three."

"And where is their father?"

"Not here with them." He hadn't asked whether there was a Mr. Dalton because it was none of his business. He suspected there wasn't, though a man was probably the source of Emilie's problems. Somewhere along the line, everything that had gone wrong in her life could probably be traced to a relationship turned sour.

"It's unfortunate she didn't let Herbert know she was coming this weekend," Corinna said. "He could have arranged for the utilities to be turned on."

"She's not staying long. She was planning to leave today, but her car won't start and the valley's snowed in. Which reminds me . . ." There was a part of him that didn't like butting into other people's business, but, hey, he was a cop. Looking out for the people in the community was part of his job. "I think they're traveling on a pretty strict budget and she wasn't counting on car trouble, so if you have any extra cookies or milk or casseroles to spare, they could probably use them."

Both sisters' eyes lit up. He hadn't been kidding when he'd told Alanna they would get a kick out of cooking for them. They were probably already planning the next few days' meals for the Daltons, and they wouldn't take no for an answer, no matter how Emilie might try to give it.

After leaving his cup in the sink, he picked up the cake carrier. "I'm going home now. Thanks for the cake."

Agatha stopped her work long enough to press a kiss on his cheek. "Thank you for shoveling the driveway, dear."

At the front door, Corinna echoed her thanks and gave him a kiss, too, then closed the door behind him. They were sweet old ladies, and the closest thing to a family he would likely ever have. They treated him like family, too, though they had their own. Agatha had never married, but she'd taken in a young relative or two. Two of Corinna's four children lived in town, with kids of their own, and there were three or four generations of cousins around. But they made room for him in a way his own family never had. For however long the Daltons stayed, the sisters would make room for them, too.

At home, he changed into dry jeans, then settled at the breakfast table with instant coffee and a slice of coconut cake. Diana had been a great cook, but she'd hated coconut. She'd hated carrot cake, too, but she'd baked a few of those because it was Mike's favorite. Her explanation for his favorite when she refused to make her husband's had been lame—Mike was his friend and a guest in their home—but, like a fool, Nathan had bought it. Only later had he discovered exactly what kind of friend Mike Pizzetti had been. By then, it had been too late for all of them, but especially Mike.

With a heavy sigh, he contemplated the kitchen around him. When he was really tired, he looked forward to extra days off, but when he got them, he didn't know what to do with himself. His mother had taught him to pick up after himself daily, so the only dishes to be washed were the ones in front of him, the only work to be done was a load of laundry, and the only way to pass his time was alone. In warmer weather, he could drive up into the hills and go fishing, help the sisters with their yard work, or take his rifle to the forest and go hunting. Even if he never tried to shoot anything, it got him out of the house and away from bad memories. But in this weather, all he could do was brood.

In direct contradiction to his thoughts, the doorbell rang. Through the frosted sidelight, he could see a shadow, too slender for Corinna, too tall for Agatha, and just right for his new neighbor. When he opened the door, he saw that she hadn't slept nearly long enough to ease the stress lines that etched her face or erase the dark circles underneath her eyes. Why had he thought she might? She had kids to take care of and an unlivable situation to make livable. Why should she rest just because she looked ready to collapse from exhaustion?

She huddled inside her coat, her arms crossed over her chest with her bare hands tucked underneath them. Her smile was tentative. "Hi. Alanna said you offered to take us to the grocery store." Her voice lifted a bit at the end, and so did her eyebrows when she looked at him, seeking confirmation that he'd made the offer and it still stood.

"Give me a couple of minutes to get my shoes on. Come on in."

Hugging herself a little tighter, Emilie stepped a few feet over the threshold, where she stopped, fingers laced loosely together, and watched as he sat down on the stairs to put his boots on.

The house was still, as if no one else was home. She

wondered if he was married. He wasn't wearing a ring, there was no sign of a woman in the part of the house she could see, and no one seemed to have a prior claim on his time on his day off. On the other hand, he was a good candidate for marriage. He was in his thirties, settled in a small town, living in a family-size house in a neighborhood of families. He had a steady job, and he was certainly handsome. His jaw was strong, a little stubborn, and his mouth, if he ever really smiled, just might be his best feature. In Atlanta, some smart woman would have snapped him up years ago.

*Atlanta.* She'd been homesick since the day she'd driven away a year ago. Sometimes, when she first awoke in the morning, she thought for one sweet moment that she was there. Other times—like now—she thought she would never get back there. The longer they were delayed, the better the chances of getting caught. If the shelter hadn't yet reported their absence to Social Services, they would know first thing Monday morning when the social worker showed up to take the children. She would report their disappearance to the judge who had rescinded the custody agreement. He was a hard man, fresh out of sympathy for weak women, unfit mothers, and hard-luck aunts. He wouldn't look kindly on her defiance of his order and would surely direct the authorities to send out bulletins all the way from Boston to Atlanta.

That was the reason she'd chosen such an out-of-the-way route. The logical travel plan would have taken her south out of Boston and down I-95 close to the coast. Instead she'd gone west, intending to turn south sometime before reaching Buffalo, in the hope that whatever effort was made to find them was centered on the eastern route.

She refocused her attention as Nathan finished lacing his boots, then took an armful of items from the closet. The parka and one pair of gloves he kept for himself. The rest—two knitted caps, a scarf, and more gloves— he gave to her. "I'll get the truck and meet you across the street. Do you want to bring the kids or leave them with Agatha and Corinna?" When she hesitated, he went on. "I can vouch for their trustworthiness. They both taught school for forty years and Sunday school for fifty. They're widely respected in town."

She didn't doubt that. Her concern was with the kids, not the character of their prospective baby-sitters. Alanna would be careful, and Brendan wouldn't talk to strangers, but Josie . . . If she got comfortable, she just might blurt out everything—and all it took to make Josie comfortable was something sweet to eat, a glass of milk, and a little adult attention. "I'll bring them," she murmured, and he shrugged as if it made no difference to him.

"Get them ready. I'll be over in a few minutes."

"Thanks for these." She held up the gloves and the knitted warmers. "We'll be waiting." She slipped out and returned to the Pierce house, tugging his gloves on along the way. They were black, thick, way too big for her, and a necessity in this weather. Though the girls' coats had hoods, they were too big—like the coats themselves—and slipped off with every move they made. They could put the caps to good use.

Her smile was tinged with bitterness. Keeping three kids and herself in gloves and hats for winter shouldn't be a challenge. Last winter's gear had been lost or outgrown, so this winter she had outfitted them all again. Unfortunately, it had been an unexpectedly warm day when they'd moved out of the apartment, and, since they weren't wearing the gloves and hats, she had tossed them into the nearest box, on top of the kids' sad collection of toys. Of no use to teenage punks with no qualms about stealing from the newly homeless, they were probably in a landfill somewhere now, and there was no money to squeeze from their budget for replacements.

She let herself into the parlor. "Come on, kids, let's get your coats on."

Alanna's eyes brightened, and she jumped to her feet and grabbed two coats from the rack. "Are we leaving? Did you get the car started? Can we go—" One look at Emilie's face made her excitement fade. "Are we going someplace with *him*?"

"Mr. Bishop is taking us to the store so I can get enough groceries to tide us over until we can go. Aren't you hungry?"

"I want a hot dog," Josie piped up. "Like last night."

Disappointment made Alanna's voice sharp. "We can't go out to eat. We don't have the money. Don't you understand that?"

As Josie's lower lip started to tremble, Emilie slid her arm around Alanna's shoulders. "I think we can probably manage hot dogs. Maybe we can even roast some wieners and marshmallows in the fireplace. Come on now. He'll be here any minute. Josie, get your coat. Alanna, help Brendan with his." After pressing a kiss to her niece's forehead, she pulled a cap down over her hair, then did the same with Josie on her way to the fireplace.

She shoveled ashes over the logs until the flames were banked, then moved the screen into place. Next she removed one glove so she could count the money in her wallet, even though she already knew the amount—one hundred twenty-one dollars and a handful of change.

Panic gripped her. She would manage, she'd told Alanna. But *how*? There was no one she could call for help. She hadn't had a single friend in Boston, and the friends she'd left behind in Atlanta had been just everyday friends. Even under the best circumstances, there wasn't anyone she could borrow money from, and certainly not less than a month before Christmas.

There wasn't any family to call, either. Her father was probably out there somewhere, but the last she'd seen or heard of him was twenty-four years ago, on the day he'd turned her and Berry over to the social workers in Atlanta, then walked away without a look back. Berry had run after him, crying and pleading, and it'd taken both women to hold her back. Emilie had simply cried. Only a few days later the same women had taken Berry away, and Emilie had stopped crying.

So what were her options? She could tell Nathan to forget the shopping trip and take them straight to the police department—not a very appealing choice. Or she could continue her deception and pray that no one in town discovered the truth before they escaped. More appealing by far, if she could do it. If she could keep telling lies without slipping up. If she kept her stories simple. If she was unconditionally honest about everything else in her life except the absence of an aunt named Miriam.

But how would she find a job in a snowbound town without transportation? What would she do with the kids? Could she enroll the girls in school without the local school contacting Boston for records? Would the Boston police notify the old school that the girls were missing? And what about Brendan? Where would she find a baby-sitter and how would she pay?

Plus there was the house. Living without electricity, water, and gas was okay for a few days, but could they do it indefinitely? Would the authorities let them? Nathan knew what the conditions were, and he was a police officer. If he thought the kids' welfare was at risk, he was obliged to take action.

If it came to that, she would just have to persuade him otherwise, because the simple fact was, she didn't have a choice. As long as there was *anything* she could do to keep the kids together—beg, borrow, lie, cheat, or steal—she had to try.

Outside a horn sounded, and Josie raced to the window. "It's a man in a truck," she announced before spinning around and racing toward the door. Alanna caught her just in time.

"Remember, Josie: Aunt Emilie is our mom, okay? You call her that, and don't you say *anything* about our real mom."

Josie jerked away. "I know how to play your dumb game, Lannie. I bet *you* mess up before I do." Sliding around Alanna, she opened the door and hit the hall at a run.

With a silent prayer for the best, Emilie wrapped the scarf around her neck. It was navy blue, over five feet long, and smelled enticingly of aftershave. Of Nathan. For one weak moment, she wanted to gather the long dangling ends and bury her face in them. Instead she swung Brendan into her arms and followed Alanna out.

Nathan's black Blazer was parked in the street. Josie, who had stopped at the top of the steps, jumped to the ground once she knew Emilie was nearby and struggled through snow that was half as deep as she was tall.

Alanna stayed close to Emilie's side. "We shouldn't be doing this," she whispered. "He's a cop. We should stay as far away from him as possible."

"He's helping us, honey." Although she agreed with the girl's last statement. They *should* stay away from Nathan, but that would make him suspicious. If he got too suspicious, he might run her through their police computers or find out who really owned the house. "It'll be okay. Just keep Josie under control, will you?"

By the time they reached the street, Nathan had opened the passenger door, and Josie had climbed into the backseat. Alanna slid in next, and Emilie handed Brendan to her before climbing in front. When she settled beside Nathan, she caught a whiff of the same fragrance on the scarf. It was musky, spicy, subtle. After she'd worn the scarf a while, the scent would be on her coat and her skin.

She found the idea too intimate for her own peace of mind.

"Kids, thank Mr. Bishop for the hats," she directed as they pulled away from the curb.

"Thank you." Josie's response was quick, glib, and verged on insincere, but it was better than her sister's. Alanna yanked the cap from her head and tossed it onto the console between the front seats. "You can have this one back. I don't need it. It messes up my hair."

Before Emilie could give her a warning look, Nathan met her gaze in the rearview mirror. "You stay out too long in this cold without something on your head, you'll get frostbite, and your ears will fall right off."

Holding on to the back of his seat, Josie popped to her feet and leaned around. "Are you kidding? Can ears really fall off?"

"They really can."

"Then she'd have to wear her stupid hair long all the time to cover up the holes in her head." Her giggle ended in an angry exclamation when Alanna yanked her back into the seat.

"Be quiet and put your seat belt on or I'll pinch your ears off, you big baby."

"Mama, make Lannie quit calling me that! I'm six whole years old! I'm not a baby!"

Emilie gave the girls a sharp look, and they settled down. Then she turned to gaze out the window. They were still in a residential area, but she could see businesses ahead. There was the square on the left, a big stone building that surely must be the courthouse, blocks lined with shops of every kind, and, on the right in the next block, a grocery store. Nathan didn't turn into the parking lot, though. At the next corner, he made a left turn, passed the square, and turned left again onto Main Street.

There was no shabbiness. The bows on the streetlamps weren't drooping, the holly hadn't dropped its berries, and the nutcracker soldiers were as bright blue, red, and green as they had appeared last night. If the town suffered from economic depression, it certainly didn't show. She'd been wrong. Bethlehem really was a Norman Rockwell painting come to life. It was beautiful.

When Nathan parked and shut off the engine, Emilie found they were in a familiar place: in front of the diner. She thought of the money in her purse and she gave him a wary look. "What are we doing?"

"Having lunch."

She had intended to eat lunch at home. Groceries, she could manage, as long as she was penny-conscious, but the eleven dollars another restaurant meal would cost was eleven dollars more than she could afford. With her face red and her throat tight, she faced him. "I can't afford . . ."

"My treat," he said as if treating an indigent woman and her kids to a meal was an everyday thing.

"I appreciate your generosity, really I do, but . . ." It embarrassed her and made her feel beholden to him. She'd spent much of her life beholden to strangers for everything from clothes to food to a bed to sleep in, and she'd sworn that when she got out on her own, she would provide for herself. She had, too, for eleven years. Until recently. "I can't pay you back."

"I don't expect you to."

Of course not. He had enough money. To him ten or fifteen dollars for a meal was negligible. To her it was everything. "*I* would expect me to."

He gave her a steady, stubborn look, then shrugged. "Then you can invite me over for dinner sometime. Fair enough?" Without waiting for an answer, he got out, then slid the seat forward so Josie could jump out. With hot dogs and sundaes on her mind, she did so without a glance at Emilie.

Brendan was trying unsuccessfully to undo his seat belt so he could join Josie outside, but Alanna sat motionless in the backseat, looking at Emilie for guidance. With a little shrug, Emilie opened her door.

There were few customers in the diner, though Nathan seemed to know everyone. The attention made her uncomfortable. She'd spent most of the last year living in anonymity, and she would prefer to continue that way, unseen and unnoticed, at least until her problems were resolved. But everyone in the place had given them a look or two, and the waitress, the older one who'd been working last night, looked extremely interested as she brought menus and coffee to their table.

"Morning, Nathan. I see you've got company."

"New neighbors. Maeve, this is Emilie Dalton, Miriam Pierce's niece."

"Miriam—Well, goodness. Harry, this is old Mrs. Pierce's niece. Welcome to town, Emilie. The holidays are a perfect time to come to Bethlehem. We may be little, but we've got a name to live up to, you know."

Maeve was joined by the gray-haired man from last night, who wore an apron around his middle: "Harry

Winslow. I own this joint. Emilie, is it? Miriam used to tell us what a pretty girl you were. She sure was right." With a wink and an elbow in the waitress's ribs, he went on. "Not much of a family resemblance, is there, Maeve?"

"To her benefit," someone murmured from a nearby table.

"Oh, Miriam was a good woman."

"If not a handsome one," the same someone added.

"Don't mind him." Maeve gave the man a warning look, then smiled. "These your kids, honey?"

Emilie rattled off the kids' names. Alanna simply nodded, and Brendan buried his face against Emilie's shoulder, but Josie grinned brightly. "I'm six years old, and I want a hot dog and a strawberry sundae."

"Yes, ma'am." Maeve executed an impressive salute. "I'd better get back to work."

Once their order was in and they were alone again, Emilie stirred sugar into her coffee. She hated deceiving nice people, accepting their friendly gestures when she didn't deserve them. When this was over and she made it home, she was going to have to do some heavy penance to make up for this and all the lies left to tell.

The next one came all too soon.

"Where did you go for Thanksgiving?"

"Nowhere."

Nathan raised one brow. "You said home is in Massachusetts. You're in New York. You obviously went somewhere."

She tried to think quickly. She'd never indulged much in untruths and wasn't at all good at thinking them up on the spur of the moment. If repairs on the car were going to take longer than she hoped, she would have to get better at this lying business, or she would be found out for sure. "We were coming here."

"To spend one night, then turn around and drive back to Massachusetts this morning?"

"To see M—Aunt Miriam's house."

"Why not plan on staying today and tomorrow and going back Sunday? Why make the trip in such a rush? Is someone waiting for you at home?"

"No."

"No Mr. Dalton?" In the back of his mind, Nathan had been wondering about that ever since the sisters had asked. Not that it mattered to him. After all, her stay in Bethlehem was temporary.

"No."

"Was there at one time?"

When she glanced at the kids, her message was clear. She didn't want to talk about the kids' father in front of them, even though only Alanna, looking anxious and angry, was paying attention. Josie was on her knees, gazing out the window and paying them no mind, and Brendan lay sprawled on the bench. As Emilie spoke, his gaze moved back to her.

"You ask a lot of questions. Is that an occupational hazard? You're suspicious of everyone?"

"Just curious." But, to some extent, Nathan supposed it was suspicion, and it had little to do with his job. Diana and Mike had taught him everything he needed to know about trust and betrayal. When two of the people he'd loved best could fool him so completely, who knew what some stranger could do given the opportunity?

"Is there a Mrs. Bishop?"

It was his turn for discomfort and sudden restlessness. He shifted on the bench and heard the vinyl crackle. "Only my mother and my brothers' wives."

"How many brothers?"

"Three brothers, three sisters-in-law, and seven nephews."

"You're lucky."

"I've never met most of the nephews, and I haven't seen any of the bunch in eight years. The sisters-in-law send cards at Christmas to keep in touch. We're not exactly a close family." He saw by the change in her expression that the subtle sarcasm in his last remark didn't go unnoticed. "Where is your family?"

She offered no answer beyond the shake of her head. Did that mean she didn't know, didn't have one, or was estranged from them? He could identify with all three possibilities. If not for his sisters-in-law, his parents wouldn't know where he was. They were definitely estranged, and he'd never felt a part of a real family, except for the six years he'd been married. Even that had been an illusion.

Before he could ask another question, she brought up one of her own. "If I wanted to find a job here, where would I start looking?"

Nathan considered the question. The diner already had a new waitress. The high school was looking for a new football coach; while she would undoubtedly please the team members, he doubted she was quite what the school board had in mind. There were no openings in the police department, nothing he'd heard about in the city offices. However, there was one possibility. "The wife of one of our officers works over at the inn. She's pregnant and due to quit any day now. December and January are Holly's busiest months, so she'll be hiring a replacement, if she hasn't already."

"What's the job?"

"Housekeeping." There was an apologetic tone to his voice. Hotel maid wasn't a job many people aspired to, but everything about Emilie said that she was desperate enough to take *any* job.

"I clean up after these guys for free. Getting paid for it might be fun."

Josie turned around and dropped down on the bench. "Lannie said you're a cop."

"I am."

"Where's your gun and your badge?"

"Here's my badge. My gun's at home. I didn't think you were so dangerous that I needed it." He removed his credentials case from his pocket, flipped it open, and offered it for her examination.

Drawing her feet onto the bench, she rested the case on her knees, studied the badge, then turned her attention to his ID. Finally, she handed it back. "You look mean. I can look mean, too." She screwed up her face and bared her teeth, making her brother smile and her sister scowl. "You ever shoot anyone?"

"No."

"If I was a cop, I'd shoot everyone." Rising onto her knees again, she drew an imaginary gun from its holster and pointed it directly at Maeve, who responded with exaggerated alarm.

"Don't shoot. I bring hot dogs."

Josie holstered the gun, then leaned forward, and whispered loudly, "I wouldn't really shoot you."

"Well, that's good to know."

"At least, not till I get my strawberry sundae."

Nathan watched her plop down on the seat and await the plate Maeve had for her. By choice he hadn't had much contact with kids since moving to Bethlehem. In the beginning every little kid he'd seen had reminded him painfully of Elisabeth, the innocent victim in the mess his marriage and life had become. So many years had passed since he'd seen her. The last time he'd held her she'd been barely three months old, chubby and solemn, with her father's dark hair and eyes.

Now she was a year older than Josie. Did she still look like Mike, or were some of Diana's features more noticeable? Did she like hot dogs and ice cream? Was she a tomboy who could be dissuaded from shooting a waitress with a bribe of food or the prissy sort who would sit primly with her hands in her lap?

Diana would see to it that he never knew. Legally he had no right. It didn't matter that, from the moment Diana had told him that she was pregnant, he'd planned for and anticipated Elisabeth's birth, that he'd held her even before her mother had, that for three sweet months he had believed she was his daughter. It didn't matter that he was listed on her birth certificate as her father, because Diana would easily prove in court that he wasn't. It didn't matter at all that he had loved her. He had no claim to her. End of story.

When Maeve cleared away the dishes and asked about dessert, Emilie answered first. "You guys don't need ice cream in the middle of the day, do you?"

"Oh, but, Mama," Josie began, and Brendan echoed her protest. Then, with a sly grin, Josie turned to him. "You ask her."

Emilie gave him a steady look, waiting for him to intervene, and he looked right back, his gaze cataloging features—long blond hair that surely must be as soft as silk. Blue eyes edged with the wariness that came to someone whom life had dealt a bad hand. Fair skin, a straight nose, finely structured bones, and a mouth too tempting by far. There was an overall impression of fragility about her, but it was misleading. She might look like china, but it was just veneer. Underneath it, she was strong and determined.

He liked that in a woman.

Fortunately for the kids, in this instance, he was more determined. After one long moment stretched into another, she relented. "All right. You can have them this time."

After taking sundae orders from the kids and a request for coffee from Nathan, Maeve turned to Emilie. "What about you, hon? I've got some pumpkin and mincemeat pies."

"No, thanks."

"Coffee?"

She smiled. "No. I'm fine."

After Maeve left, Nathan commented, "You should do that more often."

"What?"

"Smile." It wasn't a dazzler of a smile, though he suspected she was capable of those, too. In fact, it was a little sad around the edges, but it was better than the worried look she wore the rest of the time.

Her expression sobered, her mouth forming a thin, grim line. "Sometimes there's not much reason to smile."

"I can think of three."

She looked at the kids, and the smile and the sadness came back.

After Maeve served them once more, Nathan sweetened his coffee, then settled back to ask a few more questions. "Do you have a job waiting for you back home in Massachusetts?"

Her gaze turned dark. "Not anymore."

"What did you do?"

"I was a secretary there. I've also done some bookkeeping and worked as an office manager."

"What happened to the job?"

"My employers decided that the best way to increase profits was to leave town in the middle of the night, taking our paychecks with them."

"Were they ever found?"

She shook her head. "None of us suspected a thing. Everything seemed to be fine. They'd promoted some people, given some raises, promised everyone a Christmas bonus. Then they disappeared. There were no raises, no bonuses, no jobs. We didn't even get paid for our last month's work." Her fingers knotted tightly around a paper napkin, tearing it into pieces. Dropping it onto an empty plate, she glanced around the table at the empty dessert dishes. "I believe we're about ready to go."

"I'll pay while you get the kids into their coats."

As she began cleaning Brendan's sticky face and fingers, Nathan went to the counter. By the time he returned, they were ready.

The parking lot at the grocery store was packed with snow and fewer than half a dozen cars. Except for employees, the store appeared to be empty. They didn't see another shopper as they followed Emilie, with Brendan in the child seat, up and down the aisles. She picked her purchases carefully, choosing mostly generic labels, buying foods that needed no refrigeration or could be frozen, looking for things that could be served at room temperature or heated over an open fire. With so many considerations, it wasn't an easy task.

The kids were better behaved than any he'd ever seen in a store. They never questioned their mother's choices, never asked for any treats, never even looked longingly at something on the shelves. They seemed to understand all too well the limitations of too little money. It was a hell of a way for anyone to live, but especially kids.

In the bread section, Emilie chose a package of hot dog buns, then studied the rows of packaged muffins. She was reaching for one when he spoke. "The Winchester sisters make the best blueberry muffins around."

"I'm sure they do." She picked up the package.

"They'll probably bring you some later today. And some cookies. Maybe a cake and fresh bread." He told himself he had nothing to feel guilty about—the sisters would have offered her food anyway because it was the neighborly thing to do—but his face grew warm under her steady gaze. "They like to cook, and there's no way they can eat everything they make, so they give it away. They'll be giving some to you."

Looking embarrassed again, she returned the muffins to the shelf.

He touched her arm to get her attention. "Accepting a casserole or two from the sisters isn't going to threaten your independence, Emilie. They feed me all the time."

"There's a difference, though. *You* don't need their help."

And she did. It went unsaid, but it was clear in the tears that unexpectedly filled her eyes, in the unsteady quiver of her chin. He tried to make a joke out of the conversation at his own expense. "Obviously, you've never eaten my cooking. It's pretty awful."

"Emilie's a *good* cook." That came from Alanna, who immediately paled and turned away. Within a second or two, she turned back. "I'm sorry, Mama. I know you told me not to call you by your name. I won't do it again."

With a somber nod for the girl, Emilie finished her shopping. Nathan watched her as the checker rung up her purchases. Every price that flashed on the scanner made her droop a little lower. The total wasn't much, only a fraction of his weekly grocery bill even with the Winchesters supplying most of his meals, but it was too much for her.

He could help her. With no one but himself to provide

for, frequent free meals, and a ridiculously low rent, he had money to invest as well as a comfortable cushion in the bank for emergencies. He could move them into Holly's place for the weekend, where they'd have the necessities of heat and running water. He could pay to get their junker fixed and get them back home to Massachusetts and not even miss the money. *If* he thought there was a chance she would let him. Considering her reaction to the lunch and the sisters' upcoming offer of food, he figured it was more likely that the snow would magically give way to summer heat in the next half second.

They loaded the bags into the trunk and made the trip home in silence. He pulled into the Winchester driveway, since hers was still blocked by snow, and shut off the engine. By the time he'd opened the rear window to get the groceries, the girls had scrambled out and, with Emilie, who held Brendan on one hip, were lined up waiting to take the bags. He gave Josie the lightest one and Alanna the next two, then held on to the rest himself. Emilie looked for a moment as if she might protest, but instead smiled weakly and followed the girls through the snow to the porch.

Who had let her down, and how many times, to make her so determined—almost desperate—to get by on her own? he wondered as he brought up the rear. What had happened to convince her that she *must* do everything herself, with no help from anyone? How many times had she been disappointed by someone she should have been able to trust?

He knew about disappointment and distrust, but Bethlehem had taught him a lot about generosity, about being neighborly and looking out for one another. If Emilie stayed long enough, maybe it could teach her, too.

On the porch, she put Brendan down, then unlocked the door. The kids disappeared inside immediately, but Josie returned, offering him a grin from underneath the cap that fell over her eyes. "That was a good hot dog. It was nice of you to buy it for me."

"I'm glad you liked it."

As she took off again, Emilie took the grocery bags from him. "It *was* nice of you."

"I'm a nice guy. This is a nice town."

She looked past him at what little of the town she could see. "Yes, it is." After a moment, she shivered. "Thank you for lunch. And for taking us to the store. And for the gloves and stuff. And for the firewood. And—"

"You're welcome." For another moment, they simply looked at each other, then she shivered again, and he realized that he was cold, too. "I'll see you."

She nodded, backed through the doorway, then closed the door, leaving him standing alone on the porch.

# Chapter Four

Monday morning found Emilie standing in the drive-way, watching a tow truck pull her car away. She had explained her situation to the driver, hating every second of the shame and the feelings of worthlessness. In response, the young man had popped his chewing gum, shrugged, and said no problem. The garage owner—his father—would work it out with her.

It was the first day of December, and they had survived the weekend in good shape. No one had come knocking at the door with warrants, and there'd been no other slip-ups since Alanna's mistake in the grocery store. They'd been safe for three days, but she didn't feel any confidence. Today was the day the social worker in Boston would discover, if she hadn't already, that Emilie had fled with the children. Today the warrants and bulletins would surely go out.

She couldn't worry about it, though. Right now she had a job interview to get to. When the sisters had visited Saturday and again yesterday, they had brought with them food and an offer to set up a meeting with Holly McBride. They had also arranged to keep the children while she was gone and had even offered the use of their car. She had gratefully accepted the food and their baby-sitting services, but had turned down the car. Her experience in driving on snow-packed streets was limited to Thanksgiving's flight from Boston. Smashing up her own car was one thing, but smashing someone else's was another entirely. For her own peace of mind, she couldn't risk it, especially when she was going only a few blocks.

She hadn't walked even a block and a half when a truck slowed beside her. It was black and white, with a light bar on the roof and a gold badge on the door. Bethlehem Police Department circled the seven-pointed star in bold, black letters.

Nathan rolled the window down. "Hop in. I'll give you a ride."

The pleasure that seeing him brought was unexpected. Life had been so tough the last year that she had forgotten there could be enjoyment in simply looking at someone. She had become too accustomed to greeting others with the expectation of trouble. That was what the lawyers, the judges, the social worker, and the landlord had brought. That was *all* Berry had brought.

She stepped into the street and stopped beside the trunk. "I'm not going far." She didn't offer the comment as a refusal, though, but merely a chance for him to drive on without feeling obligated. He didn't.

"Then it won't take long. Climb in."

She obeyed, settling in the seat and fastening the belt while he rolled up the window. She had never been in a police car before, and she looked with more than a little trepidation at the radio, the handcuffs dangling from a knob, and the shotgun locked into its mount. "Did Agatha call you?"

"Corinna. The first lesson you have to learn in dealing with the sisters: you can't beat them. No one is as stubborn or determined as they are. However, you do appear to come close." There was a pause, only a moment, then, with his gaze fixed on the street, he asked, "Why is that?"

She, too, stared at the street. "I prefer to call it independent."

"There's no shame in needing help from time to time. The shame is in being too stubborn—excuse me, too independent—to accept it."

"And when have *you* ever needed anyone's help?" Her voice was heavy with skepticism. He was a man, a cop. If someone had left him with three kids to take care of, he would have done it, and without losing his job and his home. He wouldn't have been reduced to kidnapping the kids and stealing a house and lying to people who were kinder than she deserved.

He didn't answer as the street narrowed and passed through a white board fence, becoming no more than a gravel lane on the other side. It climbed gently through a stand of trees, around a pond, and past open fields before circling under a porte cochere at the inn's main entrance. There he stopped, then faced her. When he spoke, there was a challenge underlying his words, an effort to shock her, a dare to her to try to top the story he was about to tell. "There was a time I could barely make it out of bed without help. It was seven years ago. My best friend got killed, and my wife accused me of letting it happen because I'd found out about them. Problem was, I *hadn't* found out. I didn't know they'd been having an affair, didn't know it'd been going on for more than a year. I didn't know they were planning to go away together as soon as he got enough money, and I sure as hell didn't know that the baby I loved more than anyone else in the world was *his* daughter, not mine. You think your life has sunk pretty low? Darlin', I guarantee you, mine's been lower."

Emilie sat in silence. He'd wanted to shock her, and he had. How awful to lose your best friend, only to discover that he'd been no friend at all. To learn that he'd betrayed you, and with your wife, no less. To love a child, believing she was your own, only to find that she wasn't yours at all but was living proof of that betrayal.

How did a man deal with all that grief and sorrow, all that rage and heartache?

Nathan had dealt with it the same way she was dealing with her problems: by fleeing. Except that she was running to home, and he had run away from it.

"I'm sorry," she murmured. The words were woefully inadequate, but all she had to offer. She was sorry she had asked the question. Sorry he'd felt compelled to answer. Sorry she'd made him remember such a painful time.

He didn't try to brush it off. "So am I." He looked away for a long moment. When he turned back, most of the grimness was gone, but not all. There was still some sorrow in his eyes, some bitterness in the set of his mouth. "I'll try to stick around, but if I have to leave, ask Holly— Never mind. I'll talk to her myself."

The inn was an old farmhouse, according to Noelle, and was white with black shutters. Every window was draped with swags of greenery and red velvet bows, and the columns supporting the porte-cochere roof were wrapped with pine boughs. Workmen on ladders were stringing lights along the roofline. The nearest one greeted Nathan by name and gave her a friendly hello.

Inside, cinnamon and cloves perfumed the air, and a fire burned in the fireplace. The long counter that served as a front desk was decorated and loaded with enough potted poinsettias to cover the entire top surface. Somewhere among them, Nathan located a bell and rang it, bringing a woman from down the hall.

Holly McBride was about Emilie's age, pretty, auburn-haired, and elegantly dressed. If her inn hadn't already intimidated Emilie, she would have finished the job. Her sweater alone probably cost more than Emilie's entire wardrobe, and the jewels on her ears, around her neck, and on her fingers were emeralds. The finished product was enough to make Emilie feel like a scarecrow ready for the fields.

Holly greeted Nathan with a kiss, then offered her hand. "You must be Emilie. Nice to meet you. You plan to stick around during the interview, Nathan?"

"I thought I'd get a cup of coffee."

"The cook's got a fresh batch of mulled cider on the stove. Help yourself."

"I will. If I get called out before you're done, have Tommy give her a ride home, will you?"

"Sure. Let's go into my office, Emilie."

The office behind the counter was all windows on two sides, the view enough to distract the most conscientious of workers. Holly didn't even glance at it as she seated herself. "Miss Agatha tells me you're new in town and looking for work. I'm already shorthanded, and one of my housekeepers is quitting next week. You'd be doing a little of everything—cleaning, decorating, setting tables, waiting tables in a pinch, helping in the kitchen, maybe even in here. I'd need you from eight to five, Monday through Friday and every third weekend. Would that be a problem with the kids?"

"No." The sisters had been so sure Holly would hire her that they'd already made plans. They would get Alanna and Josie off to school if necessary and keep Brendan all day, then the girls would go to their house after school and stay until Emilie got home. The only real problem would be getting herself back and forth. That long, meandering driveway turned her no-problem-it's-only-a-few-blocks walk into a problem. She would have to get the kids up early and would be walking home alone after dark. Like any native-born Atlantan, she wasn't thrilled with the idea, but she could do it. She could do anything when she had no choice.

"How old are your children?"

"Three, six and nine. One boy, two girls."

"We're having an open house the thirteenth of this month. I'll need you to help with that, but the children are welcome, too. Christmas is so much nicer with kids around." She flashed a smile. "They must be getting excited about it."

Emilie murmured agreement. Truth was, the kids weren't excited because they'd never known a real Christmas. There'd been little money for gifts, none for decorations. Christmas parties, parades, and pageants held little interest for Berry. As often as not, she'd been in the process of uprooting the kids when Christmas came, moving from one town to the next, from one man to the next. Just last Christmas Emilie had had to teach them the words to "O Little Town of Bethlehem."

This Christmas they were living there.

She wished she could give them one memorable Christmas with decorations, parties, lights, visits to Santa, shopping, gifts under a tree, and a traditional dinner. Just one holiday that they could look back on with fondness in the years to come. She would do her best to buy them a gift or two, but there was no money to spend on the rest of it. Every other penny she earned here would have to go toward food, the mechanic's bill for the car, and their eventual trip home.

The rest of the meeting passed quickly. Holly gave her a few forms to fill out, told her to dress casually, and asked her to start the next morning. With a tremendous feeling of relief, Emilie left the office and followed Holly's directions to the kitchen at the back of the house to find Nathan.

When he saw her, he swallowed the last of his cider, rose from the table, and met her in the hall. "Better watch it. You're almost smiling."

"I smile."

"Not often enough. I take it things went well with Holly."

"I start tomorrow."

"Good. So now you need to get the older kids enrolled in school. We can pick them up on the way."

"Are you sure your boss doesn't object to your using the city's time to run my errands?"

"I'm available for calls. He doesn't mind."

He held the front door open, and she brushed past, trying to ignore the anxiety the mention of school conjured up. She had already faced the fact that the girls had to go to school. It would arouse too much suspicion if they didn't. Still, she wished she could ask him what procedures Social Services would follow once they'd learned the kids were gone. She wished she knew which of her fears were legitimate and which weren't worth the worry.

She wished she knew beyond a doubt that she wouldn't find herself standing in the school office with Nathan at her side when the principal got off the phone with Boston and said, "Those kids aren't hers. She's kidnapped them."

They were halfway down the drive before he spoke again. "Don't you get child support?"

"No." Berry had never figured out who Brendan's father was, and she'd lost track of Alanna's and Josie's fathers years ago.

"Why not? Where is your ex?"

"I'd rather not talk about this."

"You are divorced, aren't you?"

Unable to face any lie that wasn't necessary, she hedged. "I'm not married. The kids' father—" one imaginary father, as opposed to three real ones "—hasn't been around since before Brendan was born."

"He must have been a real sweetheart."

"Yes, he was." Then she changed the subject. "The garage picked up my car this morning. Thanks for calling for me. They're supposed to have an estimate ready later today."

"It might be more than the car's worth."

"I know. It's a piece of junk but it's our junk, and it's paid for."

"Why don't you sell it and use the money as a down payment on something else? Then instead of paying Lloyd six or eight hundred dollars, you can be paying that on the new car."

*Six or eight hundred dollars.* Was that an educated guess based on what he'd seen under the hood Friday morning, or had he picked those numbers out of the air? Lord, at the salary Holly had offered, she would have to work a month or more to bring home that much— longer, since she would also be buying groceries and lunches. She whispered a silent prayer for a repair bill she had a hope of managing, then responded to his question. "Sell it? To whom?"

"There's a salvage yard south of town."

A junkyard. The car was the only possession she had, and it was good only for scrap metal. It was enough to make a weaker woman cry. "Buying another car means getting a loan. What bank's going to give me a loan? I have nothing."

"You have a house and a job."

A house that wasn't hers and a temporary job in a town where she couldn't stay. No, foolish or not, she would get the car fixed and hope it made it to Georgia before falling apart once and for all.

"Emilie?"

She murmured absently.

"We're here."

Blinking, she realized that they were sitting in the Winchesters' driveway. Hastily, she got out and went to the door. She expected to take Brendan, too, but he was asleep on a pallet, Ernest snuggled under his chin and cookie crumbs dotting the quilt around him. After a whispered conversation with the sisters, she ushered Alanna and Josie out.

Nathan watched as they negotiated the steps. Josie skipped along, cheered by the prospect of school. Alanna looked worried, too old for her age. He hadn't yet seen her laugh, smile, crack a joke, or do anything else kids should do. Maybe if the job at Holly's place worked out, they could stay long enough to give the kid some stability in her life, and maybe then she would revert to the behaviors of the child she was.

Emilie looked a little worried, too. She was keeping secrets. He'd noticed the way she'd avoided answering about her divorce. I'm not married, she'd said, not,

Yes, I'm divorced. Maybe she'd never been married. Maybe she'd had a long-term relationship with some guy and marriage had never been in the plans, or maybe the kids were the results of three short-term flings that hadn't lasted beyond the moment. Maybe she was still married, and the husband was back in Massachusetts wondering where the hell his family had gone.

Maybe the secret didn't involve her marital status but the kids. When she'd lost her job and her home, maybe the court had seen fit to give the children to their father, and, on their holiday visit, she'd fled the state with them. If that was the case, there would likely be an attempt-to-locate broadcast sent out sometime today. That was one more thing to check when he got back to the station today.

Josie climbed into the backseat and fastened her seat belt. "Mama says you're taking us to school. I like school. I'm in the first grade, and I know how to read."

"You're a smart kid."

"Yup. I'm smarter than Lannie. I read better than her, and I'm prettier, too." The last was said with a sly grin, calculated to bring a response from her sister. She wasn't disappointed.

"Shut up, Josie. You're not supposed to talk all the time, especially to strangers." Alanna slammed the door and scowled.

"Mr. Nathan isn't a stranger. We had lunch with him

and went to the store. He bought us hot dogs and ice cream. Don't you remember?"

"Of course I remember. Geez, you're such a child."

Nathan closed his ears to their bickering and focused instead on their mother. When the kids had gotten in the truck, she had gone to their house. Now she was returning with an envelope in hand. School records, he assumed, as she slid in beside him.

The elementary school was at the opposite end of town. Getting the girls enrolled was easy enough—a few forms and a telephone request to their old school for their records. He didn't try to disguise the fact that he was listening to the conversation between Emilie and the assistant principal, but he learned nothing new beyond the fact that they'd come from Boston.

After giving each kid lunch money and a kiss, Emilie waited until they were outside to give a soft sigh.

"What was that for?"

"Relief. I have a job, the kids are in school, and I have reliable baby-sitters for Brendan. Things usually don't come together this easily for me."

He didn't ask how things usually went for her. He knew from personal experience that once a person's luck turned sour, it could be a long time before anything went right again. He also knew that that time *did* come. It had for him. Maybe getting snowbound in Bethlehem had been the turning point for her.

When he stopped at the end of the driveway, she opened the door, then glanced back. "Thanks for everything."

"I'll give you a ride in the morning." When she started to speak, he raised one hand. "I know it's not necessary. I know you'd rather walk, freezing all the way, but a human icicle isn't going to be of much use to Holly."

She got out, faced him, and smiled. It was enough to make a man stop and stare, to warm the air between them, to brighten the day like the sun coming out after endless rain. "For your information, I was going say, 'Thank you, Nathan. I would appreciate the ride.' " She closed the door, and he watched her every step of the way to the house, half-wishing he could follow her and half-glad he couldn't. He was starting to enjoy the time spent with her too much, and that was as good a signal as any that he needed time away.

Besides, he had a little matter at the tax assessor's office to take care of.

He felt guilty when he walked into the small office on the courthouse's second floor, and the feeling annoyed him. It wasn't as if he was doing anything wrong. He was just making certain that the people occupying a certain piece of property had a legal right to do so. He was doing his job.

The office was quiet, the counter empty. After a moment's wait, he called out and heard a rustle around the corner before a young man appeared, half of a sandwich in hand. "I'm sorry. I didn't hear anyone come in." He looked around, then left the sandwich on a corner of the nearest desk, dusted his hands, and approached him. "What can I do for you?"

"Where's Art?"

"Mr. Blocker is in a meeting, and Dorothy had a doctor's appointment. Is there something I can help you with?"

Dorothy Campion was the only clerk to work in this office for longer than Nathan had been in town. He hadn't realized that the county had hired someone new. Slight of build, bespectacled, and wearing a sweater vest and a bow tie, the guy couldn't have looked more like a geek if he'd tried. Even his hair, light brown muddied with some other shade, was worn like a geek's, parted on one side, combed straight across, and heavily oiled. But his smile was friendly enough, and his eyes . . . Behind the thick lenses of his glasses, his gaze was the clearest and most direct Nathan had ever meet, as if he could see straight into a person.

"You're new in town, aren't you?"

"I've been here a while. What can I do for you?"

"I'm looking for the owner of a house over on Fourth Street. The number's 311."

"I can get that for you," the clerk said with confidence before giving the various files around the room an uncertain look.

Nathan gestured toward the wooden card file sitting on one countertop. "It should be in there. They're filed by address."

"Thanks. I'm kind of new at this." He thumbed through the contents of first one drawer, then another, then turned with a *Eureka!* flourish. "Here it is. 311 Fourth Street. The owner's name is Emilie Dalton, but the tax bill goes to Herbert Thomas, an attorney just down the street. I'm sure he can help you locate her. Here, would you like to see?"

Nathan scanned the card, skimming over the billing information and the assessed value of the house—not a bad sum if Emilie chose to sell—and going straight to her name, there in black and white. No mistake. Emilie's claim to the house was valid. "Thanks. Thanks a lot."

In contrast to the guilt that accompanied him into the office, he felt a definite relief as he took the stairs one flight down to the police department. He would've hated like hell to find out that she wasn't the owner, to have to remove her and the kids, knowing that they had no place else to go, especially only three weeks before Christmas.

He was on his way back to the desks set aside for the patrol officers' use when Sadie in the dispatcher's shack called his name. "I hear you've got a new neighbor."

"Yeah, Mrs. Pierce's niece has moved in."

"I also hear that you took her to lunch at Harry's Friday and that she's very pretty."

Warning bells sounded. Though she hadn't found wedded bliss herself after three tries, Sadie found being single an unnatural state for anyone else. She thought it her God-given duty to play matchmaker whenever she got the chance. Schooling his voice into casual disinterest, he said, "Really? I hadn't noticed."

Her laugher overshadowed the clatter of the printer as a batch of teletypes printed from the terminal. When the printing stopped, she tore the paper away, scanning and sorting the messages as she talked. "Nathan Bishop not noticing a pretty woman? That'll be the day. You've been out with every pretty one in three counties."

"Did you also hear that she's got three kids?"

"Hmmm. How do you feel about an instant family?"

He'd been asked that question before, whenever she'd found a prospective mate for him—or any other single officer in the department—who came with kids. "She's just a neighbor, Sadie."

She skimmed the last page before looking at him. "How old are you, Nathan?"

He'd been asked that, too. "Thirty-four."

"And married once, no kids."

He thought of sweet, dark-eyed Elisabeth and how she had wrapped one tiny hand around his thumb every time he'd given her a bottle, how she had wrapped her tiny self around his heart every time he'd looked at her. "No. No kids."

"At least you were lucky there. I had two when my first husband left me and one more when my second walked out. It's been at least six years, Nathan. You can't let one bad experience scare you off for good. It's time to try again."

Keep trying until he got right. That was Sadie's advice, but he had no intention of taking it. The end of his marriage had cost him too much. He didn't have enough left to try again. "I don't think so. Once was enough for me."

"You're too young to be a cynic. Someday the right woman's going to come along—maybe already has—and you're going to fall hard, and you'll never regret it."

Her words called to mind a picture of Emilie and that cut-him-off-at-the-knees smile, and he shook his head to clear it. "I've got work to do. See you later."

As he walked away, Sadie picked up the teletypes. Only a couple were of any interest to the department. The rest she absentmindedly fed a sheet at a time into the shredder next to her desk. When the telephone rang, she adjusted her headset and pressed the button. "Bethlehem Police. Do you have an emergency?"

As she listened to the caller, the final page of the discarded teletypes scrolled into the shredder. She was occupied with her call and didn't even notice that it read: *From the Boston Police Department: Attempt to locate the following missing persons: (1) Emilie Marie Dalton, white female, blond hair, blue eyes, age twenty-nine, and the following minor children . . .*

Agatha Winchester stood at the window, one lace curtain lifted for a view of the street in front of the Pierce house. Behind her Corinna was on the phone on version three of the same conversation. The young clerk on the other end was resistant, but she would come around, or Corinna would simply go over her head to her boss. That was what had happened at both the water and the gas offices.

"What does her mother's maiden name matter? The woman is dead. If Mrs. Dalton doesn't pay her bill, you're surely not going to collect it from her mother." Corinna's voice turned stern. "I have no time for this nonsense, dear. Let me speak to Timmy . . . Timmy Mc-Fadden . . . Yes, *Mr.* McFadden to you. That's the one."

Agatha smiled. Tim McFadden had been in her sixth-grade class. He fancied himself as having outgrown his old nickname, but it still came in handy at times.

Outside a yellow truck bearing the city seal edged a few feet into the Pierce driveway. The gas company truck was right behind, and no doubt, once Corinna finished with Tim, the electric company truck would soon follow. They hated to poke their noses into Emilie's business but, after discussing it at length, had decided that they had no choice. If the girl's budget was so tight that she could barely afford food, then she surely had no money to spare for the utilities deposits. But those babies couldn't live in an unlit, unheated house without water, not in this weather.

If Emilie protested too much, then she could pay back the money when she was on her feet again. Pride was important, and hers had already suffered from the circumstances she'd found herself in. They didn't want to add to her feelings of failure. They just wanted to help.

"Thank you, Timmy. I knew you could get things done. Give my best to your parents." Corinna hung up with a satisfied smile. "The power will be turned on as soon as a truck can get over there."

"The water and gas people are there now. Do you suppose we should go over?"

"And give her a chance to tell us no?"

"What if she tells the workers no and sends them away?"

"After the discussions I had with their bosses, do you think either of them will leave with the job unfinished?"

"No, of course not. Besides, Emilie isn't foolish. She's just trying to do the best for her babies." As one, they looked at Brendan, playing quietly with his bear. He hadn't cried for his mother, not when she'd left him with his sisters and not when he'd awakened to find the girls gone. He hadn't spoken much, either, just an occasional yes or no and one whispered thank you. Agatha was used to kids who chattered, like Josie, like her own grandnieces, and -nephews. Brendan was so quiet that it was sad.

"I suspect Emilie will be over to see us soon enough. When she does come, the least we could do is have lunch ready."

"It's only neighborly," Agatha agreed, letting the curtain drop. She crossed to Brendan, offering her hand. Instead of accepting it, he extended Ernest's hand. With the bear swinging between them, they went into the kitchen, where she settled him on a tall stool beside the counter.

Within a half hour, the breakfast table was set for four, with a salad at each place and chicken pot pie steaming in the middle, and Emilie was ringing the doorbell. Agatha settled Brendan in a booster seat kept handy for family dinners while Corinna escorted their guest to the kitchen. "We were just sitting down to eat. Take off your coat and sit there beside Brendan," Corinna directed.

"No, really, I—" Realizing that Corinna was already sliding the coat off, Emilie broke off and obeyed. She seemed a nice young woman, Agatha thought, but so afraid of imposing and just a little too determined to manage on her own. Of course, when you found yourself on your own with three children and no money, a little independence was a good thing. But she needed to learn that people weren't meant to be totally independent. Everyone needed somebody. The children needed

Emilie, and Emilie needed *them*—Agatha and Corinna, Nathan, Holly, and everyone else who wanted to welcome her to the community.

Emilie took the seat next to Brendan, bending to give him a kiss. "Hey, sweetie, how are you doing?" After Nathan had dropped her off an hour ago, she had intended to pick up her nephew and heat a can of soup over the fire just as soon as she'd gathered more wood. Then the water guy had come and the gas company guy, and she'd known the power company people wouldn't be far behind. She had sat down to wait and had ended up crying. She'd told herself they were tears of despair, but the instant she'd felt warm air blowing from the nearest register, she'd known it was sheer relief. No more hauling logs, putting together makeshift meals without a refrigerator or stove, or melting snow for the bathroom. No more worry about bathing, washing clothes, or getting a decent night's sleep on a pallet on the floor.

Just more debts to repay in the future—and so much more to be thankful for. She had a job, and the girls had enrolled in school without any hitches. They had heat, lights, and water. And she would be seeing Nathan every morning. Life was looking better.

"About the utilities . . ."

Apparently expecting a protest, Corinna stopped her quickly to explain. "We were just trying to help."

"I know. Thank you very much."

"It was our pleasure," Agatha said sincerely.

"I will repay you."

"Please do. The next time you see someone who needs help that you can give, give it."

All of her adult life, she had done that, donating regularly to her favorite charities. But it was better to give than to receive, the Bible said. She had learned that lesson painfully well during her years in foster care, and she was learning it all over again. Giving made her feel warm and kind inside. Receiving made her feel ashamed and unworthy. Even though this situation wasn't her fault, even though she'd done the best she could, she still felt responsible. It was a quirk of her personality, just as Berry's personality allowed her to feel not one bit of guilt, even though she was overwhelmingly at fault.

But Emilie was going to learn to accept help graciously. She might hate needing it, but the simple truth was that she *did* need it, and she'd been blessed to find people willing to give it. She would accept their assistance with reminders to herself that this situation was temporary. Once they got to Georgia, she would get back on her feet, and she would no longer need charity.

When the meal was over, she helped with the dishes, thanked the sisters for keeping an eye on Brendan, then took him home to explore the warming house. It was a luxury to turn on lights in every room she entered, to twist a handle in the bathrooms and see water come out, to walk from one long-unoccupied room to another without the bone-aching shivers she'd almost become accustomed to.

Downstairs, in addition to the parlor, dining room, and kitchen, there was a formal living room filled with canvas-covered antiques. Upstairs she found another bathroom and four bedrooms, all sparsely furnished with faded Persian rugs, furniture of mahogany and cherry, dark drapes, and darker wallpapers. If it were her house, she would claim the room at the back for her own, give Alanna and Josie each a room of her own, and turn the last room into a bright-colored haven for Brendan.

It wasn't her house, of course, but since she had already borrowed the first floor, surely it wouldn't compound the sin too much if she also borrowed two bedrooms. When the owner discovered what Emilie had done, she wasn't likely to ask how many rooms they had appropriated. It wasn't going to lessen her anger if they'd used only the parlor, the bathroom, and the kitchen.

She chose the room nearest the stairs, with its twin beds, for the girls and the one directly across the hall for Brendan and herself. She cleaned them, made the beds with linens from the hall closet, and unpacked their bags. Next she cleaned both bathrooms and was finishing the kitchen when the school bus stopped out front and the girls got off.

Josie chattered endlessly about her day, her teacher,

and her five new best friends. Once she finally ran out of steam and went to play with her brother, Emilie sat down on the hearth beside Alanna. "How was your day? Did you meet anyone?"

She shrugged. "I don't know why we have to go at all. It's not like we're going to be here very long. We're leaving as soon as the car is fixed, aren't we?" When Emilie didn't offer confirmation, panic slipped into Alanna's voice. "Aren't we, Aunt Emilie? You said we would stay until the car was fixed, and then we would go on to Atlanta. We *can't* stay here. This place isn't ours, and if they find out, they'll arrest you and send us back to Boston!"

"We're not staying, honey, not permanently." Though some part of her liked the idea, in a fantasy sort of way. Bethlehem was a lovely little town—the small-town-America ideal, with little crime, no poverty that she could see, a strong economy, and friendly neighbors eager to lend a hand. It was the sort of place that people in big cities believed no longer existed, the sort of place where parents—or aunts—could raise their families in a healthy, safe environment.

"When are we leaving?"

"I've got to earn some money first. The garage won't fix the car for free, you know. We've got to eat, and we need money for gas, motels, and meals on the trip. We need money when we get there, too, so we won't have to go to another shelter."

"*When* are we leaving?"

"New Year's Day." Emilie made the decision right that moment. It brought her fear and, in an odd way, hope. It held only fear for her niece.

"That's a whole month! We can't lie and pretend for that long! Aunt Emilie, the longer we stay here, the better the chances we'll get caught. Don't you know the police are looking for us!"

"Don't you know they're looking for us in Atlanta, too? They knew I was from there. They have to suspect that that's where I've taken you." She smoothed the girl's hair. "Alanna, right now we have a place to live, and I have a job. I can get enough money to get us home, and the kids can have a real Christmas for once in their lives. It'll be okay, honey. Don't worry."

"But—"

"No buts. Worrying is my job. Getting your homework done before dinner is yours. Listen, girls." She waited for Josie's attention. "Tonight we're sleeping in real beds. Your room is the first door on the right upstairs. Why don't you go take a look?"

Josie raced upstairs and was back quicker than Emilie would have guessed possible. "Hey, there are two beds in there. Is one of them mine?"

"One for you, one for Alanna."

"A bed just for me? For real? I've never had a bed of my own." With that she was gone again, her shoes thudding on the stairs. Still looking morose, Alanna followed her.

Josie's amazement made Emilie's chest tighten. The kids had had so little in their young lives—no decent home, no real Christmases, no stability to speak of. She had made promises—to them, to the judge, to herself— that she would change that. She would do it, or go to prison trying.

She was hanging the girls' coats on the tree she'd re- turned to the front hallway when someone knocked at the door. She opened the door, wondering as she did if she would ever be free of this niggling little discomfort at the sound of a knock.

Not yet. Not when her guest was dressed in a police- man's uniform, complete with a badge, handcuffs, and a gun.

"I see you've got the utilities on."

She glanced at the yellow bulb glowing outside the door and flipped the switch that turned it off. "The sis- ters' doing." She gestured for Nathan to come in, then closed the door behind him. She was happy to see him, even if she did prefer him in jeans and a sweatshirt. She liked to forget what thin ice she was skating on where he was concerned.

"Are the kids home from school?"

"They're upstairs doing homework."

"And you've been cleaning."

"Is that a lucky guess, or do I have cobwebs in my hair?"

"Actually, the house smells different, although you do have a bit of dirt right here . . ." He drew his finger across her cheek. His finger was cold. Her face was suddenly warm. "Do you need to take the kids out this evening for school supplies or anything?"

"I don't know. I'll ask them."

"Let me know by eight. Most of the stores are closed by nine." He withdrew a folded sheet of paper from his pocket. "I stopped by Lloyd's on my way home and picked this up."

The estimate on her car. She hadn't forgotten it. She'd intended to go next door and borrow the sisters' phone to call the garage, but she'd been busy cleaning, and then the girls had come home from school, and she'd had to talk to them, and . . . Truthfully, she'd been delaying the bad news as long as possible, because no matter how much—or, please, God, how little—the repairs might be, it was too much.

Now she couldn't delay any longer. She accepted the paper from Nathan, whose expression gave away nothing, and unfolded it. She scanned the list of work included, but the handwriting was bad and the words foreign. What she could make out, she couldn't understand.

She understood the total, though, every penny of it. She read it, blinked, then read it again, but the numbers didn't change. The decimal point didn't move a space or two to the left. Thirteen hundred and ninety-five dollars.

Her stomach queasy, her palms damp, she sank down on a stair step. There was no way she could come up with that kind of money, not if she worked at Holly's inn until *next* Christmas rolled around. Even if she could get the money, only an idiot would sink it into an old clunker like the wagon. Nathan had been right earlier. The car—the only thing she had of any value—wasn't good for anything but the junk heap. "These are the minimum repairs necessary to get it running again?" She sounded hollow and stunned. She *felt* hollow and stunned.

"It's an old car, Emilie, with a lot more than that wrong with it." He sat down two steps below her. His voice was quiet, somber. "There are a couple places in town where you can pick up a better car for less. With the house as collateral, there shouldn't be any problem getting a loan."

How could she ask for a bank loan? They would want references she couldn't provide and collateral she certainly couldn't give. It would mean proving that the house was hers, when she hadn't known Miriam Pierce from the man in the moon. Besides, what if, somehow, some way, it got back to the authorities in Boston that she had applied for a loan? Would they come knocking at her door themselves or would they ask the local police—maybe even her neighbor—to take her into custody? Getting arrested would be a bad ending to the worst year of her life, but getting arrested by Nathan would be worse.

"You don't even really need a car in Bethlehem, not right away, at least. The girls will ride the school bus, and I can give you a ride to and from work. You can do your grocery stopping when the Winchesters do or with me on the weekends. You can get along fine without a car."

Tamping down the fear and frustration that made her tremble inside, she smiled weakly and folded the estimate, then crumpled it in one hand. "Thanks for bringing this over. I'll decide what to do—" her voice quivered before she got it under control—"and I'll let Lloyd know."

# Chapter Five

After work Thursday, Nathan changed out of his uniform, then picked up the Dalton kids at the Winchesters'. Josie was happy to come along, Brendan willing to follow wherever she went, but Alanna resisted. "This isn't a good idea," she protested as Josie dragged her down the driveway. "Mama didn't say anything about you picking us up. We're not supposed to go off with strangers, and definitely not without her permission."

"Then you can get it when we pick her up. Brendan, let me carry you across the street."

The boy darted away and held his arms up to Alanna instead. Giving Nathan a scowl, she swung her brother onto her hip. "Why are you doing this?"

"We're surprising your mother. We're going out to dinner and then to the Christmas parade."

Josie spun around. "Christmas parade? I *love* Christmas parades."

"How would you know? You've never even seen one." Alanna's scorn didn't dampen Josie's spirits at all.

"But I know I'll love it. Will Santa Claus be there, Mr. Nathan?"

"Santa and a few of his elves."

"Oh, I especially love Santa."

"Why? He's never brought you anything, not once," Alanna scoffed.

"That's because he didn't know where to find us. This year he'll know—I'll tell him—and he'll come."

Nathan considered their conversation as he helped Josie into the truck. He had assumed that Emilie's financial trouble was a recent problem, but apparently that wasn't the case. He couldn't imagine anything besides lack of money that would keep her from giving the kids a Christmas.

Though her mother was broke, Josie was right: Santa would come this year. The sisters would provide something, and he could, too. He hadn't bought a Christmas gift in seven years, not since he'd spent half a month's paycheck on more toys, books, and clothes than a three-month-old could possibly use. In her anguished fury, Diana had ripped the paper off the gifts, torn pages from books, smashed toys, and thrown one red velvet dress out the window. His own grief over Mike's death numbed by the discovery of his betrayal, Nathan had watched until she'd exhausted herself, and then he had walked out. He'd spent the night on the streets, in the cold and the rain, and when he'd gone home the next morning, Christmas morning, Diana and Elisabeth were gone. All that was left was the remains of their ruined Christmas.

He hadn't celebrated the holiday since. Here in Bethlehem, he always attended the parade, the party for city employees, and the open house at Holly's. He showed up for the sisters' Christmas Eve celebration and the midnight service on the square, but he'd only been going through the motions. None of it had really meant anything.

This year it might be kind of fun to shop again. It might make him feel better about the holiday, the last seven years, and Elisabeth.

Emilie was waiting at the inn door when they arrived. He knew from Lloyd that she'd taken his advice to junk the car, receiving $110.00 for it—and even that, according to the mechanic, had been generous. Too bad she needed so much more.

Surprised to see the kids, she immediately asked, "Is something wrong with Miss Agatha or Miss Corinna?"

"No, they're fine. We're going out to dinner before the Christmas parade."

Her response closely mirrored Josie's. Her eyes brightened, and she looked about ten years younger. "A Christmas parade? Tonight? I love Christmas parades."

"Santa Claus is going to be there," Josie piped up, "and I'm going to tell him where we live so he can find us this year. I know he will." The last statement was accompanied by a snort from Alanna.

"I'm sure he will, honey." Emilie settled comfortably in the seat. "I haven't been to a parade in . . ."

"If you have to think about it, it's been too long."

"It has," she murmured. "Much too long."

Since Nathan had left work at four o'clock, the streets making up the parade route had been closed to traffic. All the parked cars were gone, and a half dozen booths were set up along the square and down Main, selling snacks to wash down with hot chocolate and mulled cider. All the shops were open late, and the sidewalks were crowded with serious shoppers and those just passing time.

"You'll never find a parking space down here. We should have walked from the house."

"You forget who I work for." After waiting for a crowd of teenagers to cross the street, he pulled into the lot reserved for police department employees.

They stood in line for a table at Harry's, skipped dessert, and headed for the nearest booth for candied apples. With time to spare before staking out a spot, they walked down the street, Emilie holding Brendan's hand while Alanna kept a tight rein on Josie ten feet ahead.

"This is nice." Emilie's smile banished the weariness

from her face, giving her the same wide-eyed look of
wonder that Brendan wore. "It's like something out of a
Hollywood fantasy."

It was pretty fantastic, with all the lights and decorations, the brightly lit windows, good-natured shoppers,
and cold air scented with cider, pine, and woodsmoke.
As she'd said, it was like some lavish movie set, the
country's favorite holiday as envisioned by Capra or
Disney. "Christmas is a big event here. With a name like
Bethlehem, it has to be."

"Miss Agatha said you moved here several years ago.
Do you have family here?"

"I had never even heard of the place until I decided it
was time to leave the city. I started looking for a job, and
Bethlehem was hiring. It was clear across the state, so I
took it." He didn't say clear across the state from what,
but the sympathy in her eyes showed that she knew.
Diana. Elisabeth. Memories of Mike.

"And you've never regretted it."

"Maybe a time or two. It's a great place for families,
but if you're alone, sometimes you can feel a little left
out."

"I know the feeling."

He looked at her quizzically. "You have a family. You
haven't been alone for nine or ten years."

She flushed as if she'd said something she shouldn't
have, then shrugged and lamely explained, "I was alone
a long time before Alanna was born."

She couldn't have been older than twenty when Alanna was born. She must have had some time before that with Alanna's father, and before him there would have been her own family. He was about to ask about them when Brendan spoke for the first time in his presence.

"Oooh."

Emilie stopped walking, swung him into her arms, and followed his pointing finger to the main display window of the combination hardware store and hobby shop. The entire space was filled with a model railroad that wound its way through a snow-covered village. There were lights on in the houses, and the Christmas tree in the square blinked in multicolored flashes. Two trains circled the town, crossing bridges and disappearing into tunnels, belching gray smoke and sounding a long, low whistle as they approached the crossings. Oooh, indeed.

"Little boys and trains," Emilie said, then looked up at him and laughed. "Big boys, too, huh?"

"Trains are neat, aren't they, Brendan?"

"Neat," the kid echoed. But that was all. He didn't plead to go inside and get a closer look. He didn't say, I want that. Just, *Oooh. Neat.*

There was plenty of room in their house for a train set, not so elaborate, of course. Just a train and track, some crossings, lights, and whistles . . .

Abruptly, Emilie whirled around. "Where are the

girls? They were ahead of us, and I forgot to tell them to wait—"

Nathan laid his hand on her shoulder. "It's okay. Nothing's going to happen to them here. This isn't Boston. Alanna will realize we've stopped, and she'll bring Josie back."

She didn't relax. Even through her coat and his glove, he imagined he could feel the tension that had streaked through her, but maybe that was his own tension. Maybe it was frustration because he *was* touching her and couldn't tell it. Maybe it was his desire to try it again without the coat and the glove.

Deliberately he removed his hand. "Why don't you and Brendan go inside so he can see the train up close, and I'll catch up to the girls. Alanna may not like me, but she'll come back with me."

Her eyes shadowed with concern, she nodded and went through the wide doors. The last glimpse he had of her, she was setting Brendan on the floor where he could press close to the pint-size picket fence that protected the village. She was holding tightly to the hood of his coat, but she was searching out the window.

Moving through the crowd was slow going, but after more than a block, it thinned, and he was able to see Alanna ahead, standing on tiptoe and looking worriedly for her mother. When she saw him, he would've sworn that she looked relieved for an instant, but by the time he reached her, she was scowling again. "Where's Mama?"

"We stopped to look at something, and you guys got away from us. They're waiting for us back at the hobby shop."

Josie pulled away from Alanna and tucked her hand inside his as they headed back. "Tell me about the parade. Is there something beside Santa Claus?"

Alanna hadn't been kidding earlier. Josie never had seen a Christmas parade before. "Lots of stuff. There'll be some bands, the winter festival queen from the high school, and plenty of floats."

"What's a float?"

He considered trying to explain it on a six-year-old level, then opted for the easy out. "You'll have to wait and see. There's your mom and Brendan. We need to find a place to watch. The parade will start soon."

They settled on an unoccupied patch of sidewalk across from the square. The snow had been cleared away from both the street and sidewalk, though there was still plenty left elsewhere. Over in the square, kids were making snowmen and angels, and on the far side, older kids were engaged in a snowball fight. After a discussion, Emilie let the girls cross the street to join school friends in a blanket-covered huddle, then turned the conversation to a remark he'd made earlier. "What makes you think Alanna doesn't like you?"

"She always frowns when I'm around. She's more

than a little on the sullen side. She doesn't want anything to do with me, and she doesn't want Josie even talking to me."

His answer gave her an unhappy look. "I don't think it's anything personal. I'm afraid Alanna doesn't hold a very high opinion of men in general."

"Because of—" He started to say *your husband*, but veered away. It seemed easier to talk about the kids' father than her husband, to think of the man who fathered the children and not the man she had loved and wanted to spend the rest of her life with. "Because of her father."

"Him, among others. Let's face it—a lot of men don't deal well with the responsibilities of children and marriage, and when they leave, the children always suffer." Emilie watched the girls, thinking grimly about the men who had influenced her niece's opinions. It had started with Bill Dalton long before Alanna was even born. He'd selfishly given away his own daughters. If he had kept them, if he had loved them, things would have been so different. Emilie would have grown up knowing that there was a place she belonged and people to count on, and Berry would have known that someone would always love and want her. She wouldn't have turned to all those self-centered, abusive men, and Alanna wouldn't have turned cynical at such a tender age.

"Women leave, too, you know."

Nathan's voice was low, quiet, drawing her gaze to him. For an instant, there was such sorrow in his eyes. It had been so hard for him, losing his best friend, wife, and daughter all in the same day. Such betrayal wasn't an easy thing to forgive, and impossible to forget.

Before she could think of anything to say, before she could do more than brush her gloved hand across his, a low murmur traveled through the crowd. Down the street a flash of red-and-blue lights atop a police car signaled the beginning of the parade. People moved in closer around them as she picked up Brendan.

One of Nathan's fellow officers came first, followed by the mayor in an antique jalopy. There was a fire engine, the middle-school band, kids dressed as gifts in brightly wrapped boxes, and floats—more floats than she would have expected from a town twice Bethlehem's size. Emilie alternated watching the parade herself and watching the kids' reaction to it. Brendan was awed, Josie delighted, and even Alanna was enjoying it. For the first time in too long, they were simply normal kids, having a good time. For the first time in too long, *she* felt like any other woman, able to put her cares aside and enjoy the moment.

During a lull in the parade, Nathan bent close, his mouth brushing her ear. "You do like parades, don't you?"

Intending a smile as her answer, she looked at him and found him closer than she'd expected, mere inches away. Slowly her smiled faded. So did his grin, until he looked so serious, so intent, so . . . heaven help her, so handsome and strong and kind. All her life she'd dreamed of finding a man who was strong and kind, a man she could count on, a man who would never let her down. She'd gone out with too many frogs, looking for just such a prince, but had finally accepted that he didn't exist.

But he did exist—just not for her. Her stay in Bethlehem was only temporary, and, for the children's sake, she couldn't prolong it any longer than absolutely necessary. She couldn't continue to deceive all these good people. She certainly couldn't get involved with anyone, especially a cop, right in the middle of her deception. It wouldn't be fair to him, letting him believe that she was something she wasn't, or to her, tempting herself with something she couldn't have. There was no reason to be disappointed or sad. It was just the way things were.

But she *was* disappointed and sad. She felt cheated and more alone than ever before.

Once again, sweet Brendan saved her. Patting her face with one hand, he pointed to the float passing by. "Oooh, neat. Trains."

She forced her gaze from Nathan's and to the float, a flatbed done up in red, green, and gold and featuring a train running in circles around a Christmas tree. Although he needed clothes badly, maybe she could squeeze enough money out of the budget for a small train set. The only toy he owned was Ernest, who'd gone past shabby to threadbare, and you couldn't really play with a stuffed bear. Of course, in Ernest's defense, you couldn't exactly snuggle with a train set.

When the sounds of "Jingle Bells" filtered down the street, the crowd pressed forward. It was the high-school band, and behind them was Santa. He was in a wagon made to resemble a sleigh and pulled by horses instead of the traditional mounted-on-a-flatbed approach she was used to. She liked Bethlehem's way much better.

"He'll circle the block," Nathan said in her ear, "then go into the square and let the kids come sit on his lap. Josie intends to be one of those kids."

"I tried to take them to see Santa last year, but . . ." She couldn't remember now which calamity had prevented the trip to the shopping-mall Santa, only that Berry had been responsible.

Santa passed, waving and calling, "Merry Christmas!" As everyone began leaving, Emilie shifted Brendan to her other hip. "Want to see Santa Claus?"

"I seed him."

"Want to see him up close, maybe sit on his lap?"

Wide-eyed, he shook his head, then wrapped his arms tightly around her neck for good measure.

"It's okay, baby. You don't have to."

"Why don't you grab the girls and get in line over there?" Nathan suggested. "I'll get us something to drink. Cider or chocolate?"

"One cider, three chocolates." She watched him nod, then walk away before she crossed the street to the girls.

While they chatted with their friends, she glanced back to see Nathan, standing in line at the nearest booth, talking to Holly. When he laughed and slipped his arm around her, Emilie felt a strange little twinge in her stomach. She'd been jealous of other people's jobs, their families, and all the riches they'd been blessed with that were denied her, but she'd never been jealous of a man's attention to another woman. She had never been involved enough to care.

Tonight she cared. Even though she didn't think there was anything between him and her boss. Even though she knew there couldn't be anything between him and her.

"Let's go," Josie pleaded, tugging hard. "I want to see Santa Claus, and everybody's in line already. If we don't hurry, we'll be left out, and he'll forget us again."

"Okay, hon, let's go."

Soon after they got in line, Nathan joined them, passing around the drinks. The cider was hot and gave the illusion of warmth, though in reality her feet were frozen and she was beginning to shiver uncontrollably. Fortunately, the line moved pretty quickly, and soon it was Josie's turn. Suddenly shy, she hung back. When her coaxing failed, Emilie looked at Nathan, who shrugged, carried her the few feet to the sleigh, and lifted her inside.

Josie stared at the man seated in front of her. He had white hair and a long, white beard, and his cheeks were red, just like in the picture book Aunt Emilie read to them. He was big, even bigger than Mr. Nathan, but he had a nice smile and was only the littlest bit scary.

"What's your name, sweetheart?"

"I'm not supposed to talk to strangers, but I don't guess you're a stranger if you're Santa Claus. I'm Josie Lee Dalton, and I live at 311 Fourth Street. That's over that way. It's a big house with a chimney and everything, right across the street from Mr. Nathan's house. You can't miss it."

"I'm sure I won't. How old are you, Josie?"

"Six. I turned six just last month, but Lannie—that's my sister—she still tries to treat me like a baby. She's only nine, but she acts like she's all growed up." She thought about sticking her tongue out at Alanna, but decided it wasn't the best idea, not in front of Santa Claus.

"Have you been a good girl this year?"

She inched closer, resting her hand on his knee. "I've been *real* good. Well, most of the time. Except when Lannie calls me a baby. Then sometimes I get mad and make her yell. But when we went to the shelter on account of we got 'victed 'cause Mama lost her job, she said me and Brendan and Lannie were the bestest kids ever. How long is it till Christmas?"

"Three weeks. What would you like me to bring you?"

"You mean, I get to pick?"

Santa laughed. "You have to give me some ideas

about what you want. Do you like dolls? Games? Maybe a soccer ball?"

She moved a step closer, then, trying not to be noticed, slid onto Santa's knee, the way the other kids had. He didn't push her away but put his arm around her instead, like Aunt Emilie was always doing. "I think maybe a game—something that we could all play. And could you bring Lannie some books so she can learn to read better? And get Brendan . . ."

"A train set," Nathan said, and Josie nodded vigorously.

"Brendan loves trains. He used to watch from the apartment—well, before we got 'victed. I like trains, too. I seen one in a store over there. . . . But it's way too much. Just a little one that he can watch go around. And that's all."

Santa was giving her a funny look that made her worry. Nobody had ever asked what she wanted for Christmas before. Had she answered all wrong? Was she supposed to say she didn't want anything? "Is that too much?" she asked anxiously. " 'Cause you could just bring the train for Brendan, since he's the baby. Lannie and me wouldn't care."

Santa gave her a hug. "No, Josie, that's not too much. I'll see what I can do." He took three bags off the seat and gave them to her. "Here's one for you, one for Brendan, and one for Lannie. You be good, remember?"

"Wow, thanks Santa." Her arms full, she slid to her feet and walked to the side of the sleigh. When she turned back, he was grinning.

"I won't forget. Three-eleven Fourth Street."

Nathan lifted her to the ground, watched her run to her family, then glanced back at Santa, also known as Mitch Walker, chief of police. "What she said about being evicted . . ."

"I won't repeat it. Are they planning to stay here?"

"I don't know. I don't think Emilie's looking beyond trying to get back on her feet. She's got a long way to go."

"If they stay . . ." Mitch looked over at Emilie, then gave a commiserating shake of his head. "Son, you're in trouble."

Nathan didn't ask what he meant, but said good-bye and moved out of the way of the next kid in line. Any reasonable person could take one look at Emilie and understand exactly what Mitch had meant. She was a beautiful, vulnerable woman, and, like most men, Nathan was a sucker for beautiful, vulnerable women.

Back at the truck, he turned the heat to high, then switched on the interior lights at Josie's request so she could empty the contents of Santa's bag on her lap. The women's groups at the churches had sewn the red net bags and stuffed them with a few pieces of candy, an apple or orange, a clothespin nutcracker soldier, and an ornament. Josie's was an angel, wings extended, dressed in a flowing blue gown, with silvery brown hair. "Isn't she beautiful, Mr. Nathan?"

Actually, the ornament was cheap and looked it, but

she was thrilled with her first-ever gift from Santa. "She's almost as pretty as you are," he agreed as he backed out of the parking space.

At the Pierce house, he shut off the engine, and he and Emilie followed the kids to the veranda. There she sent the children inside, with instructions for Alanna to get them ready for bed, then closed the door and leaned against the jamb. "This was a very nice evening."

"I take it Josie was pleased with the parade and Santa Claus."

"What did she ask for?"

"A game for herself, books for Alanna, and a train for Brendan."

"I guess I'll try to get them."

"Let me."

"Oh, Nathan . . ."

"Look, I don't have anyone to buy for, and I'd like to. Just a couple of things. I won't overdo it."

Her smile was sad. "I should be able to do this myself."

"No one expects you to do everything except you. I'm just talking about a few gifts, Emilie. That's not too much to accept, is it?"

She drew a deep breath, then managed a smile less sad. "No, it's not."

For a time they both stood there. He tried to find the words to say good night, but they wouldn't come. She reached for the doorknob a couple times, but her fingers never made contact. They were both waiting. He knew what he wanted: one kiss. One brief, sweet, innocent kiss that held the promise of possibilities. He just wasn't sure what Emilie wanted.

Well, he couldn't stand here all night trying to second-guess her, or they would both freeze. Closing the distance between them, he lifted her face and brushed his mouth across hers. She didn't recoil or run away screaming. In fact, she gave a little sigh and sank back against the door, and so he did it again. This time he made a real kiss of it, and it was everything he'd wanted. Sweet, innocent, and full of promise, so much promise that it could scare a man.

It took all the strength he possessed to end the kiss, murmur good night, and walk away. With every step he wanted nothing more than to return and kiss her again, a hundred times again. He wanted to kiss her everywhere—on the porch, in the hall, in her bed, everywhere, all over. He wanted . . .

Too much. Too soon.

Mitch surely had been right. He was in a world of trouble. If God was in the mood to take requests, he wouldn't mind admitting that this was the kind of trouble he would like to stay in for a long, long time.

Emilie watched him climb into the truck and lift one hand in a wave before she went inside and locked the door. For a time she simply stood there, listening to the sounds of the kids' bath upstairs and feeling pleased, scared, shivery, and sad all at once.

There had been a lot of years when she'd been looking for someone like Nathan, when she'd been free to pursue a relationship, with no kids and no lies to take responsibility for. Why couldn't she have met him then? Why now, when she was up to her neck in trouble and sinking deeper every day, when the best she could hope for was a broken heart?

Wearily, she locked up and headed upstairs in time to sweep up a naked Brendan as he escaped the bathroom and Alanna's towel. He giggled when she swung him around, then hugged him tight. Whatever else happened, *this* was her priority—these kids. Falling in love, dreaming about falling, or even just a hot and heavy affair couldn't interfere.

As soon as Alanna and Josie finished their baths, Emilie tucked them into bed. Dragging Ernest along, Brendan climbed in at the foot of Josie's bed and slid under the covers. In the middle of their first night upstairs, Emilie had awakened to discover him gone from the bed they'd shared. He had wandered across the hall to his sister's bed and had slept there every night since.

She kissed the younger two first, then sat down on the edge of Alanna's bed. "Did you have a good time tonight?"

"Yeah, it was fun."

"It wouldn't hurt if you told Nathan so the next time you see him."

Alanna lay on her side, facing the window. "Aunt Emilie, do you believe in angels?"

Emilie followed her gaze to the three ornaments hanging from the curtain rod. Next to Josie's angel was Brendan's star, shiny gold on one side, silver on the other, and Alanna's angel, with the same face and hair, the wings tucked neatly back, and a scarlet dress. "Yes, darlin', I do."

"Do you believe in miracles?"

"Hey, we're still together, we've got a place to stay, and we saw our first Christmas parade tonight. If that's not a miracle, I don't know what is." Emilie brushed Alanna's hair back. "Do you believe?"

"I don't know. I used to pray for Mama to get better, but she never did. I'd pray for her to quit drinking, and she'd come home drunker than ever. It's kind of hard to believe when things keep getting worse."

"I know." What could she say to make Alanna feel better? How could she explain that sometimes prayers went unanswered?

Before the first right word came to mind, though, Alanna changed the subject. "You like him, don't you?"

" 'Him'? Is that how you refer to someone?"

"Nathan. Mr. Bishop. You like him."

"Yes, I do."

"Does he like you?"

"I think so. And you and Josie and Brendan."

"If you make him like you a lot, you know, the way all those men liked Mama, maybe we won't get into trouble. Maybe he'll help us."

"Honey, you don't use someone who likes you to stay out of trouble. That's wrong."

"Living in this house is wrong. Letting everyone believe you own it is wrong. Running away from Boston was wrong." Alanna turned onto her back and fixed her gaze on Emilie. "You're not going to, like, fall in love with him, are you?"

"You worry too much. I hardly know Nathan. I'd like to know him better, but don't forget, Lannie—we're only going to be here a few more weeks. Go to sleep now. Morning comes early." She tucked her in, shut off the lamp, then stood for a moment in front of the window.

Moonlight shone on the star and the angels, highlighting the serene smiles. It had been incredibly long since she'd managed serenity. She was nowhere near it tonight.

She did believe in angels and miracles and the power of prayer, but she knew better than to expect a clear answer or the answer she wanted. If she thought she could have whatever she wanted, she would be praying right now. *Please let us stay in Bethlehem. Let me resolve these problems without losing what we've found here. Let me have a chance with Nathan—just a chance. Let us have this place where we can belong, all of us, and have friends and be loved.*

It wasn't so much to ask. If God could create the universe, then surely He could erase a few pesky legal problems in Boston and a few well-meant lies here. Surely He could find a way to wipe out all the bad and let the good remain.

She touched one wingtip, and Josie's angel swayed from side to side. These few days in Bethlehem had made her greedy. All she'd wanted last week was to make it safely to Atlanta and a chance to fulfill her promises to the kids. Now, seven short days later, she wanted safety, security, an escape from the consequences of her lawbreaking, a place to belong, and a man to belong to. She wanted everything.

The angel grew still. It wasn't the real thing, she reminded herself. It couldn't grant wishes or offer peace. It couldn't even transport her prayers to God. It was just a Christmas tree decoration.

She left the kids' door open, shut off the hall light, and made her way by moonlight to her own bed. It had been a long day, and tomorrow would come early. She was ready to sleep and to dream—of kisses, angels, and miracles.

Long after Emilie left the room, Alanna lay awake, the covers pulled to her neck. Josie was snoring, and from time to time Brendan would murmur, but other than that, the house was quiet.

She wondered if it was quiet at the hospital where her mother was. There were a lot of sick people there, and on the times when the doctor had said it would be good for them to visit, it had scared Alanna. The place had smelled bad, and there had been a lot of noise and people crying. Brendan had cried and clung to Emilie when Mama tried to take him. She'd looked thin and edgy, like she might yell at them just for being there. She hadn't yelled, though. She had cried, too.

Josie was the only one who'd enjoyed the visit. She had told Mama how pretty she looked and how much she missed her. She had chattered the way she always did about the things they would do when Mama came home. She hadn't known—still didn't know—that Mama might never come home, at least, not to stay. She'd gotten clean before, but it had never lasted, and Alanna didn't know of any reason to believe that this time would be different.

Unless you were six years old and believed in Santa Claus.

Josie had had fun at the parade, and she'd talked all through her bath about Santa and the presents he was going to bring. She didn't know that Santa had been wearing a wig, a beard, and padding. She didn't know that his name was really Mitch something. His niece, Susan, sat next to Alanna in school and had shared her blanket at tonight's parade, and she'd told Alanna so in a whisper. But it was okay for Josie to believe. After all, she was just a kid.

Alanna wished there really was a Santa Claus or an angel or anyone with the magic to make things right for them. If they stayed in Bethlehem, they were going to get caught, but they had no choice. Emilie was convinced that their luck could hold another twenty-seven days, but Alanna wasn't. In less than twenty-seven days, Emilie had lost her job, they'd been evicted, and Social Services had told her to give the kids back. In twenty-seven days, the real owner of the house could come back, Emilie could be arrested, and the kids could be taken away and separated forever.

If there really was a Santa Claus, she would climb on his lap, even if she was too old and too big and didn't believe, and she would beg him to make everything all right. Mama would be better and never get sick again, and she would join them in Atlanta. Emilie would have babies of her own, and they would all live together— Mama and her children and Emilie and hers. Just one big happy family.

None of them had ever been part of a happy family. This, with all their worry about getting caught and going to jail and foster homes, was as close as they'd gotten. They deserved to be happy. Santa Claus couldn't do it, but maybe an angel could.

Between the moon, the streetlamps, and the snow, it

was pretty bright outside, bright enough to see the angel's smile. Alanna had never known anyone who could smile like that—like she didn't have a care in the world. Where she came from, there were always troubles.

Slipping from the bed, she raised her hand until the angel's bare feet rested in her palm. In the quiet night, she half expected to feel something—some little shock, something angelic and magic. Silly. It was just a pretty-painted piece of plastic meant to hang on a tree. It didn't have any magic powers. She didn't believe in angels, even if Emilie did, and as for miracles . . . She'd have to see one to believe it.

Still . . . "It's a neat idea—having someone special looking out for you and keeping you safe," she whispered, stroking the tip of her finger over the folds of the deep red dress, feeling the texture of the wings where they rose out of the back. "I guess that's why we have mothers—and aunts. 'Cause we can't have angels. If we did have an angel, we'd keep you pretty busy. We're in so much trouble that it'd take you and about a million more to get us out of it."

She let her hand drop, gave Brendan's star a twirl, then scurried back to the warmth of the bed. As she huddled under the covers, she looked at the angel once more, smiling in the night, and wistfully whispered, "It's a really neat idea."

# Chapter Six

"I knew I would find it if I looked hard enough." Smiling broadly, Agatha slapped a photograph on the table in front of Nathan. As Corinna refilled his coffee, he looked at the snapshot, dated ten years ago on the back. It was a picture of the Pierce house with snow piled to the top of the porch steps.

"Nice shot."

"That's all you have to say? Don't you see?"

"It's Emilie's house in the snow."

"Not the snow. If you want to see Emilie's house in the snow, just look out your window. I'm talking about this." She tapped one finger on the porch. "The decorations."

It was decorated for Christmas, with lights along the roofline, garlands on the porch rail, and wreaths with big red bows on every window. "Pretty."

Exasperated, she sank into the chair opposite him. "It's Christmas, Nathan. Every house on the street is decorated except Emilie's and yours. Your isn't decorated because you're pretending you're Scrooge, but Emilie's isn't done because of money."

"She isn't going to let anyone buy her a bunch of decorations." He had persuaded her to let him buy gifts for the kids. He wasn't going to push his luck on things like lights, garlands, and wreaths.

Corinna stepped into the conversation. "The point Agatha is trying to make is that Miriam was a budget-conscious woman."

"I can make my point just fine. She was a dear woman, but she was a skinflint. She kept every decoration she ever had, and she didn't like throwing away money unnecessarily. Those wreaths and garlands are artificial. They're surely still in the attic over there."

"If someone wanted to climb up and get them—"

"Then Emilie could decorate for Christmas."

"Without spending a penny."

"For the children."

He studied the sisters while sipping his coffee. He hadn't decorated a house for Christmas since he'd lived at home and been in charge of climbing onto the roof to string the lights. The last time, he'd fallen off, landed on his mother's prize shrubs, and broken his arm. "You know, that house has a full attic with regular stairs. Emilie's perfectly capable of going up there herself."

"Why would she? She doesn't even know the decorations are there."

"So you want me to tell her."

"And bring the boxes down, of course."

"Maybe help her with the lights."

"And the wreaths for the upstairs windows. It would be a shame if she tried to climb out on that roof and fell."

"And it wouldn't be a shame if *I* fell off the roof?"

Both sisters blushed. "Of course it would, but that would never happen."

"Besides, Emilie's got those children to take care of."

Lately, he'd had the odd feeling that *he* had three children to take care of, and their mother, too. Even odder, he didn't mind the idea at all—and *that* bothered him. If he'd gone looking for someone to get serious with, he certainly wouldn't have chosen a down-on-her-luck mother of three who didn't plan to stay in town any longer than she had to. A relationship with Emilie was bound to turn sour, and it was hard enough when that happened without bringing children into it.

Finishing his coffee, he stood up. "Okay. I'll tell her about the decorations, get them out of the attic, and break my fool neck hanging them for her. By the way, the cake was good, but the next time you intend to bribe me, I want cheese Danish."

"We'll remember that," Corinna said with a smile that was equal parts satisfaction and smugness.

"As long as you're going over there, how about delivering this?" Agatha pressed a large tray into his hands. Covered with clear red plastic wrap and decorated with a bow, it held squares of fudge, chocolate-dipped candies, and other treats.

He delayed taking the tray long enough to pull his coat on. After saying his good-byes, he left the house and crossed the snow to Emilie's. Alanna answered the door, muttered something about mother and kitchen, and headed upstairs. The house was quiet as he made his way down the hall. Passing the parlor, he realized that it was a lack of background noise. At his house the television was always on, and the sisters always had the radio playing. He hadn't seen any sign of either in the station wagon a week ago.

Brendan was sitting at the breakfast table, navigating a matchbook around salt and pepper shakers with the chug-chug of a locomotive. Josie was as still as he'd ever seen her, sitting sideways on her chair, eating dry cereal, and staring out the window.

Emilie, washing dishes, noticed him first. "If you'd come five minutes earlier, you could have had breakfast."

"I ate next door."

"What is that?"

"A gift from the sisters."

She dried her hands and peeled the plastic away to pick up a piece of chocolate. "Fudge? I love fudge."

The short list of things he knew she loved grew by one: her kids, Christmas parades, and now fudge. Pretty good company to keep. "I'm going to the grocery store later. Want to go?"

"Sure. The kids will appreciate it. We ran out of milk this morning."

Silence fell, the same odd, anticipatory silence that had preceded Thursday night's kiss. He tried to think of something to say, but couldn't. She tried to occupy herself, but didn't. Finally, reminding himself that the kids were across the room, he cleared his throat, but the hoarseness remained. "Agatha and Corinna wanted me to tell you that your aunt's Christmas decorations are still up in the attic. They thought you might want to use them."

"My aunt . . ." She sounded vague. He wasn't the only one whose mind had been on other, more intimate matters. "Oh, yes. Miriam."

"I have instructions to carry the boxes down and to crawl out on the roof with the wreaths if you're interested."

"There's snow on the roof. What if you fall?"

He had the strangest sensation that he was already falling. "I promise not to break more than a few bones."

"I think we can do without any broken bones. But if you're willing to get the boxes, I'm willing to do my part. The attic is this way."

He followed her upstairs, to the end of the hall, and

through a door that led to more stairs. Considering that it had never been used as living space and hadn't been touched for seven years, the attic was remarkably clean but none too organized. There were trunks and boxes stacked all around the perimeter, and not one single label.

Emilie walked slowly around the room. "I guess she knew where she had stored everything and never thought about whoever would move in after her."

"Did you know her well?"

She paused in front of a cheval mirror but didn't look at her own reflection. "No."

"Whose sister was she? Your mother's or father's?"

"She was— Oh, look. Isn't this pretty?" Ignoring the dust, she knelt on the floor in front of an antique cradle, giving it a rock. "When I was little—no more than five—I had a doll with her own little wooden cradle. I always thought it was so neat, and when I grew up and had babies of my own, I swore I would have one exactly like it."

"Did you?"

She wiped a cobweb away, ran her hand over the wood, then stood up with a sigh. "No."

"Things didn't turn out quite the way you'd planned, did they?" At her embarrassed look, he shrugged. "You think when I got married, I intended for my wife to fall in love with my best friend, pass his daughter off as mine, then divorce me after he was killed?"

She dusted an old trunk, then sat down. "What happened?"

Mitch Walker was the only other person in town who knew anything about Mike's death. When he'd interviewed for the job, Nathan had felt it was the chief's right to know. It could have given Mitch second thoughts about hiring him.

Now Nathan was having second thoughts about having confided in Emilie. He didn't want to talk about it, didn't want to remember the pain. He didn't want to think about what it meant that he'd told her—not his friends, not the people he considered family, but a stranger he hardly knew. But he answered, and in some perverse way, it felt good.

"Mike and Diana and I had known each other since we were kids. She and I started dating when we were sixteen, and we always doubled with him and his girlfriends. She never cared much for him, but she put up with him because of me. I thought it was generous of her." He heard the bitterness creeping in, felt the resentment building, and tried to ignore both. "Mike and I moved to New York together, got hired by the department, and went through the academy. A year later Diana came up from Pennsylvania, and we got married. In the beginning, we fought a lot about the job, the hours, the pay, but after a while, that stopped. From the time she got pregnant right up to the end, we'd never gotten along so well. She was attentive, sweet, loving. I thought . . . Jeez, I thought I was the luckiest man in the world. I actually felt sorry for Mike because he didn't have a woman like Diana in his life.

"One day, not long after Elisabeth was born, Mike came to see me. He admitted that he'd been gambling and was in pretty deep. His bookie was starting to suggest other ways he could pay him off—providing him with a little information, a little muscle. I told him he had to talk to the sergeant, but he refused. He was panicked about the possibility of losing his job. He said he could handle it, so I let it slide. I covered for him. I lied for him because I didn't want to get him into trouble.

"Things got worse until finally I gave him an ultimatum: he could turn himself in or I would. He pleaded with me for one more chance. He was going to fix everything. He asked for twenty-four hours, and I agreed. I knew it was wrong. I was supposed to be one of the good guys, for God's sake. I wasn't supposed to look the other way just because he was my friend." But Mike had begged. He'd been wild-eyed with fear and desperation. He'd sworn that everything would be all right, but he'd been wrong. So damn wrong.

"The next afternoon he was dead. His big plan to get out from under his bookie was to kill the guy. He was a cop. He thought he could do it without getting caught. While he was at it, he planned to take whatever money he happened to find and use it to make a new start with Diana and Elisabeth. Unfortunately, his target was the better shot." He went to sit on the nearest windowsill, the glass cold against his back. "I'm partly to blame for it. I knew he wasn't going to straighten out on his own. He was breaking the law, and I looked the other way. I made it possible for him to continue breaking the law, and, in the end, it killed him."

Emilie shivered in the gloomy room. He wasn't responsible for Mike's death. Mike was. Nathan had only tried to help a friend. It wasn't his fault that the friend had tried to take the wrong way out.

But that wasn't the reason for her shiver. Thursday night she had wished, hoped—prayed—for a miracle, for a chance with Nathan, for some resolution to their troubles that wouldn't destroy the new relationships they'd started here. She had thought that perhaps these people who were so kind and generous might also be forgiving, that once the truth was out, they might understand and not hate her for the lies. But not Nathan. He'd been understanding and forgiving once, and it had cost him dearly. If he trusted her, if he got involved with her, then discovered that she—like his best friend, like his wife—had betrayed him . . .

She shivered again.

Swallowing hard, she left the trunk and went to stand in front of him. "It wasn't your fault. You can't control what other people do. You did what any friend would have done: you gave him a chance. The fact that he blew that chance is his failing, not yours."

"If I'd been a *real* friend, I would have turned him in. I would have stopped him before he did something stupid."

She reached for his hand. "Don't kid yourself, Nathan. He'd already done plenty of stupid things. He'd fallen in love with your wife. He'd helped pass his own daughter off as yours. He'd gotten into serious trouble. Desperate people do desperate things." *She* was living proof. "Mike made his choices. The responsibility—the guilt, the blame—lie with him. Not you."

For a long, silent moment his fingers tightened around hers, and his gaze, dark but faintly hopeful, locked with hers. He wanted to believe, she knew. He wanted very much to believe that he hadn't played some role in his best friend's death. He just wasn't quite able.

After a time, he released her hand, rose from the windowsill, and went to the nearest stack of boxes to open the first one. She started at the opposite end, blowing off dust, pulling open flaps. Lucky for Miriam that she'd had this huge attic, because evidently she had never thrown anything away. Emilie found clothes out of style long before she was born, a stack of newspapers from the forties, and piles of letters and pictures. "Some of this stuff should be in a museum."

"Bethlehem has a historical society. You can give it to them if you want. It's yours."

She wished that were true. If this lovely house and all its contents had been hers, the court never would have revoked their custody agreement. If it were hers, she would be disgustingly happy, because it would mean that she had a place to belong. It would mean that she stood a chance with Nathan.

They checked the top boxes in every stack, meeting in the middle. He picked one up to move it to the floor, and she tapped him on the arm. "Look."

On the side that had been against the wall, the word Photographs was written in a neat hand. The box next to it was marked Correspondence. Every single box was labeled, for some reason on the back. Maybe Miriam had done some rearranging, then had died before putting everything right. Whatever the reason, they sorted out the Christmas boxes, then carried them two at a time downstairs to the dining room, away from curious little hands.

The boxes were treasure chests for Emilie. Many of the items were heirlooms, and everything looked costly. Even the artificial wreaths and garlands, at least seven years old, were of the best quality and looked pretty darn real. A few pieces she looked at in their boxes, then immediately returned to the packing carton—the blown glass ornaments so fragile that a firm grip might shatter them, the figurines in boxes adorned with names she'd long heard but could never afford, especially on the antique market. A number of the items were probably worth a pretty penny to a collector—

"You could probably sell some of this stuff."

She gave Nathan a sharp look. "But that would be wrong. It would be—"

"Wrong? To sell things that belonged to an aunt you barely knew when you and the kids are just barely getting by? It's practical, not wrong. Just a few of these things could replace your car, buy the kids a new wardrobe, and give you money in the bank for your next emergency."

She closed a box of the exquisite, expensive stuff and set it aside for a hasty return to the attic. "I couldn't do that. These things have been handed down from generation to generation. They belong in the family." A family that wasn't hers.

"Sentimentality's real nice, sweetheart," he said softly as he brushed behind her. "But you can't eat it, wear it, or live in it."

He was right, of course, and if these things truly belonged to her, she would take his advice. She would never let the children live in poverty while valuable heirlooms languished in the attic awaiting their once-a-year use. But he could never know that they weren't hers to sell, so she let the conversation drop.

She sorted through the last boxes, then looked over what she'd left out. Yards of garland and clear lights lay neatly coiled at one end of the table. There were a dozen wreaths and two dozen red velvet bows, each so carefully packed that, after seven years in storage, they were wrinkle-free, and an angel to place on the mantel. Her dress was gold satin with a swath of brocade that circled above her wings and cascaded down. She looked very old and delicate and more than capable of watching over the parlor.

Working together on the lights, they switched bulbs and fuses and managed to get about half the strings working, enough to line the railing and the roof. Outside they hung the garland first, then attached the wreaths and bows to hooks hanging above each window. The wreaths for the upstairs windows remained inside. No way was she risking her neck or Nathan's just for a few pretty wreaths.

Clasping her gloved hands to keep them warm, Emilie asked, "What about the lights?"

The look Nathan gave her was curious. "Haven't you ever done this before?"

She shook her head. If her own parents had ever decorated for Christmas, she couldn't remember it. Some of her foster families had, but it had always been such a family event, and she had been left out, by their choice or her own, of most family events.

"We'll hang the lights tonight. How else are we going to know if we've got them right?"

It seemed pretty clear to her. After all, the lights would simply go straight across the roofline, then loop along the garland. But if Nathan's tradition involved doing them at night, who was she to argue? Besides, spending the evening, even just a small part of it, with him was such a pleasant prospect. "Why don't you come over for dinner? I make a pretty good chili, and we can have Agatha and Corinna's fudge for dessert."

For a moment he simply looked at her, then, with the faintest of smiles, he accepted. "I'd like that." The smile disappeared immediately. "Get the kids and let's go to the store. We'll have lunch first."

She gave only a second's thought to refusing yet another free meal, not because she'd spent the last five days learning to be gracious about accepting help but simply because she wanted to go. She wanted to sit across from him and share a meal. She wanted to spend every minute with him that he was willing to offer. After all, in a few more weeks, she would be hundreds of miles away and would never see him again. "Give me a minute."

He waited outside, making final adjustments to the garland. She hustled Josie and Brendan upstairs, out of their pajamas, and into clothes while Alanna watched from her bed. "Come on, Lannie," Josie urged. "We got to go. Mr. Nathan is waiting."

Alanna ignored her. "Can I stay here? I'm not really hungry."

"No, darlin', you can't."

"Why not? Mama used to leave me alone when I was a lot younger than I am now."

That was true. When Alanna was six years old, Berry had deemed her responsible enough to be left in charge of Josie and baby Brendan, sometimes overnight. But Berry's judgment had been affected by the drugs and alcohol. "I'm not saying you're not responsible, Alanna. I'm saying you can't stay today. Nathan invited us all to lunch, and we're all going."

"But, Aunt Emilie—" Scowling, she broke off and yanked on socks and shoes. "You're not so different from Mama. Every time a new man came around, we all had to do whatever he wanted."

Emilie grew still. So it wasn't just Nathan's job as a police officer that put Alanna on edge. She had lived through too many of Berry's relationships, where the man always came first, where his desires and needs received priority over the children's, and she was afraid. Emilie longed to wrap her arms around her and hold her tight, to make her believe that no one would *ever* come between them. She would give anything to erase all the hurts and fears, to give Alanna and the others the sort of normal, loving upbringing that every child deserved.

But she couldn't undo the harm Berry had done. She could make their future better, but there was no magic wand that could rewrite the past. All she could do was love the kids as if they were her own, be there for them always, and give them some measure of stability that they could count on. It would take time, though, and a lot of it, before she won Alanna's unconditional trust.

Nathan would have to wait a little longer. This was too important to put off until later. "You know I love you guys and your mom more than anything in the world, don't you?"

Grudgingly, her gaze cast down, Alanna nodded.

"You're my family, and family comes first. No one can change that."

"Men can always change it," Alanna whispered. "Right now it's easy for you to say that you love us most, because there isn't anyone else. But what if there was? What if you fell in love? What if you fell in love with *him* and got married and had babies? Then *they'd* be your family, and you would love them more. What would happen to us then?"

"We would still be a family—just a bigger one. Do you think I could ever fall in love with anyone who didn't love you, too?" A few weeks ago, she would have added more. She'd had ten years on her own to fall in love. If it hadn't happened then, it wasn't likely to happen now that she had the responsibility of a family.

But a few weeks ago, she hadn't met Nathan. She hadn't known that the possibility of love still existed for her. Except, because of her past, because of his, the possibility was an *im*possibility. "We're only going to be in Bethlehem another three weeks—"

"And four days."

"And that's not long enough for falling in love and making a new family." But her words were a lie. Three weeks and four days was long enough to fall in love. It was more than long enough to get her heart broken. "Quit worrying and let's eat, okay?"

"Okay." But Alanna didn't look any less worried—or any more reassured—as she dragged out of the room behind the younger kids.

Emilie paused in front of the window, where she gave the twin angels each a pat. She was hoping to buy Alanna a couple of outfits for Christmas, and Nathan had offered to buy her some books, but she needed something so much more important—faith that she was loved, that she was wanted, that she would never be turned away. But how did you gift-wrap faith? How could you make someone believe who'd never had any reason to?

The angels had no answers for her.

She joined the kids on the veranda just as Nathan pulled into the driveway. As usual, Josie raced ahead. Brendan tried to follow, but his legs couldn't manage the snow, so Alanna swung him up into her arms. Fifteen or twenty years from now, she was going to make some lucky kids the best mother in the world . . . unless she reacted to all this childhood mothering by having no children of her own. If that was the case, Emilie thought grimly, it would be one more blame heaped on Berry's head. One more regret they would all have to live with.

Nathan offered a choice of restaurants, and Josie voted loudly for Harry's Diner. Brendan followed her lead, and Alanna simply shrugged. No matter where they went, she would be happier, Nathan knew, if he weren't along. He was sorry she felt that way. He didn't require everyone's approval, and he'd certainly been on the receiving end of emotions stronger than dislike, but he could be a good friend, and he figured Alanna could use one.

Besides, of course, there was the matter of Emilie. If he was going to be spending a lot of time with her—and he was—it would be easier if her daughter didn't get hostile every time he came around. He didn't expect her to share Josie's wholehearted enthusiasm, but he would like a little more acceptance.

Maeve greeted them at the diner with a wink and a comment about new traditions. Though her optimism was misplaced—traditions couldn't be built in the short time Emilie was planning to stay—he liked the idea of family traditions. Little routines like sitting down to dinner every evening with no interruptions, attending church together on Sundays, or having lunch every Saturday in the same restaurant held a reassuring appeal all their own.

All three of Emilie's kids—but especially Alanna—could use such reassurance.

After eating their hot dogs and fries, the kids, at Josie's request, moved to the counter barstools for dessert, leaving an empty bench curving what seemed a long distance between him and Emilie. Next Saturday, and for however many Saturdays remained, he was going to rearrange the seating order. Josie was fine company, but he'd rather sit close to her mother.

"What do you do on Saturdays when you're not chauffeuring us around?"

"Go to the grocery store, watch football games on TV, do my laundry. Nothing special."

"Do you ever work?"

"Only if it's a holiday or everyone's out sick."

"And you go out on dates."

"Occasionally."

"And are they special?"

"Occasionally. What about your dates?"

Her shrug was casual. His interest in her answer wasn't. "I don't date. I have three children, remember?"

Most men would rather pass up an evening with a beautiful woman than risk falling for someone with a ready-made family. That had been the deciding factor in a few relationships he'd decided not to pursue—that, and the fact that he'd had no interest in trying again. "Of course, a husband makes it kind of difficult to date. Although," he added cynically, "my ex-wife managed."

Emilie was looking at him with sympathy that made him wish he'd kept those last words to himself. He wanted a number of things from her, but sympathy ranked low on the list. When moments passed without any comment from her, he asked, "*Is* there a husband?"

"No."

It was a variation of a conversation they'd had before. Her answer today left him as unsatisfied as it had that day. "So you're divorced."

Her gaze shifted to the street outside. As answers went, it wasn't enough.

Her refusal to say, Yes, I'm divorced, nagged at him, but how far should he push it? If there was a husband back in Massachusetts looking for her, he needed to know before it was too late, before he found himself in the same situation that had led to the end of his marriage—and Mike's life. On the other hand, if there was a custodial *ex*-husband back home looking for his kids, did he want to know? When he would have to report her to the authorities in Boston?

"You know there's something between us, Emilie. Before it goes any further, I need to know the truth. No carefully worded answers, no guilty evasions. Is there someone, anyone, I should know about?"

Her gaze was steady and—he would stake his future on it—honest. "No. I told you, Brendan's father took off before he was born. I haven't been involved with anyone since then."

The answer gave him a tremendous sense of relief, but it didn't ease the niggling little doubts. He wished she would be forthright and straightforward about it just once, and then they never needed to discuss it again. Maybe she was embarrassed because she'd had three kids with the guy and apparently never married him or because he hadn't wanted her enough to stick around through his son's birth. Maybe she simply didn't trust him with her past, the way he had never trusted anyone with his. Until her.

He wanted her trust. *Really* wanted it. "How long did you live in Boston?"

"What makes you think it wasn't forever?"

"You don't have the accent."

"No accent at all?" She looked surprised, almost disappointed.

"No Boston accent. Something more Southern. Alabama?"

"Georgia. I was raised there."

"And you came north . . . ?"

"Because I had family here."

"Are they still here?" If they were, why hadn't they helped when she lost her job and got evicted? Why had she wound up in a homeless shelter?

"No." The word was pinched and withdrawn, like her expression.

"Do you have any family anywhere?"

"No."

"What about their father's family?"

"There's no one."

At first thought, it was hard to imagine being so completely alone, but his own situation wasn't so different. He had parents, brothers, in-laws, plus aunts, uncles, and cousins, and yet he was alone. His only family was here in Bethlehem—the Winchester sisters—but there were no blood ties between them, just affection, respect, and love.

"How long do you plan to stay in Bethlehem?" It was a question he should have asked earlier. Before spending the morning with her. Before kissing her.

"Until New Year's."

Less than a month. That wasn't long enough for anything . . . except winding up lonelier and more alone than he'd ever been. Except getting attached to her kids and losing them, the way he'd lost Elisabeth.

Though maybe it was long enough to change her mind. If this thing between them was worth developing, if it held the promise of any sort of future, she could be persuaded to stay. *He* could persuade her.

"Where will you go?"

"Home."

"That's Boston, right? You drove down just to see your aunt's house and to spend one night, and then you were going back to Massachusetts. That's what you told me last week."

Suddenly restless, she began stacking the dishes— plates here, silverware there, napkins and straw paper over there. He slid his own dishes out of her reach.

"What do you have to go home to? You lost your job. You lost your home. You were living in a shelter, for God's sake."

Her eyes widened, and her face paled. She looked as if she might dissolve into tears at any moment. "How do you know . . . ?"

Embarrassed that he'd blurted out her secret, he shrugged. "Josie told Santa after the parade. It happens to a lot of people, Emilie. It's nothing to be ashamed of."

"Oh, really. When was the last time you were evicted? Or your brothers, your friends, your neighbors? Have you ever actually known anyone who's been evicted, or don't you associate with that kind of people?" Without waiting for an answer, she got up, picked up an armful of coats, and called, "Alanna, Josie, Brendan, let's go."

"But, Mama, I'm not finished," Josie protested as Alanna obediently slid to the floor and began wiping her brother's face and hands.

"Me, neither," Brendan added. "Go 'way, Lannie. Not finished."

Emilie didn't hesitate. She kept her coat, dropped the others on the bench, and left. Nathan grabbed his own jacket and pulled it on as he crossed the room. "Alanna, keep an eye on the kids. Maeve . . . ?"

The waitress nodded sympathetically. "They'll be fine."

Emilie was halfway to the bandstand in the square by the time he got across the street. He followed, kicking the snow off his boots as he climbed the wooden steps. "I'm sorry."

Her back was to him, her voice none too steady. "For what?"

"I shouldn't have said anything. I knew the morning we met, when I saw the stuff in the car, that you didn't have a home to go back to. Josie just confirmed it. I'm sorry."

"You don't know what it's like to find yourself in a shelter. I'd never accepted charity. I'd always taken care of myself. Then things started going wrong. We had bills, unexpected expenses. We moved to a cheaper apartment, and then to an even cheaper one, but my income couldn't keep up with the costs of living. Suddenly one day we were homeless. Everything we owned was in that stupid piece-of-junk car. We had $173, no place to go, and no one to help. It was either the shelter or sleep in the car." She turned, and he could see in her eyes the tears he'd heard in her voice. "Do you know how people look at you when you're homeless? When you can't feed your children, when you can't give them a place to sleep? It's like you have some sort of disease that everyone's afraid of catching. They treat you like an outcast, like someone to be shunned. They make you ask—*beg*—for the basic necessities, for food and a bed, for things everyone is entitled to. It's not bad enough that you've lost your job and your home. They take your pride and dignity, too."

That explained her reluctance, her great difficulty, in accepting help, Nathan thought grimly. But there was a difference between a helping hand and a handout.

"Where were you planning to go last Friday if you'd been able to leave? Why didn't you come here to stay? You have a house here."

"I didn't want to stay. I just wanted . . ." She broke off with a shrug that indicated she couldn't explain or he couldn't understand. He *couldn't* understand, but he didn't have to. All he had to know was that she was here now. All he had to do was convince her to stay.

He crossed the bandstand, buttoned her coat, pulled her gloves from her pocket and held them while she slid her hands inside, then wrapped the dangling scarf around her neck twice. Still holding the ends of the scarf, he drew her closer. "People have bad luck, Emilie. That's all that's happened to you. It doesn't mean you're a failure or undeserving of dignity and respect. It also doesn't mean that you have to do everything on your own just to prove you can. It's okay to accept help. It's all right to let someone else be strong for you until you're back on your feet yourself."

"There's never been anyone else to depend on."

She said never as if she meant it, as if not once had there ever been anyone to turn to. The thought that she truly could have been so alone forever was stunning. It made his voice husky and low. "There is now."

For a long time, neither of them moved. They stood too close, but not close enough, gazes locked, neither willing to break the contact. He thought about kissing her—wanted it more than he wanted his next breath—

but he didn't bend closer, didn't brush his lips across
hers, didn't pull her so close and so tight that he couldn't
tell where he stopped and she began. Instead, with his
fingers knotted around the scarf, his chest tight, and a
quivery, quavery sensation deep inside, he simply
looked at her.

The sound of a horn on the nearby street reminded
him where they were. Forcing his fingers to uncurl from
the wool, he released her, took a step back, and turned
away. As he drew a deep breath of frigid air, he swore
he heard a soft, disappointed sigh behind him. Without
turning, he extended his hand. After a moment, she took
it and let him pull her to his side. "You're going to be
okay."

Her fingers tightened around his. "Yes, I am."

Without further conversation, they returned to the
diner. Emilie chose to wait outside while he went in to
pay the check and collect the children.

"Is everything all right?" Maeve asked as she counted
out his change.

"Yeah, it's fine." Considering that he hadn't kissed
Emilie, even though he'd wanted to, even though she'd
wanted him to.

"She's got three real sweet kids. That Josie's a pistol,
isn't she? Brendan's a little doll, and Alanna . . . That
girl's going to break some hearts someday." She smiled
as she watched the kids head outside to join Emilie. "I
just wish Alanna didn't worry so. The whole time you

were gone, she sat in the booth, with this anxious look on her face that made her look ninety instead of nine. It's just not right for a child so young to have such cares."

Nathan gave her the singles for a tip, then dropped the change into the need-a-penny cup. "They've been alone a long time. She's had to grow up quicker than a kid should."

"They need a good man in their lives," she said with a sly grin. "It'd make all the difference in the world."

"With opinions like that, you don't have many feminist friends, do you?"

"Feminism has nothing to do with it. Men need women, and women need men. That's the way God intended it. This old world would be a better place to live if everyone had someone to love."

Nathan followed her glance to the long window that looked into the kitchen, where Harry was busy at the grill. He didn't comment, but said good-bye and went to the truck. Emilie had already settled the kids in back and was fastening her own seat belt when he got in.

"Hey, Mr. Nathan, why did you guys go for a walk without us?" Josie asked.

"Because you were eating ice cream like a little pig."

She gave a credibly piggish snort, then giggled. "What is that place you went to?"

"A bandstand."

"What is that?"

"Every summer they have concerts there. People bring picnic dinners and quilts and chairs, and they eat on the grass, and the kids play games."

"That sounds neat. Will you take us?"

"He said in summer, goofball," Alanna said with less than her usual scorn. "We won't be here then."

Her statement made everyone's smiles fade. It made even Josie sink into silence for the short drive to the grocery store.

If she wanted to do what was best for the kids, Nathan thought, Emilie would stay. They needed stability. They needed to know that they had a home not just for now but for next month and next year and the next twenty years. This was their fourth home—five, counting the shelter—in recent months. That was a hard way for kids to live. It was a hard way for her to live.

At the grocery store, Josie climbed halfway out, then paused, her gaze fixed on the distant corner of the parking lot where the snow was still untouched. "Mr. Nathan, could we stay outside and build a snowman while Mama buys groceries?"

"If your mother says so."

She twisted to face Emilie over the top of the truck. "Can we, Mama? Please, just one snowman? You said we'd only see snow once in a blue moon, and since we're going home from here, it don't matter if I get my shoes wet. They'll be dry before school Monday."

Emilie and Alanna exchanged looks. Alanna nodded first, then Emilie did. "Come on, Brendan, you go with me."

He struggled to free himself. "Doan want to. Want to build a 'nowman."

"He can stay, too. If they get too cold, I'll bring them in." Nathan watched her go inside, then started across the lot, a few feet behind the kids. So they could stay in his care as long as Alanna was there, too. If he didn't know better, he'd think Emilie didn't trust him.

But he did know better. He knew the one time he'd been alone with Josie, she'd blurted out something Emilie hadn't wanted anyone to know. He'd bet money Alanna's job wasn't to make sure he took proper care of the kids but to ensure that Josie didn't offer any other personal tidbits that might embarrass their mother.

Insisting they needed no help, Josie and Brendan went straight to work on the snowman. Alanna leaned against the shopping-cart corral, hands stuffed deep in her pockets, and watched her brother and sister while Nathan watched her. After a moment, she twitched, shifted, and turned away, then whirled back. "What?"

"What is it you don't like about me?"

"I don't even know you. It doesn't matter, anyway, because we're leaving in twenty-five days."

"Are you so anxious to get back to Boston?"

His question put her on guard. Suddenly she couldn't

meet his gaze, and she found it impossible to stand still. "I want to get someplace where we can stay."

But that place wasn't necessarily Boston. Had Emilie told him it was? Last week she had implied it. Today she'd said they would go home when they left Bethlehem. His assumption that home meant Boston had made her uneasy, like Alanna. Was she planning to settle someplace else—maybe back in Georgia? Someplace where they would see snow only once in a blue moon? But if that was the case, why didn't she simply say so? Why act as if she had something to hide?

Maybe she did. Maybe she was playing him for a fool, and everything she'd told him so far—every piece of information he'd dragged out of her—was a lie.

He didn't believe that. Maybe he wasn't the best judge of character around, but there was something about Emilie that he was convinced he could trust—some basic decency, some innate honesty.

"You don't want to stay in Bethlehem."

Alanna shrugged. "It's a nice town."

"You like the school?"

"Yeah."

"Have you made some friends there?"

"A couple."

"But you don't mind leaving them."

She didn't answer. She probably did mind, as any child would, but felt it would be disloyal to her mother to say so.

"What do you do for fun?"

Her only answer was a big, awkward shrug.

"I guess you've outgrown playing with dolls. Do you like to read? Play games? Work puzzles?"

Another shrug was accompanied by unexpected honesty. "I like to read, but Josie was telling the truth for once. I'm not very good at it."

Without looking up from the base she and Brendan were making for their snowman, Josie said, "Lannie, I *always* tell the truth. Well, almost always. Sometimes I tell more truth than I'm supposed to, like the time I told that woman her hair was ugly."

"She was an important lady, and you were rude to her."

"But her hair was *orange*. Ladies' hair isn't supposed to be orange."

"It *was* pretty ugly," Alanna admitted with the beginnings of a smile. "Mama said it was the color of a rotted pumpkin. You'd think an important lady would know better."

What made a woman important in Alanna's eyes? Someone with the authority to evict them from their home? A prospective employer for their mother? Maybe a clerk who could approve or disapprove them for public assistance.

He returned to their subject before Josie had joined in. "You know, Miss Agatha and Miss Corinna both used to teach school. If you asked, I bet they'd help you with your reading."

For an instant she looked hopeful, then a no-big-deal sort of look settled across her face, matching her shrug. "What does it matter? Except for schoolbooks, I don't have anything to read."

"You could get a library card. They've got plenty of books to read."

"Even if we don't really live here? Even if we're only going to be here twenty-five more days?"

"Even if. When you go to Miss Corinna's after school Monday, ask her to take you to the library and help you get a card."

"Do you think they'll let her?"

He laughed at the idea of anyone trying to tell the old lady no. "There's only one hard-and-fast rule in Bethlehem, Alanna: *no one* stands in the way of what Miss Corinna or Miss Agatha wants. They'll let her. All you have to do is ask."

# Chapter Seven

The night was still and quiet. Emilie sat in the front yard in a place where the snow had blown away to manageable proportions. The bench had come from the veranda, ornate wrought iron and dusty wood slats. Her old brown quilt covered the wood, and the blankets from their beds were spread over and around her, Josie, and Brendan.

Fifteen feet away, Nathan and Alanna were in the process of hanging the last strings of lights. The garland and three-fourths of the porch roof were already aglow with dozens of tiny white lights. It was a lovely sight.

"It's the prettiest house in town."

Emilie smiled at the reverential tone of Josie's voice. Every day she had second thoughts about the wisdom—and the honesty and decency—of what they were doing here. Every day she regretted the loss of the car that prevented them from continuing their flight to Georgia. But moments like this made the risk worth taking. Hearing the awe in Josie's voice when she talked about her visit to Santa, seeing the wonder in Brendan's eyes every time he saw the Christmas decorations around town, and watching Alanna interact even just briefly with Nathan without open hostility were worth it all.

Being with Nathan in itself might be worth it all.

This wouldn't be the richest Christmas, in material terms, but it would be a memorable one because it was a season of firsts—their first parade, Josie's first visit with Santa, their first real gifts, their first time in a place where they didn't belong but were welcomed anyway. It was the best ending they could have to a less-than-joyous year. If only Berry could share it . . .

She wished she could call her sister and tell her that they were all right, but it wasn't possible. The authorities could be monitoring any calls Berry received. Depending on her mood and the level of her desire to escape the hospital, she might blurt out whatever she knew to whoever happened to be around. She would just have to trust in Emilie's ability to take care of her children, and please, God, don't let that trust be misplaced.

Holding tightly to her blanket, Josie rose to her knees and brought her mouth close to Emilie's ear. "I wish Mama could see this."

Emilie pulled her onto her lap, snuggling her under the quilt she shared with Brendan. "I do, too, baby."

"If she could live here, she would be all right. I just know she would, 'cause this is such a nice town, and all the people are nice, and she would be happy and would get well and would never be sick again."

Emilie hugged her tight. "Maybe she would." Bethlehem had worked its magic on Nathan, and, if only they could stay, it would do the same for them. Maybe it could help Berry, too. Maybe here she could find whatever it was she'd been searching for all her sad life. Maybe here she could rid herself of the demons and appreciate all the wonders of her life, starting with her three beautiful children.

There was a thud on the porch as Alanna jumped down from the railing where she'd balanced to string the lights. She and Nathan joined them on the bench, Alanna lifting Brendan to slide underneath him, Nathan squeezing in on the other side of Emilie. It was a tight fit on a bench made for two, but it was cozy.

"Isn't it pretty, Lannie? Don't you wish—"

Under the blanket, Emilie gave Josie a warning squeeze.

"Wish what?"

"Nothing." Josie laid her head back on Emilie's shoulder and gave a deep sigh. "I wish we could live here forever."

Before the solemn sentiment could make Emilie teary-eyed, Josie slid underneath the blankets to the ground, knocking her cap off in the process, leaving her fine hair standing on end. "I'm cold. I want fudge."

"Fudge won't make you warm," Nathan teased.

"Of course it will. Fudge cures all the world's ills." Emilie scooted forward. "Let's go in. We'll have hot cocoa and fudge and warm up by the fire."

Alanna stood up, lifting Brendan with her. Before Emilie could do the same, Nathan caught her arm. "You guys go on. I want to talk to your mother."

She watched them go, then slowly slid back on the bench. When she would have moved down to put room between them, he pulled her snug against him. On a quiet, frigid, Christmas-lights night, it was exactly where she wanted to be.

Moment after moment passed in silence. Whether he really had anything to say or just wanted a few minutes alone, she didn't care. At that very moment, she couldn't care about anything beyond his arm holding her close, his body strong and solid beside her, the faint musky fragrance of his aftershave, and the slow, steady rate of his breathing.

"When I was a kid, we always decorated the house for Christmas. I was the one who went up on the roof and outlined it in colored lights. The year I was eighteen, I had finished with the lights and turned away to the ladder when I fell. I grabbed at the only thing handy, which happened to be the lights I had just hung, and took them down with me. I blew out half a dozen strings, damaged a couple of my mother's bushes, and broke my arm."

"What a Christmas present. I bet you played it for all it was worth."

"It wasn't worth much. My father was annoyed because he had to buy new lights and hang them himself, and my mother spent more time worrying about her bushes than me."

"Doesn't sound like the ideal family."

"We weren't mistreated or neglected. We had a nice house, clothes, spending money." He shifted and somehow moved her just a bit closer. "It was kind of like how I imagine a foster home to be. Our needs were taken care of. There just wasn't much love."

The white lights seemed to fracture and twinkle in the cold night air. Watching them, she answered thoughtlessly. "Not quite like any of the foster homes I knew." The instant the words were out, she stiffened. So did Nathan.

"What do you mean?"

Wrapping herself in a blanket, she moved to the opposite end of the bench and faced him. "I don't suppose you'd be willing to forget I said that." Of course not. Things couldn't be that easy. Drawing a deep breath, she offered a silent apology to Berry for cutting her from the explanation. "When my mother died, my father didn't want to raise a daughter by himself, so I lived in foster homes for several years."

"What about your aunt?"

Would Miriam Pierce have taken in a niece whose only parent didn't want her? If she were as dear as the Winchester sister's claimed, probably. "She didn't know. She and my father weren't close." The words came haltingly, each one forced out, and she hated them. They weren't exactly a lie, not in the strictest sense. But they were in every other sense—especially the unforgivable one.

"What was it like?"

She wanted to sugarcoat her life, to say it wasn't bad, little different from his own upbringing, but she was already drowning in untruths. She needed every bit of honesty she could manage. "Sometimes I was nothing more than household help. They gave me food, clothes, a place to sleep, and in exchange I cleaned the house, cooked, and baby-sat their own children. Most homes were better, but I was always the outsider, the one who didn't belong, the one whose own family didn't want her."

"Didn't Social Services try to contact your aunt?"

"I couldn't tell them about relatives I didn't know existed." The social workers had asked her father the day he'd left them, but he'd said there was no one. Berry believed he had lied, and she'd told the social workers about a grandma whose name she didn't know who lived in a faraway place she had never been. They had thought it was just a lonely child's fantasy.

"It must have been hard. When your own father lets you down, it's tough to trust someone else." He caught hold of her blanket and pulled, drawing her along the bench and onto his lap. "But I'm not your father, Emilie. I'm not going to decide one day that you're more trouble than you're worth. I'm not going to walk away."

She wished she could believe him, but she knew so much that he didn't. She knew the truth about the kids, this house, and, worst of all, about herself.

He removed one glove and touched her face. His fingers were warm against her skin, and they made her tremble. She should stop him, should run from him as far and as fast as she could, because whatever there was between them—and he was right; there *was* something—couldn't last. Once he knew what a fraud she was, he would never forgive her. He could never love her.

But when she raised her hand to his, she didn't push him away. When he tilted her head back, she let him, and when he kissed her, she let him do that, too.

*A kiss is just a kiss,* the old song went, but it was wrong. The only kisses she'd experienced had been perfunctory—good night, thanks for the date, we don't need to do it again—or hot and hard, demanding sex, promising physical pleasure and nothing else. She'd never been kissed like this before, never so lazy that it made her bones melt, never so sweet that she wanted to cry.

She'd never been kissed as if she mattered.

Nathan deepened the kiss, coaxing her mouth open, seeking to taste more, connect more. Her acceptance matched his need degree by searing degree. Her hands came to his face, then slid inside his coat and the open collar of his shirt. Her fingers were icy cold but left heat and awareness everyplace they touched, and they made him long—damn near ache—for more.

There had been a point to the kiss—that he wanted her—and he was making it clear. His arousal pressed hard against her hip. His breathing was uneven, his blood so hot that the immediate area was in danger of a premature thaw. He wanted to kiss her harder, to make her feel the same raw hunger, the emptiness, the sweetly tormenting need. He wanted to hold her tighter, to get lost inside her and never find his way free. He wanted . . . Sweet hell, he *wanted*.

Under the cover of her blanket, he loosened two buttons and slipped his hand inside her woolen coat. Underneath she wore a sweatshirt over a white cotton shirt. He maneuvered his way under the fleece shirt and fitted his hand to her breast. The intimate caress made her stiffen, made a tiny groan catch in her throat. The sound was pure need, pure pleasure, the most erotic sound he'd ever heard.

In desperate need of air, he drew his hand free and ended the kiss with a series of smaller kisses. For a moment she remained still in his arms, a little dazed, a lot aroused, as beautiful and still as the night. After what seemed like forever, she breathed, a great ragged breath that shuddered through her, and finally she opened her eyes.

He expected desire, pleasure, some small bit of affection. He got all that and more—sorrow so exquisite that it turned him cold all the way through. "Emilie?"

She looked as if she wanted to weep, and, for a moment, when she pressed her face against his neck, he thought she might. But then the sadness, if not gone, was at least banished to the outer edges. "I'd better go in."

*I*, not *we*. An invitation to go home couldn't be any clearer. He let her stand up and watched her haphazardly fold the blankets. "What's wrong, Emilie?"

"Nothing." Except she wouldn't look at him. Except that she'd gone from hungry, willing, and damn near steaming in his arms to so cool that the night couldn't compete.

"Please," he said impatiently. "Don't lie."

The look in her eyes turned aloof, distant. This afternoon, Josie had taken offense at her sister's implication that she wasn't always truthful. It was a trait she apparently shared with her mother. Emilie picked up the blankets, clutching the thick pile to her chest, and gave him a frosty look. "Nothing's wrong. It's late, I'm cold, and the kids are waiting for their cocoa. Thank you."

"For what? Carrying the boxes down from the attic?

Taking you to lunch? Hanging the lights? Or turning you on?" He didn't like the sarcasm—it was ugly and it made her look ashamed—but it was hard to control.

"For everything."

She was turning away, preparing to go inside the house and shut him out. Forcing the frustration aside, he blocked her way without touching her. "It was just a kiss, Emilie."

"No. I've had plenty of just-a-kiss kisses. That wasn't the same. Not even close."

The admission sent relief rushing through him. "Does that scare you?"

"Yes, it does. All my life I've wanted . . ." With a shrug, she left it at that. *Wanted.*

"Me, too," he admitted quietly.

"I've got those kids. They're my first priority."

"I understand."

"Everything I've done—and everything I *will* do— has been for them. I can't change that."

"I expect that. But being a good mother doesn't rule out having a life of your own." He moved a step closer and, when she didn't back away, slid his arms around her. "Just give us a chance, Emilie. That's all I'm asking."

"You know I'm planning to leave in a few weeks."

"I know. I've been warned. But you could always change your mind. Come on, Emilie. Just a chance."

The sadness was still in her eyes, with just a bit of hope that flared, then faded. "You might regret it."

"I might. But I'll definitely regret it if we don't try, and so will you."

"You're crazy."

He more than agreed. Pursuing a romance with a mother of three who intended to leave town in a few short weeks . . . That wasn't just crazy. It was certifiably insane. But it felt *right*. "Just give me a couple of weeks."

After a time, she smiled, a rueful, against-her-better-judgment sort of smile. "All right. Three weeks and four days."

Twenty-five days. It sounded like a lifetime, but he knew it could pass in the blink of an eye. It was long enough to fall in love and long enough to break a heart. If he couldn't change her mind, it was all they would ever have. But if he could, it would be the beginning of a miracle.

That was all he needed—a miracle. But, hey, it was Christmas. The season for miracles.

"Come in for cocoa?"

He nodded, took the blankets from her, and followed her inside. The kids were in the parlor, Alanna flipping through a well-thumbed book of children's stories while Josie told Brendan a story about a very well behaved bear named Ernest.

Emilie made the cocoa, and he carried the tray of

candy into the parlor. While they ate, the conversation was easy, relaxed, unimportant. It was the kind of evening he had once envisioned sharing with Diana, Elisabeth, and the other children they would have. It was nice. Special. It made him want more.

At eight-thirty, Emilie sent the kids up to get ready for bed, then stretched out on the floor, her head resting on one hand. The room was dimly lit, the fire sending its woodsy scent into the air with every crackle and pop. It would be a perfect seduction scene if not for the empty cups, napkins, and candy crumbs between them, if not for the sounds of kids splashing in water drifting down from upstairs.

It was a damn good seduction scene in spite of all that.

"I love fires."

He smiled faintly. The kids, parades, fudge, and fires. Maybe someday he could add himself to that list. "Then you'd better not go back to Georgia. It's too hot and muggy there for a good fire—though that didn't stop Sherman when he burned Atlanta."

"And we've never forgiven you Yankees for it." Abruptly, her smile faded. "I never said I was going to Georgia."

"No, but Josie did. It was the once-in-a-blue-moon comment, added to the facts that you're from there and you never actually said you were returning to Boston."

He grinned. "Don't forget—I'm a cop. I figure things out for a living."

She murmured something that sounded suspiciously like, "I wish I could forget," but before he could question her, the younger kids raced into the room. Josie was wearing a T-shirt with one shoulder halfway to her elbow and the hem hanging past her knees, and her brother was naked, his skin glistening where it was still wet.

Carrying a towel and looking exasperated, Alanna followed them. "He wouldn't do this every night if you didn't think it was cute," she complained as Brendan climbed astride Emilie's hip and gave her a damp hug.

"And you wouldn't let him do it every night if you didn't think so, too."

Josie dropped down beside him. "Tell us a story, Mr. Nathan."

"About what?"

"Have you ever shot any bad guys?"

"You asked that last week."

"I thought maybe the answer had changed. What kind of policeman are you if you don't never shoot anyone? Did you ever arrest a bank robber?"

"No."

"Did you ever see a dead body?"

An image of Mike the last time he'd seen him flashed into his mind. The other officers on the scene had told him Mike was dead, had tried to keep him away, but he'd insisted on seeing for himself. He had knelt on the floor beside him and prayed, God, had prayed so hard and so desperately. But it hadn't been a mistake. The best friend—the worst friend—he'd ever had really was dead. And that had been just the first shock of the day.

It had been one hell of a Christmas.

"You're so gruesome," Alanna said scornfully.

"I am not!" Then, "Mama, what is gruesome?"

"It's asking questions like that at bedtime."

"Oh." Josie's responding grin stretched from ear to ear. "Then I *am* gruesome. Mr. Nathan—"

Alanna grabbed a handful of Josie's oversize shirt. "Come on, it's bedtime. I'll read to you."

Protesting loudly all the way, Josie let Alanna drag her backwards to the door, where her grumbling magically stopped. "Good night, Mr. Nathan. Good night, Mama. I love you."

"I love you, too, baby." She rubbed Brendan's back for a moment, then tapped him on the head. "You'd better go, darlin', or you'll miss Lannie's story."

When he was gone, Nathan lay down at right angles to Emilie and returned to their earlier discussion. "Why do you want to go to Georgia?"

"It's my home."

"You don't belong there." Belonging, he thought, especially now that he knew about the foster homes, was a big thing to her. She hadn't belonged in those other people's homes, hadn't belonged in Boston, and she wouldn't belong back in Georgia. But here in Bethlehem, she could make a place for herself and the kids—had already done so. She could have family here, like the Winchesters. Like him.

"Of course I belong there. As we say at home, 'I'm American by birth but Southern by the grace of God.'"

"I was born and raised in Pennsylvania, but I don't belong there. There's nothing there for me now. What will you do in Georgia?"

"Find a job and support my family."

"You already have a job here—not a great one, I know, but there's always something opening up. Where will you live?"

"I don't know. I'll find a place."

"You already have a place here. What about a babysitter for Brendan? You can't leave him with just anyone."

"I'll find someone."

"But—"

"I know. I already have someone here." She stared past him into the fire. "If things were different, I'd stay in a heartbeat, but . . ."

"What things? Talk to me, Emilie."

She gave him a smile that was sweet and sexy as hell. "Kiss me, Nathan."

She was manipulating him. He knew that and didn't care. He had three weeks and four days to talk her into staying—or to discover that he didn't want her to. Tonight he was more than satisfied simply to kiss her.

Emilie was in the inn's laundry room Monday afternoon when Holly came looking for her. "The McKinneys are gone, thank God. You can do their suite when you get a chance."

"I'll take care of it as soon as I finish here."

"Are you guys settling in okay?"

Emilie shook out a towel and folded it neatly. "The girls are happy in school, and Brendan likes spending his days with the Winchester sisters. I'm sure they're spoiling him rotten."

"And you?"

She reached for another towel. "I like it here."

"I bet." Holly smiled slyly. "I saw you at the parade with Nathan. And I heard you had lunch with him at Harry's on Saturday."

"I saw *you* at the parade with him, and all five of us had lunch Saturday." But it had been just the two of them on the bench Saturday night, just them alone in front of the fireplace.

"The Winchesters have been trying to find a wife for Nathan ever since he moved to town. They even set me up with him a time or two. He's a nice guy. You could do worse." Her smile turned wry. "Believe me, I *have* done worse. I'll be in the office if you need anything."

According to staff gossip, Holly had dated every single man in town and maybe one or two of the married ones. Whatever she was looking for, she hadn't found it. Emilie, on the other hand, had found what she wanted within minutes of driving into town. She just couldn't have it, at least not for more than three weeks and two days, and she felt guilty for taking that much. It wasn't fair to Nathan to let him believe that he had a chance of convincing her to stay when nothing in the world—besides the dropping of all criminal charges and custody of the children—could do that.

But he insisted he was prepared to deal with her leaving. And he'd been right: she would regret not taking what little she could have. Who knew? Maybe they would discover that this thing between them was nothing, and she could leave with her heart intact and he would be happy to see her go.

Yeah. And maybe she would awaken tomorrow to green grass, birds singing in the trees, and roses in bloom.

What she was doing *wasn't* fair to Nathan, but she had to give it a try. Hadn't she prayed for a chance with him? Hadn't she asked Alanna's angel, God, and anyone else who might care for just a chance? What if this was it and she turned away from it because she couldn't see the future? What if Christmas did bring a miracle, and she wasn't in a position to accept it because she had kept Nathan at a distance?

And if there were no more miracles? If this temporary safety was the only miracle she was entitled to? At least she would know that there was a place where, even briefly, she had belonged and someone she had belonged with. It wasn't much, but it was more than she'd ever had.

She carried the towels up the back stairs and retrieved the cleaning cart from the closet before tackling the McKinneys' suite. The two rooms and bath were pure luxury and cost more per night than she made in a week. There had been a time when she'd envied people who could afford such expensive getaways, but she had a finer appreciation for money now. She didn't want costly vacations, elegant clothes, luxurious surroundings, or a fortune in gems. She did want an entire wardrobe for each of the children that didn't contain one single hand-me-down unless it was in good shape and properly fitted. She wanted to treat them to birthday parties and Christmases with trees and gifts without having to choose between that and food. She wanted to give them a place to come home to now and for always.

If she were really greedy, she'd want to give them an uncle and cousins to come home to. But that was too fragile a dream to toy with. It could shatter too easily and leave her utterly alone.

Switching the television to a music channel, she cleaned the rooms to the cheery sound of Christmas carols. She missed music in their lives. Berry had never been able to hold on to a television—it was too easy to pawn when she needed a few bucks—and the compact stereo Emilie had taken north with her had been stolen from the apartment less than a month after she'd arrived. Coincidentally, Berry had disappeared at the same time.

Emilie didn't miss the TV, but music made life easier, burdens lighter. She'd needed a little lightening for a long time.

By the time five o'clock arrived, she was ready to go home, put her feet up, and veg for the rest of the evening. She couldn't, of course, but it was a nice fantasy. So was Nathan, waiting outside to give her a ride home.

"You look tired."

"I am. I made eight beds, scrubbed eight bathrooms, washed ten loads of sheets, towels, and napkins, polished six miles of stair railings, and helped unpack twenty-seven boxes of ornaments."

"Does Holly have her tree yet?"

She looked wide-eyed at him. "That's the biggest tree I've ever seen indoors. It must be at least twelve feet tall."

"She likes to have the biggest one in town. You should get a tree for the kids."

"You should have one for yourself."

"How do you know I don't have one?"

"Because I've been in your house." The first Saturday

when she crossed the street to reluctantly ask him to take her to the store, she had stood in the living-room doorway long enough to notice that it was neat, with not even a magazine out of place, and definitely empty of anything that had ever grown outside.

Lately, when her thoughts wandered across the street, they didn't waste time in the living room but marched right on up the stairs. She wondered if his bedroom was as clean as the downstairs, if his bed was big and sprawling or just right for two, and how many women had shared it with him.

"Want to come over tonight?"

In the bed in her mind, all the ghosts of other women were banished by his question. There was only the two of them, hot, naked, together. Wishing for a little winter's chill to cool her face, she answered without looking. "For what?"

"Dinner. Miss Agatha brought a pot of beef stew over when I got home from work. There's a loaf of fresh bread to go with it. Okay?"

She smiled just a little. "Okay."

In her driveway, he turned to look at her. "The kids have gone to the library. Miss Corinna will bring them home when they get back. Come on over whenever you're ready."

Now, she wanted to say. *I'm ready now.* But instead she nodded mutely and climbed out of the truck. From the veranda, she watched until he'd driven around behind his house, then went inside. No sooner had she hung her coat on the tree than the doorbell rang. Expecting Nathan or the kids, she opened it with a big smile but found herself facing a stranger.

He was a handsome young man, probably about her own age, wearing a black wool overcoat and dress shoes dusted with snow. His smile was warm and charmingly chagrined. "I hate being unprepared for meetings, but I've been out of town, and now my uncle's out of town, and . . ." He broke off and drew a breath. "I'm Alexander Thomas. May I come in?"

She hesitated. Life in Atlanta and Boston had taught her caution, but Bethlehem was neither place. Besides, the children weren't home. If this man was dangerous— an idea she could hardly imagine—at least he would be dangerous only to her.

Once in the hall, he didn't show any interest in going farther. Instead, he peeled off one black glove, reached in a pocket for a business card, and offered it. The title underneath his name was simple and direct and made her hands tremble. Attorney. Noelle said a trust maintained the house, and lawyers administered trusts, didn't they? Did this lawyer handle Mrs. Pierce's trust? Did he suspect she was an interloper? Had he come to throw her and the kids out?

"My uncle, Herbert Thomas, was your aunt's attorney for many years. He retired not long after her death, but he still handles her account. He would have come to greet you himself, but he's gone off for one of his botanical symposiums, so he asked me to welcome you. That's why I don't know your name. My secretary forgot to get it, and I don't have access to my uncle's records until he returns."

She had to try twice to swallow over the lump in her throat, had to draw a breath to steady her voice. "I'm Emilie Dalton."

"Nice to meet you, Emilie." He glanced down the hall and up the stairs. "Uncle Herb has kept the grass mowed in summer and had the house painted two years ago, but then it's built like a rock. It hasn't needed much in the way of maintenance. However, if you have any questions or problems or need help in any way, please give one of us a call."

"No, I . . . Everything's fine."

He treated her to another smile. "My wife and I drove by last night on our way home from church and saw the lights. It's nice to see someone living here again."

"We're glad to be here." She meant it. For all her guilt over appropriating the house for her own, for all her misgivings and all its wrongness, she was very happy to have it.

"The trust your aunt set up covers taxes and maintenance. Uncle Herbert also said that if you need a little cash for getting settled, arrangements can be made."

"Thank you, but that won't be necessary." She sounded stiff and knew he would attribute it to pride, but it wasn't. She had already borrowed Mrs. Pierce's house. She wasn't going to borrow her money.

"Well, then . . ." He pulled his glove back on and smiled again. "If you need anything, give me a call. It was nice meeting you, Ms. Dalton."

Murmuring a good-bye, she closed the door behind him, then tucked his card into her purse. He seemed efficient, capable, and compassionate. If he handled criminal cases, too, she just might have need of his services someday soon.

She walked through the house, her footsteps echoing on the wood floors, muffled on the rugs. It seemed so empty and lonely without the kids. How things had changed in a year.

When she had first received Berry's plea for help, she'd had a few misgivings. Her sister's previous requests had always been for emergency cash, but this time she'd wanted Emilie to act as a surrogate mother while she got herself straightened out. What did Emilie know about mothering? She'd had a few intimate relationships, but she'd never been faced with the awesome responsibility of motherhood, and this situation would be even harder than motherhood by the usual means. She was accustomed to living alone, to being responsible for no one but herself. No matter how she loved the kids, they weren't *her* kids. They had a mother living right there with them—a mother who was impossible to deal with at times, who screamed at them, frightened them, and wavered between gratitude for Emilie's assistance and resentment for her interference.

Considering all the odds stacked against them, Emilie thought she'd done a pretty good job. Although they missed Berry, the kids seemed happy with her. They loved her, and she loved them in a way she hadn't thought possible, as if they were her own. Always, no matter what happened, they would be a part of her. She worried about them and missed them when they weren't around.

She settled in the parlor with a magazine borrowed from the inn's library, but the glossy pages held little interest for her. After laying it aside, she was looking for paper to leave a note for the kids to go to Nathan's when they arrived with a thunder of pounding feet and armfuls of books. Pink-cheeked and breathless, Corinna brought up the rear.

Josie skidded to a stop and bumped into Emilie. "Look, look, we got library cards! Lannie's got one, and I got one, but not Brendan, 'cause he's a baby."

Still bundled in his coat, Brendan stuck his tongue out at his sister. "Doan care. Got books anyhow."

"I don't care," Corinna corrected. "And we don't stick our tongues out at people, do we?"

Emilie hid a grin as Brendan solemnly shook his head. Maybe she hadn't done such a great job, after all. She was so happy to hear speech from her nephew that she'd never thought to correct him, and she'd thought tongue-sticking-out was perfectly acceptable, considering that they could be punching, kicking, and screaming instead.

Alanna claimed Emilie's attention. "Look how many books they let me check out. Before we leave here, I'm going to read these and a whole lot more." She started toward the door, then returned and gave the elderly woman a hug. "Thank you, Miss Corinna."

"You're welcome, dear." Corinna waited until Alanna was gone, then loosened her coat and sat down. "She's a bright child. It won't take long to get her reading up to snuff."

"What's wrong with her reading?"

"She's just a little behind. Classes can be so large these days that it's difficult to give much individual attention, and I'm afraid that changing schools as frequently as she has didn't help any." There was a hint of apology in Corinna's voice, as if she feared offending Emilie. "Nathan suggested that she ask Agatha and me for help, so we're going to spend a little time with her after school each day."

Emilie was dismayed. "How did Nathan know she was having trouble reading when I didn't?"

" 'Cause I told him." Josie answered from in front of the fireplace without looking up from her book. "I told him I can read better than Lannie and I was prettier."

"Why did you tell him that?"

"I said I can read better because I can, and I said I was

prettier because it made her scrunch her face up like this." She mimicked a fierce frown that resembled Alanna's before turning back to her book.

"Why didn't either of you ever tell me?"

"You were always so tired from working. Lannie said don't bother you. But it was okay to tell Mr. Nathan 'cause he doesn't live with us, so it's not his problem."

Emilie pulled Brendan's coat off and laid it over the sofa arm. "I don't care how tired I am. I want to know everything about you guys, okay, Josie?"

"Okay, Mama."

"It's hard being a single parent, isn't it?" remarked Corinna gently.

"Harder than I imagined." Especially when she suddenly discovered she wasn't doing such a great job after all. "Maybe someday I'll get the knack of it."

"Maybe before someday comes, you'll find the right young man and no longer have to do it all alone." With no more than a smile, the old lady brought a flush to Emilie's cheeks. According to Holly, the sisters fancied themselves matchmakers. If they thought they'd made a match for Nathan, they were wrong. Three weeks and two days. That was all the time she had.

She gazed at the satin-gowned angel on the mantel. She believed in miracles, she did, and she wanted to believe that this mess could turn out happily for them all. But if she believed and her happy ending didn't materialize, it would be even more heartbreaking. On the other hand, if she hedged her bets by always preparing for the worst, didn't that mean her faith wasn't strong enough?

"I imagine you're having dinner at Nathan's this evening."

"Was that your idea or his?"

"All his, I assure you." Corinna smiled again. "He's a very intelligent young man. He knows exactly what he wants."

So did she. She also knew that she couldn't always have it.

"Well, dear, I'd better get along. Josie, remember to bring a book with you tomorrow. Brendan, you bring one too. We'll institute a regular reading time."

The shy little boy who hid his face from most people he encountered put aside his picture book and raced across the room to give Corinna a hug before she stood up. Amazed, Emilie walked outside with her, shivering on the porch. "I don't know how to thank you and Miss Agatha for all you've done."

"You know, Emilie, most people in this world are more than willing to help if they just know what needs to be done."

Not in her world, she wanted to protest. She'd never met anyone less helpful than their landlord, Berry's lawyer, the social worker, or the judge who had revoked the custody agreement. They'd all known that she was doing her very best, but none of them had cared.

Corinna patted her on the arm. "Everything will be all

right. You just wait and see. Go on in now, dear, before you freeze."

She obeyed, checking on the kids, then heading upstairs. This evening was far from a date, but it wouldn't hurt her to change clothes, maybe fix her hair and do a little makeup. Before turning into her room, though, she caught sight of Alanna, stretched out on her bed, concentrating fiercely on her book, her lips moving silently as she read. Emilie knocked at the open door before going in and, when Alanna made room, stretching out beside her. "I appreciate your not wanting to worry me, but I wish you'd told me about this."

Alanna shrugged. "You had enough to do already. I thought maybe after we got to Atlanta . . ." Her voice turned flat before trailing off. A week ago she had been as anxious as Emilie to get to Georgia. Now she sounded reluctant.

"You'd like to stay here, too, wouldn't you?"

Marking her place in the book, she laid it aside and turned to face Emilie. "It's a nice place, and I like my teachers and friends, but I understand why we can't stay. Is Atlanta a nice place?"

Most of the three million or so people who lived in the metropolitan area probably thought so. Heavens, Emilie had thought so . . . until she'd gotten a taste of Bethlehem. Her huge, sprawling, gridlocked, crime-infested hometown couldn't begin to compare to little, old-fashioned, bandstand-in-the-square Bethlehem. "It's big. Busy." Anonymous. They could get lost there, so the authorities couldn't find them—but neither could the good people Corinna had been talking about.

"Maybe we could stay, Aunt Emilie. You've got a job, and we could get a little house or apartment, and then we wouldn't be doing anything wrong, and you could prove to the judge that you can take care of us. He would let us stay with you, and he wouldn't arrest you, and we could live here forever."

It was a sweet dream. Unfortunately, it fell in the impossible-dream category. With what she earned at the inn, she could cover their expenses, a small Christmas, and save for bus tickets to Georgia, but right now their expenses didn't include rent or utilities. If she had to pay the full costs of their living, her job wouldn't cut it. Besides, she was neither young enough nor naive enough to think that the courts had any mercy. She had defied the judge's order and fled the state. At best she would be charged with contempt and violation of a court order. If the judge wanted to make an example of her, she would be charged with kidnapping. That wasn't a little nothing charge that was going to be forgiven just because she had a job and a place to live.

"I could go to school with the same kids for longer than a couple months, and Miss Corinna and Miss Agatha could help me learn to read better, and Brendan would start talking more, and Josie—well, Josie will be happy wherever we live. And you. You could still see

Mr. Nathan, and—" Abruptly, she broke off, and the light faded from her eyes. "But, of course, we can't. That's okay. We'll like Atlanta, too. I'm sure we will."

Emilie wanted to hug her, to bring the glow of hope back to her face. More than anything she wanted to tell her, sure, they could stay and everything would be all right, just as Corinna had assured her. But they were empty words, and while she might have to lie to everyone else in her life, she wouldn't lie to Alanna. She wouldn't fill her with hope, knowing it would be taken away. "We may not like Atlanta as much. But at least we'll be together, and that's what counts."

# Chapter Eight

Wednesday morning Nathan pulled into Emilie's driveway, glanced at the house, then, upon giving it a second look, burst into laughter. Somebody had come visiting during the night and left Emilie and the kids a present right in front of the door. He tapped the horn once, then climbed out. As he approached the door, Josie yanked it open, then gave a squeal of delight. "Look, look what we got, look what Mr. Nathan bringed us!" Dropping to the floor, she wriggled underneath, jumped to her feet, and gave him a tight hug. "Thank you, Mr. Nathan. How did you know Brendan and me wanted one all for our very own?"

He lifted her into his arms, then faced Emilie on the opposite side of the tree. "I wish I could take credit—especially after a hug like that—but it's not from me."

"Then who?"

"I didn't hear anything after I went to bed last night. Did you?"

Alanna, wearing her coat and carrying her and Josie's books, squeezed past with a pine needle sticking to her hair. "The way Josie snores, who could hear anything?"

"Maybe it was Bill Grovenor. He owns the tree farm outside town. Or the sisters. Or Holly." Or Mitch, who had a soft spot for kids like Josie, or any of a number of other people in town who were easy touches for kids at Christmas. "Maybe it was Santa."

"Santa, huh?" Emilie was looking at him as if she believed that *he* was Santa. It was a role he wouldn't mind filling for her. "Well, if you see Santa, tell him thanks."

Josie slid to the ground and grabbed her schoolbooks as the bus stopped across the street. "I'm going to tell Mr. Lucas that drives the bus and Wendy and Mickey and Amber . . ." The list trailed off as she flew across the yard. Alanna followed behind at a more sedate pace.

With much effort and more than a few scratches, Nathan and Emilie got the tree, complete with stand, into the parlor. The last time they'd been alone in here, they'd wound up necking in front of the fire until the heat in his body had at least matched the heat in the blazing logs, until he'd been forced to go home, aroused and frustrated, because staying any longer was too risky. There had been something sweet about the frustration, though—the anticipation of not yet having something he very much wanted, the promise that it was worth waiting for, the certainty that Emilie was special, because he'd never waited before.

This morning there was no fire burning, sunlight brightened the room, and they weren't alone. Brendan and the tree kept them company. Situated in front of the windows, it was about seven feet tall and full around the bottom, perfectly shaped without so much as a needle out of place. It filled the parlor with its sweet pine scent.

Emilie stood back and stared, hands on her hips. "Now what am I supposed to do with it?"

"I can believe that you'd never put up lights outside before, but surely you've decorated a Christmas tree."

"Of course I have, but what am I supposed to decorate it with?"

"All those boxes of ornaments we carried down from the attic. All that pretty glass stuff you took one look at, then shoved back into the boxes."

"All the expensive, breakable, irreplaceable stuff? With Brendan and Hurricane Josie? I don't think so."

"Fine. Tell the sisters you'll be late today, and we'll go shopping after work. We'll get some popcorn, flour, salt, paint, and construction paper. The kids can make their own ornaments." He tugged her hand. "Come on, we're late."

For a moment she resisted, standing her ground. "Tell me the truth, Nathan. Did you do this?"

"Would you give me a hug like Josie did if I said yes?"

Her only answer was a smile full of sweet promise that made him want to lie, to claim credit for the tree and anything else in the world that might give her pleasure.

"It wasn't me, and I can offer only about seven thousand guesses. People do this sort of thing around here, Emilie. It makes them feel good. It's all part of the holiday. Just accept it in the spirit in which it was offered and enjoy it."

Bundled up in his coat, Brendan opened his arms wide as if to embrace the tree and buried his face in its branches. Looking at them, he grinned from ear to ear. The sight was enough to melt the coldest heart . . . and Nathan's was far from cold.

After filling the bowl of the stand with water, they locked up and left. Brendan ran ahead, climbing the steps to the Winchester porch, ringing the doorbell, and calling out, "Miss Corinna! Miss Agatha! There's a tree in our house!"

"He's always been such a shy little boy," Emilie remarked. She waved when Corinna opened the door, then walked to the truck with Nathan. "He's coming out of it."

"And he's turning out to be more like Josie than Alanna."

"Good." Suddenly she looked guilty. "Not that there's anything wrong with Alanna, of course. It's just that Josie's so optimistic. It hasn't yet occurred to her that there might actually be someone in this world who's not convinced that she's the prettiest, brightest, funniest kid that ever lived. With that attitude, life is a little easier for her. But Alanna has her strong points, too. She's very mature, capable, and independent."

"Like her mother. None of them look like you, but I can see a little of you in them.

"They all look like me—blond hair, blue eyes."

"Sweetheart, there's a lot more to looking alike than hair and eye color. My youngest brother has blond hair and blue eyes, but he doesn't look anything like you."

"Well, my kids *all* look like me. I'm surprised a cop who figures things out for a living can't see that."

"Was their father blond, too?"

She knotted her fingers together and looked out the side window. "Yes, and blue-eyed and irresistibly charming." She didn't say the words as though she meant them, but with mockery, making fun of herself for falling under his spell.

"Tell me about him."

"There's not much to tell."

"You were together six years. You had three children. There must be something. Where did you meet him?"

"At work."

"What was his name?"

"Alan."

Alan and Alanna. The names alone told him that she'd been very young or very much in love. He preferred the former but suspected the latter. "What was he like?"

"I really don't want to talk about this."

He drove through the gate onto the inn's private drive, then stopped and faced her. "Then tell me one thing. Were you and Alan ever married?"

She was silent for a long time, staring out the window, her breath fogging the glass, then, finally, gave an answer. "No."

"Why didn't you just say so the times I asked if you were divorced?"

"Where I come from, nice women don't have kids without getting married at least once, and smart women don't have second and third children when the father hasn't yet accepted responsibility for the first."

He didn't ask why she had. Alan had wanted her, and she'd needed to be wanted. After living in foster homes, she must have been in need of affection and someone to share her life. She must have thought she'd found both in Alan, and, in a way, she had. Maybe he'd been a disappointment, but he'd given her three kids whom she clearly loved.

He wanted to ask if she still loved Alan, if she'd be willing to give him another chance even though he'd run out on them. At the same time, he didn't want to know. He would find out sooner or later, when he saw just what kind of chance she was willing to give *him*.

He just hoped, when he found out, it wasn't too late for him.

At the inn, she climbed out, looked back at him as if to speak, then smiled faintly and closed the door. He watched the glass door swing shut, saw her walk out of sight down the hall, then abruptly he shut off the engine and went inside. Holly was coming from the kitchen, a tray of muffins in hand.

"Have you seen Emilie?"

"She went that—And good morning to you, too, Nathan."

He passed through the kitchen and into the laundry room, where Emilie was gathering fresh linens from the shelves. He caught her arm and pulled her around to face him. "I don't care whether you were married once, five times, or never, and I don't care about anyone else's expectations."

"Oh, come on. Tell me you weren't surprised, just a little, that all three of the kids are illegitimate. Tell me the thought didn't enter your mind, even for a moment, that I'm in exactly the situation I deserve for bad judgment and immoral behavior."

He slid his arm around her waist, holding her close when she would have pulled away. "Actually, I was relieved. When you kept avoiding my questions about divorce, I thought maybe you had a husband or an ex-husband back in Massachusetts looking for you and the kids. I couldn't get involved with a married woman, not after what I went through with Diana, and I'd really hate to fall for someone, then have to arrest her later for kidnapping her own kids." Now that he'd said it aloud, the idea sounded silly. He smiled. She didn't.

Instead, she laid her head against his shoulder. For a moment she leaned against him. Then, with a shudder, she drew back, removed her coat, and picked up the sheets. "You'd better get to work."

"Have dinner with me tonight. Just you and me."

"We can't."

"Emilie—"

"We have a tree to decorate, remember? Do you want to tell the kids it'll have to wait so you and I can go out? After the hug Josie gave you? After that grin on Brendan's face?"

"All right." He gave in with a scowl. "I'll see you this evening."

"Nathan?"

Pausing in the doorway, he looked back.

"Maybe tomorrow night? Just you and me?"

"I'd like that." He left her in the laundry room, filched a muffin from the tray at the front desk, and gave Holly a bear hug. "Good morning to you, too." When he walked out the front door, she was laughing.

By the time he reached the station, the muffin was gone. He got a cup of coffee to wash it down, then knocked at the door of the chief's office. Mitch motioned him inside. "Seems we had a prowler in the neighborhood last night."

"Was anything stolen?"

"Nope. In fact, he left something behind—one of Bill Grovenor's finest trees, complete with stand. Stuck it right in front of Emilie's door. That's 311 Fourth Street, you know—big house with a chimney and everything. Right across the street from me."

"I remember. Josie's directions were quite clear." Mitch didn't look the least bit concerned. "Hardly a police matter, is it?"

"No. I just thought you might be interested." Nathan started to turn away, then looked back. "By the way, what happened to your hands?"

His face turning red, Mitch looked at the scrapes.

"Bill's trees can get kind of scratchy, can't they?" Nathan asked softly.

"Don't tell anyone."

"I won't. By the way, the kids were thrilled, and Emilie sends her thanks."

"She's welcome."

She certainly was, Nathan thought on his way out. If he could only convince *her* of it.

Josie sat on her knees at the kitchen table, her lip between her teeth, and brushed blue paint over her angel's dress. She'd made the decoration all by herself, except for Aunt Emilie mixing the dough and Mr. Nathan helping her shape it and Aunt Emilie baking it. She'd done everything else, though—had made the round face and the long hair and the feet sticking out from under the dress. They weren't tiny little feet like on her angel upstairs. Lannie said they looked like giant shoeboxes and there was no way she could fly with them because they weren't aero-something, but Mr. Nathan said she could fly anyway, 'cause angels had magic.

She loved angels. She'd already made six, but with Christmas only two weeks away, she figured she couldn't have too many. They needed a lot of magic to keep the police from taking Aunt Emilie and to stop the orange-haired lady from making them live with strangers. She wanted to stay right here in this house, with Miss Corinna and Miss Agatha next door and Mr. Nathan across the street. Aunt Emilie had promised they would stay until after Christmas so Santa would know where to find them, and Josie tried to be happy with that, but she really wanted to stay forever. It was a nice place, and she loved it.

Leaving her angel to dry, she went around the table to stand next to Mr. Nathan. "That's an E, for Emilie," she announced, pointing to the letter he was making out of dough. Leaning closer, she whispered, "I'm not supposed to call her that. I'm supposed to call her Mama. Make a J, for Josie."

He rolled out some dough and made a pretty J—not the printing kind she did in school but one with loops.

She asked for an A and a B, then finally an N. When he was done, she eased closer and traced one finger over the letters. "Can we paint these after they're baked?"

"Sure. What color do you want your J?"

"Brown and blue," Lannie said in a mean voice, just 'cause all Josie's angels had brown hair and blue dresses.

"Do not. I want red-and-white stripes, like a candy cane." Josie stretched under the table and kicked Alanna before Mr. Nathan lifted her into his lap. "Do you like kids, Mr. Nathan?"

"Nope, not at all."

His answer made her giggle. "You do, too. You like me."

"You think everyone likes you," Lannie said.

"So? Everyone *does*." She stuck her tongue out at Lannie before snuggling a little closer. "So if you like kids, Mr. Nathan, why don't you have any?"

The room got real quiet. He didn't move at all, and, from over at the stove, Aunt Emilie gave her a look like she'd done something bad—not the mad look Mama, her real mama, used all the time, but the sad one that was just Aunt Emilie's. Lannie was giving her the mad look.

Embarrassed 'cause she'd done something wrong and confused because she didn't know what, she slid to the floor. "It don't matter. I just thought you might be a good daddy to some little kid. But it's okay. Miss

Agatha don't have any kids, and—plenty of people don't, and—"

"Hush," Lannie whispered in her bossy voice, and gratefully Josie did.

Finally Mr. Nathan picked her up and put her on his lap again. "You're right, Josie. It doesn't matter. I was married once, back before you were born, and I thought we were going to have kids—we really wanted them—but we didn't."

"Instead you got divorced." Practically every kid she knew in Boston was divorced and lived with just their mamas. Some of them saw their daddies, but most didn't, like her. She didn't even know her daddy's name, and she couldn't remember if she'd ever seen him. Sometimes she wondered where he was and if he would play catch with her or maybe take her fishing. She thought about whether he had hair like hers and a deep voice and a nice smile, like Mr. Nathan's, or if he drank too much and got mean and yelled in a scary voice like Mama. Once she had asked about him, and Mama had gotten mad, then cried, and Lannie had made her promise never to ask again. But she still wondered.

She patted Mr. Nathan's hand. "It's not too late. You can still get babies. You're not too old." Looking at Aunt Emilie, she grinned. "Mama likes babies." She liked him, too. Josie had been peeking the other night when they'd kissed in the front yard, like it wasn't cold and late and there wasn't fudge and hot cocoa inside. When she had giggled, mean old Lannie had made her get away from the window and pretend that she hadn't seen a thing. But pretending didn't make it so. If Aunt Emilie liked him well enough to kiss him, maybe she'd want to have a baby with him, and then they could stay here, and Mr. Nathan could be their pretend-daddy, at least until Mama came to take care of them.

Aunt Emilie came to clear the table. Her face was pink, like stirring the spaghetti sauce had made her hot. "Enough talk about babies. Go wash your hands so we can eat dinner."

"But I just washed my hands when we started."

"And they need it again." Lannie lifted Brendan to the floor, then took hold of Josie's collar and pulled her into the bathroom. Lannie washed her hands first, then Brendan's.

Moving up to the sink, Josie let the water run between her fingers. At first it was blue from the paint, then it ran clear. "Lannie? Can I tell you something?"

"Sure. Use soap."

"I wish . . ." With her foot, she closed the door, then lowered her voice to a whisper. "Sometimes I wish Mr. Nathan could be our daddy, and I wish Aunt Emilie really was our mama."

Lannie stopped drying Brendan's hands and stared at Josie in the mirror. She looked surprised and scared all at the same time, and quickly, scared herself, Josie said, "Not always. Only sometimes. Is that bad?"

After a long time, Lannie laid her hand on Josie's shoulder. "No, it's not bad."

"Don't never tell anyone, okay?"

"I won't."

" 'Cause it would make our real mama cry."

"I said I won't. Now let's eat dinner."

As Emilie cut Brendan's spaghetti into bite-size pieces, she watched the girls return to the table. Josie looked subdued, as if Alanna had chastised her for her conversation. Emilie knew she hadn't meant any harm. It was just Josie as usual.

As she ran around the table and climbed into the empty chair beside Nathan, Josie's somber mood disappeared. "Do we get to decorate the tree after dinner? We got plenty of stuff made. It's going to be the most beautiful tree in the world."

"It won't have any lights," Alanna said glumly.

Emilie shared her disappointment. Back home in Georgia, her trees had twinkled and glowed with hundreds of tiny colored lights. When she had packed to move to Boston, the boxes of decorations had gone into a storage locker. She had fully intended to go back home as soon as she persuaded Berry to move with her. But Berry had refused, and Emilie had been unable to leave her and the kids. She had also been unable to keep up the rental on the storage unit. Six months ago everything there had been sold at auction. The entire lot hadn't been worth much—the dishes, the linens, the knickknacks. Even the ornaments hadn't held much dollar value, but the sentimental value . . .

She forced herself to forget and to smile. "Maybe after dinner, Nathan will take you to the store to buy a string or two of lights." The pleasure it would give the kids was well worth a few bucks, and she could squeeze the money out of the budget.

"I want to go, too," Josie announced around a mouthful of food. Brendan repeated her demand.

"Why don't we all go?" Nathan suggested. "You can get your lights, and the kids can look at the toys and get an idea what they want Santa to bring."

"Oh, I don't think they need any ideas." No use getting their hopes up. She had limited money to spend on gifts, and it would be too depressing to see all the things she couldn't give them. "You guys go ahead. Brendan and I will stay here and clean up the kitchen."

Brendan vigorously shook his head. "I go, too."

"You stay with me, darlin'."

His eyes doubled in size, and his lip trembled as he squeezed out one perfect fat teardrop. "I want to go with Nathan."

"That's Mister to you," Josie corrected him.

In a heartbeat, he went from truly sorrowful to sweetly manipulative. "I want to go with Mister. Please, Mama."

"He said please," Josie helpfully pointed out, as Alanna promised, "I'll watch him."

Nathan added his own assurance. "He won't be any trouble."

Emilie scowled playfully around the table at Brendan and his chorus of supporters. "All right. All of you go."

As soon as the meal was over, the kids bundled up, shot out the door, and headed for Nathan's truck. He lingered for a moment in the front hall with her. "I'll take care of the kids."

"I know you will." She adjusted the scarf around his neck, brushing his jaw, his cheek, then drew back. "You'd better go."

"You could come with us."

She considered it for a moment. She could go and have a good time sharing him with the kids. Or she could stay, clean the kitchen, move all the decorations into the parlor, and, once the tree was decorated and the kids were in bed, have the rest of the evening alone with him. It was no contest. "Go. Have fun." From the doorway, she watched him leave, waved to the kids, then returned to the kitchen.

Cleanup took little time. With the leftover spaghetti sauce in the freezer and the dishes stacked in the drainer, she carried the decorations into the parlor. In addition to the baked-dough ornaments, there were chains of construction-paper loops, strings of popcorn and cranberries, three-dimensional paper snowmen, paper snowflakes, and foil-covered cardboard stars. It would be a homemade Christmas tree, no doubt, but, as Josie had insisted, it would be beautiful.

She settled in the armchair, her feet propped on the table, only seconds before footsteps sounded on the porch. A moment later, Josie and Brendan came rushing in, talking at the same time. "We got lights—pretty lights—in all different colors, and we saw a train—you know the train—with little houses and little people— and smoke and a whistle—and Mr. Nathan—that's Mister—got you something."

Brendan gave Josie a shove. "Not supposed to tell. You promised."

Josie clapped her hands over her mouth, garbling her words. "I didn't tell, did I? But, oh, Mama, it's so pretty. Wait till you see."

"No, darlin', you didn't tell." Emilie watched Alanna and Nathan come into the room, both carrying bags. She'd given Alanna money for the lights, but there was no way her ten dollars had bought three bags' worth of decorations. Of course Nathan hadn't been content simply to chaperon the shopping trip. He'd had to contribute. But that was all right, she told herself, and realized with a bit of pleasure that it really was.

Though the last box of Christmas lights was no different than the three that preceded it, the kids showed her each one before diving into the second bag.

"They picked out one each," Nathan said with a shrug. "I figured you wouldn't mind too much."

He had bought each of them a box of ornaments. Brendan's was satin balls painted with cartoon characters. Josie had chosen a mixed collection of ceramics—a drum, a horn, Santa, and a reindeer, among others—and Alanna was holding tightly to a box of icicle shapes in iridescent glass. They were beautiful, exactly what Emilie would have chosen herself.

Nathan laid the bag he carried on her lap.

"What is this?" she asked.

"An early Christmas present. A belated housewarming gift. Whatever."

The bag held a box, and the box held a tree topper: yet another angel. Her hair was blond, but she had the same smile, the same serene beauty, as all the others. Her wings were spread wide, arching high above her head, and her ivory gown flowed over the insert that fitted over the tree top. She was simple and beautiful, and Emilie would treasure her forever.

Nathan was standing behind the couch, patiently unwinding a string of lights from its packaging with an occasional expectant look her way. Carrying the tree topper, she circled the sofa and pressed a kiss to his cheek. "Thank you."

"You can do that again later," he murmured. "After the kids have gone to bed . . ."

In spite of the warmth in the room and the heat radiating from him, a little shiver slid down her spine. Oh, the things they could do after the kids were in bed. Share kisses, arouse desires, touch, explore, learn. They could go too far too fast, yet it wouldn't be far enough or fast enough to satisfy her. They could indulge, seduce, gratify.

They could start breaking her heart. Barring a miracle, it was bound to happen, and her life had been remarkably short of miracles. Instead of dwelling on the inevitable, though, she smiled and accepted his invitation. "After the kids are in bed."

Decorating the tree was truly one of the memorable moments in Emilie's life. Sometimes she helped, but for the most part, she leaned against the back of the couch and watched, gathering memories of Nathan and Alanna stringing the lights and Josie and Brendan hanging the popcorn, cranberry, and colored-paper loops. They handled their homemade ornaments with the same care given to the store-bought, choosing each location with great deliberation. Nathan offered help when they needed it but spent the rest of the time standing beside Emilie, his hand clasping hers.

How many times in her childhood had she watched similar scenes and felt the unbearable ache of loneliness? How many times had she promised herself that, when she grew up, Christmases would be different? That she would have a husband, a home, children, and love? How many times had she dreamed dreams exactly like this?

Too many. Every Christmas since she was five. All those years she'd been on the outside looking in, and all the years since, she'd been on the inside but all alone, decorating a tree for one, fixing a holiday meal for one. But she'd never managed to change it. She'd never found the man who would give her the family, the love, and the home.

Until now, when everything else in her life was wrong.

Finally, perched on Nathan's shoulders, Brendan hung the last of the ornaments. It was time for the angel. Josie dragged in a chair from the kitchen, and Alanna carefully handed the angel to Emilie. Nathan beckoned her to the chair, helped her up, and steadied her with his arm around her waist as she leaned on tiptoe to slide the angel over the highest needle-covered finger of the tree. She hadn't even straightened when suddenly the lights went off, plunging the room into darkness but for the four hundred twinkling lights on the tree. He lifted her into his arms and carried her back a dozen feet, behind the kids, before slowly letting her slide down his body to her feet.

"Beautiful." Josie's whisper was soft and awed, followed by Brendan's own seal of approval.

"Oooh, neat."

Her arms around Nathan's neck, Emilie was staring at him in the colored shadows instead of the tree, but she echoed their sentiments. Beautiful. Neat. And just plain *Oooh*.

# Chapter Nine

The station was quiet when Nathan returned to clock out Friday afternoon. He'd gotten tied up on a call and had missed the shift change by twenty minutes, but he didn't mind. The hour between his quitting time and Emilie's was wasted anyway. He changed out of his uniform, then usually just hung around his house watching the clock or, lately, waited at the inn.

This evening they had been invited to dinner at the Winchester house. Tonight marked the beginning of the Bethlehem Women's Club annual Tour of Lights, and Agatha and Corinna, founding members of the club, always celebrated with a party. For fifty years the club had been sponsoring the tour. For six years Nathan had avoided it. This year, though, he was looking forward to it. A cozy seat snuggled in the back of a hay wagon with Emilie . . . What wasn't to enjoy?

Sadie was still in the dispatcher's shack when he passed. Twice a week she worked a double shift, long hours for a woman her age—for a person of any age— but she claimed it beat sitting home alone in front of the TV. Having spent far too much of his own time in exactly that way, Nathan knew she was right.

"What are your plans for this evening?" she asked as he stopped in the doorway.

"We're doing the tour of the town."

"You and Miss 'She's-just-a-neighbor-Sadie'?"

"Yes, Emilie. And the kids."

"You ever get out without those kids?"

"Occasionally." Last night they'd gone to dinner alone, while the sisters baby-sat. They had gone to Mc-Cauley's Steakhouse but had been back home in time for the kids' eight-thirty bedtime. The rest of the evening had been spent on the sofa in Emilie's parlor, talking, listening for the kids, just looking at the tree, and kissing. Not a lot. Not enough to tempt themselves to do anything more.

"I hear you were buying toys on your lunch hour."

"Jeez, Sadie, you have better sources than any cop I've ever known."

She patted her graying hair and smiled, as if his comment were the most effusive of compliments. "I do my best. How do you like her children?"

"They're good kids."

"Can you see yourself playing daddy to them for the next ten or twenty years?"

Easily enough that sometimes he worried. He had never wanted an instant family, had never wanted to play father to another man's children. Been there, done that. In the end, losing Elisabeth had hurt worse than Mike's death or his and Diana's betrayal. There was too much potential for pain and loss in raising another man's kids. Still . . . yeah, it was a risk he could take for the Dalton kids. For Emilie.

"They're not planning on being here for the next ten or twenty years." He had until New Year's, less than three weeks, to change Emilie's mind. If he succeeded, great. If he didn't, there was a lot of potential for pain there, too. "I'd better get going. See you Monday."

"Have a good one, Nathan."

He drove home, changed into jeans and a sweater, then headed for the inn, where Emilie was waiting at the door. Her expression brightened when she saw him. Ordinarily he didn't kiss her in the morning or the evening, saving it for when they were alone. This evening, even though Holly was at the desk and there were guests in the lobby, he leaned across and gave—took—one slow, sweet, welcoming kiss. When he drew back, Emilie caught her breath, then gave a shaky laugh. "I like the way you say hello."

He would like the chance to find out how she said good morning, would like to wake beside her, to see her sleepy and soft in his arms. It wasn't going to happen, though, not without a little outside help. He didn't know how she felt about making love with the kids across the hall, but the idea made him uncomfortable. What they needed was some kind soul to arrange a sleepover, but he couldn't imagine the slumber party that could include both girls and Brendan.

He *could* imagine a few hours some weekend morning, though. The sisters could supervise a trip to the library or maybe the kids could accompany them to church one Sunday. Surely he and Emilie could work out something. Provided she wanted to.

"How was your day?"

He glanced at her. "Quiet. It's always fairly quiet."

"You don't miss the excitement of police work in the city?"

"I had eight years of excitement. That was plenty for me. Do you miss the city?" He was more than happy to trade the city's hustle for small-town peace, but he'd made the transition voluntarily. Emilie had been stranded here through no choice of her own. Maybe she preferred having a million or so neighbors, most of whom she would never know, over the everybody-knows-your-business life in Bethlehem.

"No."

"So maybe you'd be interested in staying in Bethlehem."

She looked away, but not before he saw the sadness in her eyes. "I can't."

"Why not?"

"I just can't. Please, Nathan, don't . . ."

He didn't say anything else until they got home. There, when she would have gone to her own house, he caught her hand. "Come inside with me."

"The kids—"

"Are having a good time with the sisters. We're going over at six, so it can't hurt to let them stay until then. Come in."

She let him pull her up the back steps and through the laundry room into the kitchen. The items he'd purchased on his lunch-hour shopping trip were stacked on the table there: a model train set, a stack of board games, and a half dozen books that the clerk had assured him were perfect for Alanna. Emilie touched one book, the top game, then ran her fingers over the molded plastic that covered the train cars. When she turned, her eyes were teary. "I don't know how to thank you."

"It's not your place. The kids can say thanks after Christmas."

"They'll be so excited. They've never had much of a Christmas before."

"Then why did you keep the house?" After the silent ride home, he hadn't meant to bring up another topic that created tension between them, but the question just popped out.

She looked at the wrapping paper, then a bag of bows, then shoved her hands into her pockets. "I never really needed the money. We never had a lot, but we got by."

"You need the money now."

"This is a temporary setback. All I really need is time. I can get back on my feet, but if I sell the house, I can never get it back. Once it's gone, it's gone forever."

"But why struggle and deprive the kids when that place would bring enough money to support all of you for years?"

"We don't *need* it," she insisted stubbornly. "If we really, really did, I'd do it, but not until then."

So the house was brick-and-wood insurance against the worst possible financial disaster. Selling it would be a last resort, absolutely-no-other-way-out solution. What he didn't understand was what, in her mind, constituted really, really needing the money if her current situation—no job, no income, no place to live—didn't. "Then why don't you live in it? Instead of going to Georgia and renting a place there, why not stay in the house you own?"

"Do you really think we can afford to live there? Even with all the unused rooms closed off, it costs a fortune to heat all that space. Atlanta's my home. It's where I belong. Jobs are easier to find there. I can make better money, and I can rent a decent apartment for less than the cost of living in that house. Maybe later I can rent out the house and make a little money that way, but I can't sell it, and I can't continue to live in it."

"But—"

Her expression closed in, and she withdrew, both emotionally and physically. "I'd better go."

He blocked her escape. "Stay. Help me wrap the presents, and we'll put them under the tree while the kids are next door. Please?"

For a moment she looked as if she wanted nothing more than to dash out the door. When it passed, she took off her coat and removed the plastic wrap from the wrapping paper. He gathered scissors and tape and, for the most part, merely watched her. She worked methodically, measuring the paper against each package, creasing it for a straight cut, and making sharp, precise folds on the ends. She circled the first package with ribbon and curled it, added a bow, and passed it to him for the gift tag.

"I haven't bought Christmas gifts in so long that I'd forgotten it could be fun."

She spared him only a glance. "Since you were married?"

"Yeah. I spent a fortune on Elisabeth. It all wound up in the garbage. Diana refused to take any of it when she left."

"Where are they now?"

"Pennsylvania, I guess. That's where she was when she filed for divorce."

"It must have been tough for her."

He accepted the second package, wrote Alanna's name on a tag, and secured it to the ribbon. "She was the one lying and cheating, the one having the affair, the one passing off another man's kid as mine, and you feel sorry for *her*?"

"Do you think lying to you was easy for her?"

"She did it pretty damn well for a long time."

"But she didn't want to. She just had no choice."

Nathan stared at her. "She had a choice, sweetheart. If she couldn't live without Mike, she could have come to me and said she wanted a divorce. She could have stopped telling me she loved me and working so hard to make me believe it. She could have told me from the start that the baby wasn't mine. She made a number of choices, Emilie. Unfortunately, for me, they were all bad."

She wrapped a length of paper around the train set and secured it with a piece of double-sided tape. "You don't believe love and lies are compatible."

"Gee, call me strange, but I happen to think that someone who claims to love you should be honest with you, especially about important things like affairs and kids. Don't you?"

"Yes." She said it very quietly. Then, "You don't believe she could have loved you both."

"No." Love wasn't supposed to be that way, not easily divided and parceled out to different men. Oh, with kids, sure, and parents and friends, but not with husbands. A person was supposed to love her husband—or his wife—to the exclusion of all others.

"Then I guess she was just a lying, scheming witch who deserves no sympathy." She fixed the last bow in place and slid the package across the table to him.

Instead of taking it, he caught her hand and pulled her onto his lap. "*I* deserve your sympathy. I was the wronged party."

"And Elisabeth. She lost out on a great father."

"Two great fathers. It must have been hard for Mike, seeing me with her, hearing me talk about her, and knowing that she was *his* daughter, not mine. He would have loved her. He would have been a good father." It was the first generous thought he'd had about Mike in seven years. Emilie must have suspected as much, because she gave him a tight hug, and for a long time he let her hold him. Then, reluctantly, he gently moved away from her. "It's six. We'd better get going, or the kids will come looking for us."

They carried the gifts across the street, where Nathan arranged them under the tree while Emilie went upstairs to change. When she returned, still in jeans and wearing a cheery red sweatshirt, they walked next door to the Winchester house. The kids greeted her with hugs, then Agatha took her away for a round of introductions. Nathan said his own hellos before wandering into the kitchen, where Corinna was mixing up a batch of eggnog.

"We wondered whether you and Emilie would make it," the old lady said with a sly smile. "We thought you might have forgotten."

He gave her the easy sort of hug he'd long ago shared with his grandmother but never his mother. "Forget your party? I'd never do that."

"I don't know. We've been inviting you for six years, and you've always accepted, but this is the first time you've ever actually come. Why is that? Could it have something to do with your date this evening?"

"It doesn't quite qualify for a date when you've got three kids tagging along."

"No, I suppose not. You know, you're going to need some time alone with her if you're going to convince her to stay here. Agatha and I will see what we can do."

Taking two cups of eggnog with him, he went in search of Emilie. With Corinna and Agatha on his side, the odds of his success had just increased. After all, as he'd told Alanna last weekend, no one stood in the old ladies' way. They *always* got what they wanted, and, in this case, that meant he would get what *he* wanted. He hoped.

Emilie was talking to Mitch's wife Shelley when Nathan handed her the eggnog. She gave him a smile of thanks as he went on to join Mitch near the door.

"Emilie won't have any secrets left by the time Shelley gets through with her," Mitch said. "She's so good at getting information from people that I've sometimes wished we could let her interrogate our suspects. They would all confess."

Nathan responded and carried on a normal conversation, while his thoughts remained across the room all the while. *Was* Emilie keeping secrets? Now that she'd admitted she and the kids had been homeless and she and the long-absent Alan had never married, he wasn't sure. Rather than secrets, he thought there were just some quirks to her personality—like her refusal to sell the house. Maybe it had to do with the years she'd spent in the foster-care system. Maybe, having lived so long without family, she was overly determined to hold on to the last connection she had to them. He didn't understand, but maybe he couldn't unless he'd lived her life. Frankly, not understanding didn't affect his feelings for her one bit.

Once the last guest arrived, they filled their plates, then Nathan squeezed onto the window seat with Emilie and Brendan. "You have nice friends," she remarked as she balanced Brendan's plate for him.

"Uh-huh." That was all he let himself say. No pointing out that they would be happy to be her friends, too. No mention that nice friends made for a nice town or that a nice town was the perfect place to raise her kids.

Emilie gazed around the living room as she ate. Everyone she'd met had been warm and welcoming.

There'd been no suspicion, no probing questions—just a little polite curiosity. These were people she could be friends with, people she could genuinely care about . . . if she weren't lying to them. God help her, she hated the lies, but she apparently had a knack for them. Everyone seemed to believe her. No one but Nathan questioned her, and, while he might not understand her, even he believed her.

Once the truth came out, he would hate her most of all. Call me strange, he'd said, but someone who claims to love you should be honest with you, especially about important things like kids. All her lies had stemmed from her need to protect the kids, but she didn't think that would make much difference to him.

Once the truth came out . . . If God was with her, that wouldn't be until she was settled in Atlanta, until she'd earned enough money to pay for the use of the house and the utility bills she'd run up. Then everyone would know how she had deceived them and how little she had deserved the friendship and trust they had offered. Then Nathan would know that she had lied about the important things, and he would hate her.

And her best chance for having a family of her own would be lost. So would Nathan's, because after being deceived twice by women he'd trusted, he might never try again.

It was all her fault. She should have stood up to Berry a year ago, should have *demanded* that she send the kids to Atlanta where Emilie could take care of them. But, no, she had let Berry wheedle and manipulate her, and now they were all paying for it.

"What's wrong?"

She didn't look at Nathan for fear he'd see too much. "Nothing. I'm having a wonderful time."

"You look like you're about to cry."

"No, not at all." She wouldn't cry, not until she and the kids were on a bus to Georgia. Then she might start and never stop.

After dinner, she left Brendan with Nathan and sought out Agatha and Corinna. "I can come back this evening and help with cleanup."

"Oh, no, dear, we won't do it tonight."

"It can wait until morning. Tonight we're going to celebrate."

"The girls and I will be happy to help tomorrow."

"We appreciate it. Why don't you all come over for breakfast first? Around eight?"

"Better yet . . ." Corinna looked as if she'd had a brilliant thought. "Why don't you let the children spend the night? We can bring them back after the tour, and you and Nathan won't have to cut your evening short, as you did last night."

"Oh, I don't think—"

"What a wonderful idea, Corinna. We haven't had little ones in the house overnight in so many years."

"But—"

"Now don't fuss. I bet the children would enjoy it. Brendan already has Ernest, and they can run home before you leave and get their pj's and any other snugglies they might need." Corinna patted her arm. "It's all settled then. You and Nathan can enjoy all the celebrations over at the park, and you won't have to worry that the children are cold or up past their bedtimes."

Emilie had her doubts that it was so easily settled. Josie would be more than happy to spend the night away from home, but neither Alanna nor Brendan would embrace the idea as readily. However, she said nothing when Agatha called the kids over and announced the plan.

Josie, predictably, was happy, and Brendan was willing to sleep wherever Ernest and Josie slept. After a look at Emilie, then around the room, Alanna shrugged. "Fine with me."

Surprised—and a little hurt by their eager defection—Emilie shrugged, too. "All right. Alanna, why don't you come with me to get your stuff, then we'll go to the park."

They slipped out of the house and into their own house. "Did you have a good day at school?" Emilie asked as she packed Josie's pajamas into a gym bag.

"Yeah. Did you have a good day at work?"

"Yes." As good as it got making beds, doing laundry, and vacuuming.

"The teacher asked me to take part in the Christmas pageant."

"How nice."

Alanna looked up at her, hope in every line of her face. "You mean I can do it? Really? It'll mean practicing after school until four, so I would miss the bus, but maybe Miss Agatha wouldn't mind picking me up, or I could walk home—it really isn't so far—or maybe Mr. Nathan . . ."

"We'll figure something out, honey. Don't worry about it." Emilie gave her a hug, grimacing while her face was hidden. One more favor to ask. But she wouldn't deny Alanna this opportunity for anything. "What are you going to be in this pageant?"

"The ghost of Christmas Present. The pageant's, like, for everyone. There's Scrooge, then Christmas carols, then Mary and Joseph and the baby Jesus. They use a real-live baby, Aunt Emilie. It's going to be really neat. It's a week from last night. That's the last day of school, too, before Christmas." The animation disappeared from her face, and she hastily turned away to get clean clothes from the closet.

The last day of school, which meant the last time she would see her teacher and all her new friends. Christmas vacation would last into January, until they were already packed up and gone. She would be starting in a new school in a strange place, having to make new friends all over again. How many friends could she leave behind before she decided against making new ones? How many moves had it taken for Emilie to reach that point? Three? Four?

In the last year, Alanna had already made that many and more.

Emilie wrapped her arms around her again, holding her tightly. "If I could find a way to stay here, honey, I swear, we would. But the only way would be to tell the truth"—and trust that the good people of Bethlehem might someday forgive them—"but we can't do that. I can't lose you guys."

She had meant to comfort her niece. Instead, Alanna comforted her, patting her back reassuringly. "I know, Aunt Emilie, and it'll be all right. We'll be happy in Atlanta. We'll find a good school, and we'll make new friends. Everything will be all right."

That was the hope Emilie clung to. Everything would be all right. Not perfect—perfect would be staying here with Nathan and the sisters—but all right.

Alanna wriggled free and left, returning with three toothbrushes wrapped in a clean washcloth. "I've got everything, Aunt Emilie. Let's go."

Back at the Winchester house, Corinna stowed the bag in a closet while Emilie got Josie and Brendan bundled. Agatha gave them two quilts, and Nathan got a third from his house before they piled into the truck.

City Park was located on the west side of town, where the edge of the valley gave way to the hills that ringed it. Its snow had been trampled and dirtied, turned into snowmen and forts, and littered by the remains of snow- balls. The parking lots were mostly full, but Nathan found a spot near the snow-sculpted playground.

"So tell me about the Tour of Lights," Emilie re- quested.

"It's a winter hayride. You'll see more of Bethlehem than you ever wanted."

"I doubt it. So far, I haven't seen anything but down- town, our block, and the inn." She slipped her hand into Nathan's. On the other side, Josie did the same.

"It's an opportunity for everyone to show off their Christmas decorations. Some people do really elaborate displays with lights, music—well, you'll see."

They got tickets, then joined the crowd around a blaz- ing bonfire. Off to one side stood the six wagons, each hitched to a team of horses, the beds filled with blanket- covered hay. People were sitting close enough in the wagon being loaded to share blankets and body heat. They were laughing, in such high spirits that it was im- possible to be otherwise around them.

Their turn came on the third wagon. Agatha and Corinna were helped in first, followed by a large group of children. Emilie found herself snuggled between Alanna and Nathan. They spread the quilts out, then she settled comfortably against him, and he put his arm around her as if it were the most natural thing in the world.

Once the wagon was loaded, the driver climbed onto the wide seat. According to Nathan, his name was Sebastian Knight, and his four-year-old daughter Chrissy was sitting on Agatha's lap. He murmured the names of the rest of their companions, usually with some little bit of information, into her ear. He pointed out places of interest and kept her warm under the cover they shared.

Their first stop was in front of a corner church with twin spires stretching into the night sky. On the steps a choir was gathered, dressed in Victorian-era costumes and singing carols. The living Nativity scene nearby featured a camel that brought Josie bouncing off the floor to lean over the side. "Mama!" For one stunned moment, it was all she could get out. "Look, Mama, a camel! A *camel!* Is that a real camel, Mr. Nathan?"

"Looks real to me."

"Does he have one hump or two? Can I ride him? Where does he live?" Without waiting for answers, she stepped back and sank down again. "Wow. This is a pretty neat town."

"It is a neat town," Nathan agreed.

Emilie gave him a warning look. "What are you? Chamber of Commerce cheerleader?"

"Nope. Just a man—" Too soon he broke off, then substituted another answer. "Just a satisfied resident."

There were plenty of ways she could finish his sentence. Just a man who preferred to see signs of life across the street instead of a lonely, abandoned house.

Who appreciated having someone besides the sisters to do his good deeds for. Who liked his town and wanted others to like it, too.

And, of course, a few ways she would like to finish it. Just a man who had gotten more than a little fond of her. A man who didn't want to see their relationship end prematurely. A man who wanted her to stay, to be a part of his life, as much as she wanted to.

She couldn't rebut his argument. Bethlehem *was* a neat town. The oldest structures dated back to the 1880s, but they showed little wear and tear. The neighborhoods were clean, the houses well cared for. The people were friendly, the streets safe, and Santa was singing carols in the square. It was the sort of place people got nostalgic for, even if they never knew it existed, that, once she left, she would miss forever.

Maybe someday she would come back, when Berry was better or the kids were grown. She could make a home for herself in one of the little houses or apartments on the south side of town and torment herself between the kids' visits with heartaching might-have-beens and should-have-beens.

Or maybe she should just stay in Atlanta.

Some of the decorations on the tour were elaborate, as Nathan had promised. There were Clauses and Mrs. Clauses who turned from side to side, waving and ho-ho-hoing, reindeer on rooftops, miniature villages, showers of stars, and nutcracker soldiers made entirely of lights. All too soon, though, the ride was over, and the wagon headed back to the park. With her head resting on Nathan's shoulder, Emilie gave a great sigh. "This was nice." Magical. An evening to remember.

"Are you cold?"

"A little."

"I can think of a few ways to get you warm again."

So could she, especially since the kids were sleeping next door tonight. A few minutes in his arms. Just one of his sweet, hungry kisses. Maybe a little touching, a little caressing, a little—

"Ten minutes beside the bonfire and a cup of hot cider should do the job."

She poked him with her elbow. "That's all you had in mind? Where's your sense of romance?"

He placed his mouth just above her ear. "Crawl up here on my lap, and I'll show you exactly where it is."

The suggestion was out of the question, but darned if it didn't give her an image that went a long way toward turning up the heat. Her throat tight, her voice husky, she whispered back, "Ask me when we get home."

"Home." He repeated the word the way Alanna sometimes did, as if it were foreign and strange but he liked it anyway. It was funny how the concept worked. She'd had her own apartment for ten years, but it had never really felt like home. She was living in the Pierce house illegally, and she would be forced to vacate it soon. She didn't belong there at all, and yet she felt as if she did. It was a real home, thanks in large part to her neighbors.

The horses drew to a stop and waited patiently for everyone to unload. After a few minutes around the bonfire, the kids gave Emilie a good-night kiss, and Josie offered one to Nathan.

"Where are you going?" he asked, crouching down to her level.

"We're spending the night with Miss Agatha and Miss Corinna, and I'm going to sleep in a bed with curtains over it—"

"A canopy," Alanna interrupted.

"Yeah, what she said, and in the morning, Mama's coming over for breakfast, and then we're going to clean up after the party." Clasping her hands behind his neck, she gave him a loud smack on one cheek. "Good night."

"Good night."

She started off to meet the sisters, then turned back. "Hey, Mr. Nathan. Are we going to have hot dogs tomorrow?"

"Sure."

With a satisfied, "Good," she skipped away.

Emilie faced the fire, holding her hands to the flames. In the wagon, she truly hadn't realized that she was cold until Nathan had asked. Now she was all too aware that her hands and feet were frozen and she'd lost a little sensation in her toes.

Nathan slid his arms around her from behind. "Just this afternoon I was thinking how nice it would be if someone invited the kids for a sleepover. Some wishes do come true."

"It was Miss Corinna's idea."

"And, knowing you, you probably said, 'Oh, no, that's too much trouble. The kids won't want to leave me. We couldn't impose.' "

"I wasn't sure the kids would want to." But they did, and for the first night in more than a year, she was free to do exactly what she wanted. She'd had hundreds—thousands—of nights like that back in Georgia and hated them. Because it was such a rarity now, she intended to make the most of it. "Miss Corinna said we could enjoy all the celebrations at the park. What was she talking about?"

He turned her toward a ring of lights in a distant corner of the park. "A lot of people go over there after the tour. You can buy hot drinks and snacks, sit around the fire and relax, or skate."

"Skate?"

"On ice. You know, like you see on TV."

She laughed. "Where I come from, that's the *only* place you see it."

"Surely a city the size of Atlanta has an ice rink."

"Probably so, but I've never been near it. Do you skate?"

"Of course. Want me to teach you?"

She thought about taking off her shoes in this cold, lacing on skates, and trying to balance on two thin little blades on a surface she could barely manage with both feet, and shook her head. "I don't mind watching, but I don't think I'm up for learning tonight."

"What are you up for?"

She would like to go home, build a fire, turn off the lights, and nuzzle on the couch. She would like to talk about things of no consequence, would like to not talk at all. She would really like . . .

"This is the first night I've had without the kids in longer than you'd want to know." She drew a deep breath before turning to face him. He kept his hands loosely clasped around her waist. "I'd like to go home."

"All right." They said their good-byes as they made their way through the crowd, then walked to the truck in silence. After he helped her in, he said, "I would want to know. How long has it been since you've had a night on your own?"

She could answer the question he'd asked, or she could give him the information he really wanted: How long had it been since she'd had a reason to spend the night away from the kids, since she'd spent the night with someone else? "A long time. Too long ago for me to remember." His name had been Mark, and they'd met on a blind date arranged by his cousin, but she wasn't sure exactly how long ago it had been. Two years, maybe three. Mark had been easy to forget.

Forgetting Nathan would be impossible.

At home, he parked behind his house. "Want to come in?"

"I need to be home in case—"

"The kids aren't going to need you. Not tonight."

"I know, but I still need to be there." She clasped his hands in hers. "Come over."

For a long moment he looked at her, as if trying to make a decision. Finally he nodded. "Let me go in for a minute."

"I'll wait out front." She followed the driveway to the sidewalk, then stopped in the middle, waiting no more than a moment before he came out. Without breaking stride, he looped his arm through hers, and they crossed the street, stomped off the snow, and went inside.

He built a fire while she settled cross-legged on the rug with her old quilt wrapped around her. When the logs were blazing, he grabbed a couple of pillows from the couch, then stretched out on his side behind her. Fingering the quilt where it covered her thigh, he asked, "Did you make this?"

"No. My mother did, shortly before she died." Actually, she'd made two in the same pattern using the same fabrics. Thirteen years later Berry had identified the materials for Emilie. Now, turning to face him so the heat of the fire was on her side, she did the same for Nathan. "This was one of her old dresses. She'd spilled bleach on it, then cut it up for quilt pieces. This one is from my father's work clothes. This was from some curtains she hated, and this was from a coat I'd outgrown."

"Is it the only thing you have of hers?"

She nodded. Just the quilt and a few photos. Age had distorted the colors, but the faces were frozen in time. There were several of the three of them—Berry, her mother, and herself—and one of her parents together. Secured in inexpensive frames, they had followed her from home to foster home, a meager legacy of a life she little remembered but missed so much. Usually they hung in a place of honor, but here they remained packed away. In the event that they had to leave quickly, she couldn't risk leaving them behind. She also couldn't risk Nathan's inevitable questions about Berry.

"What was she like?"

"She sang a lot, and she smelled of jasmine. When she cooked, she wore an apron with a ruffle around the edges, and she had a wonderful big laugh."

"How did she die?"

"She was on her way home from the store. She ran a red light, collided with two other cars, and was killed instantly.

"How old were you?"

Deliberately she avoided his gaze. When she'd told him about the foster homes last weekend, she had misled him about how long she had lived there. It was one thing to admit to a few years of not being wanted, another entirely to acknowledge that she'd lived most of her life that way. But Nathan could be trusted with the truth. He wouldn't pity her or wonder what was wrong with her. "I was five."

Nathan stared into the fire. Living only a few years in the situation she had described was bearable. After all, she would have already done most of her growing up with a mother who loved her and a father who had at least provided for her. She would have already had a solid foundation for her life and a strong sense of herself. But thirteen years . . . She'd been little more than a baby, younger than Josie, and had lost her mother, her father, and her home all at once. She must have been terrified, bewildered, and so alone.

"Most foster homes are good places. I had some good parents, but they weren't *my* parents. It wasn't my home or my family."

"It must have been tough."

"Kids cope in different ways. Some just naturally fit in. Some are so desperate for permanence that they'll do anything, please anybody, to find it. Some are so used to rejection that they reject the families first. And some of us . . ."

Were quiet and afraid. They accepted responsibility, did everything that was asked, but shied away from too much affection. Having lost too much already, they kept their distance, afraid of losing again. They remained apart from the families, dutiful and obedient guests who could be gone on a moment's notice.

It was a hell of a way to grow up, Nathan acknowledged. And when they did grow up and were on their own, what happened? Who did they share holidays with? Who congratulated them when they succeeded or comforted them when they failed? What did they do about family?

Emilie had gone out and made her own. She had left her last foster home at the age of eighteen. Soon after she'd been pregnant, and soon after that she'd been a mother. Finally, in Alanna—and later, Josie and Brendan—she'd found someone who needed her and loved her unconditionally.

He wanted to tell her how sorry he was, to kiss her long and hard and make her forget. He wanted to convince her that there were people who wanted to be part of her family, who would ensure that she would never be alone again. He settled for simply touching her.

After a time, she raised her gaze again. "I believe there was something you were supposed to ask when we got home."

Where's your sense of romance? she had asked in the wagon, and he had responded with an invitation. *Crawl up here on my lap, and I'll show you. . . .* He had been grateful that she hadn't taken him up on it. The ride hadn't been long enough or the night cold enough to deal with the consequences that were sure to arise.

Now they had all night.

"You want romance?" The only lights burning were

the four hundred tiny lights on the Christmas tree. The fire was burning brightly, its smoky scent mingling with the smell of sweet pine. It was late on a Friday evening, and he was alone with Emilie. He couldn't think of anything much more romantic.

He touched her cheek, gliding his fingers over heated skin to her jaw. Seeking, exploring, they moved lower, down her throat to the barrier of the quilt, brushing it aside, reaching the soft cotton of her shirt. He watched her face as he flattened his palm, then slowly moved it lower, lower, between her breasts, across her middle, to the bottom of the shirt. There he reversed direction, sliding underneath the sweatshirt, opening his fingers wide.

Her skin was soft and unbearably warm. When he inched higher, she sighed. When he brushed the bare underside of her breast, she caught her breath. Her eyes were closed, her skin a warm gold in the firelight's glow. Her lips were slightly parted, and she looked . . . Dazed. Aroused. Beautiful.

He freed his hand, then grasped both edges of the quilt and pulled her to him. She came willingly, stretching out alongside him, bringing her body into close contact. When she tilted her head back, he kissed her—nothing intimate, mouth against mouth, no tongues, no pressure, no urgency. Rolling onto his back, taking her with him, he kissed her again, catching her lower lip between his teeth, stroking his tongue across it, and then he kissed her for real. His hands were in her hair, and her hands were knotted in his sweater. She opened to the kiss with no coaxing, and he thrust his tongue inside, tasting, teasing, arousing. She was sweet and enticing, and for the first time all evening, he was way beyond warm and too close to steaming.

Reluctantly he broke away to take a badly needed breath. She looked exactly the way he felt—stunned. For a moment she stared at him, then touched her lips to his again. It was a sweet kiss, not inexperienced but achingly innocent. It awakened a new level of sensation—fierce need tempered by tenderness, hunger controlled by an overwhelming desire to protect her. It made his chest tight and his body hard, heated his blood and turned his breathing ragged. It created the sweetest pain he'd ever known and promised the purest pleasure.

The kisses continued, gentle, easy, tentative, demanding, until finally she pulled away. She sat up and scooted back, clutched the quilt tightly enough to turn her knuckles white, and drew a deep, shaky breath. "I think—" She sat on the hearth, then stood up. "I think you'd better go now."

By the time Nathan got to his feet, she was halfway to the hall. He caught up with her as she started to open the front door and stopped her with his hand flat against the wood. "I don't want to go, Emilie." His voice was deliberately calm, even. "Ask me to spend the night."

"I can't—I'm not prepared—I don't have . . ."

He pulled three plastic packets from his pocket,

stacked them one atop the other, and pressed them into her hand. "Ask me."

She stared at them before meeting his gaze. Desire was evident in her hazy blue eyes, along with insecurity and just a little fear. "Are you always prepared?"

"No. But tonight I was hopeful."

She closed her fingers around the packets, hiding them from sight, then locked the door. When she shut off the hall lights, he relied on only the dim light from down the hall to see her move toward him, and then she was kissing him, and he didn't care about seeing anymore. Her lips pressed to his, her tongue inside his mouth, she began backing away, pulling him with her, not stopping until she reached the steps. There she offered a slow, lazy smile and an invitation he would have to be dead to resist.

"Make love with me, Nathan. Make a little magic for me. Spend the night with me."

# Chapter Ten

Emilie's bedroom was all shadows and moonlight. The air was cool, but it felt good on her heated skin. It eased by a degree or two the fever that had spread through her body and cleared her mind of passion induced haziness. For the moment, she was thinking clearly enough to know that, whatever happened later, however her lies ended, she wanted this with Nathan— this intimacy, this night, this fantasy. She needed it.

There was a fireplace in the room, but she'd never bothered to carry wood up the stairs. She regretted it now. She would have liked to make love with him by firelight, to feel the fire's heat warm her skin the way his kisses warmed her blood. She would have liked to see his body, naked, strong, and aroused, painted golden by the flames, to feel the need and hunger consuming them the way the fire consumed the wood.

But they didn't need the heat from the fire. They generated enough of their own. They didn't need the light because instinct would guide them, and the consuming would come with the joining. It had already started.

Holding both of his hands in hers, she stopped beside the bed, and he immediately kissed her. He stroked her hair, her back, her breasts. He held her tight against his arousal, stirred her own arousal into a trembling, breath-stealing ache, and made her go weak, clinging to him in a way she had never clung before.

He pulled her sweatshirt over her head, and the cool air made her shiver. His hands on her breasts chased away the chill, feeding the hunger, making her hot now, so hot that her skin was slick with it. He helped her remove the rest of her clothes, then stripped out of his and followed her down onto the bed.

"I need . . ." His voice was harsh, thick. Giving up on words, he loosened her fingers and took one of the packets. The others fell to the bed. While he dealt with the condom, she touched him, marveling at his power and at her own power to make him tremble, to suck in his breath, to groan in a low, tortured, tormented voice. Then he filled her, and it was her turn to tremble, to gasp, to indulge in a soft moan of pleasure.

He was greedy, demanding, moving inside her, deep, hard, fast, and yet he gave as much as he took. Every touch, every thrust, that pleased him fed her, building, pushing her to such arousal that she couldn't think, couldn't speak. All she could do was react, rising to meet him, making her own demands, insisting, claiming, begging with frantic moves and voiceless pleas.

Satisfaction washed over her, intense, toe curling, heartbreaking, shuddering from his body through her own, coming in great waves that slowly, slowly receded into tiny ripples. With each little ripple, the tension eased, then built again, a little higher each time, a little stronger, a little greedier.

Murmuring soft words, sharing soft kisses and impatient touches, they made love again, a little less frantic but no less needy and no less satisfied when it ended. They remained together, her body tight around his, his sheltering hers. After a moment's recovery, he gave her the sweetest, gentlest kiss, and she felt a frightening rush of guilt, regret, sadness, and sorrow. There was no doubt about it. This relationship, this man, and all these lies were going to break her heart.

"Emilie, I—"

She pressed her hand over his mouth. "Don't say anything."

He nipped her palm, then soothed it with the slow, coarse stroke of his tongue. Such a simple thing to make the muscles in her belly tighten. Before she could fully consider wanting him again, though, he pressed a kiss to her forehead, then left the bed. Closing her eyes, she listened to the pad of his footsteps, down the hall to the bathroom, then past the bedroom again and down the stairs.

For one instant when he had spoken her name, she had thought, hoped—feared—that he was about to make a confession of love. As much as she wanted to hear it, it would have been more than she could bear. She would have burst into tears and quite possibly confessed everything. It would have ruined everything, would have brought the heartache inevitable in the future right here between them.

But he had obeyed her plea and said nothing, and that was almost more than she could bear.

He returned with her quilt and an armload of firewood. She turned onto her side and watched him lay the fire, watched the flames send shadows leaping across the room as he wrapped the quilt around himself. When he offered her a silent invitation, she didn't hesitate. They lay curled together, his body warming her back, the fire and the quilt warming her front.

"So your last time was too long ago to remember, huh?"

Her mind was too dazed, her body too sated, to recall any memory of the last nothing-special time she'd shared someone's bed. At this very moment, she'd lost even the details she had earlier remembered—the man, the name, the date. At this moment, all she could think about was Nathan, how very special he was, and how desperately she was going to miss him. Just the thought brought tears to her eyes that she blamed on the woodsmoke as she blinked them away.

Accepting her silence as answer enough, he changed the subject. "What do you want for Christmas?"

"More of that." His hand was sliding over her hip to her waist, then back again, stroking, tickling, warming.

"I'm serious."

"So am I." It had been so long since she'd experienced such a casual pleasure as a lazy rub. She wanted to stretch like a cat, to arch against him in silent request for more. She wanted to feel his skin grow warm against hers, to feel his arousal swell hard where they touched. She wanted to pretend that there was nothing sexual about his caresses even as they both grew hotter, harder, needier, until her body tingled, until his throbbed, until they couldn't bear one second, one stroke, one breath, longer apart.

His fingers slid up to her waist, then dipped down, rippling across her stomach before returning to glide across her hip. "I've got the kids' gifts. I want to get you something, too. Tell me what you like."

"I like you."

Chuckling, he nuzzled her hair from her ear. "Sweetheart, you've got me."

"I like Christmas and snow. And hayrides in the night. And bonfires." She liked this house and her job, this town and her neighbors. She liked seeing Alanna with friends and Josie wide-eyed with wonder over Santa and a real camel with one hump or two. She liked watching Brendan open up, playing with kids other than Josie, talking to people other than family.

She liked everything about this town where she couldn't stay.

"Snow? A Southerner by the grace of God likes snow?" His fingertips brushed her breasts, making her gasp in mid-giggle. "Do you collect anything?"

"Blond-haired, blue-eyed children."

"You have anything against brown hair and brown eyes?"

She caught her breath again, but it had nothing to do with his wandering caresses. Blinking furiously to keep the tears at bay, she rubbed, long and lazy, against the entire length of his body. "At this moment, I have a lot against someone with brown hair and brown eyes."

He nipped her earlobe before giving it a soothing caress. "Do you like to read?"

"Uh-huh. I read about the poky little puppy and the cat in the hat and green eggs and ham every night."

"Do you like music?"

"I love music."

"How about diamonds and emeralds?"

"Nah. Then I'd have to get a new wardrobe and a new life."

He shifted her so she lay on her back, then swept the quilt back and studied her in the firelight. "I think you'd look beautiful in diamonds and emeralds and nothing else."

She captured his hand when he would have touched her and clasped it tightly in hers. "You've already given me a gift. I don't want anything else." But it was a lie. She wanted him, this intimacy, and a houseful of brown-haired, brown-eyed babies forever and always.

He raised her hands to his mouth, kissing each one, then slid his hand free and resumed his caresses. Every brush of his skin against hers spread heat and hunger. She'd never known fingers across her stomach could be so erotic, had never recognized the ribs as an erogenous zone. At last, when her muscles were taut and her nerves were twitchy, when even his breath against her shoulder made her heart thud, he worked free of the quilt and rose over her, his muscles straining as he supported himself only a breath away.

"Where are the condoms?" His voice was rough, ragged.

So was hers. "On the bed." She wished they didn't have to use them, wished they could reduce their love-making to the bare basics, just the two of them, no barriers, no protection, no safeguards. She wanted to tempt fate, to take with her when she left the dream—the hope—of a child, brown-haired and brown-eyed, who could fill her arms and help heal her heart.

But she was in no position to indulge her dreams. She already had three children to take care of alone. She couldn't handle a fourth. No matter how badly she wanted to try.

After leaving a trail of kisses across the swell of each breast and the flat of her stomach, he pushed himself to his feet and recovered the condoms from the bed. She watched with unashamed interest—and regret—as he unrolled one latex sheath in place, then joined her again, joined with her again.

Golden light, heat that sizzled, passion and pleasure and pain. Their breathing grew raspy, their skin slick, their arousal unbearable. Emilie clung to him, her movements instinctual, her body seeking, demanding satisfaction that came in an explosion of light, of moans and helpless cries, of heat and damp and clenching, quivering muscles.

Trembling, Nathan rested against her, and she held him, stroking his hair, his back, his strong arms. What did she want for Christmas? This: to be with him. It would be every Christmas gift, every birthday present, every dream and wish all wrapped up in one. And she could have him for nineteen more days. Less than three weeks of perfect in twenty-nine years of so-so. It wasn't much.

But it had to be enough.

Saturday morning Nathan awakened in a cold room in a strange bed with a warm body snuggled close behind. He gazed at the ashes in the fireplace, at the quilt still on the floor and the plastic wrappers discarded alongside and smiled. Just yesterday afternoon he had wished for a sleepover to take the kids away and leave Emilie to him for one entire night, and his wish had come true. Maybe his luck would hold and he could wish for her to forget about going home to Georgia and to make a new home for her family here with him.

Maybe if he subtly encouraged her, if he made sure she saw how happy the kids were, if he showed her how easily they fitted into the community . . . Maybe he couldn't change her mind, and when January first was gone, Emilie and the kids would be gone, too. But maybe he could have one miracle. Just one, and he would never ask again.

He had asked favors of God before. The first time he'd faced a suspect with a gun. The time one of those suspects had taken a shot at him. The Christmas Eve when Mike got shot. The moment he'd seen his best friend's body. That night when Diana had screamed out her secrets and the next morning when he'd realized that she and Elisabeth were gone. He had prayed plenty of times, and sometimes he'd gotten the right answer. Sometimes he hadn't. Somehow, some way, Emilie was going to be the right answer.

He slid out from under the covers and reached for his jeans. He would like to spend the entire rest of the weekend in bed with her, but it was a quarter of eight, and the kids were expecting her next door for breakfast. He didn't think the sisters would let them come to wake her, but if they slipped away without Agatha's and Corinna's knowledge—something he wouldn't put past Josie—he didn't want to cause questions that Emilie might not be ready to answer.

He got dressed, then sat on the bed. "Emilie?"

She murmured and burrowed deeper under the covers.

"It's morning, sweetheart, and breakfast is in ten minutes."

She opened her eyes, and her scowl dissolved into a sleepy, sexy, enticing smile. "Good morning."

He resisted the urge to stretch out beside her, to slide his hands under the covers and reacquaint himself with the body he'd come to know well in the last twelve hours. "Have you considered sending the kids to church with the sisters tomorrow morning?"

"And what would I do while they're gone?"

"You could invite your friendly neighborhood cop over and make mad, passionate love to him."

"Send the kids to church so we could have sex? There's something wicked about that."

There was something wicked about what they had done in this bed last night. Wicked and wild, addictive, and sweetly, purely pleasurable. He didn't dwell on it, though, not when he was already dressed, fresh out of condoms, and ready to face her children, who didn't know what they'd done last night, and the sisters, who had made it possible. He kissed her, then forced himself to back away, not stopping until he reached the door. "I'm going home to change, then I'll see you at the Winchesters'."

The last thing he saw as he turned away was a flash of long legs and bare hip as she slid out of bed. Swallowing hard, he took the stairs three at a time, pulled on his coat, and headed out into the cold.

After a shower and clean clothes, he left once more. If he needed an excuse, he could say he'd come to help with the cleanup, but neither sister would ask. He ate breakfast at their house about three Saturdays out of four.

Josie answered the door and somehow managed to climb up into his arms. "Hey, Mr. Nathan, Miss Agatha says you're taking us to a party today."

It took him a moment to remember the open house at the inn. Emilie would be working, helping Holly play hostess. It was a good opportunity for her to meet a hundred or so of Bethlehem's friendly citizens—an opportunity to see yet again that this was a place where she could belong. "That's right. I am. But not until after lunch."

"Hot dogs at Harry's. But no sundaes, 'cause Mama says Miss Holly will have sweets at the party." As he carried her into the dining room, she opened her arms wide. "I'm glad you're here. I'm hungry, and we waited for you."

"I can see that." He deposited her in her chair, in front of a half-eaten waffle. Crumbs from a muffin littered the tablecloth, along with a few bits of bacon.

"We didn't wait, but we did save you some food. Have a seat." Agatha gestured to the empty setting across from Emilie, whose smile was tentative and shy, 180 degrees different from the sucker-punch smile she'd given him in bed a short while ago.

He was polishing off his own waffle when Brendan, on his left, laid his hand on Nathan's arm. "Hey, Mister." His voice was little more than a whisper. "I sleeped over here last night."

"I know you did. In the bed with the canopy?"

Brendan looked to Josie, whose head bobbed, then mimicked her response.

Nathan leaned closer. "Do you know what a canopy is?"

Wide-eyed, Brendan shook his head. He drew his hand back, saw it was fuzzy with lint, and tried to clean it before holding it up for Nathan's inspection. "My hand's sticky."

So was the sleeve of Nathan's sweatshirt. The boy realized it at the same time Nathan did, and his grin faded as his lower lip trembled. "Sorry," he whispered, shrinking as far away as the booster seat would allow and clutching Ernest to his chest. "I sorry."

"Brendan—" It was Emilie who spoke, starting to rise at the same time Agatha did. Nathan beat them both, though, scooping Brendan and the bear up as he stood. "It's okay. Come on. Let's clean up in the kitchen."

Both women sat down again as Josie's matter-of-fact voice filtered through the doorway into the kitchen. "He makes dumb messes all the time. He's just a careless baby."

Nathan's curiosity was stirred as he turned on the water, then settled Brendan on the counter. The kid had clearly expected to get into trouble, and Josie's comments had sounded like a direct quote from someone with little patience for little boys' messes—certainly not Emilie. Maybe a baby-sitter? Back in Boston, Emilie must have left the kids with someone while she worked—probably a neighbor whose prices were cheap and whose services, apparently, were worth about what she was paid.

As he washed the syrup from Brendan's hands, arms, and face, the kid leaned forward, putting his face close to Nathan's. His expression was intense, his tone belligerent. "Not a baby."

"No, you're not."

"Not careless."

"No."

"Or dumb."

"Of course not. Josie didn't mean that. She was just talking." Finishing with Brendan, he used the washcloth to clean his sleeve, then Ernest.

"Josie talks a *lot*," Brendan said, then laughed, and

the last bit of worry disappeared from his eyes. He held
his arms out, and Nathan swung him to the floor. Dragging the bear by one arm, he ran from the room, chant-
ing, "Josie talks a lot. Josie talks a lot."

"Do not!" came a denial from the dining room.

"Do too. Mister said so!"

"You've done it now," Emilie said in a quiet, amused
voice. "Josie will use up half the oxygen in the room
denying that she talks too much." Taking advantage of
their moment of privacy, she slid her arms around him
from behind, and he clasped his hands over hers.

"Who told Brendan he's a careless baby who makes
dumb messes all the time?" Tension tightened her body
against his. When she would have pulled away, he held
her hands while turning to face her. "His baby-sitter?"

She sighed heavily. "Berry sometimes kept him while
I was at work."

And who was Barry? A neighbor, a boyfriend, a
lover?

"Ordinarily, she was a sweet, loving woman, but
sometimes she just didn't have much patience. Sometimes it was hard for her to deal with a three-year-old
acting like a three-year-old."

His jealously eased with the knowledge that Berry
wasn't a man, someone special to Emilie, someone who
knew the soft little cries she made when sexual tension
was splitting her apart, who had watched the flush of or-
gasm color her cheeks and spread down her throat to the

tips of her breasts. At the same time, his dislike of any adult who couldn't deal with a three-year-old sprang solidly to life. "Why did you leave him with her?"

"I was doing the best I could, Nathan. She wasn't my first choice, but sometimes she was the only choice."

"At least here you don't have to worry. You'll never find better baby-sitters than Miss Agatha and Miss Corinna."

Shadows darkened her eyes, and she pulled her hands free. "No, I won't."

And that subject was closed for discussion. But only for the moment.

Cleanup from last night's party took little time, while baking and decorating gingerbread men passed the rest of the morning. At lunchtime, the kids said their good-byes, and they headed for Nathan's truck and hot dogs at Harry's. Seated on her knees and talking between bites, Josie said, "Miss Agatha said the party's a open house. What's a open house?"

"It means the doors and windows are always open," Alanna replied.

"Oh. But don't it get cold?"

Emilie tugged Alanna's ponytail. "It means that there's no set time for the party. People can come any-time after three o'clock and leave anytime before six."

"What time are you going, Mama?" Josie asked.

"I have to be there at two."

"And what time are we going?" She directed the question to Nathan.

"Probably around four."

"Is Santa going to be there?"

"You planning to remind him where you live?" At Josie's solemn nod, he shook his head. "He won't be there, but you don't have to worry. Santa's got a good memory. He won't forget."

"Of course he won't," Alanna murmured. "He spends enough time there." Her gaze, as blue as her mother's, was directed at Nathan. He wouldn't call it unfriendly, but it wasn't exactly friendly either. It was measuring. Speculative.

No one had ever referred to him, however obliquely, as Santa Claus before. He could think of worse names Alanna could call him. He could also think of a few better. Like Dad.

Emilie tugged her hair again. "Hush now. Not in front of the kids."

Alanna's gaze didn't waver. "Can I ask you something?"

He wasn't sure he wanted to hear it, but he shrugged and waited.

"My teacher asked me to be in the pageant next week, but practice is after school. I would miss the bus. If Miss Agatha—" She broke off, squirmed a little, and looked at her mother as if hoping she would finish for her.

When Emilie remained silent, she turned back to him. "If Miss Agatha can't pick me up . . ."

He knew what she wanted and what his answer would be, but because her feelings toward him were ambivalent at best, he waited for her to ask.

Alanna drew a deep breath. "If Miss Agatha can't pick me up, could you?"

"Sure. When and what time?"

"Monday, Tuesday, and Wednesday at four."

"I'll be there."

"Thank you." Her words were quiet, but the relief in her eyes was enormous. Moving around the way they had the last year probably hadn't given her many chances to take part in school activities, so this one must be special. He hoped she had the best role, remembered her lines perfectly, and was the star of Bethlehem Elementary. She deserved to be a star at last once.

Alanna slumped back on the bench. Asking hadn't been so hard. Of course, she'd been practicing in her head all morning, and still the words hadn't come out right. She was awfully glad he had said yes. But if he hadn't, Aunt Emilie probably could have talked him into it. He looked at her like a man who really liked what he saw. At first, Alanna hadn't liked him because of that. Too many men had looked at Mama like that, and she and the kids had paid for it. But Emilie wasn't like Mama, and Nathan wasn't like those men. He arrested people instead of getting arrested himself, and he didn't drink, use drugs, yell, or punch.

She also hadn't liked him because he was a cop and could cause trouble for them. But he seemed nice enough, and he acted like he didn't mind having them around. He didn't yell at Josie for always talking or want to spank Brendan for getting his shirt dirty this morning. He hadn't gotten mad at any of them even once.

He could be the answer to their problems. If he and Emilie fell in love and got married, then everything would be okay. He wouldn't have to ever know the truth. The judge back in Boston wouldn't arrest her when he found out she was married to a cop, and they could all stay in Bethlehem forever. They could have a real home, and Emilie could have babies of her own, and they could be one big happy family, just like she'd promised.

If Emilie fell in love with Nathan, everything could be perfect. Considering that her aunt was looking at him in the same way he looked at her, Alanna would guess that maybe they were already halfway there. Now if they would just fall all the way . . . And before Christmas, please, she added in a silent request to God, the angels, Santa Claus—whoever might be listening. Having a real home and a pretend-father and friends and no worry about jail and foster homes was the best Christmas present she could imagine.

After lunch, they skipped the grocery store and went home so Emilie could get ready for work. Josie was the first one in the door and the first one in the parlor, where she stopped so suddenly that Brendan and Alanna ran into her. "Look!" Her eyes big, her mouth open, she pointed across the room.

Afraid that the tree would be gone or their pretty decorations had been ruined or stolen, Alanna didn't want to look. When she did, she gave a great sigh. The tree was where it belonged, and so were the ornaments, her glass icicles, and Emilie's pretty angel. Everything they'd ever had in Boston that was worth stealing had been stolen, but not here. Bethlehem was different.

She wanted more than she could say to stay where it was different.

What had stopped Josie in her tracks was the presents under the tree. They'd never had many presents before—just a few from Emilie each year. Sometimes Mama had traded them to a neighbor for a bottle of booze or worse. This year they had a tree *and* presents— a big one for Brendan, some medium-size ones for Josie, and some smaller ones for her.

"Mama, Mama, Santa Claus came!" Josie darted to the fireplace, got down on her knees, and stared up inside. "How'd he do it? How'd he get down our little chimney with those big boxes? I thought he only came on the night before Christmas."

"He does," Emilie answered from the doorway. "You

know how Miss Agatha and Miss Corinna have presents under their tree?"

They had a *lot*, Alanna thought as Josie nodded, all wrapped in pretty paper with lots of ribbons and bows. It looked like something out of a Christmas fairy tale.

"Those are presents that they've bought for their family and friends, and presents that people have bought for them. These are presents that Nathan bought for you. Santa will deliver his gifts on Christmas Eve."

Alanna had known the presents were from Nathan, even though the FROM place on the tags was blank. Maybe he really didn't mind having them around. Maybe he even *liked* them. None of Mama's boyfriends had ever liked them, but Nathan had said he'd wanted kids when he was married, and since he didn't have any of his own, maybe he wanted them to be his pretend-kids.

Or maybe he just liked Emilie an awful lot and was willing to put up with them to have her. She could live with that.

Josie crouched in front of the tree, looking at the boxes. "So when do we get to open these?"

"Christmas morning. Think you can wait that long?"

Josie's grin stretched ear to ear. "Oh, yes. Until then, I can look at them. Our tree doesn't look so lonely anymore, now that it's got presents."

Emilie went upstairs to change, and Nathan sat down on the sofa. Brendan crawled up to sit beside him, and

Nathan put his arm around him like it was the normal thing to do. Alanna couldn't remember any man ever putting his arm around her, not even her dad, who had left when she was a baby and had never come back.

Alanna took the chair. "Did Mama say who'll keep us while she's gone?"

"Since you're going to the open house with me, you might as well stay with me. We'll go shopping or something."

"For what?"

"A gift for Miss Agatha and Miss Corinna, maybe something for your mother. You have any suggestions?"

Alanna shook her head. She knew plenty of things Emilie wanted—a husband, a family of her own, a home that no one could make her leave, an easier life without so much worry—but they weren't things that could be bought in a store and wrapped under the tree. But they *were* things Nathan could give her, if he wanted. If she could be talked into taking them. "She needs a lot of stuff."

"I don't want to give her something she needs. I want to get her something she wants."

She wasn't sure exactly what the difference was, but she didn't have a chance to ask him to explain because Emilie was coming down the stairs. A moment later she came into the room. Nathan was looking at her like he'd never seen her before, because he hadn't, not like this. Her hair was pulled back with a black velvet bow, and she was wearing black shoes, black pants, and a top in glittery gold with a matching sweater. They were clothes that she'd brought from Atlanta with her, dress-up clothes that she'd never worn in Boston, and she looked beautiful.

Josie looked up from the tree and its presents. "Oh, Mama, you're so pretty." That was what she'd told their real mama the last time she'd seen her. Mama's hair had looked like it hadn't been combed in days, her eyes had been red with big dark circles under them, her nose was sniffly, and she'd been wearing a yucky hospital gown and a robe with the tags sewn on the outside, and Josie had said, "You're so pretty, Mama," and she'd really meant it.

She *could* be pretty, like Emilie, if she only tried. She was trying now to get better so she could be their mother again, but only because the judge made her. Once when she and Emilie had argued about her quitting the drugs, Mama had said that she didn't *want* to quit, and Alanna had known then that she probably never would. Nothing was more important to her, not even her kids.

She pushed the memory back where she didn't have to notice it, to where she kept the pain of how much she missed her mother and how bad she wanted to see her, and made herself smile. "You do look pretty, Mama."

Nathan told her so, too. Brendan just grinned.

They took her to the inn, where she told them all to behave and touched Nathan's hand before getting out.

Alanna wished she had kissed him, even if it would have made Josie giggle.

"Can I sit in front, Mr. Nathan?"

"Not this time. Alanna's going to, then you can later."

Making a face at Alanna behind his back, Josie plopped down and put on her seat belt again. Alanna quickly climbed into the front seat and fastened her own seat belt. It was silly to feel nervous—they'd been alone with him before—but she did anyway.

They drove back downtown to one of the stores that sold toys and the sort of things people gave for gifts. While the kids played with the toys, Nathan stayed close to Alanna. She wished he would go off and pay attention to Josie, but she was also kind of glad that he didn't. Josie got enough attention—and everyone else's.

"Is there any special reason your mom wants to go back to Georgia?"

She looked at him only from the corner of her eye and answered stiffly, "It's her home. It's where she's from."

"Don't you think she could be happy someplace else?"

He meant here, with him. The knowledge made her stomach flip-flop. "Maybe."

"What would it take to convince her of that?"

"I don't know."

"What would it take to convince you?"

Finally she did look at him. "I like Bethlehem. Josie

likes it, too, and Brendan. We'd stay here if Mama said we could, if it was possible."

"Why isn't it possible, Alanna?"

She shrugged guiltily. If she tried to lie, the truth might slip out, and then all of Emilie's fears—all of her own fears—would come true. If he knew everything, maybe he would help them, but probably he wouldn't. Probably, because he was a cop, he would tell the judge in Boston where they were, and the orange-haired lady would come to get them, and the police—maybe even Nathan—would take Emilie to jail for not doing what the judge told her to.

No, for them to be able to stay in Bethlehem, he couldn't ever know about the judge or the orange-haired lady or Mama, not unless someday Mama got better and came for them. Alanna didn't think that would ever happen, not for a long, long time, but if it did, by then Emilie and Nathan would have been together too long, and he would love her way too much to arrest her.

She looked at him once more. "Can I ask you a question? Do you want to marry my mother?"

He looked surprised, then kind of stubborn. "I think maybe I do."

"It's okay with us if you do," she replied, then walked away to join the kids with the toys. When she glanced back, he still looked surprised and stubborn. More than ever, he looked like exactly the right answer to their problems.

# Chapter Eleven

"Why are we going to church? We've never been to church, not once, have we, Lannie? And we turned out good, so why do we have to start now?"

Emilie pulled Josie between her knees and held her there while tugging a dress over her wriggling niece. "You'll enjoy it. Miss Agatha will be your Sunday school teacher, and you'll see some of your friends from school there."

"But, Aunt Emilie—"

"She doesn't care about going to church. She just doesn't want to wear a dress." Alanna finished tying her shoes and stood up. "Aunt Emilie, do you think maybe I could have a new pair of shoes for Christmas? Something a little nicer than tennis shoes?"

That was the first time in Alanna's entire nine years that Emilie had heard her ask for anything. Even on her last birthday, she had acted as if it were just another day, nothing special. She'd had no expectations of a party, a cake, gifts, or even a card. Unfortunately, except for a home-baked cake and heartfelt wishes, she'd gotten nothing special. "I think so. We'll see, okay?"

"If church is so much fun," Josie asked with a pout, "why aren't you going? Why do you get to stay home in comfortable clothes while we have to go?"

Because Nathan was coming over as soon as the Winchester car turned the corner, and they were going to spend the next two hours or so indulging in a little wickedness. Just the thought made her face warm . . . but not with desire. She felt that, too, but this was embarrassment.

"Because she's been to church. She doesn't need it like you do. We'll be downstairs." Alanna took Ernest's hand and, with Brendan holding the other, left the room.

Josie twined her arms around Emilie's neck. "I'm a good girl."

"Yes, you are, but going to church might help make you better."

"But I don't want to be better. I'm happy just being good."

Emilie gave her a hug before standing. "Don't forget—Christmas is less than two weeks away. You don't want to get on Santa's bad side this close, do you?"

"No." Her scowl indicated displeasure. Did Santa give credit for good behavior that was greed-induced? Emilie wondered as they joined the others downstairs.

Bundled in her coat, she stood on the veranda while they hurried next door, where the sisters were coming out to their car. She waved good-bye as they drove away, then shifted her gaze across the street. Just as she'd expected, Nathan came out of the house only a moment later. He greeted her with a kiss that made her forget the cold, her earlier embarrassment, even her own name. "The kids are gone," she said unnecessarily.

"I know. Want to go out for breakfast?"

"Nope."

"Want to go for a drive?"

"In the snow?"

"I have four-wheel drive, remember?"

She thumped her fist against his chest. With all the padding between them, it had no effect.

"Want to . . ." Positioning his mouth over her ear, he murmured sweet, sinful suggestions that made her tremble. By the time he finished, her legs had gone weak, and she was clinging to him for support. Wearing a sexy, knowing grin, he waited for an answer, and she gave it breathlessly, greedily.

"Yes."

He pulled her inside the house, locking the door, and into the parlor. This morning's fire was dying, but a few tinder-dry logs brought it back to life, sending out warmth with every crackle and pop. They stretched out close enough to feel its heat, Emilie on her back, Nathan on his stomach beside her, leaning on his elbows so he could gaze down at her.

"What did you think of the open house yesterday?"

"It was nice." She hadn't expected to have much fun. She was an employee, after all, not a guest, there to make sure everyone was comfortable and that neither their plates nor their glasses went empty for long. But no one had treated her like a servant. They had acted as if she were just one more of their friends and neighbors. How she wished that was true.

"The mayor was sweet on you by the time he left."

"Oh, right." The pudgy little man was old enough to be her father and had been accompanied by his pudgy little wife whom he clearly adored.

"I'm sweet on you. I have been for a long time." He turned onto his side and toyed with the top button on her shirt. "Ever since the day I came in here and saw you asleep right here."

"What day?"

Finally he unfastened the button and turned his attention to the next. "The first day. While I carried in the firewood, you came in, wrapped up in a blanket, and fell asleep in front of the fire. You looked . . ."

Pretty? Appealing? Femininely helpless?

"Exhausted."

So much for ego. "If exhaustion appeals to you, you can have your pick of the single mothers of the world."

"I've already picked the one I want." The second button slid open, too, and his fingertips rubbed the skin there, raising goose bumps and making her breath catch, before he moved to the next button, securing the fabric between her breasts. Already it was a little tighter than normal. Already her breasts were swelling, her nipples hardening.

"No response, huh?"

"Darlin', if you can't feel my response, then you're not trying." As the button popped free, she guided his hand underneath the fabric, sliding it until it covered her breast, until her nipple was pressed tantalizingly against his palm. With a long, lazy sigh, she closed her eyes and gave herself up to the pleasure of his touch.

"You know what I'm talking about."

She arched her back, rubbing against him. "Were you talking?" She knew what he wanted, of course—some response to the announcement that he wanted her. No, not just *some* response. The right response. *His* right response. It broke her heart that she couldn't give it.

"Atlanta's not so great, you know. It doesn't have anything that you can't find here."

She kept her eyes closed to hide her tears. He was right. Everything she wanted—everything she needed—was right here in Bethlehem. Everything she couldn't have. "Please stop, Nathan," she whispered. Pushing his hand away, she moved to sit on the hearth, in sudden need of the fire's heat.

"Alanna says staying here isn't possible. Why? What is so damned important—"

"Alanna says? Is that what you do when you're alone with the kids? You question them about me?"

"No. Yes. I just wanted to understand. . . ." He scowled as he sat up. "The kids are happy here. You're happy here. Why the hell are you so determined to leave?"

Rather than give answers he couldn't accept, answers that didn't make sense even to her, she shifted the focus of the conversation. "Do you realize how arrogant you're being? You knew from the start that we would leave here after Christmas, and yet you got involved with me anyway, believing that I would change my mind, my plans, and the kids' futures simply because you want me to. What if I insisted that you leave Bethlehem? What if I expected you to quit your job, leave your home and friends, and move to Atlanta? You wouldn't think that was such a great idea, would you?" Bethlehem was as important to him as it could be to her. This town and its people had played the major part in his healing after his friend's death and his wife's betrayal. It would be impossible for him to leave.

"You don't know what I'd think," he said quietly, "because you've never asked."

It was true. She had never considered the possibility of asking him to move to Atlanta because it *wasn't* a possibility. Before she could ask him to give up his life in Bethlehem and move with her, she would have to tell him the truth, and once he knew how she had deceived him, he would no longer want her. He believed that loving someone required honesty, and, although she'd limited her lies only to those necessary to protect the children, she had been anything but honest with him.

Still, she couldn't resist tormenting herself with the fantasy. "So, Nathan, you want to move to Atlanta?"

"No." He sat down beside her. "But I would think about it. I wouldn't rule it out without any consideration. I wouldn't make a choice and stubbornly stick to it, regardless of whether it was right or very, very wrong."

And to his way of thinking, her decision *was* very, very wrong. Of course, he didn't know that she had lied about the important things—the kids, this house, the trouble in Boston, her very identity.

"I'm sorry. I guess I'm just not as rational and logical as you. I make mistakes, a lot of them. Coming here was a mistake. Staying past the weekend was a mistake, and you—" She broke off before she could tell one more lie, but it was too late.

"I'm a mistake, too? Spending time with me, making love with me, letting me fall for you and your kids— were those all mistakes, Emilie?"

It would be easier in the long run for both of them if

she said yes, if she hurt him now once and for all, if they spent the remaining two and a half weeks apart. But it was one lie she couldn't tell, one hurt she couldn't inflict. "No," she whispered. "You're the best thing that's ever happened to us."

For a long time he sat still and silent. When he finally looked at her, she couldn't meet his gaze. "But it doesn't change the way this is going to end, does it?"

"I warned you that there was no future."

He touched her, his fingers gentle on her cheek. "Hey, you can't blame a man for hoping. It's Christmas, and I've been very good. Who knows what Santa might bring?"

Her smile was shaky and reluctant, but Nathan considered it an improvement over the tears that had threatened a few minutes ago. It was enough to help ease the ache he felt inside. It was enough to keep that little bit of hope alive.

It was also enough to force a decision. There would be no more talk about staying or going, no more pressure to change her mind. If this one month was all they got, then he was going to make the most of it. When it was over, when January came and she was packing her bags, then he would argue, plead, beg if necessary. Then he would consider making one more move. Until then, all he intended to do was give her plenty of reasons for staying.

"I wish I'd known you . . ."

She didn't finish, and he didn't press her. "You know me now. That's what counts."

She slipped her hand into his, shyly, tentatively, the way Josie sometimes did. "You're a good man. Santa should be generous."

He would have to be, since Nathan's wish list consisted of only one thing—a family, *this* family, his forever. It was a lot to ask—too much, according to Emilie—but he wasn't asking her. He was asking the miracle-makers.

"Speaking of Santa . . . The city employees' Christmas party is this Friday afternoon. The kids will be out of school, and Holly wouldn't mind if you took off a couple of hours early. Will you go with me?"

"Yes." She answered with a catch in her voice, as if she didn't want to go almost as much as she did.

"Good. I could use the support. Santa always puts in an appearance for the kids, and he's always played by someone in the department. Since I'm the only one who's never done it, Mitch thinks it's only fair that I take my turn. And since I need a little practice—" he pulled and she came, sitting astride him—"why don't you sit right here—" she wrapped her arms around his neck—"and let me try my best—" and rubbed her body against his—"ho-ho—"

The last "ho" was lost in a kiss, hot, wicked, and needy as hell. She thrust her tongue into his mouth, slid her fingers into his hair, and squeezed her hand between their bodies to stroke him, and, like *that*, he went from only vaguely aroused in the way that he was always vaguely aroused around her to hard, hot, and desperate for more.

She broke the kiss only long enough to pull his shirt over his head, then touched him, gliding her palms everywhere while her hips rocked against his. He wanted to be inside her, wanted to strip off their clothes and fill her, fast this time and hard, and maybe the next time, too. He wanted passion, frenzied need, and loss of control. He wanted longing intense enough to shatter them both and satisfaction perfect enough to put them back together. He wanted . . . needed . . . would surely die without . . .

She peeled off her clothes. He kicked off his jeans, then removed the condoms from the pocket before tossing them aside. She yanked one from its package and worked it on with fingers that trembled, fumbled, and made him groan, and then she took him inside her, no sliding, no easing, no bit-by-bit acceptance, but a sudden, hard thrust, taking all of him all at once. He gripped her thighs, his fingers dark against pale skin, holding her still while her body worked to accommodate him, while his body worked to regain some control.

The fire was hot behind him, but it couldn't compare to Emilie. Where they touched, they sizzled, their skin heated and slick. She moved with him and against him, taking more than he could afford to give, giving more than he could bear to take. His muscles quivered and knotted, and his chest burned with each labored breath, until, with a dazzling burst of sensation, she brought him to completion.

Cradling her, he eased to the floor and stretched out beside her. Her eyes were closed, her lips parted. He kissed her, and she slowly smiled. "You *are* good."

"I try my best." He stroked her face, her throat, down to the swell of one breast. She shuddered and pushed his hand away, but he brought it back immediately, sliding down past one sensitive nipple to her ribs and beyond. "You're a beautiful woman. For a mother of three, you look damn good." Her skin was smooth, pale, unmarked by the weight gain each pregnancy had caused. "When she was pregnant, Diana—" The muscles in her belly tightened beneath his hand. "Does it bother you—talking about Diana?"

"No." But she pushed his hand away again and turned onto her side, snuggling so close that he couldn't see her face. "What about her?"

"She was afraid of getting stretch marks. She went through a ton of cocoa butter while she was pregnant. Our bed smelled like a damned tropical island."

"My doctor says that doesn't help. Either you get them or you don't. Maybe it's genetic, or maybe it's just luck." She touched her tongue to the center of his chest. "Did she get them?"

"You bet. It broke her heart because she could never

wear a bikini again." A few short months later, she'd learned the real meaning of heartbreak. So had he. In a few weeks, he was going to learn it all over again.

He wanted to protest, to complain long and loud to whoever was in charge that he didn't need any reminders. The pain and loss were still a part of him and always would be. Besides, he was long overdue for some good fortune in his love life.

But he had no right to complain. Emilie had made it clear from the beginning that she wasn't staying. He had known a few weeks was all he could have, and he had forged ahead anyway. If he ended up with a broken heart, he had no one but himself to blame.

Besides, there was always that miracle. He wasn't giving up hope until January. The day he stood in the street and watched them leave for the last time, then he would stop believing. Then he would stop hoping.

Maybe. Or maybe he'd quit his job, load up his truck, and follow them.

He had no desire to live in Atlanta. He knew nothing about it, except that it was too similar in many ways to New York and too dissimilar from Bethlehem in many others. He wanted to spend the rest of his life right here, where he belonged as he never had before. But more than that, he thought he wanted to spend it with Emilie and her children. He *thought*. He wasn't a hundred percent sure.

But he would be by Christmas.

"Tell me about Atlanta."

Her muscles tensed, and the look she gave him was swift and wary. "What do you want to know?"

"What is it like? What makes it special?"

She pulled away, added logs to the fire, and watched them burn. "You know how you feel about Bethlehem? Well, that's how I feel about Atlanta."

It wasn't the answer he wanted. He wanted her to feel that way about Bethlehem, too. He wanted her to drive down Main Street and feel the warm welcome that he'd felt the very first time he'd driven into town. He wanted her to look at the businesses, the houses, and the people and feel as if, for the first time in her life, she had come *home*.

"Do you have friends there?"

"Some."

"You probably won't have any trouble finding a job."

"No."

"If I went there on vacation, what would you take me to see?"

She was quiet for so long that he was beginning to wonder if, in spite of her earlier halfhearted invitation and her assertion that he was the best thing that had happened to her, she wasn't the least bit interested in finding him on her doorstep once she moved. Finally, with a shrug, she answered. "If you come in the fall, you could see the Falcons play or, in the summer, the Braves."

He pulled her down to rest against him. "I don't think I'd go that far for a football or baseball game when I can see them on television all the time. What else?"

"You could tour the Coca-Cola museum."

"I drink Pepsi."

"Visit the house where Margaret Mitchell was born."

"I never read *Gone With the Wind*."

"See Stone Mountain, where the heroes of the Confederacy are carved in granite."

"Rocks don't excite me."

"What does excite you?"

That was a leading question if ever he'd heard one. "You do. This does." He stroked as much of her as he could reach. "So does this." Nuzzling her hair away, he kissed her ear, then worked his way to her mouth. "So does this." Claiming her hand, he guided it lower in an intimate caress, then muffled his groan with a kiss.

When finally he freed her mouth, she was breathing unevenly, and her eyes were hazy, but she returned to their original topic. "If you went to Atlanta, what would you want to see?"

"Josie, Brendan, and Alanna. You. Like this." He left her long enough to locate a condom, wishing he didn't have to, wishing he could come inside her and deal with the consequences later. Could he be lucky enough to get her pregnant this second time around? Maybe. And if she got pregnant, surely he could convince her to stay.

Surely she wouldn't choose illegitimacy for their child when she was already raising three illegitimate children.

But she *was* already raising three. What was one more?

Pushing the thought out of his mind, he slipped inside her, slow, deep. Once he had filled her, once they were as close as two people could ever be, he closed his eyes and savored the intimacy. He'd been wrong a few moments ago when he'd thought that Bethlehem was the one place he'd truly belonged. It wasn't. This—with Emilie—was.

*This* was home.

With a look out the window at the snow that was drifting down, Corinna settled in a chair and picked up her crocheting. The snow had started an hour ago, not too heavy, not too fast, the sort that might continue through the night. Bundled in their warmest clothing, the children were out in the yard with Agatha, kicking up sprays of white before falling to their backs to catch the fat flakes in their mouths.

She watched them for a moment before turning back to the work in her lap. She'd learned to crochet at her grandmother's knee, making everything from doilies to tablecloths to bedspreads. Now she was working on delicate stars, lacy snowflakes, and little rounded stockings that would decorate the packages piling up under the tree. It was a tradition she'd started when her own children were small, one that she intended to continue as long as the good Lord let her.

Outside Josie squealed a delighted greeting as Nathan pulled up. Alanna climbed out of the truck, her schoolbooks clutched to her chest. Nathan got out, too, catching Josie as she launched herself into his arms. They couldn't look more like father and daughter. Of course, the child bore no physical resemblance to him, but the connection was there. The love. Josie needed a father's love, and, heaven knew, Nathan needed a daughter's.

He set the child down, spoke to Agatha for a moment, then came up the steps and let himself into the house.

She picked up the pattern for the star, one that she'd made so many dozens of times that she needed only a glance at the instructions to recall the proper stitches. "We haven't seen much of you lately, Nathan. It seems our new neighbors keep you busy."

He sat down on the footstool nearby. "It seems they keep you busy, too. I believe this is the first time I've seen Miss Agatha playing in the snow since I moved in."

"Having children around keeps you young." She glanced outside again, where Josie and Brendan were trading snowballs while Alanna watched from the sidewalk. "How did Alanna's practice go?"

He shrugged. "Okay, I guess. She doesn't talk to me much."

"It's nothing personal, I'm sure."

"She doesn't know me, and it doesn't matter whether she likes me because they're leaving in January."

"She told you that today?"

"About a week and a half ago. On the other hand, she told me Saturday that it's okay with them if I marry their mother."

She concentrated on a combination of double and treble crochets before returning to the conversation. "Have you considered it?"

He was slow to answer, staring out the window at the children before finally offering her a vague smile. "I've thought about it. What man could spend much time with Emilie and not think about it?"

"A great many, once they see those children."

"I'm not sure it's a question worth considering. She's not staying in Bethlehem."

"Perhaps she simply hasn't been given the right incentive." Her eyes might not be as sharp as they once were, but she could see the way he and Emilie looked at each other. It was the same way her Henry had looked at her for more than forty years.

"She's not open to changing her plans. Believe me, she made that clear."

Painfully clear, judging by the look in his eyes. Sympathetically, she let the subject drop. "Have you heard the weather forecast this afternoon?"

"Snow into the night, with a warm spell later this

week—all the way up to thirty degrees." His smile was cynical. "Don't you love winter?"

"As a matter of fact, I do. I love the holidays, the cold, and the snow. When I was a young girl, I skied and skated and took more than a few sleigh rides with my beaus. That was before I met Henry, of course." Most people had a *before* period in their lives. From now on, Nathan's would be *before Emilie*. "If it weren't for the snow, dear, you might never have met the Daltons. They might have spent the night next door and been gone without our ever knowing they were here."

"Maybe that would have been better," he murmured, but she knew he didn't mean it. Rising to his feet, he kissed her forehead. "I'll see you."

Her crocheting rested forgotten in her lap as she watched him leave. Alanna spoke to him—probably thanking him for picking her up; she was good about that—and this time it was Brendan who wanted to be held while Josie walked backwards in front of Nathan and chattered nonstop. Corinna had never seen four people—five, including Emilie—who needed each other as much as these five did. Emilie would have to be out of her mind to leave a man like Nathan, and he would be equally foolish to let her go.

They were in dire need of a little help, and it looked as if would be left to Corinna and Agatha to provide it. But what to do?

\*   \*   \*

The sisters provided dinner Thursday evening, a gesture Emilie appreciated deeply. While the lasagna warmed in the oven, she bathed and dressed Josie and Brendan, then sent them downstairs to wait for Nathan while she talked with Alanna. Ever since they'd gotten home, Alanna had been curled up on her bed, not in a sociable mood.

Emilie stretched out on the bed behind her, spoon fashion, and stroked her hair. "Are you ready for the pageant?"

"Yeah."

"You know your lines?"

"Yeah."

"How was school?"

"Fine. We had a party in homeroom. Some of the mothers brought cupcakes and candy and punch, and we played games."

Emilie had already heard all about playing Pin the Nose on Rudolph from Josie. Presumably, fourth-graders played more sophisticated games. "Are you nervous about tonight?"

"Only when I think about it."

"Are you sad about not going back to that school?"

After a long time, Alanna whispered, "Yes. But I'll get over it. I'll like my new school in Atlanta, and I won't miss Susan or Lisa Marie or Mrs. Welch too much. I'll make new friends there, and I'll have a new teacher."

For all her optimism, she didn't sound as if she believed a word of it. Emilie wasn't sure she did, either, but she lied, too. "Sure, you will, honey. It'll be a great place, and you won't even miss . . . Oh, darlin', who am I kidding? It'll be hard on all of us to leave Bethlehem. We'll be in a strange place, and we'll have to make new friends all over again. But we'll manage. As long as we stay together, we can do anything."

"Can you forget Nathan? Can you find a new boyfriend to take his place?"

Emilie's eyes stung, blurring her view of the star and its accompanying angels in the window. "You don't just replace men like Nathan."

"Mama did. When one man left, it never took her very long to replace him. But Nathan's not like those men." She sighed, her breath warm on Emilie's hand. "You don't just replace a friend like Susan, either. She's the best friend I've ever had."

"I wish we could stay."

Alanna patted her hand reassuringly. "Maybe we can."

"No, honey, we—"

"It's Christmas, Aunt Emilie, and we're in a little town called Bethlehem. Don't you know anything could happen?"

The faith of a child. For a time Emilie had feared that Alanna had lost her faith. She was glad it had been restored—and hoped it didn't disappear for good when

New Year's rolled around and they headed for Georgia. "Sure, darlin', anything could happen. Like tonight, Alanna Dalton could bring the entire town to its feet with her powerful portrayal of the ghost of Christmas Present. Broadway could come calling, and Hollywood, and critics coast to coast could proclaim that a star is born."

Alanna smiled vaguely, moroseness exchanged for anxiety. Better nerves than heartbreak, Emilie decided.

"What if I forget my lines? What if I walk out there and I can't say anything? What if I trip on my costume or I throw up or—"

"You're going to be the best ghost of Christmas Present that ever was."

"But, Aunt Emilie—"

Emilie welcomed the interruption of the doorbell. "You'll be fine. Come on down, and let's eat."

By the time she made it to the front hall, Nathan was hanging his coat and Josie was unloading her burdens, sounding every bit as grumpy as she looked. "Mama made us take a bath early, and she made me put on a dress, all because Lannie's in some silly play."

"It's not silly, and this may come as a surprise, but girls are supposed to wear dresses from time to time."

"Wendy doesn't wear dresses, and Amber don't. Mrs. Mackey don't wear dresses, and Miss Thomas don't, and Mama *never* wears dresses, and—"

Emilie clamped her hand over Josie's mouth from behind. "Makes you value your peace and quiet, doesn't she?"

"Peace and quiet are seriously overrated." He leaned over Josie and kissed Emilie, warming her cheeks and heating her blood. "Where's the Christmas ghost?"

"Upstairs working on a case of stage fright."

"I've got something for her. Do you mind if I take it up?"

"No, go ahead."

Josie tried to wriggle free to follow him. When Emilie held her at the bottom of the stairs, she simply raised her voice instead. "A present? You got Lannie a present just for being in a silly play that I have to take an early bath and wear a dress for? What is it? Can I see it?"

"Has anyone ever called you nosy?"

Even as she gave a solemn shake, Brendan did just that. "Josie's nosy. Nosy Josie."

She stuck her tongue out at him, then gave Emilie a sweet, innocent smile as she was steered toward the kitchen. "Let's get dinner on the table."

"But we want to see Lannie's present."

"You can see it later. In the kitchen, now."

The table was set, and Josie and Brendan were in their seats when Alanna and Nathan joined them. Alanna went straight to Emilie and held up the necklace around her neck for inspection. "Look, Mama. Look what Mr. Nathan gave me. A star for a star. That's what he said. Isn't it neat?"

The necklace was a thin gold chain, and the pendant hanging from it was a five-pointed crystal star, faceted to sparkle like a diamond. "It's beautiful, sweetheart."

When Alanna went to show the kids, Nathan stepped close behind Emilie. Cutting the lasagna into squares, she murmured, "You're good."

"So I've been told."

"Did she thank you?"

"She was very gracious."

"Something she learned from her mother."

"Ha. Something she could have taught her mother a few weeks ago." He carried the pasta to the table while she got the bread from the oven. She was grateful for the moment alone while she transferred the bread to a basket, for the chance to get rid of the lump in her throat and the ache in her chest.

She'd known practically from the beginning that Nathan was dangerous—to her heart if not to her freedom. She'd known the risk of falling for him was too great to ignore, but she'd done just that. She'd closed her eyes to all the obstacles and problems and fallen in love with him anyway. She had suspected it for a while, but had been reluctant to put the proper name to her feelings. This gift to Alanna left her with no choice.

She loved Nathan. And in two weeks, she was going to lose him.

She wanted to cry over the unfairness of life, but she had known all too long that life wasn't fair. For twenty-four years she'd been trying to make the best of it. For the next two weeks, she would make the most of loving him, and after that, she would go back to just trying to cope.

With a smile that made her jaws ache, she joined the others at the table, where Nathan chatted and teased with the kids. Even Alanna responded, shyly at first, then with a hint of Josie's boldness.

As soon as dinner was over, they left the dishes to soak and piled into Nathan's truck for the drive across town to the high school. Mitch and Shelley Walker made room in the bleachers for them, just a few rows below Holly and a few rows above Agatha, Corinna, and all her family.

The program started promptly at seven with a welcome from the school superintendent, music from the high-school band, and carols by the middle-school choir. After a few minutes, Brendan, who had sneaked Ernest in under his coat, climbed into Emilie's lap. Less than five minutes after that, Josie gave up her seat on the wood bench and climbed into Nathan's lap, straddling one knee and leaning back to rest her head on his shoulder.

"You guys look like the perfect family," Shelley whispered between songs. "Single women everywhere will mourn when they hear that Nathan's off the eligible list."

Somehow Emilie managed to keep her smile. "Don't make any rash pronouncements. We're just . . ." Intimate friends? Star-crossed lovers? "Neighbors."

"Let's see . . . You went to the Christmas parade with him. You've publicly had lunch with him at least once every weekend since you came to town. You got him to go to the sisters' party and on the lights tour. He stayed right by your side at Holly's open house. He takes you to work every morning and picks you up every afternoon, and word is he spends all his evenings with you. And yet you're just neighbors. Well, honey, I've never seen such cozy neighbors."

As the singing started again, Emilie allowed herself just a moment to buy into the family fantasy. She imagined what it would be like to be Nathan's wife, to know that he would always be there for her, to be able to share the joys and fears of life with him. She could easily picture the five of them living in his blue house, having breakfast every morning, rushed during the week, long and leisurely on Saturdays. They would go to church every Sunday and sit down together for dinner every night. He would play soccer and baseball with the kids, and the two of them would find time of their own to make babies of their own, and they would all be disgustingly happy.

It was a fantasy so lovely that it made reality all the less bearable. She and Nathan and the kids could never be that kind of family. Two weeks from today she and the kids would be boarding a bus for Atlanta. End of fantasy.

But two weeks—that was a lifetime. For two weeks

she could know what it was like to love a man who, she was pretty sure, loved her. For two weeks she could be the happy mother in a perfect pseudo-family. She could live the fantasy.

Tramping feet on the gym floor drew her attention back. The choir were taking their seats, and the stage was set for the play. She waited impatiently for Alanna to put in an appearance. When she did, in the best stage whisper Emilie had ever heard, Josie announced, "Look, Mr. Nathan, there's Lannie. Mama, there's Lannie."

Her performance was perfect for a first-timer. She remembered her lines and spoke them in a clear, strong voice. The only indication of nervousness was her fingers, occasionally reaching up to clasp the crystal star as if it brought her luck.

It wasn't the star that was lucky. It was Nathan, who looked as pleased as any father in the building.

Was there *any* solution to their problems that she might have overlooked, any possible way she could tell Nathan the truth without losing him forever? Only if he developed an incredible streak of forgiveness, and, based on his experiences with Diana, she didn't think that was going to happen. She couldn't believe that he might love her more after only a few weeks than he'd loved the wife he'd grown up with. She couldn't hope that he might forgive her lies when, seven years after his divorce, he still hadn't forgiven Diana's. She couldn't even conceive his overlooking her flight from Boston, the court order she'd defied, and the arrest warrant that had surely been issued, not after his experience with Mike. If he knew there was a warrant for her arrest, he wouldn't hesitate to turn her in.

Truthfully, she would be disappointed if he didn't.

The pageant ended with the choir singing "The Hallelujah Chorus," accompanied by a host of grade-school angels wearing white gowns, paper-covered wings, and tinsel-wrapped halos that glittered under the bright lights. Once it was over, no one made a rush for the doors. Families gathered their children and chatted with neighbors. With Brendan drowsy in her arms, Emilie listened while Nathan talked with friends and let her thoughts drift off. In fantasy land, when they left the school, they would go home together, just like all the other couples around them. They might stop at the Winchester house to celebrate Alanna's performance, or they might go straight home and relive it all again through her excited chatter. By nine-thirty or ten, the kids would be in bed, and they would follow soon after. They would make love—quietly, so as not to wake the children—and they would fall asleep snuggled together for warmth and the simple, priceless comfort of knowing, even in sleep, that they were no longer alone.

At that moment, Nathan glanced her way and smiled a sweet, private, only-for-her smile, and her chest grew tight. The crowd, the noise, and the lights faded, leaving her trembling and happy enough to cry. She could save the fantasy for next month. She didn't need it tonight.

Tonight she had the real thing.

When they finally made it home, the children were tired. Emilie was removing her coat when Alanna spoke. "I'll get the kids to bed, Mama. Leave the dishes, and I'll do them tomorrow." She stretched up to kiss Emilie's cheek, hesitated, then gave Nathan a quick kiss, too. "Good night," she whispered before hustling Brendan and Josie up the stairs.

Looking a little stunned, Nathan watched until the kids were out of sight, then sighed. "Alanna's going to be a heartbreaker someday. Just like her mother."

"Not me. I've never broken any hearts." She tried to sound light and careless, but failed miserably.

"Sweetheart, you're breaking mine every day."

"Nathan—"

He caught her hand when she would have touched his face and pressed a kiss into the palm. "Let's do the dishes. Let Alanna enjoy her first day of Christmas break."

He washed, and she rinsed. When the drainer was full, she picked up a towel to dry the rest. The first few pieces were easy enough until Nathan, finished with his job, decided to help her. He stood behind her, hands tangled in the towel with hers, head bent to nuzzle her ear.

"I want you," he murmured, and she could feel the proof. "Ever since I looked at you after the pageant, holding Brendan, looking like everything I thought I would never have, so beautiful and motherly and so damn hot . . ."

The plate started slipping from her fingers. He laid it aside, dropped the towel, and slid his hands under her sweater to her breasts. There was something she should say, some protest she should make, but her body's only protest was for more, and her heart's only words were of love. He kissed her, taking the words, and held her tight against his arousal, rubbing against her in an erotic simulation of their most intimate pleasures, and all she could do was enjoy, crave, burn . . .

"Good night, Mama. Good night, Mister." The voices were Josie's and Brendan's, shouting down from the second floor, returning to Emilie a small part of the sanity she'd lost.

"The kids . . ." Her objection was unsubstantial and far from convincing. The kids would be asleep soon. If she and Nathan were quiet, they would never know, and, besides, it wasn't so wrong. Husbands and wives made love with their kids in the house all the time. Of course, Nathan wasn't her husband, and she could never be his wife, but she loved him and wanted him and—

"I know." He gave her one last kiss before stepping away. "Want to go out tomorrow tonight?"

"Yes."

"Ask the sisters to baby-sit. We'll have dinner at my house." He started away, reaching the door before turning back. "Emilie—" His eyes dark, his gaze intense, he gave her a long, heated look, then his jaw grew taut. "I think I'd better go now."

His footsteps faded down the hall, then the front door closed, and still Emilie remained by the sink. If only the kids hadn't interrupted, they would be naked and sweaty and frantic right here, and she would never have been able to look at a kitchen the same way again. Even though the kids *had* interrupted, she might never again see it as a strictly utilitarian room.

As she turned off the lights and made her way upstairs, she gave a soft, regretful sigh. As soon as it was out, though, anticipation replaced regret. There was still tomorrow to look forward to—a half day of work, a little shopping, the party with Nathan, and their date. Mercy, yes, their date.

# Chapter Twelve

The second floor of the courthouse housed a number of offices and courtrooms around a large central common area. No cases were scheduled for the afternoon—no work at all, except for a skeleton crew in the police, sheriff's, and fire departments. Everyone else—city and county employees alike, along with just about everyone who did business with one or the other—was gathering upstairs for the party.

Everyone except Nathan, who stood in the locker room, feeling complete aversion for the task ahead of him.

Holding the offending garments, Mitch grinned. "It's not so bad. You use these pillows for stuffing and this spray adhesive to hold the beard in place. The wig is sewn into the cap—oh, and here are the fake eyebrows."

"They look like giant caterpillars."

"Don't use too much adhesive on them. They'll pull yours off." With a rueful look, Mitch rubbed one finger across his own eyebrows. "All you have to do is let the kids sit on your lap, give 'em a ho-ho-ho, ask if they've been good and what they want for Christmas, and don't make any promises. Tell them you'll see what you can do. Then give them a gift from the bag and send them on their way. The pink tags are girls' stuff, and the blue tags are boys'. Any questions?"

"Yeah. Tell me again what I did to deserve this."

"It'll be fun. The kids'll love you."

"I'm not looking for any kids' love." He scowled at the red-and-white clothes. A man who was about to put on a Santa suit probably shouldn't be telling lies. He was looking for the affection of three kids in particular, but he was pretty sure that pretending to be Santa Claus wasn't the way to get it—well, maybe with Josie, but not with Alanna and Brendan.

The locker-room door swung open, and one of Nathan's fellow patrolmen came in. Dansby glanced at the suit, then Nathan, and snickered. "Man, are you gonna be sweating. Wearing that fuzzy whatever-it-is is like wrapping up in a dozen blankets on a hot summer day."

Mitch hung the suit on a hook. "Come on, let's get upstairs. Santa will make his appearance at three o'clock. If you need any help getting dressed, let me know."

"He brought his own help—that pretty little blond neighbor of his." Dansby gave a low whistle. "I'd be Santa if she'd help me get in and out of the suit. If only she didn't have those kids . . ."

"If only you didn't have that wife . . ." Still scowling, Nathan followed Mitch out. Quite a crowd had gathered on the second floor, and it took him a while to locate Emilie, alone in a corner with Brendan, whose face was pressed to her shoulder, and Judge McKechnie. She looked more than a little uncomfortable, but the judge could do that to people braver and bolder than she. When Nathan maneuvered her away, she gave him a grateful smile.

"I'm sure the judge is a nice man," she whispered, her tone leaving a *but* hanging.

"I'm not so sure about that."

"Oh, he is. He's just . . . intimidating."

"That's the effect he goes for. He'll be glad to hear he succeeded. Where are the girls?"

"With their friends." She gave the crowd a long look. "Who's left to conduct the business of the city?"

"One dispatcher, a couple of cops, a couple of deputies, and a switchboard operator. Everyone else is here." He looked around, too, spotting the mayor, the councilmen, and the fire chief. The head of the water department was deep in conversation with the tax assessor, whose clerk Dorothy hovered nearby. About the only person he didn't see was the new clerk, the one who'd looked up Emilie's house for him.

"There's Alexander Thomas."

Nathan glanced at the lawyer. He had known Thomas for years. They had shown up at the same functions, dated the same women—at least, until Thomas's marriage a few years ago. He liked the guy—for a lawyer, he wasn't half bad—and had never felt the slightest bit envious of him. Until now. "How do you know him?"

"He came by the house right after we got here. His uncle was Miriam's attorney. He asked Alexander to welcome us to town."

"Herbert's about eighty years old and lives on the edge of town. He has a greenhouse bigger than most people's houses, where he raises every variety of exotic flower known to man. If you don't have chlorophyll flowing through your veins and your roots firmly planted in soilless medium, he's got no time for you."

She gave him one of those killer smiles, and for a moment he forgot everything else. There wasn't much he wouldn't do for a smile like that—quit his job. Move to Atlanta. Beg. Plead.

He didn't have the chance to offer any of the above, though. Raising his head, Brendan gave the crowd a wary look before settling his gaze on Nathan. He grinned and manipulated Ernest's paw in greeting. "Where's Santa?"

"He's not here yet. Are you going to sit on his lap and tell him what you want for Christmas?"

Brendan solemnly shook his head.

"All the other kids will be doing it."

Another shake.

"I bet he'd like to meet Ernest."

He clutched the bear tighter. "Ernest mine. Miss Corinna said doan have to seed him."

"Miss Corinna's right. You don't have to." Leaning closer to Emilie, he asked, "Is Miss Corinna going to baby-sit this evening?"

She gave him another of those smiles. "Yes. As a matter of fact, they've invited the kids to spend the night again. We'll have from six-thirty this evening until I have to leave for work in the morning"

Work. He'd forgotten that her job required periodic weekend shifts. That meant lunch at Harry's with just the kids—and maybe another shopping trip. He'd bought more gifts for the kids this week, along with presents for Agatha and Corinna, but he still needed something for Emilie, and surely the kids would like to buy her something, too.

They worked their way around the room, talking, filling plates from the buffet, balancing food, drink, and Brendan. Finally, shortly before three, they left Brendan with the sisters, and Nathan took Emilie downstairs with him.

The locker room was empty, and the damn red suit

was still hanging here. He had tried for a week to talk Mitch out of this. He wasn't the Santa type. But Mitch was adamant, so here was Nathan, about to trade his uniform for the St. Nick suit. Everyone else had enjoyed the joke at his expense, and now Emilie was proving no exception.

"Maybe you'd better keep the gun," she suggested as he hung his gun belt in his locker. "You might need to defend yourself against all those dangerous little desperados."

"Don't laugh, sweetheart. Santa hasn't gotten you a gift yet."

"This can be my gift—seeing Nathan Bishop play Santa Claus and enjoy it." She watched him hang up his shirt and unzip his trousers, and her smile faltered. "Or maybe *this* is my gift."

He stripped down to his boxers, then stepped into the baggy red trousers. They were cut extra large and came with their own padding and a pair of suspenders. Next he pulled on the shiny black boots, then Emilie helped him into the coat. Like the pants, it was heavily padded, enough so that some officers didn't need additional bulk when they wore it. He would need pillows, though, or risk being the scrawniest Santa Bethlehem had seen.

Emilie inserted pillows all around, contoured to give him a jolly fat look. By the time he buttoned up and she fastened the wide leather belt around his middle, he was already uncomfortably warm. By the time the beard and brows were fixed in place, he was sweating.

She plopped the red stocking cap on his head, and the white pompom fell in his face. He shoved it back, then pulled on big black gloves while she arranged the thick white curls. "Now I know why Santa's cheeks are always red in pictures. The poor guy's dying of heat stroke."

"You look great."

He turned to check his reflection in the mirror over the sinks. He looked different, that was for sure. Sitting on the bench, he wriggled to get comfortable, spread his legs apart, then leered at her and patted one thigh. "Come sit on Santa's lap, little girl, and show me how very good you are."

"Nathan!" She sounded half-amused, half-scandalized. "That's blasphemous."

"Irreverent, maybe. Come on, give it a try. I'm new at this, remember? I don't want to dump some poor kid on the floor."

She primly balanced on his leg. "You don't even look like you."

"I should hope not."

"The kids will love you."

"I'd be happier if you loved me." The instant the words were out, he wished he could recall them. The light dimmed in her eyes, and he could feel the tension streaking through her even through his layers of padding.

Her gaze darting away, she got to her feet and put some distance between them, keeping her back to him.

"I think you're ready to go. The kids are waiting."

He followed her, pulling off one glove so he could touch her face. "Forget I said that, okay? I didn't mean—It was the suit talking. Forget it, okay?"

Her smile was quavery and her eyes bright. "So be happy," she said, then started toward the door. "And go make the kids happy."

He stared after her. It would make me happier if you loved me, he'd said. *So be happy.* Was she saying . . . No. She would never bring a declaration of love into their relationship, not when she was resistant to staying, not when she also seemed resistant to his leaving with her. No, there'd been no deeper meaning in her words. They'd just been a meaningless admonition. Be happy. Smile. Have a nice day.

Emilie led the way up the stairs, well aware of Nathan's scowl. Bless his heart, he really didn't want to do this. It made her love him a little more that he was willing to go through with it anyway.

Mitch was waiting on the landing with a big black bag filled with small gifts. He helped Nathan sling it over his well-padded shoulder.

After giving him a kiss, she went upstairs and found a place against the wall to watch. As a booming ho-ho-ho echoed through the stairwell, she took Brendan from

Agatha and directed his wide-eyed attention toward the stairs.

"That's Mitch," Shelly murmured as a shout of Merry Christmas reverberated. "I guess Nathan hasn't had much practice."

There were shouts and shrieks from the kids as Santa came into the room. He was mobbed before he'd gone more than a dozen feet by the bolder children, including Josie. Emilie watched with bittersweet pleasure as he worked his way to the thronelike chair set up in front of the windows. He engaged in good-natured banter with some adults who knew he was a reluctant St. Nick and answered the questions shouted by kids about sleighs, reindeer, and elves before he settled in, the bag at his side, and got ready for the steady stream of kids on his lap.

"He's a good sport," Shelley remarked. "I certainly wouldn't want to be Santa Claus."

"I was Santa's helper a couple of times when I was dating Paul Ivey," Holly said as she joined them. For Emilie's benefit, she explained, "Paul used to be the assistant police chief. He got a job with the Buffalo PD a few years ago."

"When Holly refused to get serious with him."

"How could I get serious about spending the rest of my life as Holly Ivey? Anyway, I couldn't believe the way those sweet little darlings behaved. One of them kicked me when I told him his time with Santa was up, and one of them pinched my bottom."

"Reverend Howard's son," Shelley said with a knowing nod. "He nailed me a couple of times, too, when I was Mitch's helper."

Talk turned to shopping, causing Emilie to sigh. In exchange for working the weekend, she would have Monday and Tuesday off, and she intended to do her shopping then. Fortunately, Nathan had gotten the kids their real gifts, so they wouldn't be disappointed if she spent all her money on necessities like clothing and shoes. But at least she could indulge in one small splurge: Santa gifts. Even though Alanna was too old to believe, even though Brendan was too young, all three of the children would have a gift from Santa waiting when they went downstairs on Christmas morning.

A nudge from Holly drew her attention across the room. Josie was sitting on Nathan's knee and talking earnestly, using her face, hands, and entire body. What did she have to say that was so serious? Surely not a list of toys she wanted. All she'd asked for before was a game, and she hadn't shown any signs of increased greed since then.

Finally the conversation ended. Josie smiled for the photographer from the *Bethlehem Courier*, who was providing snapshots for all the kids, then gave Nathan a kiss before jumping to the floor and running off.

Shelly leaned over and chucked Brendan under the chin. "Honey, don't you want to see Santa Claus?"

Though he hid most of his face, he kept one eye open and watching. "Nope."

"Do you think he's kind of scary?"

"Stranger. Doan talk to strangers."

"My parents tried to teach me that, but it didn't take." Holly grinned. "What if your mother went with you, Brendan? She could sit on Santa's lap—where she's no doubt been before—and you could sit on her lap."

"Holly!" Shelley admonished.

"Hey, we all sat on Santa's lap when we were kids. Didn't you, Emilie?" When she nodded, Holly gave Shelly a chiding look. "Get your mind out of the gutter, Shel."

"Do you want to go closer?" Emilie asked, shifting Brendan to her other hip.

"Nope." But he peeked around the man in front of them to get a better view, and when Alanna came with an offer to take him to the other side of the room—not to see Santa, but to show him off to her friends—he willingly went.

The line of waiting children slowly dwindled, Nathan noted with relief. He was craving something icy and cold when the last kid wished him Merry Christmas, waved, and wandered away. Now all he had to do was make some sort of good-bye, then he could wander away, too, and get out of this leather and fur and breathe again.

He was about to rise from the chair when a small blond boy clutching a raggedy bear slowly approached. Nathan had seen him watching, as if he wanted to come but couldn't bring himself to. Even now, he couldn't make up his mind. For every two steps forward, he took one back. Finally, he was standing directly in front of the chair. He peered intently at Nathan for a long time, then moved a step closer and thrust his bear forward. "Ernest."

Nathan shook hands with the bear. "Hello, Ernest. It's very nice to meet you."

Brendan quickly reclaimed him. "Ernest don't talk."

*Ernest's owner don't talk much, either,* Nathan thought. "What's your name?"

"Brendan."

"Do you want to sit on Santa's lap, Brendan?"

He gave a long, slow shake of his head.

"Have you been a good boy this year?" This time he got a vigorous nod in response. "What do you want Santa to bring you for Christmas?"

Brendan took a look around. Emilie was against the far wall, talking with Holly and Shelly. Josie had taken off with her friends again, and Alanna, waiting nearby, was occupied with her own friends. Assured that they had some level of privacy, Brendan took a step forward, then another. Finally, he raised his arms, and Nathan lifted him onto his knee.

"What is it you want?"

Brendan cupped his hand to his mouth, and Nathan leaned close so the boy could whisper in his ear. "I want to see my mama."

"Your mama's right over there, see?" He pointed to Emilie, but Brendan shook his head.

"That's my aunt Emilie, but I'm not supposed to tell." His voice quavering, he repeated, "I want to see my real mama. Please."

Nathan's discomfort was forgotten as a chill snaked down his spine. He reminded himself that Brendan was just a little kid, that little kids had fanciful imaginations and made mistakes and sometimes just plain lied. But Brendan's expression was as totally serious as anything he'd ever seen, and the sadness in his blue eyes was too real to be a lie.

"Where is your mama, Brendan?"

"In Boston. With sick people."

"A hospital?"

He nodded solemnly.

"How long has she been there?"

The boy shrugged.

"What's her name?"

"Berry." He turned the second r into a w, but Nathan understood. He'd heard the name before. It was Berry who'd told Brendan that he was a careless baby who made dumb messes. Berry who sometimes kept him while Emilie was working. Berry who had trouble dealing with a three-year-old who acted like a three-year-old. Berry whom Nathan had already decided he didn't like.

And she was Brendan's mother And the girls', too?

"What's her last name?"

"Dalton," he whispered. "Can you find her, Santa? Can you take me to her? Please?"

"I'll see what I can do."

For the first time, Brendan looked relieved. He accepted the gift Nathan pressed into his hands, slid down, and started to run away. A few yards away, he turned back, grinned, and waved Ernest's paw.

Nathan didn't bother with a farewell. He left the chair, crossed the room with long strides, and took the stairs two at a time. By the time he reached the police department, he'd yanked the hat and curls off. The beard came off with a jerk, taking patches of his skin with it, and the eyebrows took a fair amount of his own with them, as Mitch had warned.

The jacket landed on one desk, the pillows on another, as he pulled out the chair and sat down in front of the computer. He was one of only a handful in the department able to access the FBI's National Crime Information Center. Sadie, who had relieved the other dispatcher so she could have her time at the party, was one of the others.

"Nathan, what's wrong?" She left the dispatcher's shack and came to stand beside him.

He typed in a request for driver's license information on Berry Dalton. His hands were trembling so badly that he misspelled the name three times. Since he didn't know her birthdate, he typed in a string of nines, hit the enter button hard enough to make it echo, and waited impatiently.

"Nathan?"

The response took twenty, maybe twenty-five seconds. Using the biographical data, he ran a criminal history and got it back even quicker.

"Who is Berry Dalton? A relative of Emilie's?"

"Her sister."

"Sister? Well, my heavens, I never knew she had a sister. Miriam only ever mentioned the one niece . . . but with a record like that, maybe she was ashamed of the other. Good heavens, all those drug charges. And Emilie's such a nice girl. You just never know."

A nice girl who had lied ever since she'd come here, he thought, forcing all emotion into his scowl in an effort to ease the tightness in his chest.

He was reading the details of Berry Dalton's latest conviction—five years confinement, five years probation, with the sentence deferred pending successful completion of inpatient substance abuse and psychiatric treatment—when Mitch came into the room. "You did fine, son, up until the minute you bolted from the room without so much as a good— . . . What's wrong? Who's Berry Dalton?"

Sadie answered in hushed tones as Nathan gave the command to print a copy of Berry's record, then typed in one more name. When he pressed enter to send the request, he closed his eyes and focused his entire soul on silent prayers that the response come back not on file. In those few seconds he prayed harder and more desperately than he ever had in his life, but it was all for nothing.

"Oh, dear Lord," Sadie whispered at the same time Mitch swore.

Feeling sick and afraid, he opened his eyes and read the computer's response. Emilie Marie Dalton was wanted in Boston on charges of felony contempt and three counts of kidnapping.

*Kidnapping.* Brendan didn't have a fanciful imagination. He hadn't made a mistake or just plain lied. Emilie wasn't his mother. She had kidnapped him and his sisters and fled the state. *She* was the liar. The woman he loved.

The woman he didn't know at all.

As the party began breaking up, Emilie left Josie and Brendan in Alanna's care and went downstairs looking for Nathan. She saw him as soon as she walked through the police-department door, sitting at one of the computers. The woman beside him touched his shoulder, and he looked up. Emilie's smile was ready, but it disappeared immediately when she saw his face.

He knew. Somehow he had uncovered the truth, and he knew about her lies, about the kids, about her crimes. Some small part of her was relieved. She'd hated the lies with a vengeance and was grateful to be free of them. The larger part, though, was heartbroken. All her fears would come to pass now. She would lose the kids and Nathan and the friends she'd made in this town. She had failed Berry, and, worse, she had failed the children. They would be taken from her now, separated and sent to foster homes. When Berry got out of the hospital, she would go back to the men, the booze, and the drugs, as she always did, and the state would refuse to return the children. And when *she* got out of prison, they would never give them to her, either. She had lost her family, and they would lose each other, because she had failed.

She stopped in front of the desk, glancing at the woman, who looked sympathetic, at Mitch, who couldn't meet her gaze, and finally at Nathan, who couldn't look away. In T-shirt, suspenders, and baggy Santa trousers, he looked shocked and hurt. She hated that she'd hurt him, hated that there was no excuse for what she'd done except the one he'd probably already guessed—the children—and that wasn't enough.

Moment after moment he stared at her. Soon the surprise would pass, and the anger would come, then the hatred. She could bear almost anything except knowing that he hated her.

Except losing the kids.

Except destroying their futures.

It was his boss who broke the silence, his voice startling Nathan even though it was pitched low and grim. "You know there's a warrant for your arrest."

She nodded.

"We have to take you into custody." He glanced at Nathan as if to ask him to do it, thought better of it, and extended his hand to her. "Come this way."

She took a step or two, then faced Nathan again. "I'm sorry."

His gaze dropped to the computer screen, and the muscles in his jaw clenched tighter.

"I never meant . . ." His eyes turned cold, and she broke off. There were no words powerful or precise enough to make him understand, no words at all to make him forgive. Swallowing over the lump in her throat, she followed Mitch into a room where the sign said Booking. There he read her her rights as he began the fingerprinting process.

"What about the kids?"

"We'll have to place them with someone until we find out what Boston wants to do. I'll ask Miss Agatha and Miss Corinna since the kids already know them. They're your sister's kids?"

She nodded.

"You don't have to talk to me without a lawyer present."

"I don't mind." What did she care about a lawyer? The best lawyer in the country couldn't get her out of this mess. He couldn't make Nathan forgive her. He couldn't help her forgive herself.

"Didn't you try to get legal custody of the kids while your sister's in treatment?"

"I had it. When I lost my job and got evicted, they revoked it."

"And so you brought the kids to your place here."

She closed her eyes. God help her, they didn't yet know the extent of her lies. They didn't know that she'd stolen the house, that she'd never heard of their dear friend Miriam Pierce. "I was taking them to Georgia. That's where I'm from."

"But why not—You're not Miriam's niece, are you?"

She shook her head.

"How did you pick her house? Did you drive around until you found one that looked empty?"

Numbly she told him about their first night in Bethlehem—about the waitress and getting lost, finding herself in front of the house, and finding the key. She didn't offer any apologies or excuses, didn't use any kinder words. Stole, lied, deceived, took advantage of. Blunt and unforgiving words.

"I need your jewelry and your handbag. Are you wearing a belt? Do your shoes lace?"

She shook her head. Her purse already lay on the counter. She removed her earrings and watch and laid them down.

"These are felony charges, Emilie. You'll have to go before a judge for a bond hearing. As soon as I get you settled, I'll go upstairs and see if I can catch one of them before they leave the party."

"They're gone. Practically everyone's gone."

"I don't know if I can get anyone to come back in this late on a Friday. If I can't . . ." He looked uncomfortable. "You'll have to spend the weekend in jail."

She tried to blink away the tears forming. "Would you let Holly know that I can't come to work tomorrow so she can find someone else? And can you give the house key to Miss Agatha so the kids can get whatever they need?" At his nod, she removed the brass key from her purse. He pocketed it, then gestured toward the door behind her. Suddenly shivering, she hugged her arms to her chest and walked with him down a flight of stairs to the basement jail.

He accompanied her to the corner cell, unrolled the mattress on the steel cot, then reached for her hand. Her fingers were so cold that she could barely feel his touch. "We'll do whatever we can, Emilie."

What they could do, she thought as he closed the door with a forbidding clang, was simple enough. They could hold her here until Monday morning, when the judge would set bail that she couldn't pay, and then they could turn her over to the authorities in Boston, who would send her to prison.

A month ago the idea of prison had terrified her. Right this moment it didn't seem so bad. No matter what happened, she had already lost the kids and Nathan. The loss of her freedom couldn't possibly compare.

Upstairs, Nathan still sat at the computer, staring blindly at the screen. Some small part of his mind registered Mitch's reappearance and knew that meant Emilie had been processed and was in a cell downstairs. The larger part, though, refused to acknowledge that fact or anything else.

Mitch stopped beside the desk. "I'm going to see if there's a judge upstairs who'd be willing to have a bond hearing now."

Nathan didn't respond.

"I'm also going to ask the sisters if they'll take temporary custody of the kids. Damn, maybe I'm not the one who should tell the kids that we've got their mother—their aunt—locked up downstairs. Do you want to talk to them? They like you."

Like? Not for long. As soon as they knew he'd played a part in Emilie's arrest—God, those two words sounded so wrong together! Emilie wasn't the sort of woman who broke the law and got arrested. She was a good person, a good mother—No, she wasn't a mother at all. She was a good liar, better than any he'd ever seen. He'd thought Diana was the best, but even she could take some lessons from Emilie.

When the kids knew that Emilie was in jail and he couldn't—wouldn't—do anything to get her out, they wouldn't like him anymore. And he couldn't help. She was a criminal. She had admitted as much. She had committed the crime, and now she had to accept the punishment.

"Nathan?"

He glanced at Mitch.

"Want to come upstairs with me?"

He didn't. He didn't want to move, didn't want to do anything that might start his body functioning again and his heart beating. He wanted to stay right here, shocked, numbed, and holding himself carefully together, until he thought there was a chance he might survive this. But he did move—rolled his chair back, rose stiffly to his feet.

"You can't go around the kids like that." Mitch gestured toward the red trousers. "Go in the locker room and change, then meet me up there."

In the privacy of the locker room, he undressed by rote, pulled on his green uniform trousers, khaki shirt, and green tie. He woodenly climbed the stairs and found Mitch talking to Judge McKechnie's secretary. Looking unhappy, he joined Nathan. "McKechnie and Barber have gone to Buffalo with their wives on a shopping expedition, and Judge Fowler is on his way to visit his grandchildren in Holyoke. By the way . . ." He lowered his voice. "We may have additional charges against her. Breaking and entering and unlawful habitation of a dwelling."

"What do you mean?"

"She's not Miriam Pierce's niece. She doesn't own that house."

That startled Nathan. "Yes, she does. I checked. I went by Art Blocker's office the Monday after she came. It was her name on the papers." That was the one thing she hadn't lied about—the only thing, it seemed.

"There must be some mistake. She told me herself."

"I checked, Mitch. I *saw* the records. She was listed as the owner." He walked the fifty feet to the tax assessor's office, found the door locked, and summoned one of the janitors cleaning up after the party. When the man found the proper key, Nathan went inside, circled the counter, and thumbed through the wooden card file, pulling out the three-by-five-inch card with the same sort of flourish the clerk had used. Then he went still.

It was the same card he'd seen before, with the same smudge on the right-hand corner, the same typo in Herbert Thomas's name, exactly the same information for the owner, including the street address in Boston. But the space for the owner's name was different. It didn't read Emilie Dalton, but Sirena Grayson. He stared so hard that the words blurred. There was no way one name could be mistaken for the other, no way the card had been tampered with, no way it ever could have possibly shown Emilie's name.

But the clerk had read it aloud and then shown it to him. He'd *seen* it.

"Let me make a note of the real owner's name. We'll have to contact her and see if she wants to bring charges against Emilie." Mitch pulled, and the card slid from Nathan's fingers. Once he'd copied the information, Nathan returned it to its proper place in the files.

"We've got to talk to the sisters."

He didn't want to be a part of this. He just wanted to go home and somehow make it all go away. He wanted to wake up and find that none of it had happened, that it'd been a dream and nothing more. But it wasn't a dream. It was a living, breathing nightmare, and he was right in the middle of it.

The kids were playing on the other side of the room when he and Mitch approached the sisters, Shelley, and Holly. Nathan watched the kids, blissfully unaware that anything was wrong, while Mitch quietly explained the facts. There were gasps of surprise and expressions of disbelief, then Corinna turned toward him. "Nathan, you have to do something."

"I can't."

"Of course you can. Why, that girl's no criminal."

"The state of Massachusetts disagrees with you."

Agatha harrumphed. "*If* she did anything wrong, it was for the best of reasons."

She'd done it for the kids, trying to save them from the same fate that had caused her—and apparently Berry—such heartache, but the best reasons in the world didn't negate the illegality of her actions. They didn't make up for her deception, for all her lies.

"You know that girl, Nathan. Merciful heavens, you're in love with her. You know she doesn't have a crooked bone in her body. You know she must have been desperate."

"And desperate people do desperate things," Mitch said, drawing their attention. "Holly, she asked me to tell you that she won't be able to work this weekend. Miss Agatha, Miss Corinna, we'd like you to take custody of the children until the court decides what to do."

"What *will* they do?" Shelley asked.

"The judge will hold a bond hearing Monday. If she can make bail, she'll be released pending extradition in Boston, where she'll stand trial. If she makes bail, she'll need a place to stay. She won't be able to go back to the Pierce house."

"Of course she'll stay with us," Agatha decided.

"Not if you have the children. She may get permission for supervised visits, but she won't be allowed to live with them."

Nathan felt the weight of four feminine gazes. They all expected him to offer his house, to insist that, of course, she would live with him. Two hours ago the only way the idea could have pleased him more was if they were married first. Right this minute, he couldn't bear the thought of being around her, of living with her and loving her and knowing she'd deceived him. If the heartache didn't kill him, this awful sense of betrayal would.

"She can stay at the inn," Holly said, giving him a disapproving stare.

An explosion of giggles drew everyone's gazes across the room. The kids were involved in a free-for-all on the floor, Josie and Brendan teaming up against Alanna and Ernest. "What are we going to tell those babies?" Agatha asked sadly.

"Try the truth." The bitterness that was burning a hole in Nathan's gut was echoed in his voice. "Of course, considering that their entire lives are nothing but lies, it might take them a while to understand what truth is."

"Nathan—"

Shaking off Corinna's hand, he started toward the stairs. From across the room came Josie's voice. "Hey, Mr. Nathan, guess what—Wait, Mr. Nathan, I want to show you—What's wrong? Why wouldn't he hear me?"

Downstairs he got his gun belt and coat from the locker room, then left the building. The last thing he saw as he pulled out of the parking lot was Josie's face, pressed to the second-floor window, watching him go.

# Chapter Thirteen

Emilie assumed it was morning when she awakened after a restless night's sleep, but the lack of windows and lights that hadn't gone off all night made it impossible to tell. She also assumed there were other prisoners in the jail, but if so, they were isolated elsewhere. She was more alone than she'd ever been in her life.

She wondered how the kids had taken the news. She and Berry had passed on their fear of the foster-care system, so the girls, Alanna especially, couldn't help but be afraid of what was going to happen. At least they had a little time with the sisters first. Maybe Agatha and Corinna could prepare them.

She wished someone could prepare *her*. Even though her worst fears had already been set in motion, she wished someone could assure her that everything would be all right, wished she could pretend to believe it.

Footsteps sounded down the corridor, punctuating the sound of her name. It was the same jailer who'd brought her dinner last night, a grandfatherly gentleman with kind eyes and a gentle manner. "Emilie, your attorney's here to see you. He's waiting in the conference room."

She couldn't imagine anyone who now knew the truth going to the trouble to find a lawyer for her. Maybe Mitch Walker had contacted whoever usually represented indigent clients on her behalf. However she'd gotten him, she wished he could work a little magic and get her out of here, but there wasn't enough magic in heaven or on earth to get her out of this.

She followed his directions down the hall to a small room on the right. There was just enough space for two chairs and a table that held a briefcase and breakfast. Standing on one side of the table was Alexander Thomas, who offered a smile and gestured toward the chair on the other side. "I thought you might appreciate breakfast from Harry's Diner. I understand the food here isn't the best."

There were biscuits and steaming gravy, slices of bacon and scrambled eggs, pancakes with butter and maple syrup, and a foam cup of coffee. It was enough to feed two—or just one who had been too heartsick last night to do more than pick at her dinner. She indulged in a few bites before looking at him. "I can't afford a lawyer, Mr. Thomas."

"Don't worry about it."

As if that were even possible, when she'd spent the last year of her life worrying about nothing but money—and the children. "I know it's expensive—"

"There's no expense, Emilie. My fee is taken care of." He sat down opposite her. "How are you?"

She ignored his question and went to the remark that preceded it. "By whom? Who asked you to come here? Who asked you to help me?"

After gazing at her a moment, he relented. "Miss Agatha and Miss Corinna."

"They're paying?"

He was silent for another moment, then, with a faint flush coloring his face, he reluctantly said, "No. Business is slow around Christmas. I have some spare time. And it's the end of a good year. I need all the deductions I can get."

He was offering to represent her for free. He could call it keeping busy or a good tax move, but the simple fact was he was helping her out of the kindness of his heart. When she could swallow over the lump in her throat, she murmured, "Thank you, Mr. Thomas."

"Call me Alex." His smile was gentle. "Any other questions before we get started?"

"One. Isn't this a conflict of interest? You represent the woman whose house I took. She may want to bring charges against me."

"My uncle represents the Pierce estate, not me. We're not in partnership. He's retired, except for the few old clients he still handles. I occasionally run errands for him, such as my visit to your house—to the Pierce house—but my practice is completely independent of his. By the way, Uncle Herb has spoken to Sirena Grayson, Miriam Pierce's niece. On his recommendation, she's declining to bring charges against you for the unauthorized use of her property."

Any charges the rightful owner of the house might bring against her were the least of her worries, but Emilie was no less grateful for the woman's generosity. "Tell your uncle I appreciate his help and ask him to tell Ms. Grayson that I'll repay her as soon as I can."

"I will. Now . . . how are you?"

"Okay. How are the kids?"

"They're scared, but the Winchesters are taking good care of them." From the briefcase he removed a legal pad, a pen, and a small recorder. "Before we get started, let me tell you what's going on. The authorities in Boston have been notified that you're in custody. Monday you'll be arraigned. That's a formal reading of the charges, and you'll be asked to enter a plea. It'll be not guilty, of course. Following that will be the bond hearing, then a hearing to grant temporary custody of the children to the Winchesters. At that time, we'll ask the judge to agree to visitation. It'll be supervised, of course, but, with Christmas less than a week away, the terms should be generous. When you return to Boston, a preliminary hearing will be scheduled, and the court there will appoint an attorney to represent you. The children will eventually be returned to Boston, also, and the care of Social Services."

And they would go into foster care, and she would go to prison. Of course he didn't say so, but it was a foregone conclusion.

"Now I'd like to ask you one question, and I want you to answer it as completely and thoroughly as you can. Why did you kidnap your sister's children?"

She talked while she ate, and she took him at his word, going all the way back to her mother and father and moving forward through every foster home until finally she'd turned eighteen and had been on her own and free to locate her sister. She talked through threatening tears, talked until she couldn't think of anything else to say. Finally she finished and sat quietly. The dishes in front of her were mostly empty, her stomach was full, and her heart was as empty of hope as it'd ever been. Alexander Thomas was probably a fine lawyer, and he was certainly a generous one, but he couldn't help her. No one could.

"What kind of sentence am I facing?"

He didn't meet her gaze but shuffled pages on his pad instead. "It varies from state to state. I'm not sure what Massachusetts's sentencing guidelines are for kidnapping."

"But you have some idea."

At last he did look at her. "Let's just say that, if you're

convicted, even Brendan won't need a guardian by the time you're paroled."

If she'd had food in her mouth, she would have choked. Somehow she had convinced herself that a prison sentence wouldn't run more than a few years—five, maybe six or seven. She had never imagined . . .

"Once bond has been paid—"

She interrupted. "I don't have the money for bail."

"It's not a problem."

"What do you mean?"

"You've got friends in town, Emilie. They'll want to help."

She knew he was wrong. Everyone who had thought she was a friend knew now how she had lied to them, how she had taken advantage of their kind natures and betrayed their trust. It was one thing to ask their local lawyer to handle her case; no one was out any money except him, and he could use the tax break. But it was another entirely to risk the kind of money bail required, especially on a liar, a kidnapper, and a thief.

"Once bond has been paid," he continued, "the D.A. in Boston will let us know when they want you to appear there. Ordinarily, they allow adequate travel time and no more, but we'll appeal to their holiday spirit and see what we can get. If they allow a few days, we'll petition the court for custody of the kids until you return to Boston. Maybe, for Christmas, they'll allow it."

"Christmas." She hid her face with both hands. "I should have taken the money I got for the car and hitch-hiked with the kids to Georgia. But I didn't want to arrive in Atlanta flat broke, and I wanted the kids to have just one real Christmas. They've never had one before, not with a tree and presents. They'd never seen a parade or taken part in a pageant or sat on Santa's lap, and I thought just once . . ."

Now *their* tree was off-limits in Miriam Pierce's house, and their only presents were from Nathan, who wished he'd never met her and then wouldn't have met them, either. Now they were once again homeless and, soon after the holidays, they would be family-less. So much for their one real Christmas.

He stopped the tape and returned everything to the briefcase as she gathered the dishes. Rising from her chair, she started toward the door, then stopped. "Why are you doing this?" As he started to speak, she raised her hand. "It's not just a slack time at work or a year-end tax break. Why are you *really* doing this?"

"Do you know how many kids are neglected, abused, or abandoned by their parents? And yet you've been willing to sacrifice anything, even your freedom, for kids that aren't even yours. People like you are hard to find, Emilie, and they don't belong in prison. I'd like to do whatever I can to help you."

"Thank you," she whispered, her throat tight.

"One last thing, Emilie. When you go to trial in

Boston, you'll need character witnesses. I thought I'd put together a list of people here in town for your attorney there. Who would you suggest?"

She thought about the people she knew best—Nathan, Agatha and Corinna, Holly, and Shelley—and bleakly shook her head. "I don't know anyone who would say anything good right now about my character."

He gave her a puzzled look, then shrugged. "I'll take care of it. I know it's tough advice to follow, but don't worry, Emilie. We'll get through this together. Everything will be fine."

Only a few blocks away, Alanna wiped her hands on a kitchen towel, then announced, "I'll be right back."

Sitting on a barstool next to her, Josie grabbed her sleeve. "Where are you going?" She'd been doing that since yesterday evening, when Miss Corinna and Miss Agatha had told them about Emilie. Alanna knew Josie was just afraid, but it still made her cranky.

"I'm going to the bathroom, okay?"

With a nod, Josie let go, and Alanna left the kitchen. In the living room, she listened for a moment to the sounds of Saturday morning baking as usual in the kitchen, then tiptoed to the door. She pulled on her coat and slipped outside, jumped down the steps, and hit the sidewalk at a run. With luck she could be across the street and back before anyone noticed how long she'd been gone.

With luck, things would be looking better before she got back.

She rang the doorbell on the blue house, waited a minute, then rang it again. She was about to press it a third time when the door opened and Nathan glared at her. "What do you want, Alanna?"

For a moment she was frightened. He looked mean and not at all happy to see her. Then, touching her star necklace, she took a deep breath. "I want you to help Aunt Emilie."

He closed his eyes and looked like he was hurting, then looked at her again and shook his head. "I can't."

"Of course you can. You're a policeman. You can call the judge in Boston. You can tell him that she's got a job and we've got a place to live and that she's taking real good care of us, better than our real mother ever did. You can tell him that you'll help her, and he'll know it's okay because you're a cop, and he'll leave her alone. Please . . ."

"She committed a crime, Alanna. The judge isn't going to forget about it just because I tell him so."

"She just wanted to protect us because she loves us. Haven't you ever wanted to protect anyone? Don't you want to protect her?" Her voice shook, and tears made it hard to see him. "Don't you love her?"

His voice sounded funny, too. "I don't even know her."

"Of course you do. Whether she's really our mama or not, she's still just Emilie. You know her well enough to want to marry her—or was that a lie?"

"It was a mistake. It was all a mistake."

For a moment she stood still, then she took a step back, hurting inside the way she always did when her mother yelled mean things at her. "But . . . I thought you liked Emilie. I thought you liked us. I thought you wanted us to be a family."

"I do like you, Alanna. I like you guys more than you know." He breathed heavily. "But we can't be a family, and I can't help Emilie. I'm sorry."

She stared at him, too hurt and mad to cry. "I was wrong about you. You're no better than those men who always treated my mama so bad. You're right. We *can't* be a family. We don't need you or want you." She gave the chain around her neck a jerk, breaking it in back, then slapped it into his hand. Immediately she wished she hadn't. That was her lucky star, and, maybe it could have helped them get through this.

Nathan stared at the star in his hand as she ran away. If he hadn't been half-dead inside, he would have been hurt by her words and her actions. But he'd gotten no more than he'd deserved. She had come to him for help, and he'd given her nothing. He had nothing to give anyone.

He watched until she went into the Winchester house, then closed the door and returned to the recliner in the living room. He had spent the night in the chair, dozing fitfully, alternating between sorrow and red-hot anger—with Emilie for deceiving him and with himself for being a fool. He should have known better. Hadn't Diana taught him that he had lousy taste in women? The more he loved them, the less he could trust them.

He had loved—oh, hell, still loved Emilie most of all. He just couldn't ever trust her again.

There had been so many little signs, if he had only known what he was looking at. Her panic that first morning at discovering that they were snowed in. Her reluctance to accept his help. Alanna's overreaction in the grocery store when she'd called Emilie by her name. Her refusal to talk much about the kids' father. Her insistence that they couldn't stay here in Bethlehem, no matter what. The absence of any sign on her body that she'd given birth to three babies.

He'd been an idiot—a lovesick fool of an idiot. He was still sick to know that everything between them had been lies. Sick that he'd fallen so easily and so hard for a woman who could betray his trust the way she had. Sick that he had fallen in love with them all and now he had lost them all.

Wearily he got up from the chair, intending only to go upstairs and stretch out in bed for some badly needed rest. Instead, he passed the stairs, took his coat from the closet, and went out to the truck. He drove downtown without considering the wisdom of what he was going to do, walked past the desk sergeant and through Booking, and grimly, numbly descended the stairs to the jail.

She was the only one in the women's cells. She sat on the bunk, knees drawn up, face hidden, hands clasped over her ankles. He ignored the despair that seeing her caused and walked right up to the bars. "Emilie."

She hadn't been moving before, but somehow now she seemed even more still. After a lifetime, she raised her head, dropped her feet to the floor, and folded her hands in her lap. "Nathan."

On the way down here, the trip had seemed important. He couldn't have stopped himself for anything. Now that he was here, though, he had nothing to say. No questions to ask, no vows to offer, no apologies to make.

"How are the kids?"

"Their mother's a drug-addicted alcoholic locked up in Massachusetts, and their only other relative in the world is sitting in the local jail awaiting trial on charges that will probably send her away for twenty-five years or more. How do you think they are?"

She flinched, and he felt like a bastard. There was nothing like kicking a woman when she was down.

"How did you find out? Was it Josie?"

Josie had talked nonstop on his lap yesterday at the party about her dearest Christmas wish—to stay in

Bethlehem with their mother and maybe a father, too, if that wasn't too much to ask. From his point of view, it hadn't been too much to ask at all, especially since he'd walked past Willamette Jewelers on his lunch hour and seen a beautiful antique diamond-and-pearl ring that would suit Emilie perfectly.

"No," he said stiffly, forcing his thoughts away from the ring. "It was Brendan. He asked Santa if he could see his mother—not his aunt Emilie but his real mother."

Her smile looked as fragile as glass. "When I realized we would have to lie, he was the one I didn't worry about because he never talked to strangers. I just didn't count on Santa Claus."

He meant to rest his hand on the crossbar, but instead his fingers curled tightly around it. "When did you realize you would have to lie?"

She came to stand off on his left, where he didn't have to look at her if he didn't want to. He didn't. "We were on our way to Atlanta, and we got lost. It had been snowing all day. The kids were tired and hungry. I was tired and hungry. I thought we could get something to eat and find a cheap motel, but Noelle—the waitress at Harry's—said there weren't any motels—just the inn, which we couldn't afford. I was going to find the police station and turn myself in, but I got lost, and suddenly we were in front of the Pierce house. The waitress had told me it was empty, that no one knew the woman who owned it. I got out to look around, to delay giving up the kids, and found the key. I thought we could stay just for one night and no one would know. Then we got snowed in, and the car wouldn't start, and the sisters assumed the house was mine, and you assumed the kids were mine, and . . ." She finished with a helpless shrug. "Things just got out of control."

Obviously *he* was one of those things—or, at least, her affair with him. "After I told you about Diana and Mike, why didn't you stay the hell away from me? Why did you let me trust you when you didn't deserve it?"

"I tried to warn you. I told you I couldn't stay. I told you it could only end badly."

"Why didn't you tell me the truth?"

"Because you would have arrested me. Because protecting your feelings wasn't as important as protecting the children. And because—I needed you. I'd looked all my life for you. I knew it couldn't last, but I thought that maybe, just once, just for a while, I could know what it was like to love someone."

Suddenly angry, he turned away to leave, then swung back. "You never said it before. Why should I believe it now?"

"I said it yesterday. You just didn't hear it."

*I'd be happier if you loved me.*

*So be happy.*

The memory made him scowl. "Everything about you is a lie," he accused, and she shook her head.

"I made a promise to myself that first morning that I wouldn't tell a single lie that wasn't necessary to protect the children. I kept that promise." She moved a step closer and settled her hands on the crossbar, too, but she didn't try to touch him. He was grateful for that—and sorry, too. "I don't expect you to understand, Nathan. Things are different in your world. But I'm sorry I came here. I'm sorry I lied to you and everyone else. I'm sorry I hurt you. But I don't regret what I've done. I made a promise to Berry, the kids, and myself that I would keep the family together, and I would do anything on earth— would still do anything—to keep that promise."

"You've broken the law to keep your damn promise. What kind of person does that make you? What kind of example does that set for the kids?"

"It teaches them that family is important."

"It teaches them disrespect for the law. It teaches them that, if they want something and the law says they can't have it because it's not theirs, well, hell, take it anyway, then run away and hide and pray to God that they don't get caught."

"What was I supposed to do, Nathan? Just turn the kids over to the foster-care system? They're *my* family, and they belong with me! I was a good mother to them!"

"You made them live like criminals. You made them lie to people who loved them. What would have come next? Cheating? Stealing? No, wait, the stealing came before the lying, when you saw a house you wanted and claimed it for your own."

"It was supposed to be for just one night," she whispered, her voice thick with tears, "and I was going to pay. As soon as we got settled in Atlanta, as soon as I had a little extra money, I was going to send it to the lawyer."

"You can rationalize and justify all you want, Emilie, but it doesn't change the facts. The state was right to take the kids away from you. Keeping them away from you and their mother is probably the best thing anyone could do for them."

The color drained from her face, and for a long time she simply stared at him. Finally, sounding fragile and wounded, she quietly asked, "Feel better now?"

He didn't. He felt ashamed and petty, and the sickness in his soul had deepened. Who was lying now? Even a blind man could see how much she and those kids loved each other. Maybe she couldn't give them much in the way of stability right now, but any fool knew that, with kids, unconditional love counted for a whole lot more than coming home to the same house every day.

Her smile was fleeting, too quavery to last. "I envy you, Nathan. It must be nice to be perfect. But I'm not perfect. I make all kinds of mistakes. Apparently . . ." Her voice got quieter, smaller. "I made a mistake about you."

She turned away then, returning to the cot, wrapping the blanket around her shoulders, and sitting with her back to him. He wanted to call her back, wanted to make her face him, to take back her last words. *He* hadn't done anything wrong. He wasn't the criminal. He wasn't the betrayer.

Footsteps on the stairs made him look that way just as Mitch came around the corner. His boss didn't look happy to see him. "What are you doing, Nathan?"

He glanced back at Emilie, withdrawn and so emotionally distant that he couldn't reach her if he wanted, then pushed past Mitch. "I was just leaving."

Mitch let him go and stopped in front of the cell. "Good morning."

Ignoring the greeting, Emilie sat with her head bowed, her eyes closed, and listened to Nathan's footsteps. With each fainter sound, her energy faded, too, and depression took its place. She didn't blame him for his remarks. If he weren't hurting, he never would have said that the kids were better off without her. But the knowledge did nothing for her own pain.

"You have visitors upstairs."

She wasn't interested enough to ask who. Probably a reporter and photographer from the local paper come to do an article about Bethlehem's latest felony arrest. It wasn't often that a little town like this captured a wanted felon, not often at all that the felon was someone they had welcomed into their midst. "Do I have to see them?"

"No. You don't have to see anyone at all. But I think you'll want to."

She glanced at him. He was a kinder man than she would have given a police chief credit for. There was no disdain in his expression, no scorn or aversion—just sympathy and concern. Too bad Nathan wasn't capable of feeling either one . . . but then, she had betrayed Nathan in ways that Mitch couldn't imagine.

When she finally nodded, Mitch opened the door. "You can wait in the conference room. It's—"

"I know." She went down the hall to the small room as he returned upstairs. She was staring at the back wall when the door was flung open and Josie raced across to hug her.

"Aunt Emilie!" Her niece burst into tears—Josie, who hardly ever cried—and wrapped her arms tightly around Emilie's neck.

"It's okay, baby." She sank to the floor with Josie, and Brendan climbed into her lap while Alanna claimed her other side. They were in tears, too. "Guys, it's all right. Don't cry."

"They're going to send you to prison," Josie wailed, "and we'll have to live with strangers."

"Doan want no strangers. Stay with you." Knotting his fingers tightly in her sweater, Brendan settled contentedly against her as if nothing on earth could move him. It eased the emptiness inside her and, at the same time, broke her heart. How would he fare in a foster home? He truly couldn't imagine not being with Josie and Alanna, couldn't comprehend depending on strangers for everything from food and shelter to middle-of-the-night reassurances. How much harm would losing his family do him?

"Are you okay?" Alanna asked. "Is it awful? Did they feed you?"

"No, honey, it's not awful. We've lived in worse places than this. I'm fine here." She brushed Alanna's hair back and noticed a narrow red mark on her neck. "What happened? Did your necklace break?"

Alanna looked both defiant and ashamed. "I broke it when I gave it back to *him*."

"Why did you do that?"

The defiance vanished, and tears welled again. "Because I thought he was different, and he's not. I asked him to help you, and he said no. He said wanting to marry you and be a family with us was all a mistake. So I told him we don't need him. We can convince the judge ourselves. Once he sees how you've taken such good care of us and I can read better and Brendan is talking more, he'll have to know that you're a good mother, and he'll let us stay together and be a family, just the four of us, and we'll be happy, and we won't miss *him* at all."

*Wanting to marry you* . . . Nathan had never mentioned marriage to her, and it was lucky that he hadn't. She would have wanted it so badly that she might have considered giving it a try, lies and all. She might have gone so far as to make those most solemn of vows on a foundation of untruths and deception, and she would have sentenced herself and the kids to a lifetime of pretending to be who they weren't.

Though her tears had dried, Josie continued to hang on Emilie's neck. "Where is your cell?"

"Down the hall."

"Are there any bad guys around?"

"Just me."

Josie giggled. "You're not a bad guy, Aunt Emilie. You're a good mom. Are there bars?"

"Yes."

"Can I see it?"

"No."

"Is it scary?"

*Yes.* The idea of spending the next twenty years or more in such a confined space was scary as hell. The idea of living that long away from the kids was more than she could bear. "No, darlin', it's not scary at all."

Josie patted Emilie's cheek. "Aunt Emilie?" Her voice was unsteady and sorrowful. "I'm ready to go to Atlanta now."

"Me, too, darlin'." She might never see Atlanta again, and even if she did, it wouldn't matter, not without the kids. "But it won't be so bad going back to Boston. You guys like playing in the snow, don't you, and there's so much to do in Boston."

"But we won't be together," Alanna whispered.

And nothing else mattered if they weren't together. Still, Emilie forged on with cheerier thoughts. "But you'll have new families—a mother *and* a father, and new brothers and sisters. You'll learn to love them, too."

"I'll hate them." Josie's grip tightened uncomfortably. "I'll hate them and the judge and the orange-haired lady. I'll hate everyone but you. And Lannie and Brendan. And Mama. And Miss Agatha and Miss Corinna."

"And Nathan," Emilie prompted.

"No. I'll hate him, too."

Emilie rested her forehead against Josie's. "No, honey, you don't hate him. You're just upset. Everyone's upset."

"Don't worry," Agatha said. "She'll get over it."

Emilie looked past the kids for the first time and saw Agatha and Corinna in the hallway just outside the door. Hot with shame and regret, she eased free of the children, got to her feet, and circled the table to face them. "I'm so sorry."

Corinna came into the room first. "Of course you are, dear. Has Alexander been to see you?"

"Yes. Thank you for calling him. And for taking care of the kids." She shifted, made uncomfortable by her guilt. "I've taken advantage of your kindness ever since we came to town. I owe you so much. I—"

"Just an explanation, Emilie," Agatha said. "That will suffice."

She related yet another version of the story she'd told Mitch, Alexander, and Nathan. When she finished, Corinna gave her a hug. "Don't give up hope, dear. It's Christmas, and you've got friends to help."

"Why would you want to? I lied to you. I'm not Miriam's niece. I don't belong in that house or in this town."

"You're our friend, Emilie, and it's not as if you were trying to profit from your lies. You wanted only to protect your family, and that's a need we can all certainly understand."

"Nathan doesn't," she said glumly, and Agatha patted her arm.

"He's hurt, dear, but he'll get over it. He'll realize that your charade was forced by circumstances beyond your control. He'll come around."

Emilie thought back to his last comment—about keeping her and Berry away from the kids—and gave a sorrowful shake of her head. He was never going to forgive her.

"We have other things to discuss," Corinna said purposefully. "Of course the judge will set bail Monday—"

"Which your friends will take care of," Agatha added.

"Mitch tells us that the judge won't allow you to live in the same house with the children, so they'll remain with us—"

"And you'll be Holly's guest at the inn. Of course, with it being Christmas, you'll be able to visit as often and as long as you want—"

"Actually, the judge will set visitation limits, but there are no rules regarding how often you can visit your dear friends." Corinna smiled modestly. "Of course, you'll attend dinner at our house on Christmas Eve and the midnight service in the square."

"It's not over until late, so you'll probably have to spend the night with us, too, and then we'll have all day Christmas."

Emilie listened to their talk with a growing sense of wonder. They knew the truth about her, and they didn't hate her. They weren't eager to see the last of her. In fact, as far as she could tell, the truth hadn't changed their feelings for her in any way. Maybe her life was falling apart. Maybe her future looked unbearably bleak. But for the first time since she'd walked into the police department yesterday afternoon, she felt the slightest bit of hope, because for the first time in her lifetime, she had friends.

Emilie's arraignment and bond hearing brought a crowd to Judge McKechnie's small courtroom Monday afternoon. When Nathan slipped in the door, he saw a few empty seats beside Mitch and Shelley on the right and Agatha and Corinna on the left, but he didn't claim one. He remained where he was—where he could make a quick escape—and let his gaze skim over Holly,

Harry, and Maeve, and what must be every single person Emilie had met in Bethlehem. He did stop for a moment on the kids, seated on the front row between Agatha and Corinna—Alanna, with her hair brushed smooth and secured with a red plaid bow to match her outfit; Josie beside her, looking a little rumpled, as usual; and Brendan, just a few inches of shaggy blond hair from this vantage point. Clean, neatly dressed, and well behaved, no doubt they were present as a testament to Emilie's mothering abilities.

She *was* a good mother. It wasn't her fault that her bosses in Boston had chosen to run off with the employees' paychecks. It certainly wasn't her fault that her sister's problems prevented her from taking care of her own children. If he'd been in Emilie's situation, after being raised the way she had been, he would have considered the same route.

Considered. Not taken. No matter how understandable her actions, she had committed crimes that couldn't be excused. No matter how desperate her need to preserve her family, her lies were unforgivable.

Considering the level of support she'd received here, not everyone agreed with him. But then, not everyone else's entire future had been tied up in her honesty, her truthfulness, and her trustworthiness. Not everyone else had been in love with a woman who didn't really exist.

Although he didn't want to, finally he looked at his reason for being there. Emilie sat at the defense table next to Alexander Thomas. Her head was bowed, her hair falling forward to hide her face. She must be more than a little afraid to appear before McKechnie. She'd found him intimidating at the party Friday afternoon—but had that been because the judge liked being intimidating, as he'd assumed at the time, or because of the secrets she'd been keeping?

He had too many questions like that and not enough answers.

At precisely one o'clock, McKechnie took the bench. The formal reading of the charges would take place first, then the judge would set bail, the sisters would pay it—the reason, he figured, for bondsman Charlie Parker's presence just behind Agatha—and Emilie would be released. The sisters thought they were taking no risks, but he wouldn't count on her staying. Desperate people did desperate things, Mitch had pointed out, and Emilie was still desperate. She might hate doing it, but if she thought she could make it out of the state with the kids, leaving the sisters to pay the price, Nathan thought she would try.

It was a sure bet that this time she wouldn't head for Georgia. She would go someplace she'd never been, someplace where no one would ever find her. Someplace where *he* could never find her.

After the charges were read, the judge gave Emilie a steely look. "The purpose of this hearing today is to set bond on the charges of kidnapping and criminal contempt of court. On the first count of kidnapping, bond is set at fifty thousand dollars."

Even from the back of the room, Nathan could see her shoulders sag. Was she regretting how much money her friends would lose if she jumped bail or fearful that they weren't *that* generous?

"On the second count of kidnapping, bond is set at fifty thousand dollars." The judge continued with another fifty thousand on the third count, plus fifteen thousand on the contempt charge. One hundred and sixty-five thousand dollars, nearly twenty-five thousand of which the Winchesters would have to come up with for bail. They'd never been taken for fools yet. He hoped it didn't happen now.

"Do you have any objections, Bill?"

The district attorney shook his head. "No, Your Honor."

The judge motioned for an officer to escort Emilie out. As she left, so did Charlie Parker, sliding a check into his pocket as he passed. All he had to do was deliver a certificate of bond to the jailer, and she would be free to go. Nathan intended to be gone before then, but first he wanted to hear the disposition of the next case.

McKechnie opened the next file. "In the matter of custody of Alanna, Josie, and Brendan Dalton . . ."

Instead of leaving the courtroom, Alex Thomas remained at the defense table. "Your Honor, at this time, we would like to petition the court for an interim special custody order of the minor children, until such time as a final determination of their permanent custody can be established."

The DA stood. "The children are currently in the care of Miss Agatha Winchester and Mrs. Corinna Humphries, Your Honor. We would like to leave them there until the authorities in Boston pick them up for return to Massachusetts."

"And when will that be?"

"My office spoke to the caseworker this morning, and she's arriving Wednesday morning with plans to return the children to Boston."

In two days, they would be gone. Nathan would never see them again, just like Elisabeth. How many times was this going to happen? How many people was he going to love, then lose?

No more. He wasn't cut out for this. He couldn't deal with any more sorrow. He couldn't survive any more loss. He didn't care if living without loving was hardly living at all. It was better than this hurt.

The judge nodded toward Thomas. "I'll grant your motion for a hearing. At that time, the DA can present his witnesses. I'll expect you both here Wednesday at one o'clock."

Thomas smiled faintly. "Thank you, Your Honor. We'll also call witnesses to support our request that custody be granted to Emilie Dalton."

"In the meantime," McKechnie continued, "the children will remain where they are. Visitation?"

When he looked from one attorney to the other, it was the DA who answered. "We recommend that Ms. Dalton be allowed supervised visits at the direction of Miss Agatha and Miss Corinna."

The judge gave the sisters a look. "In other words, any time she wants for as long as she wants."

"It is Christmas, Jack," the DA pointed out.

"All right. Anything else?"

Nathan left as quietly as he'd come, snapping up his jacket, heading for the cold outside. He was almost there, almost safe, when the door to the police department opened and Emilie, escorted by Charlie Parker, walked into the lobby. For a long time, she stared at him, and he couldn't help himself. He stared back. She was so damn beautiful, and he wanted her so damn much.

But when she made a move as if to reach out to him, when she started to speak, he stiffened and abruptly walked away. He didn't stop until he reached his patrol unit, didn't let the first bit of tension seep away until he'd completed a slow circuit around the town.

Sometimes he felt so betrayed and angry that he was convinced he hated her. Most of the time, though, he just hurt. At night he dreamed about her—about holding her, making love to her—and he awakened in an empty bed with an ache strong enough to make a man cry. In so short a time she had become the best part of his life. Without her, nothing would ever be right again.

And he was without her. Right now it was his choice. While he had no shortage of pain, he was shamefully lacking in forgiveness. But after her extradition to Boston, they couldn't be together no matter how much they might want. Without some influence on her side, she didn't stand a chance against the charges. She was going to prison for a very long time.

Somehow, that knowledge hurt worse than everything else put together.

Josie lay curled on the window seat, a fat pillow under her head, and stared out at the dark night. It was snowing again, and if there were stars in the sky, she couldn't see them. If she could, she would wish on them, but she wasn't sure anymore that wishes came true. She'd been making wishes and saying prayers since Aunt Emilie got arrested, and no one had been listening. Miss Agatha said God always listened, but maybe that was only to people He knew. Josie had been to church only once, and she'd been more interested in the games they'd played and the treats they'd given out than the lessons they'd taught. If she'd known Aunt Emilie was going to be arrested, she would've been better, honest, but she hadn't known.

Laughter from the kitchen made her look over her shoulder. Everyone was making gingerbread men, putting silly faces on them. She'd done one, but instead of silly, his face had been frowny, like her own. Like Mr. Nathan's.

She missed him and wanted to go across the street to see him, but Lannie said no. She said he wasn't their friend anymore, and Josie had stuck her tongue out and kicked her and said he was, too, their friend, and Lannie had pinched her. She still had a red place on her arm right . . . Well, it was too dark to see it, but it was there. She could feel it.

Mr. Nathan *was* their friend. He was sort of almost like their daddy. He took them places and bought them hot dogs and Christmas presents. They were the only presents they had, except for the ones Santa Claus would bring on Christmas Eve when they were all snuggled in their beds and visions of sugarplums danced in their heads. Josie wasn't sure what a sugarplum was, but she *was* sure they'd be dancing their little toes off on Christmas Eve.

Anyway, Mr. Nathan *was* their friend. He didn't get mad at them, and he picked Lannie up after school every day so she could be in the play, and he made Aunt Emilie laugh. But lately she'd been crying a lot. Not in front of them—she would never do that—but when she'd come to see them this evening, her eyes were shiny red and her nose was sniffly. She was sad because they were going back to Boston, and Josie, Lannie, and Brendan had to go live with strangers. Josie didn't want to go to Boston, and she didn't want to live with strangers. She wanted to stay right here, but if they couldn't do that, she wanted to go to Atlanta. Maybe after everyone else was asleep on Christmas Eve, she would sneak downstairs and wait by the fire for Santa to come, and she would ask him to take them to Atlanta. He could do it, and he probably didn't care that she'd only been to church once in her whole life and hadn't learned anything.

"What are you thinking about, sweetheart?" Aunt Emilie sat down beside her and put her arm around her, rubbing her tummy the way she did when it hurt from eating too much. She hadn't eaten anything tonight but a bowl of stew for dinner and that frowny old gingerbread man's head.

"How will Santa Claus know to come here instead of next door?"

"Santa knows everything."

Josie scrunched up her face. "Did he know we weren't supposed to be there? Is he the one that turned us in?"

Aunt Emilie got that funny look, like she wanted to laugh but shouldn't. "No, darlin'. It wasn't Santa Claus."

"Then who? Who catched us? I didn't tell no one, honest, and Lannie didn't, and Brendan don't talk to no one."

"It just happened. It's no one's fault. You know, when you go back to Boston, I bet you'll get to see your mama. Won't that be nice?"

She nodded. She missed Mama, especially at night when she was in bed. She missed the way Mama smiled when she was having a good day and the silly games she used to play with them and the silly stories she made up for them. She *didn't* miss Mama's bad days, but after all this time in the hospital, maybe she wouldn't have any more bad days.

"Why do we have to go back to Boston? Why can't we just go to Atlanta and Mama can come there?"

"We just can't."

"But why not? You're not in jail. You can go wherever you want. Why don't we get our stuff and go, and no one will find us, and we'll stay together, and we won't have to live with strangers."

"It would be wrong, Josie."

"Why?"

"Because there are laws we have to follow, and the law says I can't take care of you."

"But you're a good mama, and you take good care of us. The law is wrong, not us."

"Maybe, but we have to obey it anyway."

"Why?"

"Because that's the way it is."

"Why?"

Aunt Emilie scooped her up and tickled her before setting her on her lap. "Because."

"That's not an answer."

"It's the only answer I have."

Because she looked sad again, Josie didn't say anything else, but she still thought it was a dumb answer. She would just have to get a better one from Santa Claus on Christmas Eve night.

# Chapter Fourteen

Tuesday evening Nathan sat alone in the silence of his house. The only lamp burning was in a distant corner of the living room, but it cast enough light to illuminate the pile of gifts on the hearth. There were toys, games, puzzles, and books. An art set for Alanna, whose salt-dough Christmas ornaments had shown more creative talent than everyone else's combined, and hand-knitted sweaters and a family gift of a compact stereo because Emilie loved music. He had wrapped them himself, pleased with the shiny foil paper and the bright curling ribbons. For a couple of days last week, he hadn't been able to walk past the room without an idiotic grin.

Now it hurt to look at them.

He'd had such hopes for this Christmas, the first Christmas he'd celebrated since Mike's death. He'd had fun shopping for gifts, decorating the kids' tree, getting into the spirit of the holiday. Some holiday. The season for miracles, once more, had become a season of sorrow.

Unable to face the mountain of gifts one moment longer, he got his coat and headed for the back door. On the way he passed the kitchen table where the message he'd received from the district attorney this morning was crumpled. The pink slip requested his presence in Judge McKechnie's courtroom tomorrow afternoon to testify for the state in the kids' custody hearing. As if everything else wasn't bad enough, now he had to help the state keep the kids away from her. She wouldn't forgive him.

That made them almost even, because he *couldn't* forgive her.

There were a couple of respectable bars in Bethlehem, the sort of places where everyone knew everyone else and no one ever overindulged. He drove past them to the Hillside Lounge on the highway out of town. This was a serious bar, a place to drown your sorrows with no one telling you you'd had enough.

The bar was dimly lit and smoky, as a serious bar should be. He ignored the other customers and went straight to the bar, sliding onto a stool and ordering whiskey. The first went down hard, bitter and stinging.

The bartender filled his glass again, then moved away. Nathan knew him only vaguely. The bar was in the county's jurisdiction, but he had backed a deputy on disturbance calls here a time or two. By the time they'd arrived, the bartender had already restored peace, and all that was left for them to do was pick up the offenders and take them to jail.

Emilie had been in jail. *His* Emilie—sweet, loving, perfect mother, perfect lover, perfect potential wife—in jail. And in a few more weeks, a few months at most, she would be in prison. It would kill him.

He drained his whiskey and signaled for a refill. The bottle was slow in coming, but the advice was not. "Don't you think you should take it easy? This stuff has a kick, you know."

The big, burly guy was gone, and in his place was a woman, a stranger of about fifty. Her brown hair was streaked with gray, her round face soft and lined, her round body thick about the middle. She looked like someone's grandmother, like she should be wearing an apron with ruffles and baking cookies to decorate with the kids, instead of tending the toughest bar in the county. But since she *was* tending the toughest bar in the county, her appearance must be deceiving. Like Emilie's. Who could ever have looked at her and guessed she was facing criminal charges and as much as life in prison back in Massachusetts?

Normally he avoided being rude, but tonight his mood was too bleak to care. "I didn't ask for your opinion. I asked for a refill."

With a shrug, she poured, stopping before the glass

was two-thirds full. "Drinking never eased anyone's pain."

"Maybe not, but passing out helps."

"Only temporarily. When you wake up tomorrow, you'll still have the same problems and a hangover to boot. Much better to deal with what's bothering you head-on and leave the booze out of it."

He glared at her. "Where's the other bartender?"

"Brent's on his dinner break. He left me in charge."

"Does he know you harass the customers when you're in charge?"

She shrugged again. "I'm not harassing you, Nathan. I'm trying to help you." Her use of his name made him scowl, and that made her shake her head. "You're a good cop, Nathan. I thought good cops trusted their instincts. Why don't you?"

"I do. If I didn't. I'd be dead by now."

She shook her head again, and her hair bobbed about her face. In the poor light, the gray took on a diffuse silvery hue. "You're not listening to your instincts regarding Emilie, or you would have accepted by now that she's the one, and nothing she's done will ever change that."

"The one what?"

"*The* one. The one you've been looking for. The one you've been destined to find. The one you're going to love until the day you die."

Her words hurt too much to be lies, but, for his own

protection, he denied them. "My instincts tell me that she's a criminal. That she belongs in prison. That she should never be allowed near those kids again."

The woman's gaze was clear, sharp, as if she could see straight into him. "You don't believe that, Nathan. If you did, you never would have fallen in love with her, and these few days since she was arrested wouldn't have been the worst days of your life—worse, even, than when Mike died."

Her casual mention of his dearest secrets made him stiffen. "She told you about that, didn't she? You're her friend."

"Hers, yours, the kids'. I'm everyone's friend. I look out for everyone."

He swallowed the whiskey and wondered why it was having no effect, why he was as stone-cold sober as when he'd walked through the door, why it hadn't dulled at least the edge of the pain eating him alive. "You look out for everyone, huh? So you're responsible for this mess."

"No. I'm just trying to help clean it up. So . . . what are you going to do about Emilie?"

"There's nothing I can do."

"You can help her get through this."

"No, I can't."

"She needs you, Nathan. She's afraid."

He lifted his glass, realized it was still empty, and pushed it away. Hell, for all the good it was doing him, he might as well be drinking colored water. The only way this stuff was going to ease his sorrows was if he poured it deep enough to drown himself.

"When did you become so hardhearted, Nathan? You used to have compassion for others. You used to see all the shades of gray. What happened?"

When he didn't answer but continued to stare at the wall behind her, she left to wait on another customer. He hoped she would preach to that guy for a while—he probably needed it more than Nathan did—but no such luck. Picking up a damp towel, she wiped her way back down the bar to him.

"Remember the shoplifter? You'd been a cop for three years. The grocery-store manager had caught her stealing, and after she ran out of the store, you caught her. All she'd taken was food and formula for her baby. You gave her money and let her go, and then you went back to the store and paid for what she'd taken. Why did you do that?"

He stared at her. He had never told Emilie that story—had never told anyone. Diana would have complained about the money, and Mike would have thought he was a sucker, falling for a petty thief's sad story. He opened his mouth to ask how she knew, but instead found himself answering her question. "She was in trouble. She just needed a little help. Besides, she wasn't stealing for herself. It was for her baby."

"Emilie was—is—in trouble, too. She wasn't stealing for herself. Everything she did was for the children."

The truth of her argument made him uncomfortable

and edgy. "What am I supposed to do? Turn my back? Cover for her? Protect her while she's breaking the law?" Bitterly he shook his head. "I did that before."

"I know. With Mike."

"And look what happened to him."

"You aren't responsible for his death."

"I gave him an ultimatum, and I didn't stick to it. If I hadn't given him one more chance, if I had gone to the sergeant like I'd said I would, maybe he'd be alive today. Maybe my marriage wouldn't have broken up. Maybe I never would have known that Elisabeth wasn't my daughter. If I hadn't tried to cover for him, maybe I would still have a family and a best friend."

"Mike and Diana made their own choices, Nathan. Diana had to live with the consequences, and Mike had to die with them. Nothing you could have done would have changed that." She filled his glass one last time, then moved the bottle out of reach. "You do have a family, Nathan—Emilie, Alanna, Josie, and Brendan. Maybe they're not a conventional family, but they're a family—*your* family—just the same. They love you, and you love them, but you're going to lose them if you don't do something."

He did love them, and he believed they loved him, too. But that didn't make them a family. They couldn't *be* a family, not after all the lies she'd told. Not after the way she had betrayed them. Not after the way he would betray her tomorrow.

"I can't help her," he said flatly. Miserably.

"Can't? Or won't?"

Ignoring the questions and the disappointment in her too-direct gaze, he stood up and pulled out his wallet. He was as steady on his feet as if he hadn't touched a drop of whiskey. "What do I owe you?"

"You don't owe me a thing, Nathan. Your debt is to Emilie. You say you love her, but where is your faith in her? Your compassion? Your understanding? Your forgiveness? Love is made up of all those things. Without them, it's a pretty sorry gift you're offering."

Scowling, he left some bills on the counter and started toward the door. Halfway there, he turned back. "One last question. How did you know—"

The woman was gone, and the big guy, Brent, was returning from the back with a case of beer. *Must be her turn for a break,* he thought as he pushed the door open. Too bad it hadn't come sooner and saved him from her aggravation.

Then, as he stepped out into the quiet, cold night, he admitted that he was beyond saving. He was in a world of hurt, and nothing could make it stop. Nothing could make it better except Emilie. If she wasn't already lost to him, tomorrow afternoon she would be, and there was nothing he could do about it.

Not a damned thing.

*    *    *

The conference room across the hall from Judge McKechnie's courtroom was small, painted pale green, and decorated with pictures of hunting dogs on the walls. Emilie sat at the table, her hands clasped tightly, and watched the second hand sweep around the clock on the wall. In three minutes she was due in the courtroom, where she would face the social worker from Boston and Nathan, who would testify for the state. Against her.

She didn't stand a chance. Oh, she might gain a few days with the kids, but she'd been notified yesterday that she must appear in Boston at nine A.M. Monday. Since that meant traveling on Sunday, a win today would give her only four days and five nights with the children. That would never be enough.

But it was better than nothing.

After another minute passed, Alexander Thomas got to his feet and gestured toward the door. "It's time, Emilie."

She was slow to rise. He had already explained to her what would take place. The district attorney would call his witnesses—only two, the social worker and Nathan—and then Alex would call their witnesses. The DA had chosen not to sequester the witnesses, so they would be allowed in the courtroom both before and after their own testimony, with the exception of Alanna and Josie. The girls had been deemed too impressionable to listen to the testimony preceding their own, so they waited next door with Alex's wife as company.

Emilie and Alex crossed the hall and went into the crowded courtroom. She tried not to, but her gaze swept the crowd, searching for Nathan. There was no sign of him, but he would show, and he would repeat what he'd told her Saturday—that she'd taught the kids disrespect for the law, that she'd told them it was okay to lie, cheat, and steal, that they were better off without her. He would break her heart again, and this time he would do it under oath, so there would be no reason to doubt whether he meant it.

The social worker was seated in the front row, her orange hair a beacon that drew Emilie's attention. As if she felt Emilie's gaze, the woman turned and watched her walk forward. Her mouth was thin, her face expressionless, her eyes sharp and critical. Was she displeased with this hearing? Probably. But Emilie didn't care as long as it didn't affect how the woman treated the children once she got them back to Boston.

Brendan, sitting with Agatha and Corinna, reached for her when she walked past. Emilie hugged him, then sat down at the defendant's table with Alex. No sooner had she gotten settled than the bailiff commanded everyone to rise for the judge's arrival. With little fanfare, McKechnie directed the DA to begin, and he did so by calling the social worker. He started with background information—her name and occupation, education and experience—before getting down to specifics.

"Ms. Petrie, how did the Dalton children come to your department's attention?"

"Their mother was convicted on drug charges and placed in an inpatient treatment program as part of her sentence. Because the children's fathers are not part of the family, the children became our responsibility."

"And what decision did you make regarding them at that time?"

"It was the mother's request that they be placed in the temporary custody of her sister, Emilie Dalton, who lived with them and desired such custody. Since our goal is to keep families intact wherever possible, we agreed and placed the children with Ms. Dalton."

"But at a later date, the custody agreement was rescinded. Why?"

"Ms. Dalton had lost her job and had been evicted from her home. She was living with the children at a crowded shelter for the homeless. We felt it was in the children's best interests to remove them from her and place them in foster care."

"Was Ms. Dalton informed that you intended to place the children in foster care?"

"Yes."

"What was her response?"

"She pointed out that the next day was Thanksgiving. She asked that the children remain with her through the holiday and promised to surrender them to us the following Monday. I saw no harm in her request, and so I agreed."

"And what did you find when you went to pick up the children the following Monday?"

"They were gone. They had fled the homeless shelter on Thanksgiving morning, less than eighteen hours after she'd made her request and given her promise."

"If the decision were yours, would you return temporary custody of the children to Emilie Dalton today?"

"Let the children remain with her through the holiday and trust her to surrender them on Monday?" She shook her head. "No, I would not."

With a curt nod, the DA sat down, and Alexander stood. "Ms. Petrie, did you do a background investigation of Emilie Dalton before you placed the children in her care?"

"Yes, of course."

"What did you find?"

"That she was employed and had been steadily employed since high school. That she'd never been arrested. That she was responsible, reliable, and dependable."

"So she was a good candidate to become a foster parent."

"There was nothing in her background to indicate otherwise."

"How did you learn that she'd lost her job and been evicted?"

"She notified me."

"Why did she do that?"

"Because, at the time she was granted custody, I instructed her to report any changes in her situation immediately to me."

"Is this a standard instruction which you give all your clients?"

"Yes."

"Do they always obey it?"

"No."

"What sort of things do they fail to report to you?"

"Arrests. Unemployment. Change of address."

"Things that might affect their custody arrangements."

"Yes."

"But Emilie didn't withhold this information. She was forthcoming with it, even though it could adversely affect her custody of the children."

The woman sat in silence for a moment, then shrugged. "No, she didn't withhold it."

"No further questions at this time." Alex sat down next to Emilie. His expression remained even, calm. She couldn't begin to guess how this first piece of testimony had gone.

At the table beside them, the DA was whispering to a young woman—his assistant, Emilie assumed. After a few seconds, she left and he faced the judge. "Your Honor, we have one more witness to call, Officer

Nathan Bishop of the Bethlehem Police Department. Unfortunately, Officer Bishop has been delayed on a call and is unavailable at this time. The dispatcher has instructed him to report to the courtroom as soon as possible."

Before Emilie could wonder what was holding up Nathan, Alex was on his feet again. "We have no objection to continuing with our own witnesses while we wait for Officer Bishop." At the judge's nod, Alex called Agatha to the stand. After a few routine questions, he asked, "How would you describe Emilie's relationship with her nieces and nephew?"

"As a healthy and happy one," the old lady said emphatically. "The children respect and adore her, and she clearly feels the same about them. I've been around children all my life, and I've never seen any better loved or cared for than the Dalton children. Oh, maybe they don't have much in the way of material possessions, but they've got all the love and support any child could need, and that is what's important."

"Do you believe the children are benefitted by living with their aunt?"

"Of course they are. For the past few months, she's been their mother in every way. She loves them, protects them, takes care of them. She ensures that they have food to eat, clothes to wear, and a place to sleep. They're well-behaved, well-adjusted children, thanks to her, because they know that, whatever else happens, she will always love them and will always, to the best of her ability, be there for them."

Emilie felt a lump growing in her throat, and her eyes grew a little misty. At least she had the comfort of knowing that dreams could come true. For a short time, friends had welcomed her, Nathan had loved her, and she had truly belonged.

Corinna was next on the stand. She answered Alex's questions, then waited patiently, unflappably, for the DA's cross-examination. "Miss Corinna, you say you believe that the best place for those children is with their aunt. And I'm sure you'll agree that a parent—or custodial aunt—must set a sterling example for the children."

"Of course I agree."

"What kind of example, in your opinion, has Emilie Dalton set for her nieces and nephew?"

"As has already been pointed out, the children are well behaved and well adjusted, in large part because of Emilie. I would call that a fine example."

"She took them when the law said she had no right to them and fled the state. She broke into an empty house right next door to you and claimed it for her own. She passed herself off as the niece of Miriam Pierce and as the mother of those children. She lied directly and indirectly to everyone she met, and she forced the children to lie, too. And yet you consider Emilie Dalton's behavior to be a fine example for those children?"

Corinna's gaze shifted from the district attorney to the

back of the room, and she directed her answer that way, as well. "Those children know that Emilie would do anything in her power to take care of them. That's how important they are to her. Her love for them is unconditional and unwavering. In their lifetimes, very few people will ever love them like that. Their own mother who brought them into this world has never loved them like that. But Emilie does."

Slowly Emilie turned and saw that it was Nathan to whom Corinna was speaking. Just in from his call, he stood at the back of the courtroom, still wearing his jacket, his cheeks ruddy, his hair windblown. A few days ago, given the opportunity, she wouldn't have hesitated to comb her fingers through it. Today she knew that she would never touch him again, and the knowledge came closer than everything else—the fear, the worry, the threat of arrest, the breaking up of her family—to defeating her.

Her hand trembling, she touched Alex's arm and gestured. The lawyer glanced over his shoulder, then gave her a smile meant to reassure. She was beyond reassurance. This hearing was simply an effort to postpone the inevitable. Maybe it would have been better all around—for her, for Nathan, God help her, maybe even for the kids—if she had volunteered to surrender herself immediately to the authorities in Boston. They could have been saved this ordeal, the kids could have started adjusting to the future that awaited them, and she could have been spared hearing Nathan speak out, under oath, against her.

After the DA dismissed Corinna and she'd taken her seat, Judge McKechnie spoke. "Have a seat if you can find one, Nathan. We'll get to you as soon as Alex finishes with his witnesses."

Nathan responded to the judge's comment with a nod, but he didn't move away from the back wall. Clearly, he didn't want to sit down.

At the front of the room, Alex called Holly as his next witness.

"Emilie's an excellent employee," she replied in response to his question. "She does her assigned duties and more. Everyone likes her, staff and guests alike. In fact, if she stayed around, I was planning—I *am* planning—to offer her a position as assistant manager after the holidays."

"Knowing what you now know about her, you're willing not only to keep her on but to offer a promotion?"

"Yes."

"You have no problems with allowing her to continue to work in your business? You have no qualms about allowing her access to the rooms and your guests' belongings?"

"Of course not! Emilie would never steal from me or my guests or anyone else!"

"But she moved into the Pierce house without the

owner's permission. She took her sister's children from Boston when the court told her she couldn't keep them."

"The court made a bad decision," Holly said indignantly. "If the court was really concerned about those kids, it should have gotten their mother help a long time ago. It should have tracked down the boss who left town with Emilie's paycheck. It should have helped her with a place to live and a little support until she'd found a new job and was back on her feet again. All she needed was a little help. Instead, the court chose to break up her family and do God knows what kind of harm to those kids."

"She's a good mother," insisted Shelley Walker, who'd taken Holly's seat on the witness stand. She'd given short, firm answers to Thomas's questions and was now doing the same to the DA's. "She's devoted to the children. She has the sort of relationship with them that all parents should strive for."

"And yet she broke the law and forced them to play a role in her deception," the DA pointed out. "You don't have a problem with that?"

"She was in a difficult situation. Maybe a few of her choices were less than legal, but, under the circumstances, I would have done the same thing."

"Would you? The wife of the chief of police?"

"I would break every law on the books if it was necessary to protect my children. Wouldn't you?" Shelley waited a moment for his response. When none came, she shrugged. "I guess that's why God made women mothers. Because we *would* do anything for our children."

Finally, Miss Agatha left the room, then returned a moment later with Josie, and Alex called the girl to the stand. She was wearing a new outfit—jeans and a turtleneck—and sneakers that squeaked on the wooden floor, and she looked both scared by the proceedings and enticed by the notion that she would be the center of everyone's attention. She climbed into the chair, sat on her knees, and gave Emilie a grin and a wave. "Hi, Aunt Emilie," she whispered loudly.

Thomas walked up to the railing and extended his hand. "Hi. I'm Alex."

"I'm Josie Lee Dalton, and I'm six years old."

"You're a big girl, aren't you?"

"Uh-huh, and pretty and smart, too. I can read real good, even if I am only in the first grade."

"Do you know the difference between right and wrong, Josie?"

"You mean like being good and behaving and telling lies and sticking your tongue out at people?" Her tone full of self-importance, she went on. "Well, you should always be good and behave, which isn't always easy, but it's not so hard right now 'cause it's the day before Christmas and Santa Claus is watching, you know. And you shouldn't tell lies or talk back or stick out your tongue or call people names or talk to strangers or pull your sister's hair or any stuff like that."

"Do you ever tell lies, Josie?"

She squirmed, clearly unwilling to make such a confession on the day before Christmas. Finally she wriggled in the seat, looked away, and muttered, "Sometimes."

"You've called your aunt Emilie Mama since you came here. Was that a lie?"

"Sort of."

"What do you mean, sort of?"

"Well, she's not really our mama, so it's a lie, but sometimes I wish . . . Sometimes . . ." She leaned forward and whispered.

"I didn't hear you, Josie," McKechnie said, his voice kind. "What do you wish?"

She stood up in the chair and leaned her arms on the judge's bench. "Sometimes I wish that Aunt Emilie really was our mama," she said earnestly. "I love my real mama. Sometimes she's a good mama, and she's funny and pretty, and she makes me laugh. But sometimes she's sick, and she cries and yells, and she leaves us alone and we don't know when she'll be back. Aunt Emilie wouldn't never leave us if you didn't make her. She loves us more than anything in the world, and she's the best mama in the world."

"If you could live anywhere, Josie," Thomas asked, "where would you choose?"

She plopped into the chair again. "Right here. This is a pretty neat town. Did you know they have a real, live camel over at the church?"

With a smile, Thomas nodded, then continued. "And who would you live with, Josie, if you could choose?"

She ticked off her answers on her fingers. "Lannie. And Brendan. Aunt Emilie. Mama. And Mr. Nathan." About half the spectators had turned to look at him when, her face fallen, Josie continued. "But we don't see Mr. Nathan no more since he 'rested Aunt Emilie. Lannie says he's not our friend, but she's wrong. He is, too, our friend, aren't you, Mr. Nathan?"

She was on her feet again, leaning around the lawyer to see him. Everyone else was looking, too, except Emilie. She didn't want to look. She couldn't.

When the DA declined to cross-examine, Josie went to sit with the sisters, and Melissa Thomas escorted Alanna in. With a nudge from the lawyer's wife, she reluctantly walked down the center aisle, was sworn in, and took a seat on the very edge of the chair. She raised one hand to her throat, to the star necklace that was no longer there, then let it drop to her lap again. She looked so nervous, Emilie thought regretfully, and so frightened. She would have given almost anything to spare the children this ordeal, but Alex had insisted that their testimony was necessary, and Alanna and Josie had insisted that they wanted to help. Now Alanna looked as if she'd changed her mind.

Alex approached the rail. "Please tell the court your name and age."

"Alanna Dalton. I'm nine." Her voice was little more than a whisper, and her expression was distressed.

"Are you nervous, Alanna?"

"Yes, sir."

"Have you ever been in court before?"

"No, sir."

"Do you know why you're here today?"

"To see if we can stay with Aunt Emilie until—until we all have to go back to Boston."

"You don't want to go back to Boston, do you, Alanna?"

"No, sir."

"Why not?"

"If we go back, they'll put us in foster homes, and we won't be a family any more. Josie and Brendan and Mama and Aunt Emilie are all the family I've got, and I'll never get to see them again until we're all grown up, because we'll all be living in different places, and Aunt Emilie . . ." Her gaze met Emilie's and turned sad. "Aunt Emilie will be in prison, when she hasn't done anything wrong."

"You know the difference between right and wrong, Alanna. Was moving into someone's house without their permission wrong?"

"Yes, it was, but we didn't break in. We just sort of borrowed it. And we didn't use anything we didn't need, and we didn't do any damage, and we were going to make it right. As soon as we got some money, Aunt Emilie was going to send it to the woman who owned the house. She promised."

"Does Emilie always keep her promises?"

Alanna nodded vigorously. *"Always."*

"She promised she would take care of you, Josie, and Brendan. She promised she would love you and keep you together and keep you safe. Has she done all that?"

"Oh, yes."

"Has she been a good mother?"

"Yes. The best."

"But she made you pretend to be her children. She made you pretend that you belonged in that house. She made you lie. How can someone who does that be a good mother?"

Alanna sat silent for a moment, looking bewildered and anxious. Finally, she drew a deep breath. "Lying is wrong. Taking or using things that aren't yours is wrong, too. I know that. But . . . My mama's been sick for as long as I can remember. Nothing's more important to her than getting drunk or getting high—not taking care of us. Not sending us to school. Not seeing that we had food to eat. Sometimes she'd go off for two or three days and leave me to take care of the others. I was always scared that she wouldn't come back. I was always afraid that she would drink too much or shoot up too much or that the people she did it with would kill her for her drugs.

"But after Aunt Emilie came to live with us, I didn't have to worry so much anymore. I didn't have to take care of everything. I didn't have to worry that she would leave us and forget to come back or that she would kill herself with an overdose or bring home some guy who hated kids to live with us. The year that Aunt Emilie's been with us has been the best year of our whole lives. So, yes, she did lie, and she asked us to lie, too, but she did it to take care of us. She did it because she didn't have any other choice. She did it because it was the only way she could keep her promise to take care of us and love us and keep us together and safe." She looked at Emilie, then at Nathan in the back before fixing her gaze on Alex. "Aunt Emilie *is* a good mother, and she doesn't belong in prison. I know, because I've had a bad mother who does."

"Thank you, Alanna. No further questions." Alex returned to the defense table.

Again, the DA declined to cross-examine. Alanna joined the sisters, and Nathan's name was called. He hated every step that took him to the front and the witness stand. The DA kept his questions short and to the point. Nathan told how he'd learned that Emilie wasn't the children's mother and how that information had led to the discovery of the warrant for her arrest. Simple, hard facts that threatened so many lives.

When he finished, Alex Thomas took over the questioning. "Prior to discovering the warrant for her arrest, what was your relationship with Emilie?"

Nathan glanced at her. Her head remained bowed, her blond hair hiding her face, as if she couldn't bear to look at him. He didn't blame her. "I wanted to marry her."

"Even though she had three children?"

"They're great kids."

"Doesn't that imply that she's a great mother?"

"Yes." Nathan didn't offer more. He didn't mention that he'd indulged in daydreams of Emilie as mother of his own children. He didn't comment on his fantasies of being a father to her three and all the babies they would have together.

Apparently, Thomas decided not to push his luck, to end the questioning with what could be taken as agreement that Emilie was a good mother. Nathan wasn't off the hook yet, though. The DA rose for another round. "Ms. Dalton kidnapped the children. She appropriated someone else's property. She deceived this entire town, including—most especially—you. Are these actions compatible with being a great mother?"

He glanced at Emilie again. She looked so small, drawn in on herself as if she needed protection from the response he would give. He wanted to reassure her, to touch her, to hold her. But all he could do was remain where he sat and answer. "She grew up in foster homes. She knows what it's like. She knows what it did to her sister. Under the circumstances, she made the only choices she believed possible. But she wouldn't make the same choices again."

"Why not? What's changed?"

"Everything. All her life she's been looking for a place to belong. Now she's found it. She belongs in Bethlehem, and the children belong with her."

At that, Emilie looked up. She hadn't expected that from him. She'd thought he would come in here, swear to tell the truth, then make the same sort of judgments he'd made Saturday. That she'd expected so little of him hurt. That he'd given her reason to expect so little hurt more.

"She doesn't even have a place to live."

"Yes, she does." He had an empty house that was made for a family and an empty heart that needed them to fill it. "She's not alone anymore. She has people to count on, people to help, people who will give her the support she needs."

The DA hesitated. Nathan knew him well enough to know that he wasn't thrilled about his role in this hearing. He had nothing against Emilie and didn't relish the idea of playing the bad guy when the entire town was speaking up on her behalf. He found no pleasure in trying to break up her family on Christmas Eve. Finally giving up his adversarial role, he quietly asked one more question. "Are you one of those people?"

Nathan looked at her. Her face was pale, her eyes

bigger and bluer than he remembered. She looked so fragile, but she was the strongest woman he'd ever known. The past five days had been so hard for her, and he could have made a difference if he hadn't been so centered on his own pain. Maybe he could make a difference now. Maybe late really was better than never. "I should have been. I regret more than I can say that I let her and the kids down. But I wanted to share responsibility for the kids when I thought they were hers, and the fact that they're not doesn't change that. I'm the closest thing to a father those kids have ever known, and Emilie's the best mother they could ever have."

"So we can assume that if Ms. Dalton's petition for interim custody is granted, you'll be sharing responsibility for the children's welfare."

He held her gaze a moment, but was unable to read anything there for the tears. He swallowed hard. "If she'll let me. If she can forgive me."

"No further questions, Officer Bishop. You can step down."

He was leaving the witness stand when McKechnie cleared his throat. "The court will recess for five minutes, while the plaintiff and the witness discuss this, and then I'll give my decision."

Emilie was vaguely aware of people moving, of the orange-haired lady leaving the courtroom, of the low buzz of voices around them, but the rest of her attention—the entire rest of her being—was centered on Nathan. She got to her feet and waited for him to approach her. He looked so serious, so intent.

When he was right in front of her, she quietly disagreed with part of what he'd said on the stand. "You never let us down."

"I didn't stand by you the way the others did."

"I didn't hurt them the way I hurt you." She raised her hand, and he wrapped it tightly in his. "I am so sorry."

"So am I."

"I love you."

The promise of a smile eased the intensity of his expression. "I know. Almost as much as I love you."

Using her hand, he drew her closer, right into his arms. She had feared she would never hold him again, had despaired of the cold, bleak life ahead of her without him, and now here he was, holding her as if he might never let go. She had only a heartbeat to savor the moment, though, before they were surrounded by a mass of small, excited bodies. Alanna wriggled into their embrace, Josie climbed into Nathan's arms, and Brendan, with help, made it into hers.

With both hands, Josie turned his face toward her. "Do you love us, too, Mr. Nathan?"

"Yeah, Josie. I do."

"Good. Because we love you, and if you could be our dad, that'd be about the best Christmas present in the whole world. Santa Claus wouldn't have to bring us nothing else."

Nathan pulled Emilie closer. "What about it? Want to marry me and make my and Josie's Christmas wish come true?"

"And mine," Alanna added, and, with a grin and a giggle, Brendan murmured something similar.

Emilie gazed at him. "I do love you." She did, more than she'd ever imagined possible. But today's hearing dealt only with the custody of the children for the next few days. She still had to appear in Boston on Monday. She still had to go to trial on kidnapping charges. How could she commit to any sort of future until she knew whether she would spend that future in prison?

He understood and held her tighter. "We'll get through it together. All five of us. As a family."

A family. Together. It was too wonderful a wish to deny. Before she could find too much pleasure in the prospect, though, from the door to the judge's chambers came a command for attention. Letting Nathan pull her snugly against him, Emilie directed her gaze to Judge McKechnie. Ms. Petrie, of the orange hair, stood at his side, and she was smiling. It was the first time in all their dealings together that Emilie had seen her smile. She hadn't been sure the woman was even capable of it.

"Ms. Petrie has an announcement to make," the judge said loudly, then deferred to her.

She stepped forward and spoke in an equally loud

voice. "You have quite a town here—quite a group of friends, Emilie. I'm impressed. So impressed that I just got off the phone with the assistant district attorney in Boston who's assigned to this case and with Judge Hawkins, who filed the contempt charges. This being Christmas Eve, I had to track them down at home," she said with a grin. "I told them about the changes in your situation, and I recommended that all charges be dropped against you and that custody of your sister's children be returned to you. This being Christmas Eve—" the grin got wider—"they agreed to accept my recommendation. Merry Christmas, Emilie. You're a free woman." Closing the distance, she shook hands with Emilie, then offered her hand to Nathan. "Merry Christmas, Nathan. You're a lucky man."

As well-wishers crowded around them, Emilie finally got the kiss she'd been craving, the kiss that had haunted her dreams. It was sweet, full of hope and love, and promised everything her heart desired—for the kids, for herself, for all time.

In spite of its late hour, the service in the square was widely attended. There had been blessings and carols and messages of peace. Now, as the last prayer ended, the bells at the nearby Baptist church began to toll the midnight hour, and shouts went up all around the crowd. Nathan pulled Emilie close for a kiss and a whispered

Merry Christmas before Josie claimed his attention. "Let's go home, Mr. Nathan, please."

"What's your hurry?" With one arm, he lifted her, and she wrapped her arms around his neck.

"It's Christmas now. We have to go home and to bed so Santa can come. We left out cookies and milk and carrots for the reindeer—do reindeer like carrots?"

"I'm pretty sure they do."

"But we got to get to bed now. If he comes and we're still awake, he might not stop and I really, really want him to stop."

"Yeah, she doesn't want to think she's been good for no reason," Alanna teased.

Josie stuck out her tongue halfway, then hastily stopped.

"Santa won't miss you," Nathan assured her. "He knows that everyone stays out late in Bethlehem, so he goes other places first, then he comes here."

"Are you sure?"

"I'm a cop, and it's Christmas. Would I lie to you?"

Satisfied, she slid to the ground as Agatha and Corinna joined them. "How did you enjoy the service, Emilie?" Corinna asked.

Emilie's smile was as bright and warm as a Southern summer day, and her eyes almost sparkled. "It was wonderful."

"It's our favorite Christmas tradition." Agatha's gaze flitted from her to Nathan, then back. "You two look as if you've already gotten your Christmas gift. Have you set a date?"

"Soon," Nathan replied.

"New Year's would be a lovely day for a wedding," Corinna mused. "The start of a new year, the start of a new life. Of course, it would take some doing to pull off a wedding that quickly, but—"

"If anyone can do it, Corinna and I can. Reverend Howard would be happy to preside over the ceremony, and Alanna and Josie could be the flower girls in lovely satin dresses, and—"

"Wouldn't Brendan make an adorable ring bearer? Of course, the invitations will have to be done by hand—"

"And Carrie Mae will do the cake—"

"And the flowers—"

Lost in their plans, the sisters started to wander off, then abruptly returned. First Agatha, then Corinna, enveloped Emilie in a hug. "Merry Christmas, dear. We'll talk more tomorrow about the wedding."

They hugged Nathan, too, then left, discussing the merits of orchids over roses.

"By the time you see them tomorrow, your wedding will be all planned," he murmured.

"Hey, it's your wedding, too."

"Yeah, but I've had one before. Besides, all I care about is the end result. This is your first—your only. They'll have you wearing Corinna's wedding gown, carrying flowers sweet-talked out of Herbert Thomas's greenhouse, and saying vows in front of a minister you've never met—"

"To the man I love more than anything. That's all that matters."

He kissed her full on the mouth, a sweet kiss that promised heat, hunger, passion, and forever, then reluctantly, remembering the crowd that surrounded them, he lifted his head. "Let's go home." At home he could be alone with her. He could show her how much he loved her and in more ways than she'd yet imagined.

When she nodded agreement, he made sure Alanna, Josie, and Brendan were close behind as they made their way through the crowd. It was slow going—everyone wanted to talk—but, as much as he wanted to be alone with Emilie, he didn't mind. It was a special night—the most special of his life—and it deserved savoring.

They had practically reached the sidewalk when Emilie stopped to chat with Holly and Shelley. Listening to their conversation, he looked around, and his gaze settled on a man nearby. Excusing himself, he left Emilie and the kids and shook hands with the owner of the Hillside Lounge. After exchanging greetings, he said, "I was in your place last night. You had a bartender working—"

"That would have been Brent. Was there a problem?"

"No, this was a woman. In her fifties, graying brown hair?"

The man shook his head. "I don't have any womer

tending bar. My clientele's too rough for most women to handle."

Nathan was puzzled. "You're sure? Maybe she was just filling in for Brent while he took a break."

"Brent's my best employee. He doesn't take breaks, and he wouldn't let anyone fill in." The man smiled as his wife came up and slid her arm through his. "Merry Christmas."

He repeated the greeting while considering the conversation. Maybe the bartender wasn't quite as conscientious as his boss believed and the woman *had* filled in for him. Or maybe the whiskey had affected him much more than he'd thought and she was a figment of his imagination. Or maybe . . .

He blamed the idea that flitted into his mind on the songs just sung and messages just preached of heavenly beings. It was Christmas, after all, and there were angels everywhere. But last night's bartender had been flesh and blood.

And a little too knowledgeable for a stranger.

And a little too familiar. Not the face—it had definitely belonged to a stranger. But there was something about the hair—brown with that unusual silvery cast— and the eyes, so clear and direct, as if . . . As if she could see straight into a person.

"Merry Christmas, Nathan."

He turned to face Art Blocker, the tax assessor. He returned the greeting, then set out to prove himself wrong.

"Hey, Art, a couple weeks ago, I stopped by your office. You were in a meeting, and Dorothy was at a doctor's appointment, and you had a new clerk working—a guy, younger than me, brownish hair, glasses, bow tie. Whatever happened to him?"

Art shook his head. "A new clerk? On the budget they've given me? I haven't hired anyone new in ten years, and even then she didn't stay any time at all—only three years, then she quit to have a baby. You must be mistaken, Nathan."

He made mistakes, he admitted as he watched Art join his family. He could have made an irreparable one with Emilie if luck, fate—God—hadn't stopped him. But these weren't mistakes. He had sat in the bar last night and had several drinks—without getting drunk—and a conversation with a bartender who didn't tend bar there, a bartender who knew things about him that no one else did. He had walked into the tax assessor's office and told a clerk who didn't exist where to find the card that proved—and later, disproved—Emilie's ownership of the Pierce house. Emilie had been told about the house by the waitress at Harry's while he'd sat in his truck outside the diner and watched them—a waitress he hadn't seen since. A waitress with oddly colored silvery brown hair—

Searching the crowd, he located Harry talking with Maeve and her family. He drew the man aside, asked the same questions, and got the same earnest answer: no new waitress. Three strangers—three curiously similar strangers—had played a role in bringing him and Emilie together—and putting them back together—but, as far as he could tell, they didn't exist.

It was almost enough to make a man believe in Christmas miracles, he thought. Then he caught sight of Emilie, Alanna, Josie, and Brendan, waiting together on the sidewalk, waiting for him, and that *was* enough to make him believe. They were his very own Christmas miracle. His very own family.